[PRE]SENT

By

Sean B. Bolton

Cover Art by Alexandra S. Umphlette

Cover Design by Casey Fontneau-Ramos

This book is dedicated to everyone who has ever had dreams they could not forget.

Prologue

Jean Luc Dubois stares down at a photograph of his wife, remembering his words, "If you walk out that door, don't bother coming back." It's the last thing he said to her before she stormed out of the house. They had been fighting for days about money, as was usually the case, and when Vivien trudged out the front door to get some fresh air, he shouted those words without even thinking about it. He didn't mean it, but he assumes she took them seriously.

As a family of French immigrants, life isn't easy. While they all speak English well, most local business owners have no interest in hiring anyone who sounds as though they don't belong. Jean Luc hates fighting with Vivien. He hates it even more when their son Francis is in the house.

Sick leave didn't exist in the 1940s. If you're scheduled to work, you show up for work. Anything other than fulfilling your duties, ill or otherwise, is all but guaranteed to cost you the job that, quite frankly, Jean Luc can't afford to lose. His wife has been missing for several days. However, at the moment that merely means Jean Luc needs to earn two incomes with his one job.

"Papa," young Francis reaches for his father as he walks away from the school-yard on his way to work. "Don't go Papa."

Jean Luc can't handle the look on his son's face as he begs him to stay. Rather than turn back to have his heart torn from his chest, he always keeps his pace moving forward, one foot after another, until the sounds of young Francis can no longer be heard. He comes close to crying almost every day, but he doesn't have time to wallow. Food isn't going to put itself on the table, and Francis needs an education.

Three weeks following Vivien's disappearance, Jean Luc is stopped by the local sheriff on his way to work. He received some information suggesting Vivien didn't simply leave following the argument with her husband. As a matter of fact, the sheriff is all but certain that Vivien Dubois is dead. The sheriff would confirm his suspicions if her body were anywhere to be found, but such a discovery has not been made.

"What do you mean she's dead?" Jean Luc asks as his knees buckle beneath him.

He sits there hunched over on the dirt road on his way to the local grocer, for whom he stocks supplies and makes home deliveries six days per week. Unable to contain the pain in his heart, Jean Luc's hands clench his chest. How could he be so careless?

The sheriff tries asking several questions about the details of their last argument, wondering if perhaps Jean Luc lost his temper and did the unthinkable to the woman who meant more than life to him. The sheriff senses the reaction is sincere, and that Jean Luc had nothing to do with his wife's death.

Once cleared as a suspect, Jean Luc receives a correspondence sealed in wax from the sheriff's lead investigator. Wrapped within the pages of a letter is a single photograph.

As Jean Luc looks at the picture of his beautiful wife, he knows that, although he didn't do it, he's entirely at fault. Vivien Dubois, an elegant young woman, appears sitting in a chair, her dress ripped and shredded in several places, yet still intact, preserving her honor; her hands draped down by her side, with a gun in her left hand, and streaks of blood running down the side of her head, with tufts of hair matted against her soft skin.

Jean Luc Dubois will never forgive himself.

Years later, well after Jean Luc drank himself to an early grave, Francis Armand Dubois learns more about his mother's disappearance. She was murdered, but that isn't good enough for Francis. He needs answers. For starters, who killed her? However, to learn the *who*, Francis may need to find the answer to the question *why was she killed*?

Francis' journey starts with a lone image, a picture suggesting that contrary to his belief that his mother was murdered, Vivien

Dubois killed herself; a revelation that Francis refuses to believe. His mother was a devout Catholic, and while she was completely devoted to her family, nothing came before God. Suicide is an unforgivable sin, one that would prevent Vivien Dubois from the glorious afterlife in heaven she prayed for. Francis knows she would never willingly betray her faith.

The more he thinks about it, several other questions enter Francis' mind. Is his mother the only victim? Murderers often get a lust for blood and kill in numbers. Did Vivien know her killer? Why hasn't her body ever been found?

These are all good questions, but what if they're the wrong questions? What if it wasn't a *who*, but a *what* that killed Vivien Dubois?

The answers are out there, and as Francis seeks them, the unfortunate truth, no matter how impossible it seems, will reveal itself...

Chapter 1

Standing five feet nine inches tall with strawberry-blonde locks flowing from her scalp like silk tassels from a Persian throw-pillow down upon her shoulders, blue eyes that sparkle like diamonds in the sun on a warm summer day, and skin as pale as printing paper and as smooth as butter spread across a cake pan, Jeanne Burns is a beautiful young woman. Grown men's hearts melt at the sight of her smile. You would never know it based on her low self-esteem, but aside from a small birthmark above her right shoulder blade, she is the embodiment of perfection. However, as is often the case in life, the cover does not define the book.

For more than five years, Jeanne Burns has felt like she is being watched. Despite the absence of roommates, pets, or any other life forms, she is never alone. People write stories about the things that bump in the night, but for Jeanne, it isn't a story. Sure, things tend to be peaceful from dawn until dusk, but when her head hits her pillow at night, Jeanne is cast into an endless pit of darkness, an unidentifiable void. Some nights she hears screams, like those of young girls suffering through tragedy; other nights there is only chilling silence.

Jeanne has sought the assistance of countless professionals, but a handful of Doctors heard only what they were trained to hear, and Jeanne was labeled a Schizophrenic shortly after high school. While her official diagnosis is Schizoaffective NOS, meaning they aren't really certain of the type of schizophrenia she suffers from, they are certain that everything she describes is in her head, and that with the right level of medication, they can make it stop. Jeanne will tell you her Doctors don't understand a thing and that the things which haunt her in the night have little to do with her mind.

Despite the previous night's torment, Jeanne Burns woke up this morning with a feeling of significance. Nothing about the salmon-colored walls surrounding her queen-sized four-post bed has changed, but for some reason she feels like today is going to be the most significant day of her life. An unexplainable smile stretches across her face as she looks at the alarm clock on her bedside table. She's three minutes ahead of the buzzer and can't wait to get up on her feet.

Full of an unusual confidence, Jeanne decides not to put her robe on and instead walks right to the bathroom, gives her reflection a wink in the mirror, and turns the shower on. Filled with bliss as streams of hot water splash upon her, yesterday's stress is washed away, and Jeanne sings along to U2's *Beautiful Day*. Lathering from head to toe, the scent of her lavender body wash fills her mind with thoughts of passion, and in an unusual moment of morning ecstasy, she bites her lip.

She remembers the first time she and the love of her life made love. The many passionate-kiss-filled nights leading up to the deed had Jeanne's blood boiling before her date picked her up. They took a nice ride out to the beach, much like they often did. It's where they had their first date. However, on the particular night in question, they went to a secluded piece of beach where, once the sun went down, they were the only two people for as far as any eye could see. They had planned the quiet picnic in the sand well ahead of time. It's something Jeanne had always wanted to do. So, when the weather was perfect and the desire was right, they went for it.

Dinner was chocolate covered strawberries, oysters on the half shell, and all the sexual tension two people can handle. Jeanne recalls the event as if it happened yesterday, when in reality it was a little less than four years ago. She sometimes wishes she could go back in time. Then again, with today being her birthday, and given the prolonged conversations about settling down with her lover, the future may be where her dreams come true.

Thirty minutes of fantasy pass before Jeanne turns the shower off. She reaches for her favorite towel, still tingling, and slowly dries her lust soaked body. Once dried, she finds herself having a typical female moment; with 1,000 outfits calling to her from a walk-in closet the size of a small corridor, she has nothing to wear. However, as hopelessness appears on the horizon, Jeanne recalls her once wise mother's wisdom.

"Honey, whenever indecision grabs you, you have to regain control. All it takes is the perfect pair of panties, and the rest will sort itself." Her mother's hoarse voice echoes in her mind.

Knowing that her mother is almost always right, Jeanne starts by selecting a matching set of undergarments. Today's destined to be great and she wants to be prepared for the luckiest of occasions, one that warrants the display of the utmost sensuality.

Jeanne slips on her black-laced silk panties, Victoria Secret's limited edition. The flower-shaped lace draws perfect lines across both cheeks, leaving just enough showing to make a religious man's heart skip a beat from staring at two perfect half-moons, luscious and full, like sinful fruits, ripe for the picking. She reaches down, places the toes of her right foot into the bottom of a curled black stocking, and slowly guides the soft fabric up her leg with her thumbs gently running along her thigh to avoid tears. Flowered elasticized lace like that of her panties stops six inches above her knee. Her left leg then experiences the same sensation.

No respectable set of undergarments is complete without a crown jewel. In this case it is a stunning black bra, with two invisible butterfly-like clasps fastened in the front, pushing Jeanne Burns' tantalizing C cups out into the world for all men, and women for that matter, in the world to covet.

She stands in front of her door-sized mirror feeling accomplished, and she cannot help but stare. Her eyes are glued to her reflection. A brief look of shock surfaces as though Jeanne has never seen herself in such a light, or has never realized just how sexually attractive she is. Looking like a professional lingerie model, there is but one outfit to wear; a black skirt that is cut off at the top of her knees, decorated with a set of thin red pinstripes, accompanied by a red top that fits Jeanne's body like a glove, with short sleeves, and a thin lace along the v-shaped neck line, which highlights her bosom in all its glory.

The skirt has a matching two-buttoned business coat, with sleeves just long enough to cover those from the blouse, which happens to go perfectly with Jeanne's favorite cherry-red lipstick. All that is missing is her favorite set of black four-inch heels and the diamond earrings she saves for the most special of occasions; and today is going to be special, she can feel it.

Once satisfied with her attire, Jeanne adds some final touches to her makeup and looks at the time glowing in the mirror from the cable box in the next room, *7:03*. She's ready in record time; she can't help but smile.

Technology has come a long way. There was a time when making a cup of coffee required water to be boiled on the stove, and toasting bread meant you had to press it into a hot pan with butter or grease to get one side nice and crisp. Today however, when the coffee pot's clock hit quarter to seven, a fresh pot brewed, and that is all Jeanne needs for breakfast.

With a feeling of pride in her chest and a fresh cup of Folgers in her hand, Jeanne Burns grabs her black wristlet, the keys to her 1983 Mustang, and heads out the front door. She nearly trips over the newspaper, which the delivery boy keeps forgetting she cancelled. She stumbles forward a couple of steps, assuming her anticipated glorious day is about to be ruined, but then her feet catch her before she falls.

Crisis averted.

In her driveway, Jeanne starts her car and lets it idle for a moment while the engine warms. She knew absolutely nothing about cars, but her daddy had always been clear, when you first start a car, especially a classic-ish muscle car, you have to let it wake up.

"Don't you need a minute when you first wake up?" He'd joke with her. "Well, cars need a minute too."

Waiting for the engine to heat, she looks at herself in the rearview mirror, and with a smile larger than any previous, speaks aloud.

"You are one sexy bitch."

Filled with all of her life's ambition, Jeanne Burns backs out of her driveway for the last time.

Chapter 2

The smell of old cheese enters his nostrils as he inhales the air coming from the filthy vents in his car. The misaligned front wheels sound like a herd of West Nile mosquitos caught in a vortex, getting louder as he accelerates. His grandfather believed he should drive any car he owned until the wheels fell off. In the case of Gregory Allen Roberts' mid-eighties Dodge Shadow, such time may be just around the corner.

Greg never wanted a Dodge Shadow. Unfortunately, a bit of bad Irish luck and a perceivably harmless comment destroyed his first car, leaving him with little choice. When you're in high school, saving the money you earn at your part-time job is one of the lowest priorities on the list.

Rolling out of bed this morning was difficult, as it is every morning. Once again, Greg had not made it through the night undisturbed, and he feels like he's getting less and less sleep with each passing night. His previous Doctor told him that just like a man who goes blind gets used to living without his sight, Greg would get used to having his sleep interrupted on a regular basis. Thus the title *previous* Doctor applies.

Every trip Greg takes in his car allows him to imagine the life he'll never have. He imagines owning a large two-story house, with a porch that wraps around the first floor. As corny as it sounds, he wants his own white-picket-fence surrounding the front yard, to highlight the garden. The back yard is a sea of green stretching for acres, and his horses roam free throughout the field. His wife is a nurse at the local emergency room, and they have two handsome sons, Aiden and Zachary, both of whom love to play baseball. As for Gregory, he's a counselor of sorts who dabbles in poetry writing in his spare time. The family breeds horses, which are kept in a barn out back, and random vacations to anywhere in the world are a common escape.

Suddenly *Highway to Hell* chimes in from blown speakers, and Greg's reminded that this is a future he will never have. Thinking about everything he won't accomplish makes each day seem pointless. He was lucky enough to finish his bachelor's degree and then make it into a field *related* to mental health.

Greg has an amazing fiancée, to whom he is unconditionally devoted. He hates that his friends all tell him he's whipped because of the negative connotation it implies. However, from their points of view, that's precisely what Greg is. At this point he knows he'd be lost without her, which may sound pathetic, but they've been through more in their few years than most couples go through in three lifetimes. She's the one who suggested Greg try this one final Doctor before quitting his search. He's doing this for her. He wants to get married and start his family, but that possibility looks less and less likely with each passing day. Expecting anything more than what he has right now would be inappropriate and irrational, and Greg knows that. He hasn't let anyone else in on that small fact, and he feels guilty for dragging his loved ones this far.

He's running late as usual, and he doesn't want to miss today's appointment. Dr. Campos is one of the most prestigious in his field, and Greg has run out of options. He's twenty-seven years old, and for the past decade, he's been without a moment of true peace in his life. The car is moving as fast as it can, but before one assumes he's hauling ass down the street, the shadow tops out at a lightning-quick forty-five miles per hour.

Between his car's ability to get him there and some of his previous experiences, perhaps Greg's subconscious is consciously delaying his arrival. The burn marks from the visit to the last "specialist" are still faintly visible on Greg's arms and chest. The Doctor had Greg sit back on a tilted exam table, and proceeded to clamp tiny wires to various places on his body. The intent was to record Greg's physiological responses to a myriad of words and shapes.

"Home," the supposed Doctor said, and Greg's left forearm twitched. "Fire," the idiot continued on, and Greg's right eye twitched. The *test* carried on until the word "failure," at which point Greg's body began to convulse. It was later determined that the dummy running the test had hooked the machine up backwards, and instead of taking readings from Greg's responses, every time a word registered, the machine jolted Greg with more and more volts of electricity.

Considering all the prior Doctors put him through, Greg wonders what will be asked of him this time around. He doesn't think there's a test currently being administered that can help him, but he understands Dr. Campos has a rare theory of his own. If he's lucky, it will go after Greg while he's there. At least then someone else will see that he's not making up his story as he goes along. At least then, there would be proof.

Greg's jaw drops at the sight of the homes lined down the street as he makes a left turn just off of Euclid Avenue. A friend had mentioned that many of the homes in the rich neighborhoods of the Inland Empire were big, but that was clearly an understatement. Every house on the block looks like Disney's *Haunted Mansion* from the outside. The driveways have tall barred gates and large brick walkways. One of the homes even has two headstones in the front yard. Many of the windows are made from stained glass and look like old English churches. Greg can't imagine what the property taxes are for these homes, but he's certain it's more than he'll ever be able to afford.

Greg parks his trusty Shadow and looks what he can see of the place over a few times before making his way towards the Doctor's home. Approaching the end of the driveway, he reaches a tall gothic-style gate held up by two massive marble columns with emerald-colored gargoyles mounted at the top.

Who is this guy? Greg ponders the thought. Since the release of Edward Scissorhands in the winter of 1990, Greg has followed the semi-demented works of filmmaker Tim Burton. Most of his films carry a sinister feeling from opening to closing credits, and standing at the end of Dr. Campos' driveway, Greg wonders if he's about to meet Mr. Burton's evil twin?

He finds a small electronic box attached to the left pillar. It's looks like small speaker, painted to match the home's outer décor, camouflaged against the marble. Greg notices a small green button on the front, and thinking nothing of it, he presses the slightly protruding knob. Nothing happens.

"Well that's disappointing," Greg says aloud, looking at the gargoyle above him, as if he expects it to respond.

He waits a moment and presses the button again, still nothing. Instead he walks back over to the gates and tries to push them open, but as soon as his hand touches the metal bars, Greg's body is jolted with a small charge of electricity, bringing those fond memories of the last Doctor back to his mind.

"Ouch!" Greg shouts at the other gargoyle.

Like many children growing up, Greg sucked his thumb, the right one. However, unlike most of those same children, as he grew older, the bad habit didn't go away. At one point he was the only ten-year-old boy sitting in class with his thumb in his mouth, sucking like it was his last meal. He doesn't remember when he stopped putting the digit in his mouth, but the pain he feels from being shocked by the front gate causes him to suck the area between his right thumb and forefinger, hoping it will make the tingling sensation stop.

Figuring he's lost the battle, Greg turns to walk back to his car, his head slumps forward in defeat.

"Who is it?" A slow, crackling, high-pitched voice asks from the hidden on the left column, causing Greg to trip over his own feet, startled.

Still staggering from being electrocuted, Greg stumbles to respond, "Um, my name is, uh, Gregory." He feels stupid using his full name. He hates the name *Gregory*. But it was his great uncle's name, and his mother idolized him, so his name is Gregory. "Sorry, it's Greg Roberts."

"What do you want, Mr. Roberts?" The whiney voice asks, causing Greg to wonder if he's at the right house.

"I have an appointment with Doctor Campos" says Greg, crinkling his eyes as he waits for the voice's rejection.

"Really?" The voice asks. "Hold on. Let me check the Doctor's schedule. Don't you go anywhere dear."

The speaker clicks off and Greg waits in silence. He looks back at the gate that shocked him and pretends to lunge his head and shoulders forward, as if to fight the inanimate bars. He feels like he's been attacked and wants to exact his revenge. How one goes about such revenge he doesn't know, but he wants it nevertheless.

Looking around the rest of the block as he waits, Greg sees many different statues. The neighbor next door has a stone sculpture of Jesus standing in a fountain, perhaps a reference to Christ's ability to walk on water, if only the water's fountain didn't stream from the Lord's midsection.

Another house has a statue of a giant eagle perched on the center of the highest point of the roof. That same house has a pole flying American, State, and P.O.W. flags at half-mast. *Did someone die recently?* However, Greg's favorite house is near the other end of the street. It's designed like a modern igloo in southern California. The main part of the house is sort of dome shaped, with a long tunnel-like walkway leading out to the street. He just likes it because it makes no sense.

A few minutes go by and Greg starts wondering if the voice from the box has forgotten him or worse, it was all in his head. Knowing the latter is more than plausible, Greg presses the button outside the gate once more and crosses his fingers. It's usually a useless gesture, but he really wants luck to be on his side for a change. A scratchy beep rings out this time, followed by a response.

"I thought I told you to wait," the cranky voice says in a fit of frustration.

"I- I'm sorry" Greg replies.

Another moment passes by without a sound. Greg feels as though he's wasting his time, and then he hears the voice again.

"Stand back Mr. Roberts," the voice says with a drawn out hiss, "I shall buzz you in."

Not knowing what will happen next, Greg steps out into the street, far enough so nothing can bite him again. He is startled a few seconds later as an alarm sounds off behind him. When Greg was six-years-old, his family moved to the south. It's a period of his life that he rarely thinks about, but as the familiar sounds of a tornado siren go off, he imagines himself right back in his mother's bathtub, praying they won't be swept away to Oz.

The eyes of the gargoyles overlooking the gate turn bright red and begin flashing while their mouths drop open, and massive streams of hot air flare out from each. The noise of hot steam escaping from a thin pipe is painful to hear. It sends a shiver down Greg's back and he raises his hands to cover his ears. The sound's vibrations shake the very earth Greg is standing upon, and he feels as though he's going to vomit from motion sickness.

Finally, the lights stop flashing and the smoke comes to a halt. There is a loud *pop* in the distance, followed by the sound of metal bending under stress. The quaking slowly subsides as well, and the gates creak, opening inward and revealing what looks like a maze just beyond the driveway. Once all of the moving parts are completely open and resting in place, the voice returns to welcome Greg in.

"You may enter Mr. Roberts," it sounds almost like a cartoon snake.

"O-Okay" Greg replies. "Where am I going?"

"Ah," the crackling voice observes, "That is why I didn't see you on the schedule. You are new." The voice pauses, as if to catch its breath. "You will walk directly forward Mr. Roberts, and when you reach the end of the driveway, you will see our door to your immediate left." The voice stops again. "I shall meet you there Mr. Roberts."

Chapter 3

Feeling almost like the gates of hell have just opened before his eyes, with the devil's trusted servant welcoming him in, Greg takes a deep breath, having little other choice at this point, and walks through the gates, his new nemesis. As he heads towards the other end of the driveway, Greg, upon closer inspection, sees that each side of his pathway is engulfed by tall green vines. The plants are wound together tight, to the point that Greg can't see where he's walking through the darkness they create. He feels a cold breeze funneling from one side to the other, chilling Greg's body to its core. Worried that he'll change his mind about the whole thing, he sprints into the shadows before him until he sees a small light approaching on the left.

That must be it.

When Greg was in second grade, he played soccer for a local recreational league. He loved soccer. Something about kicking a ball as hard as you can filled little Greg's heart with joy. However, after losing to another team in the rec league, his coach made the entire team run wind sprints up and down the field until sun went down. About half way through the punishment, Greg became winded and fell to the ground, clenching his chest, and struggling to breathe. His Doctor later diagnosed him with Asthma. As a result, two things remain true to this day; when Greg gets really excited or when he exerts a lot of energy, he has trouble breathing; and he hates soccer.

Now at the front of Dr. Campos' enormous house, Greg tries to catch his breath.

At what he perceives to be his desired destination, the door gently opens without a sound, revealing a golden archway, leading to a long and dark corridor. After the events with the attacking gates and the hidden speaker, Greg is curious to meet the crackling voice.

Without any delay, a woman appears before him in the doorway. She's remarkably short, almost a dwarf. Her hair is mostly pale with a few streaks of grayish black. She's dressed in faded black garments that drape over every part of her like curtains from a rod that's hung too close to the floor. Her eyes stare out from behind a crooked pair of glasses that are held together in the middle by a small piece of electrical tape. Greg steps forward to speak, but is cut off. The woman opens her mouth, revealing two partially rotted teeth, and addresses the guest.

"Welcome, Mr. Roberts, to the home of Doctor and Mrs Campos. I am Miss Paxon, keeper of the house. You may address me as ma'am." Her voice is even worse in person.

"Thank you" says Greg. His grandfather demanded that he be polite whenever necessary, and truth be told, the words come out as more of a reflex now.

"You mean thank you ma'am" Miss Paxon corrects him immediately.

I tried Grandpa. Greg looks up to the sky and shrugs his shoulders.

"Um, yeah. Thank you ma'am." Greg hopes he got it right. "So, where is Dr. Campos' office, um, ma'am?"

"Don't be so anxious young man," says Miss Paxon. "There are some rules in this house Mr. Roberts. You shall pay close attention and mind every detail if you want to return to this place again. Do you understand Mr. Roberts?"

Greg is puzzled by the woman's longwinded words, but can't allow it to be an issue.

"Yes ma'am, I understand" says Greg.

"Good" says Miss Paxon. "Now, listen closely. Firstly, you do not touch anything unless directly instructed to do so. Understood?"

"Yes ma'am" replies Greg.

"Secondly," says Miss Paxon, "You do not speak to anyone in this house, aside from Doctor Campos of course, unless directed to do so. Understood?"

"What about," Greg is interrupted before he can finish.

"No!" Miss Paxon shouts. "You speak to nobody. Do I make myself clear Mr. Roberts?"

Greg takes notice of Miss Paxon's succinct and direct order, recognizing that the command was given without delay.

"Yes ma'am" says Greg.

"Thirdly," Miss Paxon adds, "When entering any room in the house, whether leaving one room to enter another, or entering from the outside, you must announce your presence. Understood?"

"Yes ma'am," Greg replies, "Must I say anything specific?"

"You seem like a clever man Mr. Roberts," says Miss Paxon, "Lastly, Doctor Campos abhors interruptions Mr. Roberts. Especially while in session. Therefore, you must turn your cellular telephone off while inside this house, and I mean off Mr. Roberts. Understood?"

"Yes ma'am," says Greg. "Is it acceptable if I use it while outside if I need to ma'am?"

Miss Paxon ignores Greg's question. "Now, Mr. Roberts, follow me."

Greg remembers when he and his best friend Kent Lawson used to talk about joining the military together. They heard about a "buddy system" for getting soldiers enrolled, and Kent had been raised for military service by his father, who also served, and was now a police officer.

They took the Armed Services Vocational Aptitude Battery test, or ASVAB, during their junior year of high school. Kent's score left him with little choice; infantry or nothing at all, while Greg's score landed in the top tier, which gave him the opportunity of his choosing. However, Greg has never been one for authority, and the idea of getting berated by a drill instructor day in and day out left him without any desire to join. Miss Paxon's stern demeanor is close to his perception of a military boot camp experience.

The scraggly old woman turns around and takes three slow steps. Suddenly two double doors open, and blinding light bursts out and into the hallway like soda exploding out of a can that has been left in the freezer too long; and Greg takes a step back, throwing his hands up to shields his eyes. The initial sensation of losing his sight dissipates a moment later, and he proceeds into the next room with Miss Paxon.

"What did I tell you?" The old bag snaps at Greg, staring at him like he's child who has been caught with his hand in the cookie jar.

"Huh? What do you mean?" Greg is confused, and his head still hurts from the glaring light.

"Mr. Roberts," says Miss Paxon, "Did you, or did you not just enter a new room?" Clearly, her mind is not as slow as her body.

"Oh," says Greg, remembering the rules, "I apologize. I forgot." The near crippled woman waits for him to follow the instructions. "Is anyone here?" He asks, sure to speak up so anyone who may be in the room can hear, but silence is all there is to greet him.

"Do not let it happen again Mr. Roberts," says Miss Paxon. "Now, follow me."

Greg remains a few steps behind his chaperone, still surveying the room he's leaving. The ceiling is pointed, with solar windows to let daylight in on sunny California afternoons. All four walls are lined with bookshelves, each packed full with literary works spanning hundreds of years. There's a coffee table in the middle of the room with four matching oversized leather chairs positioned near each corner. The ivory floor has four black tiles, one in each corner of the room, with the letters "EC" sculpted in gold in the center of them. Looking up, and full of curiosity, Greg doesn't realize how long he's been in his trance.

"Mr. Roberts," says Miss Paxon, calling Greg back to attention, "This way, if you please."

The next room is bare, four walls painted *padded room white*, a floor, and a ceiling. There are no decorations and no lights. It's simply wasted space.

"Is anyone in here?" Greg says, learning quickly. Perhaps he would have excelled in the military.

With nothing to see, Miss Paxon proceeds forward.

"Okay Mr. Roberts," she says, stopping directly in front of the next door. "This is as far as I go. You will go through this door and find another room with furniture and things that don't belong to you. Remember the rules," she continues, lacking confidence in Greg's ability to be disciplined. "You will proceed to the door at the back of the room. Knock once and wait. Understood?"

"Wait for what?" Greg asks, pushing Miss Paxon's buttons.

The gruff woman sighs, almost moaning, before responding, "For an invitation to enter Mr. Roberts. Is that too much to ask?

"No ma – I mean yes ma'am." He stumbles for the right answer. "I will wait to be invited in ma'am." He looks at Miss Paxon's face, hoping he reached an acceptable response.

"I will meet you here after your session Mr. Roberts," says Miss Paxon, rolling her eyes in frustration, "Good luck."

Greg watches as the creepy old woman walks back into the room filled with bookcases and disappears through a door on the right wall. He goes through the door before him as instructed, where he finds a curious room. It's difficult to see at first. However, once Greg closes the door behind him, a light comes on in each of the ceiling's four corners. He takes a few steps into the room and comes to a halt, the heels of his sneakers screeching on the slick floor. Looking down, Greg's eyes widen with fear. There in the middle of this citadel of house, is a random cliff with a two hundred foot drop. Greg's heart starts racing.

Around the time Greg turned seven years old, his parents signed him up for swimming lessons at the local YMCA. He was excited to learn how to be like a fish, free to roam in the open water. When he walked into the room where he was to have the lesson of a lifetime, his eyes nearly fell jumped out of his head from the joy of looking at the massive Olympic-size swimming pool.

Sadly, the happiness Greg felt as he gazed upon the enormous body of chlorinated water was to be short lived. Within thirty minutes of the lesson beginning, the entire class lined up by a tall ladder at the far end of the pool. The task seemed harmless enough, until Greg got closer to the top rung, where he realized each of his classmates were stepping up to the top and diving off of a long springboard. Finally, Greg reached the top, and as he neared the end of the board, he looked down to the pool, which now seemed to be fifty stories below him. It was only ten feet, but at seven years old, ten feet may kill you.

Greg started backing up, retreating to the rear of the springboard, but there was nowhere for him to go; the line of classmates left him only one way to get down, and without any warning, and before he could protest another moment, the instructor shoved Greg off the end of the board. The fall down to the pool felt like an eternity, and all of the short-lived memories passed before Greg's eyes. Now with a twenty-year-long fear of heights, Greg finds himself standing on the edge of a cliff in the home of Dr. Campos, waiting for someone to push him.

Retreating really isn't an option for Greg at this point, but convincing his muscles to move in any direction is going to take focus and determination. Hoping to gain some composure, he takes a deep breath, closes his eyes, and thinks of anything pleasant that he can remember. It never takes Greg long to recall thoughts from the past. As a child who suffered from Post-Traumatic Stress Disorder (PTSD), he's generally able to remember significant moments from throughout his life in an instant. This time, however, Greg can't get away from the feeling he's about to plummet to his death.

Giving up on getting over the fear, Greg slowly opens his eyes to look down again, while also forcing himself to take one step back. The view changes rather oddly, giving him the idea to look up; and that's when he sees it, a photorealistic painting of a giant canyon covers the ceiling. Greg sighs in relief as his gaze makes its way back down. The floor in this room is a giant mirror, and the lights are set up at varying angles to create an optical illusion of looking over the edge of cliff. Greg is starting to hate this Doctor before he even meets him.

"Hello," says Greg aloud, somehow remembering Miss Paxon's rules. "Is anyone in here?"

Feeling like an idiot, Greg walks across the reflective floor to the door on the other side of the room. The long trip from outside the gates of hell is over. It's now or nothing.

If this guy can't help me, nobody can.

Dr. Emmanuel Campos sits in a hand-stitched-leather executive chair behind a mahogany desk, with his body slouched forward upon his elbows. His pen is waving back and forth in his right hand as he stares through a set of bifocals at his next patient's file. With little history of any known mental illness, aside from what he would consider to be a minor case of PTSD, , he wonders how Greg managed to pass the qualification screening for his services.

In his sixties and enjoying retirement, the highly reputable Dr. Campos has only recently agreed to take on his newest patient, with the potential to take on more in the years to come. During his years working at Patton State Hospital, a mental institution for the criminally insane in San Bernardino, California, he perfected what he believes to be a viable process for the treatment of night terrors. However, while perfecting this process, he discovered another potential breakthrough in not only science, but in mankind's search for an answer to a nagging question, "Are we alone in the universe?" His studies resulted in several revelations, allowing him to become one of the most successful Doctors specializing in cases involving delusions perceived by patients to be of a paranormal nature.

Looking at the antique clock in the far corner of his office, Dr. Campos hears a knock on the door in front of him and smiles.

It's time.

Chapter 4

The heavy door swings open and Greg Roberts enters. He has
seen the inside of a number of therapists' offices, but he has
never made a home visit. It's immediately obvious that Dr.
Campos had a successful career. Aside from the awe-striking
view from the end of the driveway, and the near-death cliff-side
experience, Greg also notices the Doctor's antique clock in the
back left corner of the newest room, announcing each second as it
ticks away. The wall behind the Doctor's desk is a sliding glass
door, decorated with velvet curtains. A marble fireplace sits deep
into the wall to Greg's right. The furniture is old fashioned, all
hand-sewn, and looks like it belongs in a Victorian castle. It
wouldn't be surprising to find the Doctor had his home shipped
from overseas. However, Greg *is* surprised that Dr. Campos had
agreed to see him.

"Hello Mr. Roberts," says Dr. Campos with a deep and
austere tone as he makes his way from behind his desk. He's a
tall man, much taller than Greg, and nearly two feet taller than
Miss Paxon. His skin is a light tan, like many old men who have
had their shares of alcohol, and he has a full head of salt and
pepper hair. The office smells like Aqua Velva and mothballs,
which suggests he's a man who finds something he likes and
sticks with it.

Unsure of what to expect, Greg reaches his hand out to greet
the Doctor, who, at first glance, reminds him of his grandfather.

"Please, call me Greg," he says. The Doctor's grip is firm. It
too reminds Greg of his grandfather, who explained that "nobody
likes a dead fish for a handshake." "You have quite a reputation,"
he continues, never knowing when to speak versus when to hold
his tongue. "I thank you for taking the time to see me."

The look on the Doctor's face is less than ecstatic. Then again, Greg is sure he looks like a common man compared to the Doctor's usual patients, unworthy of his expertise.

"Please Gregory," says the Doctor, struggling with his need for formality, "Take a seat, any seat you'd like."

Preferring the comfort of having his feet up, Greg chooses the doublewide cushiony seat that's really more like a miniature couch than a chair. He smiles when he sinks into the padded leather rather than bounding off from being too firm. Once settled, he takes off his shoes and puts his feet up on the accompanying ottoman.

"Before we begin," says the Doctor, taking a seat in a recliner positioned opposite from Greg's chosen perch, "Do you have any questions for me?"

Dr. Campos is a professional, and he's in the business of providing a service to those in need. Greg is, in a sense, his customer. Treating him as such is normal, if such a thing exists.

"As you've likely read in my file Doc," says Greg, choosing to be rebelliously informal, "I've been to several head-shrinkers; no two alike. What's your approach?" His over exaggerated mischaracterization is not impressive.

"That's a fair question, Gregory," the Doctor replies as he begins his newly designed semi-orientation. "Once we're able to get through the basic information that tells me who you think you are," his words cause Greg's head to do a double take, "I'll ask you more specific questions that require detailed answers. Then we'll work together to figure out what it is that's negatively impacting your life." The Doctor sounds as though he's expecting some resistance. However, Greg is still confused by the Doctor's riddle-like disposition; and, having never enjoyed the complexity of the infamous Rubik's Cube, Greg can't help but wonder if this meeting will seem like one giant puzzle.

Although a confusing stranger who specializes in crazy people, there's something about Dr. Campos' grandfather-esque presence that Greg finds inviting. It could be that the Doctor fits into Greg's general affinity for the elderly, which, in Greg's mind, is anyone over the age of fifty; he figures they've lived through and seen more than he could have in his short life, and he respected them because of it; or maybe he's too confused to know better. Whatever the reason, somehow, Greg feels secure in the Doctor's office. Perhaps this is the help he's been looking for.

"Gregory," says Dr. Campos, his favorite pen flickering in his right hand again, "Your file says that you first started experiencing your, we'll call them night terrors for now, when you were a teenager. Is that correct?" Greg is startled by the Doctor's quick leap to the greater issue.

"So much for getting through the basics," says Greg, his voice spiking a bit with wonder. "What happened to laying a foundation?" Dr. Campos isn't fazed by Greg's reply. He was deliberate in his preface to the conversation.

"Please," the Doctor continues, "Go back a ways, before the first night during which you remember having these terrors, and tell me what comes to mind."

As he does when recalling most memories, and just as he did while standing on the side of a cliff shortly before entering the office, Greg closes eyes and tries to clear his mind. He has to focus for a moment.

What was going on in my life before Its *first visit?*

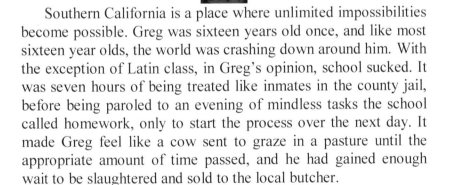

Southern California is a place where unlimited impossibilities become possible. Greg was sixteen years old once, and like most sixteen year olds, the world was crashing down around him. With the exception of Latin class, in Greg's opinion, school sucked. It was seven hours of being treated like inmates in the county jail, before being paroled to an evening of mindless tasks the school called homework, only to start the process over the next day. It made Greg feel like a cow sent to graze in a pasture until the appropriate amount of time passed, and he had gained enough wait to be slaughtered and sold to the local butcher.

However, Greg met his best friend, Kent Lawson, in Latin class. Kent won him over by bluntly referencing an opportunity to be slaves later in the year. Somehow, Greg found Kent's lack of tact appealing.

The only thing that made Latin stand out was Ms. Z, and the general threat of being pegged by a disgusting sock. She was an unusually idiosyncratic woman, average height and build, older, probably close to retiring, with paper-white hair. Her sense of humor was as dry as a can of prunes left outside in Death Valley during the summer, and she kept a long tube sock that was grey with red stripes and looked like it was made in the 1970s. That primary gym sock was filled with even more socks and kept under the overhead projector at the front of the class.

Greg doesn't know if this is what Dr. Campos is looking for, but as sad as it is to say, before the *night terrors*, as he called them, there was the dirty gym-sock.

If a student was caught doing anything other than giving Ms. Z his undivided attention, she would whip out her sock wad, and as if she were Cy Young throwing his best pitch, she'd launch the sock rocket at whoever wasn't complying with her requirements. Every time she wound up and let it rip, the airborne mass would strike her intended target directly between the eyes. By the time a pegged student realized what had transpired, he would get a whiff of what smelled like a 300-pound man's athlete's foot that had been sweating in the awful garment. At which point Ms. Z would tell him to pay attention and collect her weapon. The rest of the class would have let out a round of ground-shaking laughter, but fear of being next was good motivation for composure.

Aside from the bland class schedule, after-school-activities often felt as if they lasted forever. Wrestling practice started promptly at 1:50 every afternoon with the same routine. Everyone on the team stretched for twenty minutes and then ran "the loop," a three and a half mile stretch of road on which one would be able to find anything from old dirty mattresses to abandoned vehicles. If you saw "the loop," you wouldn't be surprised if the police one day found the mob's graveyard among the rubble. The best part of the run was the coach's participation.

Greg assumes that Dr. Campos will redirect or stop him, having traveled far enough off whatever track he was hoping to keep Greg on, but the interjection doesn't come.

Mr. E, or as Greg called him, Coach Beefy, was a 550-pound man who sported a set of glasses made in a year before Greg's mother was born, and a mustache that was most commonly associated with child molesters. His head was bald on top with a thick layer of black hair forming a skullet, which started just above one ear, wrapped around the back of his greasy head, and ended just above the other ear. During the scenic trip around "the loop," as Coach Beefy called it, he would get in his clunker of a mini-van and roll along the side of the group, offering words of encouragement along the way.

"You guys may not believe it now," Coach Beefy would yell, nasty grease from a random piece of pizza running through his pedophiliac facial hair, "But you're well on your way to becoming lean, mean, wrestling machines." The irony was maddening.

It was difficult to take anything Coach Beefy said seriously during the team jogs. Just as his words seemed to bring motivation, Greg would look to his right, and there Coach Beefy would be sitting, in his air conditioned min-van, which squealed every few minutes when it hit a bump, as if the vehicle were writhing in pain beneath the mass that was its whale of a driver.

When "the loop" had been completed, the team partook in a set of specific activities, until Coach Beefy decided everyone had put in enough work, at which point they got to stretch for another twenty minutes, and then go home. This was the routine every day of the week, with the exception that Saturdays and Sundays started in the morning.

Also like most teenagers, Greg felt like nobody understood him. His life was lived like that of a machine. Each morning started with the wretched sounds of a soon-to-be destroyed alarm clock, his ritualistic morning piss, followed by a much-needed shower. He often skipped breakfast, which was part of his determination to prove to the world's scientists that if it was as important as they all claimed, he wouldn't have been able to make it through each day like everyone who was buying into the hype.

Greg arrived at school thirty minutes before class to engage in scintillating conversations with a group of like-minded, similarly doomed friends. When the first bell rang, he'd make his way to class where he often achieved scores that further proved his breakfast theory. The day progressed with more classes until the aforementioned wrestling experience, followed by hours of cleverly labeled homework, because the teachers knew students weren't going to do it at school, and then off to a dream world where Greg would be rudely interrupted by that vile alarm again.

Greg's eyes open to find Dr. Campos sitting exactly as he had been. He has a clipboard in his lap, with a legal-sized yellow notepad fastened to the front, upon which he is making a series of small notes. Greg doesn't know what could be worth writing down. Then again, he's not the Doctor.

"Okay Gregory," says Dr. Campos, looking as if he's waiting for Greg to say more. "It sounds like you resent the days before the events we'll discuss at a later time." Greg had never thought of it that way, but he's right, Greg *did* resent school. "Are you unhappy with your early teen years because you want to be at peace?" The Doctor's questioning continues, "And do you believe that was the last time your mind was free?"

Greg ponders the Doctor's inquiries, almost taking them as suggestions for a moment. Nearly a decade has passed since Greg has known any mental or emotional peace. Again, the Doctor may be on to something.

"I wouldn't rule that possibility out," says Greg, trying to sound smarter than he feels. "My life wasn't terrible then. School just seemed like a waste of my time, and I've felt as though time is something of which I don't have a lot left." Greg didn't want to crown him as a genius, but denial would be counter-productive.

Feeling his left side start to fill with pins and needles, Greg pushes himself up so that he can rotate to a more comfortable position. It seems that no matter how fluffy a chair looks, if you sit in it long enough, your limbs will go numb.

"Gregory," says Dr. Campos, raising a single finger in Greg's direction, "You say that school was a waste of time." A brief pause allows Greg to look around the room, wondering if perhaps the Doctor was making sure someone else understood what Greg stated; but, with nobody else present, at least not that he can see, he nods his head in confirmation of the Doctor's understanding. This may be the Doctor's way of telling Greg that he's listening. Dr. Campos doesn't want to spoil the big surprise, so he chooses his words carefully.

"Aside from the larger reasons for your appointment today," the Doctor continues, "What caused you to believe that your time was being wasted?"

Greg inhales long and hard as he focuses on the most accurate answer. An example from his personal experience feels like the appropriate response. "I don't know if my file mentions it Doc," he starts his reply, "But I'm a mental health worker. I've wanted to be a mental health worker since I was a little boy." Greg's response almost amuses himself, but he holds his smile in. The look on Dr. Campos' face suggests that he's heard this story a time or two.

In geometry class, students spent a lot of time focusing on angles and distances. The instructor insisted that they'd need the skills he was attempting to teach when they made it into the real world.

The image of Mr. Johns pointing his jumbo-sized chalk at him as he lectured on crosses Greg's mind, and must have caused a day-dream to begin.

"Please, continue." The Doctor requests as he makes a brief note.

Mr. Johns' favorite part of teaching always seemed to be putting students on the spot. He was a short man with a slight hunch in his back, and the fact that his left shoe had a substantially thicker sole than his right suggested one of legs was shorter than the other. Like an evil scientist, his fingers tapped on one other as his hands both touched at the base of their palms held out in front of him. The only thing missing was a villainous laugh.

One day Mr. Johns called Greg to the front of the room, and as Greg made his way to the chalkboard, the teacher explained that he was going to walk Greg through a practical word-problem. He loved making examples of his students. Once in front of the class, he instructed Greg to grab a piece of chalk. He felt as though he should have strings attached to his limbs so the puppet master could move Greg himself. The instructions were to draw a small bird, or something similar to a bird, at the top of the board. Greg's artistic ability was shit, but he drew a small bird nonetheless. The next instruction was to draw a tree underneath the bird, and a small man to the left of the tree.

Suddenly geometry involved more drawing than art class.

After the class looked at the masterpiece for a moment, Mr. Johns had Greg draw lines along the right side of the tree from the highest point of the bird to the base of the tree. A second line went from the farthest point of the right side of the tree's base to the base of the small man, and a third line from the man to the bird. He had created a triangle.

Copperfield had nothing on Mr. Johns.

The next step was to define each side of the triangle with lengths of distance. By the time Mr. Johns defined the man's height from his shoulders to the ground, Greg could see the math accumulating. He then asked the class to calculate the angle at which the man would need to throw a stone, if traveling in a straight line, in order to knock the bird off of the tree?

"Tell me Dr. Campos," says Greg in the middle of his story, "What does knocking a bird off of a tree have to do with my line of work?"

Caught somewhat off guard by Greg's choice of an ending to the story, Dr. Campos takes a breath. "So, Gregory," he says, still composing his thoughts, "You believe that geometry was a waste of your time."

"Haha," Greg can't hold the laughter in. Who knew that psychologists could be superheroes too? Greg thought Captain Obvious only existed within ignorant people.

"Not just geometry Doc." he replies, "Most of my classes used examples equally as pointless for teaching tools." Greg's frustration is noticeable, especially as his breathing becomes more strenuous. "I should note Doc," Greg keeps talking despite his need to catch his breath, "That I am yet to use geometry since I completed the course ten years ago." He realizes he's getting out of line and forces himself to stop before he hyperventilates.

"I can see you feel strongly about this Gregory," says Dr. Campos, sensing Greg's blood pressure rising. "I'm not here to upset you," he proceeds with caution, "I simply want to get an idea of how your mind operates. Let's take a ten-minute break. You can use the restroom out in the hall, or, if you smoke, feel free to go out on the patio and unwind." It's as if the thought in Greg's mind made its way to the Doctor's mouth.

Dr. Campos stands up, clipboard in hand, and walks to the door where Greg entered.

"We'll pick things back up afterwards," he says as he exits the room.

Chapter 5

Pacing back and forth on Dr. Campos' back patio, smoking his *Kool Filter Kings*, Greg is fuming. School, in his opinion, is among the biggest problems in America. Children are told they have to go to school to get smart before they're old enough to form a sentence. It's beaten into them. If people hope to amount to anything during their lives, they not only have to get a basic education from a school, they need to pay a university for an advanced education as well. Greg doesn't see the point in talking about it. That's not why he's there. He wishes he could talk to someone, anyone; Well, anyone else. He needs to calm his nerves.

As he stares intently at his cell phone, Greg contemplates whether or not he should dial a number, and a sad realization comes to mind; he can recall the most insignificant things in his life in great detail, a gift from his PTSD. However, he doesn't know anyone's phone number; not his fiancée's, his mother's, his brother's, Kent's, not a single one. He knows he can navigate through his smartphone's menu to the list of contact's, at which point he can tell the hand-held computer to call any random person, but as he stares at the number-pad in front of him, he doesn't know an actual sequence that will cause any acquaintance's phone to ring.

"Oh well," Greg speaks to himself in a shameful tone.

It takes him a minute to get into the directory, but he smiles immediately upon hitting the "send" key. The line rings once and it occurs to Greg that she's probably at work. It rings twice and he hopes she's not too busy to take the call. By the time it rings four times and goes to voicemail, Greg lets out a big sigh and ends the call before it asks him to leave a message. What would he have said anyways; that he was pissed off about nothing important, and that much like his opinion about school, he feels like he's wasting his time? Greg will save his life-mate the grief of having to hear his pointless whining. Instead he drops his finished butt to the floor, stomps it out, and suddenly feels the phone vibrate in his hand.

She must not be too busy after all.

Some Doctors have suggested that Greg is precisely the type of person Sigmund Freud was talking about when he developed his theory on the "Oedipus Complex." Nobody's saying that Greg wants to have intercourse with his mother, but the fact that he is engaged to a younger-model version of his life-giver leaves the professionals wondering.

When Greg was fourteen, his family lived exactly one and a half miles from the local high school, a trip he made by foot each and every day, rain or shine. As luck would have it, on his way home the day before Christmas vacation, Greg ascended a dirt incline that connected the east side of the neighborhood to the west. At the top of the path was a group of classmates smoking cigarettes and picking on another student at Greg's school. There were two things he hated almost as much as he hated school, smokers and bullies.

Thinking he was some sort of heroic avenger, Greg dropped his backpack to the ground and ran toward the ruckus. If he'd really been paying attention, Greg would have seen that with basic math he could count ten attackers. With one victim to pick on, the group easily divided in two and continued beating both Greg and their first victim. One of the bullies even pulled Greg's shoe off of his left foot and smacked him across the face with it. Greg hated smokers and bullies.

Anxious to talk to anyone at this point, Greg answers his pulsating phone. "Hey babe," he greets his hopeful wife-to-be, lighting another cigarette with his free hand.

"Hi sweetie," she always addresses him with some term of endearment. "Is your meeting over already? Haha," she chuckles before whispering, "That would be a record."

"You're funny," says Greg sarcastically, taking a long drag of his menthol cancer stick, "I'm taking a butt break."

His fiancée hates when he smokes. She's heard the recap of the shoe-to-face incident, and she's heard about all of the grief Greg used to give his mother before she quit smoking herself. However, she also remembers how emotionally crippled he was when they first met. Still, no woman wants to see the man with whom she intends to spend the rest of her life aim for an early grave.

"Enjoy it while you can," she exclaims in a less than impressed tone.

Greg promised her that he'd quit by the time his birthday comes around, which gives him less than three weeks to work on lung cancer. The joshing concludes and Greg proceeds to tell her about his frustration and general lack of optimism. Luckily for him, after a few years of experience, she knows him like an assassin knows a trigger. He's sensitive.

Greg's ranting eventually tapers off, his lover slowly inhales, and though he's unable to see her, he knows she's smiling, whether she's happy or forcing it for his sake.

"Sweetheart," Greg can hear that his fiancée is preparing to impart some generic wisdom she likely got from her own mother upon him, "Everything happens for a reason. Just be patient. I love you."

Greg sees Dr. Campos walking back into his office from the edge of the patio. His almost-wife is right. He needs to be patient. After all, this is his last chance.

"I love you too baby," He responds in-kind. The call ends and Greg tries to let his caller's kind words bring him peace. He doesn't know what he'd do without her.

Break time is over, and Greg, ready to get the show back on the road, smothers the remainder of his cigarette on the concrete patio, walks back into the Doctor's office, and, remembering the rules of course, shuts off his phone.

"Hi Doc," he says, ready to make some progress, "Let's do this."

Chapter 6

Over the last ten or eleven years, Jeanne Burns has seen many Doctors, from physicians, to therapists, psychologists, and psychiatrists; none of which have been successful; yesterday's session least of all.

So, on this, her twenty-eighth birthday, Jeanne Burns decided that she is going to take the advice from the infomercial playing on the radio in her old Mustang on her way to work, and visit a local psychic. She figures that it can't hurt matters any, and who knows, as good as she believes today is going to be, it may be just the thing she needs to get back on the right path.

On the corner where Archibald Avenue connects to 4th Street, there sits a run-down strip mall in the back corner of an Ontario California parking lot where a storefront window reads, "Fortunes Read Daily."

"Perfect," Jeanne says to herself. *What could be more legitimate then a back lot prophet?*

Unable to resist, Jeanne turns into the nearly empty lot, parks her car, and struts towards the entrance. Considering how sensually dressed she is, if a police officer were to pass at this exact moment, he's likely think there is more for sale than just fortunes.

Two steps through the doorway and bells begin to ring as if Jeanne had just returned home from war and songs of victory were sounding to announce her arrival. There's a desk upon which an antique cash register sits next to a sign instructing her to take a seat while waiting. Jeanne would be glad to oblige the signs directive, but much to her surprise, there is no furniture for her to sit on. Behind the desk is what looks like a large fitting room at a clothing store smothered by dark-purple velvet drapes. Water is dripping from a large crack in the ceiling, and the wallpaper is peeling and stained yellow from years of cigarette smoke being exhaled upon it.

What am I doing here? Jeanne can't help but think she's made a foolish mistake?

"Haha," a deep laugh resonates through the semi-lobby as if made through an intercom system of some sort. Jeanne cautiously turns around in the center of the room, like a rotisserie-cooked chicken at a supermarket deli, looking for the location of the sound she just heard; but there aren't any speakers that she can see.

Someone is here.

After a moment of feeling puzzled, a woman standing less than five feet tall appears out of nowhere without a sound. She's wearing a silk robe that covers most of her stunted body. Her hair is messy and repugnant, somewhere between dreadlocks and a tattered mop. Her face is mostly smooth, with the exception of two tiny moles on her right cheek, which have a short white hair growing out from between them. The woman introduces herself as Mistress P, and asks for Jeanne's name, which, at that point causes her to feel cheated.

"Are you the fortune teller?" Jeanne asks, hoping she didn't misread the sign out front. Mistress P takes a second and looks her customer over. It's not often a woman as beautiful as Jeanne walks through the door in heels and a skirt, at least not unless they have something to sell. Then she smiles and bows, confirming her role and solidifying Jeanne's concern.

"I don't mean to be rude miss," says Jeanne in her most skeptical tone, "But shouldn't you know what my name is?" The bizarre woman doesn't even bat an eye at the question, acting as though she hadn't asked it.

Ignoring the minor detail, Jeanne shows the mistress her photo ID, and is immediately provided a list of services offered, including a written disclosure that there are no refunds, for any reason. Looking for the first good news in a long time, but not really believing in the woman's abilities given her disheartening introduction, Jeanne gives twenty dollars to the mistress, who proceeds to escort her behind the velvet curtain.

Hollywood leads you to believe that all fortune-tellers have exotically-scented candles burning to intoxicate your senses, elaborate carpeting to charm your perception, and bright crystal balls to complete the storybook experience while having your future read. Mistress P, however, has two folding chairs that are less than alluring, a stain-covered coffee table from a weekend of flea marketing, and an aroma that smells like senior citizens. Understanding why there are no refunds, Jeanne reluctantly takes a seat.

Every year a large group of quasi-actors gets together to put on a one or two-week-long medieval-themed festival called the Renaissance Fair. The participants would camp in the nearby parking lots and fields by night, and when day broke, they dressed up like members of the kings' and queens' courts and put on a fabulous show. Jousting and sword-fighting, as well as period piece plays and fortune telling were among the many historical-era events that took place while the fair was open to the public.

When Jeanne Burns was twelve-years-old, her mother allowed her to skip school during the week, and they went to the Renaissance Fair for some fun. Jeanne had her face painted; she got to wear a knight's armor, customized for a child of course; and she and her mother had their fortunes read. The oracle was a giant man with a deep bass-filled tone when he spoke, but was otherwise as kind as Santa Claus. His tent was filled with a thick mysterious fog, and random beams of colored light flickered from everywhere. He used a heavily worn deck of Tarot cards, and waved a sandalwood-scented incense stick while he talked. Mistress P is not that elegant of a soothsayer.

After a few questions about her life, the "all-seeing" mistress who is seated across the short and dirty table asks Jeanne to hold her hands out, palms to the sky. She quickly grabs Jeanne's wrists with her wart-covered fingers and pulls Jeanne's hands closer to her side of the table, dragging Jeanne's elbows through what she now realizes is not a dry stain after all.

That better wash out.

Within ten seconds the prophet grunts and releases her subject's limbs. Jeanne looks at her with probing eyes, uncertain of what just happened. A small jewelry-sized chest appears from a drawer under the mistress' side of the table, who proceeds to reach into the box and pull out what looks like the rocks you can find scattered along any beach in America. They appear to have sat in running water long enough to make them smooth to the touch, and sparkling to the eye. Mistress P rolls them onto the table like dice in a craps game at Caesar's Palace in Las Vegas. The stones come to a halt after bouncing off of the container from whence they came, and her eyes roll back in her head. The fortune-teller looks to the sky and begins mumbling things in a language unknown to Jeanne.

"Hold your hands out in front of you again," she snaps at Jeanne, her focus returning to Jeanne's stare as she grabs the tips of her fingers.

"Is everything okay?" Jeanne asks, starting to feel scared.

"Silence!" The mistress shouts, her body beginning to twitch as if she's going to have a seizure.

Jeanne does as the Mistress asks and sits in silence for a minute, then two, and eventually five. "This is stupid," she says, yanking her hands away from the outrageous woman. "I'm just going to grab my things and –"

"Aaah!" The Mistress' scream impedes on the subject's attempt to flee, as her eyes open wide, and she falls backwards out of her chair.

"Oh my God," says Jeanne, the Mistress now violently shuttering on the ground. "Are you okay?" She asks, running around the table to help.

"Get away," says the mistress with a fearful fire in her eyes. "You, get away from me now."

"What?" Jeanne asks, confused.

"Just get away!" The Mistress shouts again. "You're a cursed woman Ms. Burns." She stands herself up, still shaking, her right hand stretched out and pointing at Jeanne's face.

"I'm what?" Jeanne asks, sure she didn't hear correctly.

"Cursed Ms. Burns," the Mistress repeats, her tone even more wicked. "You have a curse on you. I don't know how long you've had it, but it's there, clear as day Ms. Burns."

"I –" Jeanne pauses, alarmed by the Mistress' words, yet sickly intrigued. "I don't understand. What do you mean I'm cursed?"

"Tell me Ms. Burns," says the mistress, gradually gaining some self-control, "How long have you felt like you're being watched, like you're never alone?" The questions cause Jeanne to choke when she gasps and her spit flies to the back of her throat.

"How could you know –" Jeanne begins to ask, but stops when she sees Mistress P pointing to the word *Psychic* on a business card taped to the end of the table. "Does that mean you know what it is?" She almost becomes hopeful.

"Aye," says the mistress, answering as if she were a pirate, "I do." Jeanne waits to see if the woman will say more on her own, but she doesn't.

"Well, then what is it?" She asks anxiously.

"Haha," the mistress laughs, "At least you're smart enough to be scared of it Ms. Burns." She stands her chair back up, takes a seat, reaches back into the drawer from which she took the chest filled with rocks, and pulls out a pack of cigarettes. "Do you have a light?" She asks.

"Huh?" Jeanne hesitates in confusion. "No. I don't smoke."

"That's okay Ms. Burns," says the mistress with a creepy grin on her face, "It's a little too late to start now." She takes a cigarette from the pack and places it in her mouth. "So, Ms. Burns, you didn't answer my question," she says, bringing her right hand up to her face, "How long have you felt as though you're never alone?" Mistress P snaps her fingers and a small spark ignites the embers at the end of the cigarette in her mouth.

Jeanne's eyes light up in amazement. "How did you do that?" She asks, thinking she's just seen a magic trick.

"You're wasting time Ms. Burns," says the Mistress, "How long?"

"I don't know," says Jeanne under pressure, also returning to her chair, "I guess it's been about ten years or so, long enough that it's hard to remember."

"And today is your birthday Ms. Burns, is it not?" The mistress asks, still grinning.

"It is," says Jeanne, unsure of what the piece of information has to do with anything, "My twenty-eighth actually. Why do you ask?"

"Well Ms. Burns," says the mistress, "I hate to be the one to give bad news, but you aren't going to see a day beyond this one." Her words hit Jeanne like a cannon ball to the stomach.

"Why would you say something like that?" Jeanne asks, furious. "What sort of scam are you running here?"

"Ms. Burns, please," says the mistress, who is quite serious, "I'm not trying to pull one over on you." She takes one long drag of her cigarette, and again Jeanne is impressed as the ash falls to the floor, leaving nothing but the filter in Mistress P's mouth. "You Ms. Burns," she continues, "Are dealing with something that almost everyone has seen."

"This is ridiculous," says Jeanne, again preparing to leave. "No I'm not. I don't know anyone who's seen what I have."

"Ms. Burns," the mistress barks, running out of patience, "I'll give you back your twenty dollars. Just let me finish."

"Fine," says Jeanne, figuring at least she can keep her money.

"Thank you," says the mistress. "Now, Ms. Burns, as I was saying, everyone has seen the very thing you've been seeing, the very thing that's watching you. However, rarely does it ever stay once someone has looked upon it. Most people have nightmares at one point or another, and every once in a while they wake up covered in sweat, scared out of their minds by what they've just seen. Often times when they're jarred awake, they'll see an odd looking shadow, like a silhouette of a man. When this happens, generally the people will shake their heads, or wipe their eyes, and then it's gone, just a figment of their imaginations."

"Okay," says Jeanne, not really seeing the point, "But what does that have to do with me?"

"Well Ms. Burns," answers the mistress, "That's where the very few people I mentioned come in." She pauses and gives Jeanne a look of helpless sincerity, "Those who continue to see the shadow, regardless of how many times they shake their heads and wipe their eyes, those are the people it has chosen." Another moment of silence passes and it's clear, Jeanne's trying to wrap her head around what Mistress P is saying.

"Chosen for what?" She asks, lost.

"It's hard to say Ms. Burns," The Mistress answers, sighing mildly, leaning back in her chair. "Whatever the reason, those who are chosen are never seen again."

"What do you mean they're never seen again?" Now Jeanne is freaked out.

"Ms. Burns," says the mistress, "Once it has chosen someone, it waits until the person's, well –" she stops to look directly in Jeanne's eyes, "In your case, today; and that's when it takes them."

Jeanne stops listening at that point. She finds the Mistress' story clever, but believes it's one she tells all the time. She figures the next person who comes in will be thirty-seven and magically *it* will wait until thirty-eighth birthdays. As far as Jeanne's concerned, it's all a bunch of codswallop. She can't stand to hear another word. So, she grabs her purse and heads for the door.

"Ms. Burns," says the Mistress, Stopping Jeanne in the doorway, who turns to listen, "I'm sorry. I truly hope I'm wrong."

Paying no mind to what she feels is bogus apology, Jeanne turns back to the exit, lets out a snippy grunt, puts on her sunglasses, and charges out the door. She's bound for a wonderful day, and she doesn't want to ruin it by being late to work.

Chapter 7

Now back in his office, Dr. Campos pours Greg a glass of water from the cooler next to his desk.

"Take this," says the Doctor handing the cup over. "If you need anything else, please, let me know."

Greg can't help but notice a change in the Doctor's demeanor. He seems spryer, like a man with a revived mission.

"Everything alright Doc?" Greg asks.

"Yes Mr. Ro –," the Doctor catches himself, "Yes Gregory. Everything is quite alright."

After years of working in the field, Professionalism is a reflex for Dr. Campos, it's part of his routine. "Talking for long periods of time tends to make me thirsty," he goes one, "And I thought you may feel the same way. That's all." He continues, pointing to the oversized puffy chair where Greg previously sat, "Now, please, take a seat. We're going to take a," the Doctor mulls his statement over, "happier approach."

When Greg was twenty-two years old, he had a platonic friend named Stephanie Schmanski. They had both experienced tremendous heartache, and talking to one another about their troubles helped them find some inner peace. They became close, but for whatever reason, things never progressed beyond a strong friendship.

Stephanie was house sitting for her parents while they were away on vacation. That Saturday, while getting ready to go on her first date since having her heart broken, she was talking to Greg on the phone. Stephanie was excited, yet nervous. She wasn't sure she'd be able to enjoy herself, but hoped she'd be able to fight through her pain. Greg was great for giving her the pep talks she needed.

A knock came at the front door, and Stephanie asked Greg to hold while she went to greet her date, placing the phone on a small end table where the family usually leaves their keys once returning home. Greg heard the door open, and after a moment or two, he heard Stephanie trying to back out of the date. Something wasn't right. Then Greg heard a door closing, followed by crashing sounds, and then screams. Stephanie was in trouble.

Greg had visited Stephanie at her folks' house once before, and he drove as fast as he could, hoping he'd remember exactly which street it was on. His memory being what it was, he arrived in record time. The Shadow barely came to a complete stop before he ran to the front door, that was still thrown open, and Greg could see the house looked like a hurricane had gone through it. Glass was scattered across the floor in little pieces, tables and chairs were flipped over in almost every room, and there was blood on the wall going up the stairs.

Greg quickly trudged up the steps to the second floor, where he noticed a cabinet was tipped over in the hallway to the left. Having helped his grandfather clean his basement several times before, it only takes Greg a moment to realize the toppled shelving unit is a gun case, and there are several opened boxes of bullets spilled across the carpet. A pit grows in his stomach.

Heading across the call from the fallen case, Greg opens the door to Stephanie's bedroom to find she's sitting on the floor in the adjacent corner. Her blouse was torn, and her pants and underwear had been ripped off. Blood was trickling down from her bottom lip because her attacker slammed her face against the wall when she ran. She had a snub nose revolver in her mouth.

"Steph," he called out to her, "Don't." Before he could get within ten feet of her, Stephanie pulled the gun from her clenched jaws and pointed it directly at Greg.

"Stay away from me!" She cried out, tears gushing down her cheeks. The man she was supposed to go out with had forced his way into the house, beaten her to a bloody pulp, and raped her. Now, with Greg standing before her, all she sees is another man, another threat, and another violator. She doesn't realize it's her good friend and confidant.

Greg stopped dead in his tracks, expecting Stephanie to shoot. She didn't. Instead, she just stayed where she was, pointing the gun at Greg, and he took a seat where he stood, and they waited exactly like that for fourteen hours. Greg wasn't leaving his friend, and he knew, sooner or later, she'd snap back to reality just a bit and see it was he who was sitting before her. He had the patience to wait.

Settling back into the large sofa-sized chair, with a glass of water in his hand, Greg puts his feet up, and thinks of the patience he showed with Stephanie. He may need some more of that patience today.

"Dr. Campos," says Greg politely.

"Yes Gregory?' the Doctor replies as he removes his glasses and sits at attention for what his patient is about to say.

"I want to apologize for being difficult," says Greg. "I know in order for this to work I must trust that you will do what you believe is best to reach an acceptable solution."

Patience.

Though he doesn't say it, Greg wants the Doctor to trust him as well.

"We haven't started discussions about my real issues," he resumes, taking his mother's advice, "and we'll never get there if I'm not patient."

The look on Dr. Campos' face appears to be that of surprise. Perhaps he doesn't think Greg is capable of accepting responsibility. Then again, it's unlikely that many of the patients at Patton owned up to much.

"I appreciate that Gregory," says Dr. Campos, still uncertain of how to respond. "Hopefully we'll be able to make our way towards the heavier burdens with which you're faced."

Greg feels a bit of relief knowing the Doctor recognizes bigger things are still to come.

"Excellent," says Greg. "I'm all yours Doc."

Dr. Campos removes his wristwatch and loosens his tie. It's time to get serious. He now has highlighters and three different-colored pens clipped to his notepad.

"What I'm going to have you do Gregory," he says, looking at Greg intently, "In just a moment, is close your eyes and tell me a story from your past."

Greg's curiosity is rising again, not sure what the Doctor is looking for.

"I don't want you to tell me just any story," says Dr. Campos. "No, instead I want you to tell me about something from before your night terrors, something from before you recognized a problem existed, however, this time, let us try something that made you *happy*."

Suddenly Greg feels like things are going way off course again.

"Perhaps you made a connection with someone," the Doctor expands his instruction, "Someone who made you feel more alive than you had ever previously felt."

Greg knows where this is headed. He's always cautious when talking about her. He worries people may not understand.

"Can you do that for me Gregory?" The Doctor asks.

Greg's heart races again, and he struggles to maintain steady breaths.

"Um," he hesitates. Greg doesn't want to make the wrong choice, but he also wants to keep her wishes in mind.

"Please Gregory," says Dr. Campos. "As you said, if I'm going to help you, you must trust me." He's right. Greg's sure if she were present, she'd understand.

"Okay Doc," Greg responds, building the courage to give the Doctor what he wants. "I'm going to tell you about a girl I met, a girl who changed my life, a girl who, though very mysterious, was perfect."

Dr. Campos nods at Greg, who leans his head back and closes his eyes once more.

This better be useful.

Chapter 8

Following the injury that ended Greg's future in the world of wrestling, he is forced to attend physical therapy every Monday, Wednesday, and Friday for six months. Being that his incident happened during a function for which the school was liable, they ar forced to foot the bill. While that saves his parents any money that would be spent on hospitals and Doctors, the school is cheap. Their priority has always been the bottom line, not the health of their student athletes. Thankfully, after two weeks without any results, Greg's mother decides to send him to a private specialist.

Dr. Vladimir Petrovic's office is located in a building with walls made entirely of glass. Greg's jaw drops in awe as he parks his Dodge Shadow in the accompanying lot. It looks like a sky-scraping mirror that starts on the ground and disappears into the crystal-blue sky. He can only imagine what a fancy office like that costs. If what he sees is any indication of the level of service he's going to get, he's in the right place.

The door gets stuck as Greg climbs out of his car, and it won't swing shut.

It's always something.

In this case, life is trying to maintain the status quo. Greg's excited about the Doctor's office, so the car needs to knock him back down a peg. Considering the reasons for needing Dr. Petrovic's services, he's unable to exert much force in an attempt to slam the door. Greg hopes fate will respond to harsh words instead. With his eyes closed he takes a deep breath and lets the world know exactly how he feels.

"Piece of shit car," he screams at the clouds above. "Can't you work with me just this once?"

Ironically, as the words flow from Greg's mouth, his body jolts from the surprise of the door thumping shut. He returns his gaze to the trusty ride and finds a young woman directly in front of him. Standing three inches taller than Greg, her long and slender, immaculately toned legs call for immediate attention, escaping from the cut of a tightly fit pale-yellow summer dress in a sharp set of stilettos. Her light-copper hair flows in waves just above her shoulders. She has lips like candy apples waiting to be tasted, and her eyes are as blue as a Hawaiian beach staring back into Greg's. Where was this angel of passion hiding when he drove in? He hadn't noticed anyone in the parking lot, but he's not going to complain about her presence now. Greg thinks he should say something before the staring gets awkward.

"Thanks," says Greg, whose sentences get shorter when he's nervous.

"For what?" She asks, batting her eyes and giving an inviting smile. Her look almost convinces Greg that she hadn't done anything, and perhaps his door closed itself. Then he recognizes that's crazy talk and knows it had to be her.

"Your triumph over my evil car," he responds moronically.

"Haha," she chuckles quietly. "You look like someone who needs a break, so consider it a gift." Her voice is soft and sensual, and elegance flows from her mouth, moved by a petite-squared jaw. Her words throw Greg for a loop. He's never met this woman before, and here she is, giving him a gift of all things? Why can't more people be this appealing?

Is she toying with me? Who is this sexy devil?

"I appreciate it," says Greg. "I'm here to see –"

"Dr. Petrovic," she finishes his sentence, and he gulps loud enough to send the two birds hovering near a small bush flying away. "You're here to see Dr. Petrovic." She affirms her words.

The smile on this girl's face fills Greg's heart with fire, while her words of prophecy set off alarms in his head, but he just doesn't care. He's smitten already.

"How do you –" Greg tries to ask.

"You dropped your appointment letter," she answers before he finishes his question. "It fell out of your hand when you shouted at the sky. It says you are seeing Dr. Vladimir Petrovic. I hope you don't mind that I saw." She winks at Greg. "Haha," she chuckles again, "Did you think I read your mind?" She stops to look into Greg's eyes. He doesn't care about the letter. "I don't want to keep you from your Doctor," she continues, "You're almost late. I'm waiting for my ride."

Greg notices a small bench by the front door where she claims to have been sitting.

"Okay," he says. "Well, thanks again." He wouldn't describe his interaction as smooth. Something about her has turned him into a guy in need of a helmet and a small yellow bus.

Inside the main doors of the building stands a sign informing Greg that he's heading to the third floor. The first floor is nothing but an open room with four elevators. Greg pushes the button to call the moving lift and waits.

While the illuminated sign counts down from nineteen, Greg looks back to the bench outside at the woman who witnessed him acting like a fool. All she did was close his door for him, and she completely blew his mind. He is mesmerized by her beauty.

Floor 12.

Greg hopes she's still sitting there when his appointment's over. It's a selfish thought, because she'll still be waiting for her ride to show, but she makes his heart flutter.

Floor 5.

He can't believe he forgot to get her name. The doors to the elevator open before him and Greg is torn between being on time and knowing what to call the enchantress' when he sees her later in his dreams. He gets on the elevator.

Chicken shit.

Greg presses the button for the eleventh floor without realizing the elevator is made from the same glass as the building walls. By the time he's half way up, he wishes he had elected to be late. The ride up is faster than the wait at the bottom.

Aside from being good at his job, there's nothing special about Dr. Petrovic. The appointment goes well, but Greg hardly notices, because he's too busy daydreaming about her, and though he's leaving an hour later than he anticipated, he has much better medical information than he had when he arrived, and he's confident he's making progress towards a swift recovery.

Stepping back off of the elevator at the first floor, his obsession with the gorgeous girl he'd met on his way in spikes when Greg notices that she's still waiting on the bench on his way back out. Hoping to redeem himself after his epic failure earlier, Greg makes his way towards her, trying to keep his hormones in check.

"Someone has clearly gone mad," he says emphatically.

"Oh," she says with a smile, "How's that?" Greg knows she sees through him, but that doesn't change his answer.

"Well," he responds, "Only someone who's out of his mind would leave you sitting here." He's hoping the smile on his face reads like a joke, though it represents a small standing ovation for having the balls to say it.

"Aren't you clever," she says as she gets up to walk closer to the charmer. She isn't running away or making up excuses; two points for Greg.

"You never know when someone such as myself is going to show up and sweep you off of your feet," says Greg with a bit of sarcasm, "or at least convince you to let me take you home." Realizing how someone could take that the wrong way after saying it, Greg attempts to recover, "Um, uh, I mean give you a ride home; to your home."

Good job idiot, he thinks to himself. "Like, where you live," he clarifies. He wishes he could just shut up, before he makes a complete ass of himself.

Convinced that his attempt to be her white knight is shot to hell, Greg turns and walks to his car, his head is slumped forward like a dog with its tail between its legs. He feels like an idiot. The door doesn't give him any trouble this time around, and as he looks up to stare at her one last time before departing, but she's gone. Greg rubs his eyes and blinks a few times, but sure as Abraham Lincoln was assassinated, she vanished.

Assuming the laws of physics still apply, Greg shuts the car door again, and heads back towards the bench. There's no sign of her.

Where did she –?

Then he hears that soft, yet vibrant chuckle somewhere behind him. Shaking his head in disbelief, Greg turns around to find the mysterious beauty getting into his trash-heap of a car, and it puts him over the edge. For all he knows, this woman really is the devil, but that doesn't faze him. He's enamored; he's in love; and he doesn't even know her name.

The ride across town is a quiet one at first. Greg's eyes keep wandering over to the passenger seat, where the cut of the exquisite young vixen's dress ridden part way up her thighs. It doesn't take much to get a seventeen-year old boy worked up, and Greg can't help but think of every dirty clip of porn he's ever watched through blurred lines on the adult channels that are distorted during the wee hours of the night.

She's willing to accept her hero's offer for transportation, but she won't tell Greg where she lives. Instead, she has him drop her off at Heritage Park, a decent sized playground with an accompanying baseball field and pool in the middle of a residential neighborhood just outside of Rancho Cucamonga, CA.

"Thanks hun," she says, leaning into the passenger window. She asks him to pick her up on Friday night in the same place. Greg's chivalry earns him a date with the red headed mystery diva leaving an impression in his mind like sunlight on undeveloped film.

Chapter 9

Prior to meeting the stunning temptress, Greg didn't care about his general appearance, and he didn't own any dressy outfits. His opinion is that anyone worth his while will like him just the way he is. Though the theory may be valid, thinking about how amazing his date looked when he last saw her, Greg has the urge to make a transformation from typical teenager to sophisticated man. He wants to catch this girl off guard and have her heart racing as fast as his did when he first saw her. His intentions are admirable, and though he's certain he's ready to become a man, reality has the finances of a high school student who works at a gas station part-time. Lucky for Greg, southern California is littered with outlet stores.

When it comes to shopping for clothing, Greg's blessed to be a male. Just walking past the women's section gives him a headache. Why a woman needs to have bras available in thirty different colors is beyond him.

Do you need more than one?

At least there are matching panties, stockings, and shoes to go with whichever choice is made. The fact that these items tend to be organized near one another in department stores makes Greg wonder if there are handfuls of women walking around in these items and these items alone? His ignorance is immeasurable at times.

At just under six feet tall, and with shoulders that are quite broad for his size, it's impossible for Greg to find pre-sized suits that fit. When he was last measured for a tuxedo for his mother's second wedding last year, the seamstress told him then that he'd have to get all of his suits tailored for the rest of his life. The key is to find a color in a style that you like, pick a size or two bigger than normal, and let the professionals with the tape measures do the rest.

Greg has always been a fan of black. Much like the advice about cars, his Grandfather always told him that a real man finds something he likes and sticks with it until the end. He never said what *the end* was, so Greg figures he wants him to love it until he dies. In black socks, black boxer-briefs, a black under shirt, black slacks, a long-sleeved black shirt complete with black buttons, to hell with the tie, all brought together by a pair of black Wingtip knock offs, he stays true to his grandfather's advice.

Handing his assortment of funeral-worthy attire to a short Hispanic holding a handful of safety pins by the fitting rooms, Greg explains his need to have his outfit ready for Friday. Sooner is okay, but later will leave him dressed in thrift store jeans and a ratty t-shirt. The older-looking sewing ninja assures him that his suit will be ready in time, and Greg moves on to his next mission.

You likely won't find any official statistics to verify the fact, but Greg assumes all teenage boys trying to be men believe they know exactly how to act in the presence of females. Being a fellow *expert*, Greg knows precisely what a woman loves; a man who smells divine. What he doesn't know is the actual scent associated with divinity. Is it musk? Does *Hugo Boss* or *Calvin Klein* fit the bill? Realizing that the answer isn't going to arrive on its own, he requests the help of a customer service representative named Molly.

"Excuse me miss," says Greg, waving his hand as if he's leaving on a grand voyage.

The sales associate is a young woman, most likely in her mid-twenties, which, in Greg's mind, means she like has plenty of experience in the field of smelling men.

"Oh, hi," says Molly with a fake customer service smile. "How can I help you sir?"

Greg has never been called sir before. He likes the sound of that. He also wonders if franchised stores have a programming factory where new workers, such as Molly, enter as untrained self-thinking people, but return as brainwashed Stepford Wives?

"This is going to sound rather -" Greg speaks, but starts to freeze in front of yet another cute female, despite her faux manners, "Um, odd; it's gonna be odd."

Molly tries not to laugh. The training struggles to hold on.

"I have a rather significant endeavor this Friday," Greg continues, "And I'm having trouble picking a smell." The look on Molly's face tells Greg he sounds as ridiculous as he feels.

Damn adolescence.

"A," she pauses, still holding the laughter in, "Smell, sir?"

"I'm sorry," says Greg, embarrassed. "I meant that I'm in search of the perfect cologne." He feels his IQ is plummeting. One or two more comments and he'll be eating applesauce out of a Playdough cup with a rubber spork.

"Haha," Molly bursts out, unable to hold it anymore, and it eases the tension, "How sweet," she says. "You're trying to smell pretty for a girl." Her smile reminds Greg of the look his grandmother gives him when she knows he wants a cookie. All that's missing now is a gentle pat on the head.

"Is it that obvious?" Greg asks, feeling like he has a sign taped to his back notifying whoever finds him of where he belongs.

"Oh, I didn't mean anything by it," says Molly, clenching her teeth to stop giggling. "I think it's cute." Greg really hopes this woman isn't paid through commission. Her sales technique rivals that of an undertaker. Then again, his pride is taking a beating standing in the aisle of a clothing store.

"How would you like me to assist you?" She asks, back in control.

Greg takes a breath and thinks to himself, *here goes nothing.*

"I've never bought anything outside of the deodorant family," he says. The theme music from *The Adams Family* plays through his head as he caps off the tune with the snap of his fingers. "I'm hoping you can tell me what sort of smell a woman likes on a guy for the first date?" Greg proceeds, submitting to the notion he isn't going to sound smart. "I feel ridiculous, but if it's going to help me win some points come Friday, your opinion is the best chance I have."

Help me Obi-Wan Kenobi. You're my only hope. He can't help but think of Princess Leia. Greg is a huge "Star Wars" fan, though the word "fan" is an understatement. His fandom is more like that of a cult member.

In the perfume aisle there are cabinets on the left for women and on the right for men. Ignoring her customer's quirkiness, really to avoid laughing at him again, Molly points to a separate shelf just beyond the cabinets and explains its purpose.

"Each fragrance available in the cabinets has an equivalent *tester* bottle located on the shelf at the end of the aisle," she says, pointing her hands from one to the other like an airline stewardess.

She gives a quick demonstration of the proper method for testing cologne, taking a small white strip that looks like the kind of bandage used to help those who snore sleep better at night, grabs a random bottle from the shelf of *testers*, sprays the nasal bandage once, and waves it in front of Greg's face.

The intense sting of chemical fumes causes him to choke and gasp for air. He tries inhaling deeply, but coughs instead. His face turns a dark shade of burgundy. He's having an asthma attack. Luckily, since he nearly died following an attack during a wrestling match, Greg always carries an inhaler. It takes him a moment to fish it out of his pocket, but once he's able to take a couple of buffs, he regains his breath.

"What was that?" Greg asks with a look of concern for his health. Again, Molly has the urge to laugh. She feels awful, but now that he's okay, it's hilarious.

"I'm – um –" she struggles to speak, and again gives in to the urge, letting out a series of quaint snickers, "I'm so sorry."

There's no way Greg's going through that again. As the struggle to breathe subsides, he asks Molly to pick any cologne she knows she likes, and that will be the bottle Greg buys. $250 later, he has a sharp outfit being altered, and a new scent. When the cashier hands him the receipt, she also gives him a comment card and asks that Greg complete the front side. The outlet store wants to know how his service was. Greg can't blame his lack of knowledge or preparedness on Molly, though she did find his near death experience humorous. With his mind focused on Friday he doesn't care that she nearly killed him with a toxic piece of paper. Greg checks the box that signifies complete satisfaction with the shopping experience and makes his way out the front doors.

Chapter 10

Friday comes after what feels like forever and Greg arrives at Heritage Park with a few minutes to spare. There's nothing more humiliating than being tardy for a first date, or so he's told. It's a pleasant spring evening at sixty-eight degrees, with a mild breeze, and clear skies. Stars are beginning to show through the fading blue sky, and the moon is nearly full. One couldn't ask for better conditions. As he takes a seat on the bench between the playground and parking lot, Greg wonders what she'll look like. He's only had the one unusual experience with her, and he doesn't know what to expect.

Will she even show?

A lot of preparation has gone into tonight. Not only did Greg shine his new shoes, he also ironed his shirt and slacks. He doesn't want to smother his date with new aroma, nor does he want to commit suicide by fragrance, but Greg used enough of his new cologne so it won't go unnoticed.

The hands on the watch show it's time, and he walks back to his car, takes a deep breath, and tells himself everything is going to be fine. Like a swimmer diving into the pool at the exact moment the starter pistol fires, the faint sound of footsteps on the pavement behind him creeps into his ears at the exact time she asked him to be there.

Greg turns around, and while his eyes adjust to the streetlight, he sees her just beyond the swings, moving with effortless grace. Witnessing each step as she makes her way towards him fills Greg with that same fire from the day they met, until they're standing face to face, speaking only through their eyes.

They look one another over from head to toe. She's wearing a sleeveless black summer dress looking as if it were designed specifically for her body, resting upon her shoulders, and cut off just above her knees. Greg takes note that she has a "style." Her matching shoes have small heels, accentuating the form of her perfect calves. She knows she looks stunning, and she can't help but smile when she sees the look on Greg's face as he does his best to pick his jaw up from the ground.

"You must have read my mind," says Greg as ignorantly as the last time they saw each other.

"How's that?" She asks in a feisty tone.

"Black," says Greg, pausing while she assesses him, "It's my favorite."

Her smile grows for a moment, and she opens her mouth to speak, but stops herself. Instead she leans in close, with her mouth pressed lightly to Greg's ear.

"We have something in common," she says, "You and I."

A shiver rushes across Greg's body as her warm breath glides along his neck. He lets the feeling set in for moment before saying anything else. Doctors may attribute what he's feeling to age and gender, but it doesn't feel like teenage hormones. Either way Greg feels like he's in a dream, which is concerning given his history, but he doesn't care. He wants to stay in this moment with her forever. They'll start with this night out and see what happens next.

"So," Greg asks, trying to spark a yearning in return, "Where would you like to go?" He has no idea what she likes; otherwise he'd make a suggestion.

"I was thinking," she says, undressing Greg with her eyes. She finds him debonair, like a teenage Johnny Cash, "Dinner's a good place to start." The look on her face says she has something else in mind, and Greg notices his palms beginning to sweat with anticipation.

"Sounds good to me," says Greg, "Have anything particular in mind?" He can see that she knows exactly what she wants.

"I've heard wonderful things about the Santa Monica Pier," she replies, trying to be helpful, "but I've never been."

Greg is surprised. Living in southern California has certain requirements, of which a significant one is enjoying the pier. . The fact that his date hasn't means Greg will be the first one to share the experience with her. This night has all the makings of a fantasy. He hopes it's not all in his head.

Depending on the route taken, the ride from Heritage to Los Angeles can take anywhere between forty-five minutes and an hour on a good day. Greg has no idea how long he's been staring at the road in front of him, but he knows his co-pilot has spent the majority of the time gazing at him. He considered doing the same, but someone should be paying attention to where they're going. It's an awkward ride, being that neither says much from departure to arrival.

As Greg drives into the Santa Monica Pier parking lot, his date's eyes grow wide at the sight of the bright lights glowing against the background of dark waters and the clear night sky. She leans forward in the passenger's seat, looking out through the windshield, filled with excitement.

Once parked, Greg jumps out of the car, runs around to the passenger's side, and opens the door to let the red headed beauty out. His grandfather lectured that treating women like royalty goes a long way, and that any object of affection should be treated with the highest level of care. Affection is definitely among the feelings Greg is filled with.

Walking into the *Bubba Gump Shrimp Co.* at the end of the pier, Greg and his date realize they might be overdressed for dinner. It's a casual restaurant known for having decent seafood, though nothing's quite like eating lobsters right from the harbor in eastern Maine. When the hostess takes Greg's name for the waiting list he quietly requests a table outdoors, to enjoy the scenery.

Waiting for a table at a restaurant in California can be a daunting task. The state's population being larger than some countries, couples can spend two or more hours waiting for a seat, especially when there's a special request. However, the time doesn't disturb the young duo one bit. The air between them is rich with warmth, as if there is an invisible force pulling them toward one another. Although they're still almost strangers, they feel like fate has brought them together; and after the quickest forty-five minutes Greg has ever seen, they have a perfect view of both the beach and the hills running along the Pacific Coast Highway.

Greg has a craving for smoked salmon, but his mind isn't concerned with what he's going to eat. He wants to know what his new favorite red head is going to have.

"What does your appetite long for this evening?" He asks with cheesy innuendo. He thinks he's being creative, when all he really wants to know is whether or not she sees anything she wants. Ah, the innocence of teenage naivety.

"I'm terrible at picking items from a menu." She answers with her eyes locked on Greg's as she makes a decision. "You seem to know what you want. I'll try whatever you're getting."

Suddenly Greg questions salmon as his choice. He's not picky, so choosing is easy for him. However, he's no longer choosing for himself. Now the choice must be suitable for her as well. He opens the menu to take another look when a voice comes from behind him.

"Hello," says the waiter, "My name is Xavier, and I'll be your server this evening."

Greg can't help but think about every other time when he's been ready to order and the waiter was nowhere to be seen. Damn Murphy and his law.

"Can I get you anything to drink this evening?" The diligent waiter asks. Greg sighs in relief. This will give him the time needed to revise his selection.

"Yes, please," he answers, looking across the table to see if she has anything in mind, knowing she's already deferred her preference to whatever Greg orders for her. "May I have two glasses of water with a twist of lemon in each and two colas as well please?" If he chooses incorrectly, at least there will be water.

"Certainly sir," the waiter responds.

With Xavier off to fetch the beverages, Greg has a moment to review the menu. However, he can't seem to stay focused on food. The thought that this all could be too good to be true won't go away. Greg looks up from the menu and sees the look in her eyes, a look filled with intent. He can feel her pulling him closer without lifting a finger. He melts in his chair as each second passes while their eyes are locked. The innocence in her stare renews the smile on Greg's face. It's early in the evening, but all he wants to do is climb across the table and kiss the lips that have danced in his mind for days.

"Do you know what you'd like to order sir?" Xavier asks. Greg didn't see him return with the drinks. Even worse, he hasn't revisited the menu.

"I, um –" Greg stumbles. The look from across the table gives him confidence, as if his date is going to love the order regardless of how it tastes. "Two smoked salmon dinners please," he says with a surprising sound of authority.

The waiter looks at Greg for a moment, takes a sighing breath, and then looks at Greg's date. He seems confused, but asks nothing else. "Sure," he says, "Two salmon dinners. Can I get you anything else sir?" He sounds hesitant, perhaps puzzled by a woman that gorgeous sitting with a young punk like Greg. Or maybe it's the casket-sharp attire they're both flaunting by the beach.

"No thank you," says Greg, "I have everything I want sitting right in front of me." The server pauses for another moment and looks at the red head again. "Huh," he mutters, and Greg can't tell if he's asking a question or talking to himself, "Sounds good sir. I'll put that in for you immediately." He's probably as glad to walk away as the couple is to see him go.

After Xavier leaves to place the order, Greg turns back to find his date's eyes fixed upon him with her head bowed.

Is she blushing?

"Is everything okay?" Asks Greg, who's notorious for putting his foot in his mouth, but has to be sure he hasn't done something inappropriate.

"Yes," his date answers. "Yes it is; great actually." Greg's happy knowing he's not the only one who stumbles for words from time to time. "It's just that–" she hesitates, "Well, it's just–" still struggling to find the words, "What you said, you know, about having everything you want right in front of you. Nobody has ever talked about me that way. It's – nice," she concludes with a tone of vulnerability.

Greg's no expert, but if he isn't mistaken he'd say she's about to cry, which is something no man shoots for on a first date.

"I'm sorry if I upset you," he says, "I–"

"No," she cuts him off, "please, don't be sorry. I'm flattered. Honestly, there's something about you that gives me butterflies. It's crazy, you know? 'Cause we've only just met. Don't get me wrong," she begins to sound uncertain, "I really like you Greg. It's just that I don't usually fall this quickly." Greg tenses up with excitement.

She's into me.

"I meant it, what I said," Greg replies, "I don't know why, but I feel like we're supposed to be here, together. Something about you, when we first saw each other outside of Dr. Petrovic's office, told me that you were right for me. Not to mention," he takes a breath and swallows, "You're, well, you know –"

Just say it already!

"You're gorgeous." He finally gets the words out. It was easier to admit to her than he expected. Then again, Greg never thought he'd be on a date with a girl who, in his mind, defines sexuality, a girl way out of his league.

Their conversation continues on. Greg tells her about his stint on the wrestling team leading up to the injury; about the near-death experience he had shopping for cologne, and about his goal to become a clinical psychologist one day. She hopes to be a physical therapist, but more than anything, she just wants to be happy. The food eventually arrives, though it's irrelevant. It would have taken something awful for them to care about the meal. The job interview phase of the date comes and goes without a hitch. It appears both wanted to get it out of the way. They enjoy each other's company; that much is obvious.

"We should ride on the Ferris wheel," she says, as giddy as a kid finding an empty milk glass and half eaten cookies on Christmas morning.

Greg's eyes nearly pop out of his head. The Pier is known for its massive wheel fitted with round umbrella-covered tubs and flashing lights. It sits on the edge of the pier while patrons ride to the top to see the town's lights, the endless stretch of the beach, and the starry night sky. Greg, however, is terrified of heights. He'll be the first to admit that the only things he fears more than death are needles and heights. He figures that either will be the cause of his demise. Now there's a problem. Greg can tell by the look in her eyes that she's going to get him on that damn thing whether he likes it or not.

"I suppose this would be a bad time to tell you that I'm scared of heights," he says in a pleading tone, hoping she'll take pity on him and suggest a nice stroll through the sand.

All girls long for walks on the beach.

Without acknowledging his claimed fear, she gets up from her seat, casually glides around the table, and whispers in Greg's ear again, "Don't worry sweetie," she says, "I'll keep you safe. You won't even know we're up there."

He doesn't know whether it's the hormones or something else, but Greg can't refuse. He has to know what makes her believe she'll keep him occupied while faced with certain death.

"How can I say no?" Greg asks fearfully.

A young man greets them at the entrance, and Greg hesitates before handing him the ticket. He can see the apprehension on Greg's face. "Enjoy the ride," he says, knowing it'll be torture. Greg wonders if he says the same thing to little girls whose parents drag them on the ride kicking and screaming through fits of snot and tears.

Greg and his date enter the umbrella-covered bucket and sit on the round bench across from one another. She can see him trembling and tries to comfort him.

"It'll be okay," she says confidently, "I promise. Thanks for bringing me here. I can't believe it has taken me this long to come."

Greg tries to listen to what she's saying, but his focus is lost as their seat begins to move. His hands fling out to each side to grab hold of the cart. A feeling of helplessness overcomes him as they slowly move towards the sky. The helplessness is soon replaced by nausea as they continue back towards the ground. He starts to recall the last time his father took him on a roller coaster. He was six, and when the ride was done, his father slapped him.

"STOP YOUR SNIFFLING!" His father screamed at him. "BOYS DON'T CRY."

Suddenly Greg's new infatuation slides around the bench until their hips are pressing against one another. She can feel his heavy breathing, which is its' own asthmatic danger. Greg stops thinking about death's approach and looks into her eyes. At that moment in the height of fear, he can see into her soul. She seems vulnerable, like a child on a quest for unconditional love. He forgets he's suspended in the middle of the air, fearing for his life. She leans in closer.

"I told you," She says softly "I'll keep you safe." She places her hand on Greg's. "I don't want to freak you out," she continues, "but I feel myself being drawn towards you, even now as we sit less than inches apart. It's our first time out together, and already I –" She pauses to take an effortless breath. "I can feel myself falling in love with you."

If he were dreaming, this would be the point when Greg would pop up in bed and realize the joke is on him. Yet, he's still there, with her, overcome with elation, and suddenly it hits him. This is the moment everyone talks about. Without any further delay, Greg leans in and gently presses his lips against hers. Then, insecure about whether or not he's made a fatal mistake he withdraws for a brief moment only to find her brilliant blue eyes confirming he's right on cue. Their lips join again. He wraps his arms around her and pulls her close. Her lips are soft and moist, like they were made for kissing. Greg tastes the mild sweetness of a nectarine as his tongue brushes across hers. Then he leans back to look at the expression on her face before responding.

"I feel the same way," he says. Before either detects it, the ticket taker is opening the door to their bucket and the ride is over. Greg forgot they were even on the Ferris wheel. Stepping back onto solid ground, he takes her by the hand, and they head back to the car.

The ride home is as silent as the ride out. They replay the kiss over and over in their heads. Two strangers a week ago who are now falling in love, it's the type of thing found in one of Nicholas Spark's books. Who could have guessed it would be this wonderful?

When they arrive back in Heritage Greg figures she'll want to be dropped off at home, but that isn't the case.

"You can drop me off at the park," she says curiously. "It has nothing to do with you Greg. The short walk home always helps me reflect on the day, and I can clear my head." As crazy as it sounds to let a young woman walk through the park alone in the dark, she seems determined to end the evening exactly where it began. Greg parks the car and lets her out. Standing there together, she takes his hands, places them on her waist, pulls herself closer, and gives him a long and lingering kiss. His heart starts racing like he's back in the air hovering over the pier.

"I had a great time tonight Greg," she says. "There are no better words to describe how I feel, but to say that I love you." A rush of delight overwhelms Greg's heart at the sound of her words. "I know how crazy that sounds," she continues, "But I can't deny what I'm feeling inside." Greg can tell by the look on her face that she means every word.

"I hope I don't scare you away," she says in a pleading tone. "I really want to see you again." Greg gives his date a big hug, and while pressed against one another, glides the hair past her ear to whisper.

"I love you too," he says, no longer scared to fess up. "To deny it is futile. You're right. It does sound crazy, but truthfully, I was almost certain I loved you the moment I first saw you." Now he prays his words don't scare *her* away.

"We should do this again next week," she says tenderly, "Pick me up right here at the same time."

The night concludes with another blissful kiss. Staring as she walks away, Greg can't help but watch each cheek move back and forth, from left to right, until she disappears beyond the glow of the street-lights. This is the beginning of a passion-filled relationship.

Chapter 11

Dr. Campos places his clipboard and pen on the lamp stand next to his chair. Then he removes his glasses and begins rubbing his eyes. Giving no initial indication as to whether or not Greg's story is useful, he stands up, places his hands on the back of his waist, and bends backwards until a loud pop echoes throughout the room, followed by a gasping exhale.

"Well done Gregory," he says, sitting back down. "Your memory for detail is remarkable. I can tell that you truly enjoyed your evening with the young lady."

Greg's glad to hear something other than patronizing words. Every other Doctor who hears about the one time love of his life tells him he's out of his mind and that he fabricated the entire thing. It's not an easy story to tell.

"Thanks Dr. C," says Greg. "I always take my time telling that story. It was a night that I never wanted to end." Even now he can feel her in his heart. "I tell you what though," says Greg, "My mouth is as dry as my father's ashes. May I have another glass of water please?"

"Of course Gregory," the Doctor answers. "It'll be good for you to stretch your legs as well. Please, help yourself to as much water as you'd like. If you want to stand for a moment, be my guest. I believe we're moving in the right direction, and I want you to be as comfortable as you can be."

In high school wrestling, teams are broken down by fourteen designated weight classes starting at just over 100 pounds all the way up to heavy weights, which is anyone over 215 pounds. Most wrestlers teeter back and forth between one pound under and one pound over their specific weight class. As a result, wrestlers will often do whatever it takes to "make weight" for tournament day.

When Greg was on the wrestling team, he varied his weight losing techniques. Some days he didn't eat; some days he forced himself to vomit like a runway model; and some days he wore a garbage bag under his sweatshirt to cause himself to sweat even more profusely than he did on a non-trash-bag day.

One year, right before regionals, Greg pushed himself hard all week. He only ate five meals in five days, forced himself to puke on three of those five, and he lined every outfit with *Hefty* bags. His determination was rigid, and as far as his weight was concerned it paid off. However, on his way to officially weigh in, Greg collapsed in the gymnasium hallway. When the trainer finally woke him up a few minutes later, he learned that he had been so dehydrated that he had to be taken to the local hospital. He missed the tournament. Coach Beefy was pissed.

There's nothing as refreshing as a glass of ice water, and Dr. Campos pays for the good stuff. Greg always chugs a glass full and then keeps another for an ongoing conversation. This isn't his first rodeo, and if Dr. Campos is anything like other head Doctors, they've only begun the journey. They still haven't discussed the biggest concerns.

Finding his way back to his seat, Greg wiggles until finding the perfect fit. Now he's ready for the next round. "Okay Dr. C," he says, feeling refreshed. "I'm good to go. Thanks again for the water." He's genuinely excited to continue.

"It's my pleasure Gregory," says the Doctor.

This guy really isn't a bad guy. The thought hits Greg out of nowhere

"I want to go back for a moment, to this woman with whom you fell in love," says the Doctor, trying to fill in the blanks. "Tell me about her family. What were her parents like? Did she have any siblings? How long were you together before she showed you her home? Give me the details about her personal life. Tell me who she is."

Greg is baffled by the onslaught of pseudo-questions, and he knows the Doctor isn't going to be happy with the lack of answers.

"Truth be told Dr. C," he says hesitantly, "She never talked about her family." Greg cringes with the anticipation of invasive questions about his lack of judgment. "Any time I tried to ask her about her parents or siblings, she either changed the subject or became frustrated with me. It was one thing she blatantly avoided discussing with me."

Dr. C looks at Greg over the tops of his lenses. "You mean to tell me that she never told you anything about her family?" He asks in disbelief, "Don't you find that to be, *odd*?" He has a point, but that isn't what matters. Greg wasn't with her for her family.

"Yes I do," says Greg, "very odd actually. I always did. Everything about her was odd, but I loved her, and if she didn't care to talk about her family, then I didn't care to push the issue. Our happiness didn't need to be sullied by a fight about her parents." Greg stops and waits to see if the Doctor is going to attack.

"That's okay Gregory," says Dr. Campos, whose tone suggests otherwise, "I'm not trying to beat you up about it. I simply wanted to know if you found it to be unusual. What about her home? When did you go to visit?"

Greg can see this is going to be a trend. Does the Doctor?

"I didn't," he answers, "Every date began and ended exactly the same. I picked her up and dropped her back off at the park. Unless she was spending the night at my place, but even that was rare. Whenever I tried to force the issue I got the same result as when I mentioned her family. She was an unusual girl Dr. C. She didn't like to use the telephone. All of our future dates were determined when the current one ended. I never found out her address, so I couldn't even drive by and physically see where her home was located. For all I knew she was living in the park. If it wasn't for the fact that she always showed up in a nice outfit, with recently shaved legs, and an intoxicating aroma, I'd have sworn she was homeless and hiding from something."

Dr. C looks concerned. Greg assumes these aren't the answers he expected. He hears a tremendous tale of a growing love, and it's followed by a world of unknowns. Greg wishes he had the answers he seeks, but he doesn't.

This is where I always lose them.

"Let me see if I understand this correctly," says the Doctor, adjusting his glasses, a nervous tick he gained somewhere over the years, "You were in a relationship with a woman, who from what I can tell, based on the little short exchange they've had thus far, you loved more than you loved yourself. However, you didn't really know anything about her. Is that right?"

You can't blame him for being skeptical. To hear him summarize it in so few words sounds pathetic.

"I wouldn't say that I didn't know anything about her Dr. C," Greg tries to recover. "I just don't know the things you want to know." Greg can't help but laugh at his own sarcasm.

"Well at least tell me you know her name Gregory," says the Doctor, irritated by Greg's quip. "You went through your whole story without calling her by name once, and I'm worried that you're about to tell me that she never told you that either."

"Don't be ridiculous Dr. C," Greg barks back. "Of course I know her name. Who dates someone for years without knowing their name?"

"Really Gregory? The Doctor has trouble believing him. "Then what is it? What is the mystery woman's name?"

"You think I'm making this whole thing up?" Greg, pushing himself off of the large cushiony chair and up to his feet, is working himself up in a fit of rage. "You think I'd waste my time to create some elaborate story just so that I can waste yours too? You've read my file; otherwise you'd never have agreed to see me. Yes, Dr. Campos, I know her name."

The Doctor stands up from his chair, seeing this is getting out of hand. He holds his hand out to freeze Greg in place like a child waiting for his father to hit him. After a momentary silence the Doctor sighs, walks over to his desk, and places his clipboard and writing utensils down.

"I think we've gone far enough for today Gregory," he says. "I do apologize for getting you all riled up, but it's necessary for me to know the things that truly matter to you. If you don't mind,

Miss Paxon will see you out, and I'd like to see you here first thing tomorrow morning. Shall we say eight o'clock?"

It's as if the whole thing was a charade. After all of Greg's shouting the Doctor seems completely unfazed, as if it didn't happen.

"Huh?" Greg asks, feeling like a bully just took the ball and left the playground. "Are you serious? That's all you have to say? I don't get it."

"Not yet you don't," the Doctor replies without looking at his patient, "but for now, yes, that's all I have to say. I'll see you tomorrow."

Chapter 12

Jeanne Burns feels a chill roll down her arm when she hangs up the phone. She knew the day was going to be special, but, before she received the e-mail she's now reading, she had no idea that the man with whom she'd been in love for almost half of a decade was going to plan a romantic night out for her birthday.

He is going to pick her up in the parking garage after work. Then, he's made a reservation at the hoity toity fine dining restaurant they've always talked about going to. Next, they will take an exclusive helicopter ride over the Hollywood hills, which, at that time of night, will be amazing. Finally, he has something *special* planned, which he's not yet ready to reveal; but Jeanne's already imagining what her ring finger will look like in the morning.

She's imagined the moment over and over for at least a year; him, in an attempt to keep the nerves at bay, mapping out his every move; them, sharing a couple fruity drinks, and a few romantic dances; and finally, her lover crouched down on one knee. She's even imagined where they'll go on their honeymoon. For now, she has to get through the rest of the workday, but the prospect is enough to make Jeanne feel like she's floating around the room.

As Beth Huard enters the office to bid farewell for the weekend, she is stopped dead in her tracks. The look glowing from Jeanne's face is enough to make her want to barf.

"And I thought I was happy for the week to end," she says. "What's got you so perky?" Given the stunning outfit Jeanne was wearing, Beth could have been referring to a number of things.

"What do you mean?" Jeanne asks. "I smile enough, don't I?" She likes playing coy.

"Please," says Beth. "I just came in here to say happy birthday, and to wish you well until Monday, but if you don't want to tell me what has those pearly whites spread from ear to ear, fine." Beth pretends she's turning to leave the room, knowing Jeanne will jump front of her to cut her off.

"I think it might happen," says Jeanne with shrugged up to her ears with joyful anticipation. "He has our whole night planned out." People have expressed less excitement while cashing in their winning lottery tickets, she's that giddy. She tells her each of the steps outlined in the e-mail her man sent.

"I'm heading up to the parking garage to meet him once I wrap things up here," she continues. Meanwhile, Beth has her head cocked to one side while she rolls her eyes. "Don't just look at me like I'm crazy," Jeanne feels judged. Beth's lucky Jeanne loves her. "I'm not crazy. Am I? Say something."

Aside from being her boss, Beth Huard is Jeanne's best friend, a bosom sister. She looks at Jeanne and can't hold it in any longer. She becomes just as foolish in the excitement. She grabs ahold of Jeanne and gives her a big bear hug.

"That's wonderful sweetie," says Beth. "It's about damn time too. I was beginning to think he was, well, you know, stringing you along." At one point she went so far as to try and convince Jeanne her lover was secretly a homosexual. "Are we sure he's not a meat lover?" She once asked.

"Oh, stop it," says Jeanne, batting her right hand at her. "He's wonderful. Besides, that's my future husband you're talking about." Jeanne has little idea as to what she wants her future to include, but she knows she wants him.

Beth got married to her sweetheart right out of high school, and at first, everything was great. They had a nice townhouse not too far from work, and they planned to start a small family. Beth got pregnant just before their first anniversary, but it was short lived. She had a miscarriage within a week of the test results. They tried again, but were unsuccessful. Eventually, Doctors explained that the internal damage Beth sustained at the hands of her mentally ill uncle left her unable to have kids.

There are always children in need of a good home, and Beth and her husband Frank were ready to offer a good home. They called adoption agency after adoption agency, but sadly, each required a ludicrous amount of money up front; money that Beth and Frank just didn't have.

They tried using a surrogate once, a woman name Vicky. She never wanted a child of her own, but always thought it was selfish of her not to use her healthy body to help provide a child to a couple who couldn't have children; at least until the child was born. Something about the process of having a child pass through her canal screamed, "You must keep this baby." Again, Beth and Frank lost out.

The fight to become parents took the strength right out from under them. The miracles performed through modern science were yet to create a solution to Beth's problem, and to avoid additional health risks later in life, she chose to have a hysterectomy.

To make matters worse, when the procedure was complete, her husband served divorce papers to her in the hospital while she was recovering. He refused to live the rest of his life with a woman who would never be able to provide him with children.

"You better call me this weekend and give me all of the little details," Beth says in a serious tone, pointing her finger. "And no holding back. Actually, if he goes through with it, you better plan to come show me the rock tomorrow. I'll make margaritas to celebrate." She now lives her life vicariously through Jeanne. "It'll be nice to fill my head with new stories of romance and passion," she adds, "So, go, have fun, and don't do anything I wouldn't."

"Haha," Jeanne laughs, and jokingly says, "That's a pretty short list at this point, wouldn't you say?" Of the two, Beth was the one whose closet was filled with skeletons.

"That's the idea," says Beth, winking. Then she walks out of Jeanne's office full of joy and closes the door behind her.

Once she recognized Beth isn't coming back, Jeanne falls back into her chair like a fresh feather floating down upon a soft cushion. Thoughts of passion and wonder fill her head as again she imagines how the touch of his hand will feel when it holds hers while he slides a ring upon her finger. With tonight being *special*, with the first dance be different? Will the first kiss taste sweeter? Will it feel like years since her last date? Will the hours take twice as long, just so she'll be tormented? She isn't there yet, but she has known today would be special since she rolled out of bed.

Jeanne looks at the clock and realizes she's daydreamed most of the last hour away. She logs back in to her computer and sends a couple last-minute e-mails, signing each with loving exaggeration.

"I think that's enough for today," she says to the silence around her.

Closing time on Friday is always a process. Jeanne has to make sure all of the computers are off and the manager's offices are locked. She walks by Beth's office and gives the door handle a good tug, then the next, and the next. Before making her way to the garage, Jeanne stops in the restroom to give herself a final once-over, looking to rid herself of any unwanted lint, stray hairs, or to touch up anything that isn't perfect. Again she's caught off guard by the stunning image in the mirror.

"This is it," she says to her reflection, "The moment you've been waiting for." She adjusts her breasts for maximum comfort, reapplies her lipstick, and kisses herself. Ready to accompany the man of her dreams to dinner, Jeanne exits the restroom, takes a few steps down the hall, and steps into the elevator. The wait is over. She's on her way to the fourth floor.

Chapter 13

Greg gets into his car and slams the door behind him. He'd grab the steering wheel, but he's too furious to drive. This isn't what he wants. He didn't seek the help of an infamous Doctor to have his love life ridiculed. Sure, there are things in his past that very well may be contributing to the present, but the Doctor doesn't have any interest in those, not yet any way. There's only a short time left before Greg turns twenty-eight, and then it's over, exit stage left, roll credits, the end.

Due to the abuse suffered at the hands of his father, George Roberts, unlike his older brother Greg, had an uncontrollable temper growing up. All it would take was for some random person to give a questionable look in George's general direction, and he'd start throwing a raging fit. Objects would often get broken, and the police would frequently be called.

As a child, and into his teen years, George lived for baseball. That may seem like a cliché, but there wasn't a minute that went buy in a day when George wasn't thinking about the sport. He was a remarkable young player too. A coach could put him anywhere on the field and know nothing was going to get past him, but if George had his choice, he'd play third base, and nothing else. While good defense is always preferable, George's real talent was hitting. He enjoyed hitting so much that he would practice his swing while standing in front of a mirror, so that he could see any deficiencies needing adjustment. His devotion to the game paved the way for a potentially amazing future.

Shortly before Greg's twenty-first birthday, he attended George's high school baseball game at the local park. Normally this wouldn't have been a big deal, except that on the particular day in question, a professional scout for the Los Angeles Dodgers was also in attendance.

Part way through the game, George was called out on a strike that he saw as a a pitch well out of the strike zone. He made his rage-filled opinion known to the umpire who made the call, and as a result, he was ejected from the game. George proceeded to walk back to the dugout, making frequent stops to turn and shout various obscenities at his enemy behind home plate. To compound the matter, George then, having finally reached the bench safely, continued his outcry by grabbing all of the bats and helmets the team had and throwing them out onto the field one by one, each with an accompanying profanity.

Having had enough of George's attitude and ridiculous actions, the umpire demanded that George leave the ballpark before the game could resume. This was not well received by the hotheaded George Roberts, who refused to comply with his enemy's demand. His teammates and coach insisted that he leave so that, at the very least, they could finish playing the game. George felt betrayed; and on his way back to his vehicle, he chose to make a decision that changed his life in baseball forever.

Before getting in his car, George Roberts, amidst his blind diatribe, picked up a baseball-sized rock, and with all of his might, launched it towards home plate, aiming, of course, for the umpire who, in George's mind, had made his last bad call. Fortunately the stone sailed beyond its target's head, and nobody was hurt. However, the damage was done. The police were called, the parents of the other players all backed George into a corner, and as an agreement to avoid going to jail, he would never play baseball again.

Following the career-ending incident, George became very active at his local church, where he learned that, through one simple prayer, if he worked really hard to do the right thing, he could control his emotions.

Greg's father was a devout Mormon. He donated several thousands of dollars to the Church of Jesus Christ of Latter Day Saints every year, and he played the pipe organ at church service every weekend. He had a firm rule that everyone in the household had to attend church each Sunday, and if they did not, they had to sit and read from either the *Holy Bible* or the *Book of Mormon* for no less than two hours.

Though his Catholic mother was against it, Greg was baptized as a Mormon at the demand of his father, which wasn't terrible in and of itself, but Greg hated church, and everything that went along with it. He got a brief reprieve when his mother divorced his father, but shortly thereafter he was forced to attend Sunday School at the local catholic church. Then, upon remarriage, Greg became required to attend service at a Christian church every Sunday. By the time he was fourteen-years-old, Greg knew one thing about organized religion; it was all a giant hoax, a clever scheme to trick people out of their money.

Several years later, knowing he can't sit in front of the Campos residence all night, Greg tries to control his nerves as best he can, at least enough for the ride home. Though he doesn't believe in God, at least not as any one religion describes him, Greg thinks that what once worked for his trouble brother may work for him.

It's not about a specific belief, he thinks to himself, *but about the focus of the message.*

"God," he says aloud, looking to the sky, "Grant me the serenity to accept the things I cannot change; courage to change the things I can; and wisdom to know the difference." Holding back the onslaught of tears, he buckles his seat belt, lights a cigarette, and puts the car in drive.

Chapter 14

It's been seven years since Jeanne disappeared without a trace and Greg hopes their paths will one day cross again. Their four years together were his happiest. There isn't a day that goes by when Greg doesn't look back and wish he could hold her one more time. He imagines her running into his arms, the feel of her body in his arms and the taste of her lips on his. If only he had a lantern with a wish-granting slave inside to will it all to come true.

BEEP! HONK! BUZZ!

Greg is startled by the sound of horns blaring from the cars lined up behind him. The light is green, but he's not moving. Caught up in his memories of his former lover, Greg forgets what he's doing.

"Sorry," he says to the other drivers, though nobody can hear him.

Twenty-three minutes, eleven traffic lights, two stop signs, and a yield later and Greg makes the last right onto his street. He lives in the fourth house on the left, 7068 Jasmine. It's an average-size single-story home built in 1984. Previously owned by a childhood friend named Jay, Greg became owner by chance. Jay fell under a forklift at work two years ago and of the five benefactors listed in his will, Greg's the only one who agreed to pay the outstanding property taxes needed to take ownership.

7068 has three bedrooms, two bathrooms, a kitchen, and a part living room part dining room combination separated by the back of Jay's couch. It sits at the top of a short but steep inclined driveway and has a garage that could probably fit two mid-sized sedans if it weren't blocked by a half broken basketball hoop hanging from the roof, and the many of Jay's old belongings still inside. With hopes that someone will be kind enough to steal his car from the curb at the end of the lawn, Greg has no reason to use his garage.

Greg doesn't see the appeal of modern decorations or furniture and is quite content with the way Jay left things upon his departure. The fridge and stove both work, there's a flat screen television atop an ironic pile of pallets, and the bathroom is fully stocked with *Calvin and Hobbes* comics.

In reality, Greg inherited a *bona fide* bachelor pad for less than ten grand.

Gourmet hardly seems appropriate tonight. After the day he's had, Greg really doesn't want to eat. No, instead he just sits on the couch staring up at the ceiling fan as it spins around and around, hoping to find solace within the blur created by the twirling blades. Dr. Campos wants to meet again tomorrow. That should be thrilling. He tries to imagine the good that may come from continuing their last conversation. Greg is all but certain that the conversation will end as they always do, in disappointment. People used to look at him like he was crazy when he said he was in love with Jeanne. What is the Doctor going to think of him? Solace is absent.

Maybe there's something worthwhile on tv.

Late night television is a waste of time. You get five, maybe ten minutes of valid entertainment followed by mindless psycho-babble and advertising. Letterman's top ten reasons to eat twelve-grain bread instead of eleven; the twelfth is enriched with magical fairy dust. Leno's headline of the week; joke dead. The newest line of aftermarket laundry detergent sold to you by the world's most annoying voice, and the silly string still won't wash off of your favorite shirt. Greg has the distinct feeling that fate wants him to lose his mind.

Tomorrow's going to be a long day and Greg wants to be ready for anything the Doctor plans to throw at him. He needs to go to bed and sleep it off. That may not be a problem for the average Joe, but for Greg it's asking for a small miracle. Even if his anger were to dissipate completely, it doesn't change the fact that he hasn't had a peaceful night's sleep in longer than he can remember. There's always something, or potentially some*one* there to torment him. But he doesn't have a choice. He must try to rest.

Greg died when he was three-years-old. His mother decided, for reasons still unknown, to test the smoke detector outside his bedroom door while he slept. She climbed up on a chair, held a lit cigarette to the detector, and it sent shrieking sounds up and down the hallway. Greg, having never encountered such a noise, woke up from his slumber and started screaming at the top of his lungs.

The sounds of the alarm and scared young Greg carried on for several minutes before his father finally entered his room and screamed at him to stop his screaming. Greg didn't hear the command and continued on with his squealing. Having had enough of the noise, Greg's father grabbed him by the collar of his pajamas, and violently lifted him up from the bed, forcefully slammed him back down onto the bed, and repeated six or seven more times. This only made Greg cry more, and much louder. Then his father picked him back up and hurled him at the nearby wall. Greg crashed through the plaster and drywall into the neighboring bathroom, where he finally landed head first into the bathtub, his skull cracking against the faucet.

Thankfully, for Greg's sake, his mother knew CPR. Though she smoked like a chimney, her breath brought Greg back from the dead a minute or two after soaring from one room to the next.

Greg decides to be proactive in anticipation of any unwanted interruptions. He walks into his bedroom, closing and locking the door behind him. He figures that if the door is locked, nobody can get in to hurt him. Then he closes his closets' double doors and props his computer chair under the handles. The Boogeyman won't be able to get out of there. He lets the blinds down over all of the windows, draws the curtains closed, and tapes their edges to the floors and wall. Nobody will be watching him sleep. He unplugs his fan, his computer, his clock, and his electric razor. The room is completely silent. If a fly were to fart, Greg would hear it. Convinced he's done all he can do to ensure a peaceful night, Greg then sets the alarm on his cell phone and climbs in bed. He closes his eyes as tight as he can, takes a couple deep breaths, and goes to sleep.

Chapter 15

"Ouch," Greg asks himself, suddenly awakened in the night. "What the hell was that?" He feels a sharp pain on the bottom of his left foot. He's been cut. "Ah, dammit!" He shouts aloud. He feels the same pain hit other foot.

I've been cut.

Greg swears someone is dragging a razor blade along the soles of his feet. He sprawls out of bed, nearly falling from the excruciating pain in his feet. With little grace, he lunges towards the wall, where he's able to turn the lights on. He immediately scans the room and then his feet to find nothing. There is nobody else there, and there is no blood to be found. His feet are fine.

"Great," he declares to himself.

"Ha – ha – ha – ha – ha," Greg can hear it's sinister laugh, echoing as if blasting from the surround sound system of the local movie theater.

"It's going to be another one of those nights," Greg says out loud, shaking his head. He switches the lights off again and gets back into bed; still feeling like blood is gushing out of his feet and dripping off the ends of his toes. It isn't real, but his body believes it is. That can't matter right now. He needs to sleep. His mind needs to let it go.

Greg eventually gets back to sleep, but it doesn't last long; a little less than an hour. He starts twitching as if he's caught in the middle of an intense dream, but that's not it. His body is reacting to a presence in the room. The blanket and sheet tucked over his body are slowly sliding off the end of the bed. However, they don't fall to the floor. Instead, they slide off of Greg and into the air, suspended as if weightless. His twitching gets stronger, further identifying the attendance of another, until he finally jerks himself awake. The blanket and sheet are now half covering his body and half lingering in air. Greg sits up and rubs his eyes, completely unaware of what's going on.

WHOOOOSH!

The rest of the covers are ripped off of Greg like a magician's tablecloth from beneath an impossible number of fragile plates and glasses, while his sight slowly comes back into focus. He gets up to turn the lights on again, but is knocked back by a ballistic blow to the gut.

Was that the blanket?

He tries to get up and is met with another blow, this time from the sheet.

"WHAT DO YOU WANT?" Greg yells.

Determined to put an end to whatever this is, Greg leaps back to his feet, and filled with the determination of a mother bear rescuing her cub, runs towards the light switch. He gets within an inch of his goal when the covers wrap around him like a mummy destined for an Egyptian tomb, and he's heaved across the room; his body bouncing off of the wall where his curtains are taped down. Greg lays there motionless, not unconscious, but unsure about what to do.

"Okay," says Greg. "I give. What do you want?"

The covers unravel like yarn from a spool and fall to the floor next to the bed. Greg can see it in the corner by his door. A black mass is sitting in the darkness.

"You," it whispers with a raspy tone like that of a fifty-year smoker's ghost. "You know what I want."

"Well then," Greg replies, "What are you waiting for?

"Ha – ha – ha – ha – ha," it laughs again.

Greg gets back to his feet and exhales a long breath. Then, like a Spartan warrior prepared to die, he antagonizes the dark being. "C'mon," he says, beating his fists against his chest, "I'm right here."

"AAAAHHHH!" It shouts loud enough to shake the whole house. The entire neighborhood rumbles when the figure leaps from its corner, throwing itself at Greg from across the room. The scream still ringing in Greg's ears.

All Greg sees is giant shadow, like the creature from his nightmares, flying towards him. He holds his arms up in preparation for what could be his last dance, when it suddenly bursts into a vapor, landing all over his body, sticking like used oil on a duck's feathers. Greg looks around the room for a sign of the mass. He has no idea what just happened. All of his fears attacked him, and then it was gone. He's breathing so hard he may vomit, and reaches to grab his nebulizer. The hairs on his arms are standing straight. Then he slaps himself in the face.

"Damn," he says, realizing he's not dreaming.

When a thing from your darkest dream attacks you in reality, there's no going back to sleep, maybe ever. Greg's alarm isn't due to go off for a couple hours. He thinks about the idea of sitting in his house, alone, in the dark, until he would have otherwise gotten out of bed, and decides to walk outside instead. He grabs his chair from under the closet door handles and carries it outside to the bottom of the driveway. He puts the chair down and takes a seat on the edge of the street.

"Howdy neighbor," a voice causes Greg to jump back up.

"Jesus Christ," says Greg. "I didn't see you there." His next-door neighbor is walking his way. Billybob Fishwright is a used-to-be hillbilly from the great state of Tennessee. He won a large sum of money last year playing poker on the Internet and decided to move out west. Lucky for Greg the house next to his was repossessed through foreclosure and Mr. Fishwright got the deal of a lifetime. Greg doesn't mind him; he just has trouble understanding what he says. Billybob may be living the high life in Southern California, but he still sounds like a redneck that was born and raised in the south.

"Oh, sorry," says Billybob, "Didn't mean to scare ya. Was a big'n huh?"

"Excuse me," says Greg. "A big what?"

"What?" Billybob asks. "Well why else'd ya be out here in the middle o' the morn'n? The quake o' course. Ain't it what woke ya?

Still thinking about the unexplainable events from inside, Greg has trouble putting two and two together.

"What quake Billybob?" He asks. "What are you talking about?"

"Greg's you josh'n me?" Billybob slaps Greg on the back thinking it's all a joke. "The quake that dun did shook the whole street's what I'm talk'n 'bout. Was kinda like back home when the tonadors come sweep'n through, 'cept my house didn't go nowhere. All I got's a busted windor in the kitchen."

The thought eventually hits home in Greg's mind, causing his heart to start racing. He hadn't noticed when he first walked outside, but now that he's paying attention he hears the sounds of car alarms and dogs barking coming from throughout the neighborhood. That's why Billybob's in the middle of the street.

"Oh, yeah," says Greg, trying to recover, "The earthquake. It was something wasn't it? Knocked me right out of bed."

"I know, me too," says Billybob. "It's my first real quake since I dun moved in last year." An odd look of excitement fills his face. "Say, y'all get lots o' these?"

"Huh?" Greg looks puzzled, thinking back to what actually happened. "Oh, no. That was probably the biggest one I've been in yet." He wants to change the subject. "You alright Billybob? Everything okay inside? Should we call the paramedics?"

"Yer a funny guy Greg," Billybob laughs. "Why'd I call the likes of them? I can tape myself up just as good as they can."

"Ha," Greg fakes a laugh so he doesn't seem rude. "You're probably right. Well, if everything's okay out here, I'm going to head back inside. I have to get ready to go." He waves to Billybob, who decides to follow suit.

The Doctor is never going to believe this.

Chapter 16

Following a night of little and frequently disturbed sleep, Greg arrives at the Campos residence ten minutes early for his next appointment. He goes through the same motions as the day before; button, lights, steam, dark and cold walk to the front door, where Miss Paxon awaits.

"Good morning Mr. Roberts." She greets him with her slow hissing drawl.

"Good morning ma'am." Greg remembers at least one rule from the previous day.

"You will be meeting the Doctor in his private study this morning. I think it's going to be a long day Mr. Roberts. Can I get you anything? Coffee? Tea? Perhaps a juice?"

"No ma'am," Greg replies. "Thank you though. I'm actually a bit anxious to get started. Will the Doctor be long?"

"I think not Mr. Roberts," says Miss Paxon as she leads him through the second room, the with décor more suited for a mental institution, and to the base of a narrow spiral stair case behind the door on the left of the room, the same door through which Greg observed Miss Paxon exit the day before. "You may go straight up Mr. Roberts. He is waiting for you," she says. "Good luck Mr. Roberts, ha – ha," even her chuckles slur, "I think you're going to need it." She closes the door behind him.

At the top of the stairs waits a tall black door with two white horses painted on each side, and a white doorknob. The dark entryway contrasts the white walls of the stairway, causing a nearly instantaneous nausea to run rampant through Greg. The longer he looks at the nefarious ingress, the dizzier he becomes, until he feels like he may pass out.

"Come in Gregory," the Doctor's voice vibrates as he opens the door at the top of the stairs; welcoming Greg into his office away from his office.

Greg's sickening symptoms disperse quickly while he makes his way into the room. Dr. Campos, dressed in his best Mr. Rogers outfit, red sweater and all, returns to his seat on a velvet sofa, where he finishes polishing his antique rifle. The room is square and very small. Two bamboo torches hang from the ceiling casting just enough light for one to see. There's an oak chest propped open in one of the corners next to a smaller velvet chair, where Greg can see another rifle similar to the one in the Doctor's hands sticking out.

"Hello Gregory," says Dr. Campos, sprightly. "How are you doing this morning? Please, come in, shut the door, and have a seat. I'll be with you in just a moment."

"Um," Greg pauses, unsettled by the Doctor's chipper tone, "I'm okay. Thanks." He checks out the room, slowly turning in a circle, much like back in his bedroom when he thought someone had sliced the soles of his feet. Greg feels like he's standing in a large furnished closet. There are no windows or air vents, at least not that he can see, and the more he thinks about it, Greg believes this room is, or at least was, the home's intended attic. He makes his way to the smaller chair in the corner and sits down. Dr. Campos finishes with his relic and stores it away with the other in the chest, now to Greg's right.

"Well then Gregory," the Doctor says, "Where should we begin?"

"I," Greg starts slowly. "I want to apologize. I got upset yesterday, and don't feel like I acted appropriately."

"Why do you think that is?" The Doctor asks. "What do you think happened?"

"Well," Greg sits upright to speak, still ready to unload from the day before, "I felt attacked. I felt as though you didn't believe what I was saying, that you were convinced I didn't know the name of the woman who stole my heart away. I'm not that creative Dr. C." He feels a little better with that off of his chest.

"Ah," says the Doctor, as if Greg has played right into his plan, "This is why it's so important for you to trust me. Some of the things I do are going to push you out of comfort, but I do it with purpose."

"I see," says Greg, who really doesn't get it, at least not yet. "So we're okay then?"

"I should think so Gregory," the Doctor replies. "You aren't the first patient I've upset. I would have been more concerned if you didn't react at all. However, I want to be rather forward with you this morning. Yesterday was merely a taste of what is to come if we are to get to the bottom of your woes. I want you to be aware that there's a good chance you won't like where things start this morning, but I ask that you do your best to remain patient. All will work out in the end." He looks at Greg's eyes, completely open and at full attention. "Are you ready to take this next step with me Gregory?"

It takes a couple of controlled breaths before Greg answers him. He hopes he won't need any puffs from his asthma inhaler.

"Okay Dr. C," he says. "I'm ready."

"Do you remember where we left off yesterday?" The Doctor asks with a straight face.

"Haha," Greg can't help but laugh, happy that the Doctor can make light of what seemed so bleak yesterday. "Yeah Doc, I remember. I thought about it for most of my night."

"Hmm," the Doctor looks down at Greg's file, "I'm not surprised. Clearly this mystery woman of yours meant a great deal to you not only then, but even now." Again, the Doctor wastes no time diving into the details.

"It's true Doctor," Greg says. "She's easily one of the most significant people I've ever known."

"I'm glad you realize that Gregory," the Doctor says. "What I need you to do now is tell me her first name." The Doctor stops for a moment, waiting to see if his patient is truly prepared to discuss this with an open mind. "Can you do that for me?" He asks in fragile tone.

"Her name is Jeanne," Greg says with ease, "Like in a bottle, only spelled differently." He'd expected more difficulty in relinquishing her name, but his answer came off almost like a reflex, as if the answer is what it is, and he doesn't care what anyone has to say about it. "May I ask why that matters Dr. C?'

He asks, having never thought about what comes after the big reveal.

"You just did," says the Doctor, still in a teasing mood. "Here is what I will tell you about the significance of you telling me her, Jeanne's, name." The Doctor looks over the tops of his lenses directly at Greg, and, switching to a serious tone, further explains, "I feared that if I couldn't get you to trust me with her name Gregory, you'd never be able to talk to me about the things causing you the most anxiety, the things that are mentioned in your file, briefly." The Doctor sits back and grabs his clipboard. Greg assumes he's writing Jeanne's name down for the record. "Now, Gregory, let's talk some more about this, Jeanne."

"Okay," says Greg. "What more do you want to know?"

"Well," the Doctor speaks slowly, "How long were the two of you together?"

"You mean how long did we date?" Greg needs clarification.

"If that's how you interpret the question, that's fine." The Doctor's sounding more and more like the riddle master from the previous engagement.

"Four years," Greg answers emphatically. "Jeanne and I spent four amazing years together."

"Wow," the Doctor seems surprised by Greg's energetic response. "And how long ago was this?" He asks.

"What do you mean?" Greg answers with a question, something Doctors usually *love*.

"The four years Gregory," the Doctor asks, "When did they come to an end?"

"Oh," Greg feels a little dumb, but sleep deprivation is a bitch. "Sorry, I last saw Jeanne a little less than seven years ago. Why do you ask?"

"Why don't you let me worry about the questions Gregory?" The Doctor gets a little snippy, hoping to curb his patient's inquiries as they proceed. "That would mean you met her more than a decade ago, would it not?" He clarifies.

"Um, yeah." Greg answers. "Almost eleven years exactly."

"Interesting," the Doctor mumbles, "Tell me Gregory, *exactly* when did you meet this, Jeanne?"

"Didn't I just say it was almost eleven years ago Doc?" Greg responds, his words laced with cynicism.

"I don't mean to be rude Gregory," the Doctor hopes he doesn't sound like patronizing his patient, "But the fact you say *almost* eleven years means it wasn't *exactly* eleven years." His eyes perk up as he enunciates the intent of his question. "What I really want to know is, do you remember specifically when you met this, Jeanne, perhaps the month and year, or even the date?"

"It was my seventeenth birthday Doc," says Greg, ignoring the fact that he feels like a third grader in grammar school.

"My, my," the Doctor sounds intrigued. "You're not far from your birthday. I hadn't realized it until just now. Do you have any big plans for the day?" He turns off course for a moment.

"Huh?" Greg's taken aback by the random detour.

"For your birthday Gregory," says the Doctor. "Do you have any big plans for your birthday? Sure, it's only your twenty-eighth, but that doesn't mean you can't celebrate."

"Um, No," says Greg, growing concerned with the Doctor's interest in his date of birth, "Why the sudden interest Doctor?"

"No reason," the Doctor replies, "I happen to love birthdays is all. I'll keep yours in mind." He makes another note on his clipboard. "Well then, back to Jeanne. Were the two of you happy together?"

"What?" Greg can't keep up with the Doctor's direction. "Yes. We were very happy; madly in love as a matter of fact."

"Really? Did you tend to get along most of the time?" The Doctor wants the whole picture.

"I thought so. We only argued about where she lived and her family," Greg says, "You know, the things I mentioned yesterday? Her home life was unknown to me."

"Yes, I remember you saying that. I wrote it down actually." The Doctor points at yesterday's notes on the clipboard, and Greg rolls his eyes. "Well, Gregory, I have to ask. If everything was going well, I mean, if you were as in love as you say you were, what caused you to break up?" Greg knew this question was coming.

They always want to know about the heartbreak.

"We didn't break up Dr. C," he replies. "I loved her more than anything."

"You didn't break up Gregory?" The Doctor's brow drops in confusion.

"Nope." Greg's reluctant to say any more.

This is where it always goes wrong.

"You haven't seen her in nearly seven years, is that correct?" The Doctor sounds skeptical in his affirmation of the facts.

"That's correct Doc," says Greg, still restraining himself from expanding his statement. "Seven years."

"Then let me ask you this," the Doctor tries again, "What caused you to go your separate ways?" He's determined to get his answer.

Greg's eyes roll back in his head while he lets out a large sigh. He considers the conversation that will have to take place if he answers the Doctors question, but isn't sure he's willing to have it. This is taking up far too much time and Greg figures he'll never get the help he's seeking if he doesn't just say it.

"She disappeared," he says bluntly.

The Doctor flips through Greg's file looking for a note from the previous therapist, but finds nothing. Greg's never answered the question before.

"Disappeared you say," the Doctor confirms his patient's response, progressing into uncharted waters. "How so?" He asks.

"I dropped her off at Heritage Park after our last date," Greg feels like he's reliving the past and starts shaking from the pain in his heart. "We made plans to go out again. Then I watched her walk into the distance, the same as always, and that was it. I went to pick her up the following night and she never came."

"I'm sorry Gregory," the Doctor apologizes. "This must be difficult for you to talk about. What did you do?" He doesn't want to stop the conversation now. They've just broken into new territory.

"I did everything I could think of," answers Greg, "The police told me I was crazy. Hell, everyone told me I was crazy."

"Crazy?" The Doctor doesn't quite get it. "Why would everyone think you were crazy?"

"It's just like what I thought yesterday," says Greg, "When I thought you didn't believe me. Nobody believed anything I said about Jeanne. Everyone told me that I made her up, that Jeanne was in my head, but she was real." Tears start to flow from Greg's eyes. He recalls the trauma as if it was new.

"That's odd," the Doctor says. "Well, let me ask you this: They all said you were crazy because you made Jeanne up. Do you know her last name?"

Greg's tears stop instantly while he glares through the Doctor's glasses and into his eyes.

"Yes Dr. C," Greg forces the words through his teeth, "I know her last name. I told you, I'm not making this up."

"Okay Gregory," says the Doctor, holding his hands up and motioning towards the floor to de-escalate the situation. "I believe you. Take a deep breath."

Greg inhales slowly through his nostrils, letting all of the air fill his longs with peace. He'll be okay.

"So," the Doctor continues, "What is it, her last name?"

Here we go.

"It's Burns," says Greg, "Her name is Jeanne Burns. Are you satisfied?"

Like a slow-motion replay under review in the NFL, Greg watches as the clipboard drops from Dr. Campos' hands and crashes on the floor. Paper disperses in every direction. Pens and highlighters fall one by one from his lap as he slowly tries to rise to his feet. His hands shake, gripping the couch's armrest. The look of shock on his face suggests the Doctor is staring at a ghost in shadows of the room. His breathing increases rapidly. He stumbles and nearly falls to the floor. Greg rushes to catch him, but the Doctor swats his hand, signaling Greg to stay away.

"Are you okay Doc," Greg asks in a concerned tone, "Do you need me to get someone, Miss Paxon perhaps? Is your wife home, Martha?" The Doctor ignores his attempts to assist.

Dr. Campos reaches his arms out in front of him to brace himself against the wall, wheezing. Every breath is more difficult than the prior. Finally, Greg decides to act.

"Martha!" He yells for Dr. Campos' wife. Hopefully he has a condition Greg doesn't know about and she'll know what to do. "Miss Paxon!" Nobody is coming.

Dr. Campos makes his way out the door and into the hallway at the top of the stairs. He turns back towards Greg, white as a sheet, still with a look of disbelief on his face.

"Don't you go anywhere Gregory," he barks at Greg through burdened breath from across the room. "Just give me a moment."

The Doctor closes the door, leaving Greg in the torch-lit room alone. This is not something he anticipated. He's never seen such paranoia exhibited by a professional.

What did I say?

Clueless as to what just happened, Greg needs another cigarette. He decides to leave the room and walk back down stairs. He remembers how to get to the Doctor's office, and he knows there's a small patio out back. At the bottom of the stairway he goes back through the door into the larger empty room, second in from the front. He turns left and goes to the next room, the one with a depiction of a faux-canyon that nearly gave Greg a heart attack yesterday. He walks through to the Doctor's office and back to the patio.

Chapter 17

"What the hell just happened?" Greg is talking to himself again, pacing back and forth across Dr. Campos' back patio, attempting to smoke a cigarette. "One minute he's pressing me for information, and the next he's in a state of shock." His hands are glossy from sweat brought on by anxiety, and he struggles to spark the lighter. "It seemed like he recognized Jeanne's name. How can that be?" He wipes the sweat from his forehead, still focusing on lighting the cigarette. "Why am I so worked up?" No answers come to mind.

Planters filled with various bushes and flowers surround Dr. C's back yard. One plant in particular stands out. A rose bush along the wall is in full bloom. The crimson-colored blossoms remind Greg of Three, one of his oldest and closest friends.

When people ask Greg about Three, before he rationalizes why someone goes by such a name, he always explains that whenever anyone places the inquiry, the same answer is given each time, regardless of the nature of the topic in question. "It's Three." Anyone whose actions are that difficult to justify doesn't have an explanation for the name by which he is known, nor does he need one.

Greg met Three as a result of both of their families living on the same street while Greg was in the eighth grade. At the time of their meeting, Three was a fan of hockey. One weekday during the first summer break from school, Three decided to practice his handling of a hockey stick in the middle of the street. This wouldn't have been an issue if a group of Greg's friends had not already been playing baseball in the middle of the same street. They tried to play around him, but without fail, he got in the way every time Greg or his friends tried to run the bases. As a result of the overlapping fun, the group asked Three to join the game.

Dressed in old tattered concert t-shirts, black slacks, and black dress shoes, people often ignored the fact that Three was built like an average teenage computer nerd, and often jumped to the conclusion that he was a psychologically disturbed devil worshipper. He believed Metallica to be the best band on the planet, and he made sure everyone knew his opinion on the matter. He enjoyed playing with sharp objects, especially while contemplating questions, often scratching his temples with a blade of some sort, and his feet reeked of rotten old cheese and formaldehyde. If there is such a thing as normal, Three was far from it.

Everyone got along with the devil worshipper immediately. Well, everyone but Greg. They all thought he was crazy, in a humorous sort of way, as opposed to a stab your sister in her sleep for eating all the green Skittles sort of way. However, Greg and Three began their friendship like two pit bulls determined to claim ownership of the only fire hydrant on the block. They got along when everyone else was looking, but for whatever reason, when they were alone, war ensued.

The battle for territory went on for the better part of eighteen months. One morning, as Greg walked by Three's house, he chose to spray Greg with his mother's garden hose. Greg, with water dripping from head to toe, stared at Three from the sidewalk, and requested that he refrain from bothering him on that particular day, as he'd been coming down with a cold, and didn't want it to get any worse. Without delay, Three shrugged off the request, and sprayed Greg again. Furious, Greg sprinted at the supposed evil one, threw him on the ground, punched him in the gut, and shoved the garden hose down his pants.

Don't be fooled by Greg's bully-like portrait. Sure, he walked away from the hose incident feeling like a made man in the local cartel, but Three always got his revenge. A couple weeks after the dousing episode, the two of them were heading to another mutual friend's house to play video games. As they arrived at the front door, Three stealthily stuck his foot out in front of Greg, tripping him, and during Greg's moment of imbalance, Three pushed him, face first, into a group of rose bushes. The thorns lacerated all of the exposed skin on Greg's right side, and he began bleeding from numerous small cuts. With a smile on his face, Three had won the battle; and, as if defeat wasn't been bad enough, their friend's mother came running out with a broom, which she proceeded to swing at Greg's head. His body had crushed her rose bushes, and he was going to pay.

Sitting on the edge of Dr. C's planter reminds Greg of Three.

A vibration in his pocket startles Greg, causing him to fall back into Dr. C's roses. For the second day in a row, his fiancée is calling.

Hopefully everything's okay.

Greg struggles to get back to his feet, thorns from the rose bushes clinging to his clothes. Looking to avoid the same lecture, he puts out his cigarette, having barely conquered the lighter.

"Hi honey," he greets her with a grin, although, the twinges from scratches on his arm are unpleasant, he says, "Is everything okay?"

His fiancée exhales slowly before responding, "Yeah. I was worried about you," she says, "You never called me last night, and I figured that you would, being that it was your first visit to this new Doctor, and given how you were doing when we last spoke. I wanted to make sure he didn't kill you, haha." Her laugh helps Greg's nerves settle. "So – how are you doing?"

"Things were going well," he says, "Though we've suddenly come to a screeching halt." How else could he describe what happened with Dr. C?

"Oh. What happened?" She asks. "Is everything okay?" His fiancée becomes concerned at the first sign of trouble in Greg's voice.

Always the worrywart.

"I'm not really sure," says Greg, "Dr. Campos asked me to talk about another time, from before, a time when I loved someone." He waits, listening for a reaction. His fiancée hates when Greg talks about Jeanne. She feels like Jeanne screwed him over by disappearing without a word, but also because she knows

Greg is still struggling to cope. She feels like they can't have their wedding until he truly gets over Jeanne.

"And –" she waits for more, but Greg isn't saying anything, "Well, what did you tell him?" There's tension in her voice, and Greg doesn't like keeping things from her. Trust is the best part of their relationship.

"I told him about Jeanne." He braces himself for the fallout, but she says nothing. "I told him about how we met and how much I cared about her, and then he started asking me questions about her past. You know how little I knew about her outside of the relationship we had." His caller remains silent. "I avoided calling her by name yesterday when I told the Doctor about her, and he became annoyed with me. He was persistent, and I don't think he believed what I was telling him."

"Really," she asks sarcastically, "I wonder why?"

"That's where yesterday ended," says Greg. "I went home angry and now I'm back here today."

"Oh," she perks up, "And how are things going now?"

"I told him her name." Greg stops, hoping his fiancée will accept this as the complete summary, but he knows better.

"I don't get it," she says. "How did this bring things to a *screeching halt* as you put it?" She isn't dumb, that's for sure. She knows her man.

"Well," Greg starts, "When I told Dr. Campos that her name was Jeanne Burns, he seemed to go into shock. He dropped his papers and started shaking. I tried calling for his wife and the housekeeper, but he managed to get out of the room before anyone came. He told me to stay put, and I've been sitting in the back yard freaking out for the last fifteen minutes." He can hear the worry sink in on the other end of the conversation.

"I knew there was something else about her, something she always kept from you," his fiancée says. "She's probably one of his patients. She's probably locked in an institution, and that's why you never saw her again, the crazy bitch." Greg pulls the phone away from his head. His caller's voice is echoing among the flowers.

"Stop it!" Greg shouts. "I'm not doing this with you. Not today." He hates when anyone says anything negative about Jeanne, especially his fiancée, who he looks to for love and support, mostly because he feels bad about mentioning her at all when she's around. "If she were locked away somewhere, I'd have found her by now. Don't go there with me babe. I'm in no mood." He only raises his voice with her when she presses the wrong button.

"Gregory." Dr. Campos slides the glass patio door open and waves for Greg to come back inside.

"I have to go," Greg says to his fiancée. "The Doctor's back, and I want to know what's going on."

He closes his phone and puts it back in his pocket before his caller can say another word. He doesn't want to hear it.

Chapter 18

In middle of the parking garage on the fourth floor, the elevator shaft fills with freezing air as the doors glide open. Jeanne Burns quickly rubs her arms to offset the shivers, which have overcome her slender body. The structure is the average slab of concrete held in place on top of other similar slabs by a countless set of rebar-enforced concrete columns along each row of spaces, sold to companies across the country to allow for extensive parking while occupying as little real estate as possible.

Stepping out onto the concrete slab, Jeanne can't see much, with the exception of a single flickering bulb at the far end of the lot. The rest of the lights are out. The weather forecast calls for temperatures in the mid-seventies without a breeze, but it feels more like a meat locker, and Jeanne is battling random gusts of wind to keep her balance.

Quickly checking her surroundings, Jeanne looks for anything, or even any*one* she may recognize. There are no cars in the lot, and not one soul in sight. Even the security booth is dark and abandoned, though at this hour, on an upper floor, that's not *too* unusual. There's a stereotypical fire extinguisher resting behind a set of ironic instructions that won't help in this emergency.

An eerie sense of helplessness fills Jeanne's head with the realization that the elevator no longer has power, and she is alone. Suddenly, she notices a sign leading to stairs just beyond the intermittent light. It's the only way out of this predicament. A nerve-calming breath allows Jeanne to focus on that goal.

"Get out of here," she whispers to herself, "Now."

Jeanne reaches down and removes her stiletto heels to allow her to run as fast as she can towards the door.

So much for sexy.

As she takes her first step, the wind dies completely, causing her to stumble. The lights in each row of the lot turn on and then back off in an alternating sequence. The elevator doors slam shut and then open again behind her. Jeanne, without a clue about what to do, leans against the wall closest to her, places her hands over her eyes, and tries to talk her nerves back down.

"This isn't happening Jeanne," she says. "Get a grip. Just get to the stairs and it will all go away." She uncovers her eyes to find that everything is dark once again. "See Jeanne. It's all in your head," shaking it in disbelief. "Maybe the Doctors were right; you *are* crazy Jeanne."

Just then, a massive gust of wind hits her with the force of a professional hockey player cross checking an opponent into the boards, slamming her against the wall. The physical pain doesn't register at first. Instead, Jeanne focuses on the sound of the wind. Another wave knocks her down, and she thinks she hears a voice.

"Who's there?" Jeanne shouts at the darkness, but there's no answer, "God dammit, Jeanne. Why are you doing this to yourself?"

With the wind subsiding again, it's time to make a move for the stairs. Jeanne drops everything she's holding, her purse, her cigarettes, her pager, her stilettos, and takes off in the direction of the blinking light, one step after another. The only thought in her mind is of the stairs awaiting her behind a steel red door, nearly 100 yards away.

Ninety feet into her dead sprint, Jeanne is reminded of her high school years, when she ran track. She was the fastest girl Etiwanda had ever seen. Then another blast of air sends Jeanne toppling down on her right side. This time she knows she heard a voice, but it's too late to stop now. She rises back to her feet and continues her flight towards freedom. Again she's knocked to the ground. Her right shin begins to bleed from a set of newly formed cuts, and feeling beaten, tears start streaming down Jeanne's face.

"Why are you doing this?" Her cries remain unanswered.

Back to her feet, Jeanne continues on, limping towards the flickering light, more blood oozing from her leg with each step. She's getting closer.

Twenty yards to go.

Fifteen.

Ten.

A brief look of success grows across Jeanne's face; she's almost there.

Then, the largest gust of wind throws Jeanne the remainder of the distance to the wall. Her body crashes against the concrete wall next to the doorway to the stairs like a lump of meat on a butcher's cutting board, and her head hits the floor.

Propping herself up on one elbow, laying on her right side, Jeanne Burns coughs, and spits a small pool of blood onto the ground in front of her; she bit through her tongue during the fall. The pain from her leg has subsided and is now replaced by a struggle to breathe. One of her ribs is broken and pressing against her lung, just one false move away from piercing through. With each exhale she spits more crimson molasses from her mouth, her eyes searching for the source of the voice she knows she heard.

Jeanne takes another deep breath, wincing in agony, and tries to push herself up onto her knees, but again she's thrown down, and her broken rib cuts into her organ like a water balloon bouncing onto a sewing needle. She'd cry out if she weren't choking on her own blood and saliva.

Then the words hit Jeanne's ears as if they were spoken within an inch of her face, "You fail me." Jeanne's heart nearly beats out of her chest.

It can't be. He can't be, the only thoughts in her mind.

She coughs harder and harder, hoping to cough up the dark rose-colored jelly stuck in her throat. Jeanne knows now that her Doctors were wrong. She isn't crazy. Her dreams aren't dreams at all.

"You fail me," spoken from nowhere again, the air still thrashing Jeanne's body.

"What do you want from me?" She mumbles through the exhaustion, blood, sweat, and tears. The lights all flash on and immediately back off, and the elevator doors slam shut again on the other side of the lot.

You can't give up Jeanne.

Despite the pain, despite the terror, and despite the wind, Jeanne will not let herself die on the fourth floor of the parking garage. She reaches forward with her right arm, and pulls herself towards the door, using her feet to help push her weight, taking deep breaths between each movement, swallowing bits of tongue mixed with blood and mucus.

Just a few more feet and we're there.

On her knees again, she reaches for the door handle to pull herself to her feet. Her arms vibrate while she uses all of the strength she has left. Jeanne moans aloud in pain, but she won't give in. Finally, she rises to her feet and is standing in front of the doorway to the stairs. Hearing the wind approaching again, she turns the doorknob in a hurry, throws the door open, and screams, "No!"

Jeanne Burns can't believe her eyes. Through all of the torture, she fought her way across the football-field-sized lot, to get to the one available exit, only to find a massive figure standing more than seven feet tall, covered from head to toe in disgusting dark rags, with nothing more than a pair of brilliant yellow eyes, glowing and blood shot, peering out, and waiting for her.

"You fail me," the monstrous being whispers with wretched breath.

"No, no, I –" Jeanne can't form a thought, let alone a sentence.

As she goes to speak again, her assailant barks once more, "You fail me!" With one swift movement, Jeanne is crushed down onto the floor, before what she believes are her repulsive attacker's feet. She just can't fight anymore; and, after one final gasp for breath, Jeanne Burns is taken.

Chapter 19

Choosing to stay in the office downstairs, Dr. Emmanuel Campos is hesitant to say a word. To be fair, Greg's not sure what he's supposed to say either. After what looked like a panic attack, Greg's not even sure they'll be able to resume with the session, or that they should. The Doctor looks at his watch, and then out the back patio door. His eyes seem to be searching for something. The file in his hand is creased down the middle from holding it too tight. Dr. Campos has something to say.

"Gregory –" the Doctor's voice has a resounding fear, "I'm going to do my best to get through these next few moments, because I need to make sure we understand one another. You witnessed my reaction to what you said a few minutes ago. While I'm aware of your inability to understand why I reacted in such a manner, Gregory, I need to show you something before we may continue."

"Okay Dr. C," says Greg, truly clueless, "I don't know what this has to do with anything, but if this will allow us to move on, then so be it." He leans forward in his seat while Dr. Campos reaches into his file. His hands are still shaking, and his skin's still pale. He pulls out a small photo and reaches forward, handing it over, face down. Greg takes the picture in his hand and flips it over. He hesitates at first, moving the photo closer to his face.

Is that? But, it simply can't be.

"What is this Dr. C," asks Greg, "Is this some sort of a twisted joke? Where'd you get this?" Now it's his heart that's racing.

"Gregory," says the Doctor, "I need to know if this is the woman about whom you spoke."

Is this why Dr. Campos freaked, because he has an old picture of Jeanne Burns?

"What's going on here Doc?" Greg rephrases his question, confused.

Nothing good can come from this. First the Doctor looks like he heard the name of a ghost when, and now he's asking if the girl in this picture is Jeanne Burns. My Jeanne Burns?

"Just answer the question Gregory," after requesting Greg's patience, it's the Doctor who's running out. "Is that Jeanne Burns?" His voice gets louder. "Is that the woman with whom you were in love? You must tell me Gregory." Dr. Campos is persistent, obsessed even. His eyes are wide, almost with rage, and frothing white spit are showing at the corners of his mouth.

"Yes!" Greg shouts, tired of the nonsense. "It's her, at least I think so. She looks a little older than when I last saw her, but yes, it's her. Now, God dammit, why do you have her picture?"

Dr. Campos lets out a groan comprised of both relief and anguish. He falls back into his chair, removes his glasses, and rubs his forehead with his free hand. He and Greg stare at one another without speaking, without blinking, without really even breathing, for a solid minute. Greg can't decide whether to leave now or wait the Doctor out.

"I have some more questions for you Gregory," the Doctor speaks first.

"No," Greg asserts, "I won't answer any more questions, not until you tell me what the hell is going on." He needs, or at least believes he's owed some answers. The Doctor is digging into a part of his past that Greg believes has nothing to do with Dr. Campos, and he wants to know why they can't move on. Why did the Doctor have a panic attack and why does he have a picture of Jeanne?

What in the name of anything holy is happening?

"This is important Gregory," pleads the Doctor, "Please, you must."

"What's going on Dr. C?" Greg asks. "You better start explaining, or I won't say another word about her." The Doctor can tell by the look on Greg's face that it's not a bluff, while the Doctor's gaze is enough to scare a blind man.

"Okay Gregory," says the Doctor softly, as if fighting himself as the words come out, "We'll play it your way." He pauses to look at his notes. "Eleven years ago, I was working at Patton State Hospital, but you already know that." The Doctor waits while Greg gives an acknowledging nod. "What you may not know is that while I was on staff at Patton, I often did community service work at the local psychiatric clinic. It was my way of giving back to the community." The Doctor sounds proud. "Well," he adds, "During my time at the clinic I met a young lady who was very disturbed."

Greg rocks forward, then back, and repeats. The anticipation is almost too much.

"After two hours of speaking with the young woman," the Doctor continues, "I determined that she did, in fact, need professional help, *my* help, as she appeared to suffer from a very graphic set of delusions. That girl, Gregory, was the woman you see in that very photograph. Jeanne Burns."

"What?" Greg asks with a stunned look. "Are you saying that you met Jeanne eleven years ago, and that she's *crazy*?"

"Yes and no Gregory," says the Doctor. "Eleven years ago, yes, we met. Crazy, was to be determined." He slowly exhales, pushes his glasses back up, and sits forward. His face is mere inches away from Greg's as he whispers angrily, "So, I need you to give me some answers?"

"Your story doesn't make sense Doctor," says Greg. "Our last date was seven years ago, not eleven, and there was nothing wrong with her, not to mention the fact that she looked younger than the woman in this photo." He finds the lack of sound in the room unsettling.

Dr. Campos grabs another file sitting on the couch to his left and opens to the last page. He turns towards Greg and reads the last sentence, "Patient reported missing to the authorities."

"Dr. Campos," says Greg, "This is a joke, right? I mean she couldn't have disappeared eleven years ago. I've seen her since then. Your information has to be wrong." Now he's the one pleading.

Dr. Campos walks to the door, pulls it open, and speaks down to someone at the bottom of the stairs, "We're ready. Send them in at once." He walks back to the couch, leaving the door open, sits back down, and folds his hands together in front of him. "Gregory," he says, "I'm not sure how to say this."

Outside of the office, a few rooms away, Greg hears the sound of marching getting closer and closer.

"I need you to listen to me Gregory," says the Doctor, "In a moment my colleagues are going to arrive, and I need you to go with them."

Greg's eyes bulge with concern, "What do you mean *go* with them Doctor?" he asks.

The noise outside the door gets louder and louder, nearer and nearer, and then, with the thud of a final drum-beat, it stops, and the office door swings open. Greg looks up to see a line of men standing in the doorway. He counts eight in total, dressed in what looks like black combat gear made for a S.W.A.T. team. Each is carrying a handgun, a set of handcuffs, and a taser, at least from what Greg can see.

"I've instructed these men to take you to another location Gregory," says the Doctor, "somewhere safe."

"What?" Greg asks in disbelief. "I'm not going anywhere with them." He begins looking for a way out short of hopping the wall out on the patio, which is blocked by rose bushes, there's only one way in or out of the room. The only way he's getting out is back through the three rooms leading to the front door, and a small army is blocking the path out. With no real options, Greg considers an attempt to force his way through the men who have come for him, but his better judgment convinces him the effort would be futile. Instead, he gets to his feet and offers his compliance.

Two of the men move towards him, while the rest funnel in behind them, forming a wall.

It's now or never.

Greg waits until the men are within a finger's reach and leaps to actions, taking off towards the door. However, the Doctor's men are prepared for Greg's pathetic attempt. He may have been a wrestler in high school, but that was a long time ago.

Each of the armed men quickly draws their side arms from their holsters. Greg stops immediately and throws his hands in front of his face, all of his muscles bracing for an assault.

"Wait, don't!" Greg yells at the men. Everyone remains still.

Dr. Campos blinks his eyes and bows his head towards his men and Greg is hit with a sharp pain in his right shoulder, then another in his right leg, followed by several in both sides of his chest. Quickly losing control of his body, Greg feels himself struggling to stay on his feet. His hands fall to his sides and he sees the men are all pointing their guns at him.

I've been shot!

With little consciousness left, Greg looks down and sees several small darts protruding from his body. Then, in a blink of an eye, he crashes to the floor, and the world goes black.

"Well done," the Doctor applauds his men. "I want to be very clear, until further notice, none of you are to harm this young man. He has information I need. Is that understood?" He stops to allow his men to acknowledge his command. "Good. Take him to the facility. I'll meet you there."

Chapter 20

It's a peaceful night as Greg and Jeanne stroll through the park under a pitch-black sky littered with specs of sparkling salt. The moon is half full and there's no one in sight. He takes one look at Jeanne and can't help but smile. She's his soul mate, and he loves her with all his being. They often take laps around random parks, talking about anything and everything their hearts desire.

"Can we remain like this forever?" Jeanne asks, offering a kiss on the cheek as payment for a hopeful answer.

"I can't promise anything forever, but I will promise you this," Greg replies, closing his eyes and imagining the bliss they'll share in their coming days, "I will love you for as long as I am able to love, whether in this life or the next. Without you, Jeanne, my life means nothing." Still with his eyes closed, he can picture the joy spreading across her face as she smiles, blushing a little. "Few people are given the opportunities to meet those with whom they share connections like ours, let alone the chances to enjoy them. What we have is rare, and I wouldn't give it up for anything."

Realizing he no longer hears Jeanne's footsteps following his own, Greg turns around to see where she's gone.

"You're sweet Greg." She's directly in front of him, a vengeful look on her face. "There's only one problem, hahahahaha," Jeanne begins laughing hysterically.

Concerned something is terribly wrong, Greg tries to approach her, but can't.

"What's going on Jeanne," Greg asks while his eyes search for answers in their surroundings, "Why can't I get near you?" He looks down at his hands, and back at Jeanne, puzzled.

"What did you expect Greg?" Jeanne's question comes in a sinister tone. "You must pay the price."

"What?" Greg doesn't know what's going on. "What price? Jeanne you're not making any sense. Please, tell me what's happening."

"You know exactly what's going on Greg," Jeanne answers, "You fail me."

Greg looks on, stunned at what he sees; Jeanne slowly drawing her right hand up from her side, she has a gun, and she's pointing it directly at him.

"Wait! No – " The gun goes off before Greg can finish his plea.

Terrified by what he's seen, Greg springs to his feet, but there's no ground beneath him, causing him to tumble onto the cold and damp concrete floor below. Landing on his stomach knocks the wind out of him, and he chokes while trying to recover. His eyes are open, but he can't see a thing.

Where am I?

When the ringing in his head subsides, Greg tries to recall the last thing that happened. He had a dream about Jeanne, but he can't recall what happened prior to that. Reaching his hands straight out in front of his body, he feels a cold steel frame, like that of a bed, only it has no legs. He runs his hands along the metal and around a corner. It goes directly into a wall.

Am I in prison? He thinks to himself. *Did I just wake up in a cell?*

Feeling light headed and nauseated, Greg makes his way to his feet, begins running his fingers along the wall. Taking tiny steps forward, he hopes to find a door, a window, a crawl space, or some way to communicate with someone nearby. The wall is coarse to the touch, with several jagged pieces, and it comes to an end in a corner where another wall shoots off to Greg's left.

Continuing along the new slab, it feels like he's been placed inside a giant rock that's been hollowed out. Neither the ground nor the walls appear to have any bricks or cracks that would indicate it's man-made, and thus far all of the sides are uneven. He reaches another corner, turns to follow along, and his knee smacks against something hard, and Greg has to lean against the wall for support in a swell of pain. Tracing his hand back down the wall, he's met by another steel object. However, this one is rounded, like a large bowl. Sliding his fingers along its surface, he comes to a knob of some sort, and pushes it towards the floor. A loud grumble disrupts the silence and the sound of flushing water fills the room.

I have a bed and a toilet, Greg thinks, *this can't be good. How did I get here? Where is here?*

The pain in his knee fades, and Greg's able to put pressure back on his leg. He blinks a few times, and a faint object appears behind a dark fog a few feet away. His eyes are adjusting. He sees a sink, a chair, and a –

A door. A way out?

Ignoring the pain shooting down his leg, Greg rushes to the end of the room, and sure enough, a large steel door is built into the wall. There's no window, and only a metal bar instead of a doorknob. He grabs the handle and pulls, but the door doesn't budge. He rubs his hands along the area of the door around the metal bar in search of a lock, but there isn't one. He uses both hands and tries to push off of the wall with his good leg, but still, nothing. Greg pounds his fists on the large sheet of steel keeping him from freedom.

"Hello?" He calls out to anyone who may be able to hear. "Is anyone there?" Continuing to beat on the door, he cries, "Let me out of here!" He alternates his breaths. Inhale. Punch the door. Exhale. Scream aloud, "Hello!" Nothing. He's trapped in a concrete room, somewhere, with no idea of how he got here. Becoming sore from all of the pounding, and out of breath from all of the screaming, which is an issue, since he doesn't seem to have his inhaler, he takes a seat in the corner next to the door, and focuses on anything he can recall.

I spoke to mom. Doc got mad. Went home, oh, and went back. Jeanne, yes, we talked about Jeanne.

"Wait," he says aloud, "I remember. The men with the guns." Suddenly, the familiar sound of marching is nearing the door. Someone's coming. The massive wave of footsteps gets closer and closer. As he presses his ear to the door, everything goes silent, and the sound of keys jingling is just outside. A set of clicks begins and Greg shuffles back. Beams of light shoot into the room as the sound of metal bending echoes through the small room when the door opens, and all Greg can see are giant shadows in the doorway.

"Where am I?" Greg asks. His grandfather always told him the first question should be the most important.

"Stand and face the back wall," the command barks out from the shadow in a deep man's voice.

"What?" Greg asks. "No. Where am I?"

"Sir," the deep voice says, "Get on your feet, and –"

Greg cuts him off before he can finish his command. "Listen," he says in his meanest tone, "I'm not doing anything until I get some answers. Where am I?" Stubbornness is Greg's favorite family trait.

"If you won't do as I say," the deep voice pauses, "We shall be forced to help you comply." Four of the shadows step forward. "I'm not going to ask you again. Sir, stand up and face the back wall."

Greg can tell he isn't joking, but at this point, he doesn't really care. He's not doing anything they ask of him. Though he knows it's going to hurt him, he offers a defying smile and says, "Assist away."

"Pick him up," the deep voice grunts. "The Doctor wants him in *the* room."

As soon as his words stop, four pairs of hands grab Greg's arms and effortlessly yank him up from the floor. He tries to resist by tugging his arms and using his feet to push back from their restraint only to find himself in a free fall. They let Greg's arms go, and his body shoots across the room from the force he exerts. Gravity kicks in, and he crashes to the ground, his head bouncing off of the concrete floor like an orange falling from a grocery bag. Stunned by the contact, Greg attempts to get back to his feet, but before he can move, the shadows pick him up and drag him out of the room.

In the hallway outside of his room, Greg sees a giant spotlight on the wall opposite his door, the same blinding light he saw before. The rest of the corridor is dark. Greg sees a dim light about fifty feet away, then again, that could be the result of his recent trip to the floor. He can't see the men dragging him along like a carcass, but he can feel the floor below him. It's not like the floor in his room. It's cold and smooth, and it feels like marble.

"So," Greg asks, "Do one of you want to tell me where I am?" He figures it won't hurt much more to ask.

"No talking!" The deep voice shouts. Greg can't tell which of them is giving the orders, but conversation is clearly out of the question.

The shadows carry him down the gloomily bland hallway and around the corner to the left, eventually coming to a halt and knocking on what sounds like the door to Greg's room. The keys jingle again, followed by another series of clicks, which Greg now presumes are locks, and the door opens. Much like his last room, this one is pitch black, and it too has a concrete floor. Once inside, the shadows drop Greg back on the floor, exit the room, and lock the door behind them. Greg can't tell if he's back in the same room, or a new one.

I don't think we went in a circle.

"Hello Gregory," Dr. Campos' voice echoes throughout the room as if spoken through a sound system.

"Where am I?" Greg asks, still determined to get an answer.

Without a response, the ground starts rumbling, causing Greg to scramble for his balance. The wall on the far side of the room begins retracting to the right, revealing another room on the other side, but it's nothing like Greg's. Doctor Campos is sitting in a giant leather chair behind an ivory desk in an office with windows for walls on all sides.

Are we in Dr. Petrovic's office?

Shocked by what he's seeing, Greg stumbles in Dr. Campos' direction. Through the windows he can see the office is surrounded by rocky hills and sandy fields on all sides, with the exception of Greg's, which looks like a small cave used for detaining, in this case, Greg. Filled with anger he charges towards Dr. Campos, only he doesn't recognize there's a remaining glass wall between them. Greg runs face first into the invisible partition and falls to the ground, blood flaring from his nose like a pressurized fountain.

"Gregory," says Dr. Campos, "Though this may appear to be one elaborate room, it is, in fact, two sound proof rooms, separated by a transparent wall." The Doctor points to an area above Greg and continues in an arrogant tone, "If you look closely, you'll find small speakers built into the ceilings, each doubling as microphones. This allows us to communicate without the threat of physical harm, at least, for the most part."

"Where am I Dr. Campos?" Greg asks, holding his shirt sleeve against his nostrils to catch the blood, repeating his question, "Where am I?"

"Where are you?" The Doctor repeats, "Tell me Gregory, where do you think you are?"

"If I knew," says Greg, his voice muffled by his blood-congested nasal cavities, "I'd be asking a different question. The last thing I remember is being in your office, the one by the patio, when a swarm of goons came in and shot me. Next thing I know, I'm waking up in a black hole. I don't know where. Hell, I don't even know when." Greg points over the Doctor's shoulder and says, "The sun is shining bright over the hills outside your office. The sun was nowhere to be seen when we were talking before, nor were the hills. So, I'll ask again Doctor, where am I?"

"That's very observant of you Gregory," says Dr. Campos, "The darts used to sedate you affect everyone differently. You've been out," he stops to think, "For a day, or thereabout. As for where you are Gregory, that's not important. All you need to know is that you're nowhere near home, and you aren't going anywhere for the time being. This facility belongs to a former colleague of mine. We use it to –" Dr. Campos stops again to consider his words, "*study*, people of particular interest."

"What the hell are you talking about Doctor?" Greg asks. Concluding that he still doesn't have all of his strength, he sits down on the cold hard floor, still plugging his nose with his shirt.

"You woke up in the room that will be yours until further notice," says the Doctor, ignoring Greg's inquiry. "It is complete with a bed, a toilet, and a sink. Meals will be given to you three times daily. When you're not locked in your room, you will be exactly where you are now. You were," he pauses again, "*escorted*, here by a group you may refer to as the Gentlemen."

"What?" Greg asks with a tone of surprise. "You can't keep me here, I have rights." He looks around the room for something, anything, to throw through the barrier. There's nothing. He gets back to his feet and goes to the door. Greg pulls on the handle with his blood-covered hands, using all of the strength he can muster, but it won't budge. Fear begins to set in and Greg becomes frantic. "Let me out of here Doctor. I don't have time for this. Let me out of here now." He runs back to the glass divider, his prior face print providing a reference point to avoid another collision. He tries to break the partition first by punching, then by kicking it, and manages to do no more than hurt himself.

"One way or another Gregory," says Dr. Campos in a demented tone, "You will give me answers."

Aside from his first time spent getting an MRI, Greg has never been scared of confined spaces; but looking at the man before him, claustrophobia sets in, feeling more and more like a suspected criminal being held for questioning in a room meant for torturing answers out of terrorists at Gitmo.

"Gregory," the Doctor says, as if he's a king, addressing his loyal subjects, or traitorous slaves, from his throne, "I'm going to tell you a story, and I want you to pay attention to the details of this particular story. I'm going to walk you through the last interview I conducted before my retirement. Though I could be wrong, I believe it will prove to be of great importance for you."

"Where's your crown Doc?" Greg asks mockingly, less than impressed by his captor's arrogant vibe. The look on Dr. Campos' face convinces Greg to return to his seat on the concrete floor, and perhaps not to push the Doctor's limits. Tired and defenseless he responds, "This should be interesting."

Dr. Campos stands up from his royal chair, and walks towards the clear wall, pulling his seat behind him, eventually stopping within a few feet of the glass partition, directly in front of Greg, where he sits back down. The file in his hands looks old.

It's a shade of faded charcoal, covered in pen marks and coffee stains, and the spine is coming apart. Dr. Campos pulled it from a box he keeps in an old storage container filled with files from his career. Greg notices audio tapes fastened to the inside cover and numerous Documents that look like medical charts. Dr. Campos flips to a specific section in the middle of the file and sifts through its pages, until he finds exactly what he's looking for. The file may be old, but the Doctor knows precisely where the information he wants is located.

"Now Gregory," says the Doctor, "As I mentioned before, aside from my primary duties at Patton State Hospital, I also worked a regular set of pro-bono hours at a local clinic." He stops to allow Greg to acknowledge the duplicated information, understanding that his patient's memory may not have fully returned. "My time at the clinic was much different than anything I did at Patton, which is why I enjoyed the extra work I was doing. However, eleven or so years ago, I met with a young woman at the clinic, a woman whose circumstances altered my life forever." He looks uncomfortable just thinking about what he's going to say. Taking a moment to wipe his mouth and adjust his glasses, he continues. "She wasn't the worst patient I'd seen by any means Gregory. While I'm sure she was schizophrenic, I had dealt with many schizoaffective disorders far worse than hers. However, her break from reality crossed into a dangerous area." He stops again, making sure Greg's following along.

Please get to the point.

"Is there a way to speed this up Doc?" Greg asks childishly.

"Please Gregory," the Doctor holds a finger to his mouth, signaling Greg to keep his shut, ignoring his patient's rude interruption. "The young woman had been coming to the clinic for quite some time," he continues without a hitch, as if he's told the story a thousand times, "and I made myself quite familiar with her file before we met. Her biggest issue was that she had convinced herself she wasn't crazy, as most insane folks do, and she wasn't taking any of the medications she had been prescribed. Normally we could have stepped in to do something, but we couldn't get a judge to sign off on a protective order at the time, and the police were stretched too thin to give the matter any attention. "Instead," the Doctor sighs, "she was allowed to live her life as she saw fit, and she went without the help she needed as a result."

"Dr. C," says Greg, irritated, "I remember you showing me a file with Jeanne's picture before you had me sedated and imprisoned. I may not be the world's smartest man, but if this isn't about Jeanne, I don't know how it's relevant."

"Please Gregory," says Dr. Campos, frustrated, "let me tell my story. This will take far too long if you interrupt me. He continues, "As I was saying, the young woman was very troubled. But you aren't going to take what I'm saying seriously, so instead, I'm going to play the recording of our last session. We'll see how cynical you are afterwards."

Dr. Campos flips back to the inside cover of the file and removes one of three tapes that Greg can see. He then stands up from his chair and walks back towards his desk, where he pushes a button that looks to be built into the desk itself.

Who is this guy?

Greg hears the sound of mechanical parts moving until a small cartridge of some sort rises out of the desk. Dr. Campos places the audiotape inside the cartridge, presses the button again, the tape is sucked into the desk, and white noise fills both rooms.

Chapter 21

"This is Doctor Emmanuel Campos," the recording begins playing overhead, "I will be recording this session with patient – please state your name and age dear."

Greg recognizes the Doctor's voice.

"Jeanne Burns," a woman's voice responds. Greg's eyes nearly pop out of his head at the sound of her voice. "Twenty-seven years old," the woman continues, "but not for much longer." Now the Doctor has Greg's attention.

"Thank you, Ms. Burns," says the Doctor, "We've never officially met before, but I have reviewed your file in its entirety, and I thought we needed to meet face-to-face. It looks like you're concerned about someone who is following you, or so you've told your previous Doctors. Is that correct?"

Greg takes notice of the Doctor's willingness to cut to the chase, something Greg originally thought would happen in his own case.

"Not exactly Doctor. I –" Jeanne's cut off by the Doctor.

"Not exactly?" Dr. Campos asks, "What do you mean?"

"I mean that I don't believe I'm being followed necessarily," says Jeanne, "It's difficult to explain, but – I – I don't know what to tell you Doctor. I'm never alone."

Greg wonders if she's confused.

"Ms. Burns," says Dr. Campos, "What do you mean by alone? Are you saying that you can't find privacy?"

Greg's a little encouraged knowing the Doctor has always interviewed with riddles.

"No Doctor," says Jeanne, "I mean I'm never alone. It's not someone who's following me. It's some*thing*." There isn't a hint of dishonesty in her tone. She believes what she's saying, and though his opinion may be irrelevant, so does Greg.

"Please, Ms. Burns," says Dr. Campos, "Tell me what is following you. What is it? Where did it come from? How long have you been feeling this way?"

It's hard for Greg to tell what Dr. Campos was thinking. He sounds like a tiger stalking his prey. He's going to wait until the perfect moment, and then make his move.

"*It* Dr. Campos," says Jeanne, "*It* is following me. There's no way to describe what it is. It just is. I don't know where it came from. All I know is that I've been haunted by these, I don't know, dreams, ever since I was a little girl. I always thought they were nightmares, but I I'm really not so sure. I'm worried that it's real. And it wants me."

Greg senses this isn't a joke. Something is wrong. Like a good mystery, he's been sucked in for the ride, until it's solved.

"I don't mean to make you uncomfortable Ms. Burns," says Dr. Campos, "But I need you to be as specific as you can possibly be. Can you do that for me? Can you describe a specific interaction with whatever it is? Can you describe it? Please Ms. Burns, this is of the utmost importance." The good Doctor sounds as though he's on to something.

"I –" Jeanne hesitates, "I can try, if you think it will help."

Greg looks down at his hands for a minute and notices his palms are sweating. If he had a seat, something other than a hard damp floor, he'd be sitting on the edge of it, filled with anticipation.

What is she going to say?

"Please do Ms. Burns," says Dr. Campos, "It'll be greatly appreciated. Do you need me to do anything before you begin?" There's a brief pause in the recording, long enough to make Greg worry the tape has been damaged, but short enough that the Doctor doesn't bother to wind the recording forward. Then it continues, "Let the record reflect that Ms. Burns is shaking her head to signify an answer of 'no' to the previous question. If you will Ms. Burns, the floor is yours."

Having made his way back to his desk, Doctor Campos stops the recording. "Gregory," he says, "I will continue with Jeanne's session in a moment, but I want to mention that the following segment is the part I believe to be of significance to you. Therefore I want you to listen closely. We will talk about this more afterwards."

"Okay Dr. C," says Greg anxiously, "I don't know how this could mean anything to me, but if this is going to get me out of here faster, let's cut the chitchat and carry on. Does that work for you?" Greg is tired of being jerked around. He has to know what she says next.

Without another word, Dr. Campos continues the playback of the recording.

Chapter 22

Jeanne Burns settles into her green-felted rocking chair and surveys the room. It reminds her of an old Kindergarten classroom. There are a few round wooden tables surrounded by cheap plastic bucket-seated chairs, small wooden shelves that look like shoe racks, and several crayon-colored pictures hanging on the walls. An old desk, much like a teacher's, sits at the front of the room near the door, and the old cracked linoleum at the back of the room is covered by a hand-made rug, the rocking chair in which Jeanne's sitting, and an old couch with knitted cushions upon which Dr. Campos is sitting. It may be by design, as Jeanne feels relaxed as her story begins.

"I know you want me to explain things in detail Doctor," she says, "But I caution you, I'm not very good at telling stories."

"That's okay Ms. Burns," says Dr. Campos. "Perhaps if you don't think of it as a story, then you'll do just fine."

"If you've read my entire file as you say you have," says Jeanne, "Then you're aware of my early childhood." She looks at Dr. Campos, who slowly blinks in acknowledgment. "You know that I was beaten by my father on a daily basis," says Jeanne, "and you know if I took one too many breaths of his air, he took anything that was near him and swung it at me. You know I was hit with electric cords, chairs, a coffee table, a telephone, you name it," again looking at the Doctor, who nods for her to continue. "You likely know that his brother, technically my uncle, sexually assaulted me, twice." The Doctor still says nothing, using his hands to encourage Jeanne to keep going. "I'm sure Doctor, as you've guessed by now, that just those facts alone left me mentally scarred."

"Yes Ms. Burns," says Dr. Campos. "Any one of those traumas can be permanently damaging, let alone all of them together. I'm not questioning your qualifications for being here, nor do I want you to think I'm discarding them," he stops to make a note in the file before adding, "Please, Ms. Burns, do continue."

"Social Services eventually stepped in and took me away from my parents," she carries on. "I was told I couldn't return to their home until either my dad got help or my mom made him leave the house," she stops to let out a boisterous exhale, "I never returned home, which I assumed meant they decided to proceed through life without me, which is fine, you know, I didn't want to be a burden."

"Perhaps, Ms. Burns," says Dr. Campos, "You were better off not returning to your parents' home."

Jeanne looks at Dr. Campos as if he'd just slapped her in the face. She says nothing in response, and instead adds, "So, I was placed in a foster home. Yay me, haha." She giggles sarcastically. "At eight years old I was given new parents, new siblings, a new family, but I don't want to talk about them."

"Is there a reason you don't want to talk about your foster family Ms. Burns?" The Doctor asks.

"It was weird living with strangers," Jeanne replies, "but that's not what I'm supposed to be talking about. You want to know about, *it*. I don't want to beat around the bush, and you don't look like a man who enjoys bullshit."

"I want you to explain things as you see fit Ms. Burns," says Dr. Campos. "It's okay if you don't want to talk about your foster family. I was merely asking if you had a specific reason for choosing not to."

The tone in Jeanne's voice changes to one of anger. She uses it to hide her fear. Greg pictures her, barely blinking, as if she's possessed. "*It* is cold Doctor," she snaps, "The coldest thing I've ever encountered. Shortly after I was placed with my new family, I began having these – I don't know – dreams I guess."

"Dreams you say," says Dr. Campos in an inquisitively arrogant tone.

"I'm not a scientist," barks Jeanne. "So, I don't know what they were technically."

"Can you describe them to me Ms. Burns?" The Doctor asks.

"All I know is that I went to sleep at night," she answers, "and after a couple hours passed, without fail, the same terrible dream would wake me up. I can still see it as if I were sleeping now. Someone, or more importantly, some*thing* is chasing me, and I'm running away for what seems like hours." Chills run down Jeanne's back just thinking about it.

"So Ms. Burns," says Dr. Campos, hinting at his theory, "this always took place while you slept."

"After dealing with the nightmares for a few years," says Jeanne, "my new parents brought me to a specialist. I can't remember his name, but I'm sure he's listed in my file. I was told that I was suffering from Post-Traumatic Stress caused by my father's and uncle's attacks," She pauses, recalling the first time she was diagnosed. "Honestly Doctor, I had to laugh at first. My father, who wanted nothing to do with me, was haunting me in my sleep without knowing it. Talk about irony, huh?"

"Do you believe your Doctor's findings were incorrect Ms. Burns?" The Doctor asks.

"At that time, Doctor, I don't know," Jeanne's voice is slightly muffled from biting her lip, mostly out of embarrassment. "After years of therapy, I was able to get past the dreams, or so I thought. Later on, in high school, I began having the dreams again. However, this time when I woke up the dreams didn't end."

"How do you mean Ms. Burns?" Dr. Campos asks, intrigued.

"I used to think I was crazy," Jeanne answers, "And who knows, maybe I am. But for the past ten years, whenever I wake up in the middle of the night, *it's* there."

"It –" the Doctor tries to speak.

"Before you go and judge me," Jeanne cuts him off before he gets another word out. "Let me tell you, Doctor, that I have thought this through, and either I'm a lunatic who needs help, or I'm not crazy, and something is watching me." She glares into the Doctor's eyes, hoping he'll believe her. "Every time I sit up in my bed," she says, "I look towards the corner of my room, across from my bed and near the doorway, and *it's* there, in the shadows, waiting, watching, in silence."

Dr. Campos stops taking notes, lingering on Jeanne's every word.

"The room fills with air so cold that I think my heart is going to stop beating, frozen in palce" she carries on, pleading with the Doctor's silence, "Doctor, it's there. I promise you it is."

Dr. Campos looks like he wants to speak, but can't find the words.

"As if that isn't bad enough," Jeanne adds, "For the past six weeks, it has been getting closer and closer to me as I pop up in my bed. I've even felt like someone was touching my legs at night. I can't get away from it, and I don't know what to do Doctor. That's why I'm here. Please tell me you can help me. *Please*."

The recording stops. Greg watches Dr. Campos remove the tape from his desk and place it back in the file. "That is all for now Gregory," he says, picking up the phone on his desk. He dials three digits. "We're all set for now. You may come take our guest," he says to the person on the other end of the line, and hangs up.

"What?" Greg asks. "No. We need to talk about this. You need to tell me what is going on."

Without acknowledging a word Greg says, Dr. Campos presses another button on the desk and the retracting wall slides back across the room, cutting Greg off from the conversation, and ending the session. Greg considers throwing another fit, but knows it's pointless. Instead he thinks about the Doctor's recording. There's no denying Jeanne was the one speaking, but what about her story?

She has nightmares like me. She's being haunted by a nearly indescribable thing. *She believed every word she said. But how can this be?*

A few minutes later, the heavy steel door swings open and eight Gentlemen enter the room, as they always do, in a single-file line. The first Gentleman turns to the rest, raises a fist in the air next to his head, and they come to a stop. Greg takes note of the leader, standing more than six feet tall and built like a house.

"Sir," says the first Gentleman, "I need you to come with us, and I'll appreciate it if you do so of your own free will." Greg recognizes his voice as the man in the shadows who ordered the men to take him from his room earlier.

"And if I don't?" Greg asks rhetorically in defiance.

"I would think prior events provide enough motivation, do they not?" The first Gentleman responds, staring at Greg intently.

"I suppose you're right," says Greg in a defeated tone.

The first Gentleman holds his hand up, swirls his index finger once clockwise, and the rest of the group surrounds Greg. They allow him to walk on his own with four Gentlemen walking both in front of and behind him. Greg is escorted directly to his room. Nobody says a word, not even Greg. The hallways are still nearly black from the lack of overall lighting, and Greg can't make out any of the structure's details. Once in front of the door to his room, two of the Gentlemen enter while the other six grab Greg and force him towards his bed. He doesn't bother resisting, at least until he sees the needle.

The week before his nineteenth birthday, Greg was still working at his local garage. He had moved up from the slave-like role of gas pumper to the luxurious role of oil changer. On this particular day, Greg was changing the oil on an old Chevy Silverado, as well as rotating the tires. He got it up on the hydraulic lift, a good six feet above the ground, changed the oil, rotated the tires, and was preparing to finish the job. That's when Hal Thomas, Greg's manager, decided to "help out."

Greg was still under the truck, collecting his tools and moving the oil disposal bucket, which Hal started lowering the lift. Alarmed by the prospect of being crushed, Greg ran for the end of the garage bay and started shouting Hal's name, flailing his arms all the way.

As if the conditions weren't bad enough, the mechanics in the shop were all big fans of *Black Sabbath*, and as was the case on most mornings, the song *Paranoid* was echoing from one end of the garage to the other, making it impossible to hear what anyone was saying. Hal didn't hear Greg screaming. However, he did look up to see Greg running, and when he realized Greg was still under the truck, he immediately released the hydraulic lift lever, causing the entire rig to shake, which resulted in the Silverado falling off of the braces holding it up for the tire rotation, and the trailer hitch at the back end of the truck came down right on top of Greg's head.

Greg probably would have panicked, but he couldn't believe what happened. Hal Thomas dropped a truck on him. Then the blood started pouring out of the two-inch gash in his skull and everyone freaked out. A couple of the mechanics fell on the ground laughing. Hal imagined the owner firing him for neglect. The cashier thought to start cleaning the blood off of the ground. However, nobody seemed to pay any attention to Greg, who seemed mere moments away from passing out.

Finally, Christy, the owner's wife, convinced Greg to get into her car, and she took him directly to the emergency room. Once there, Christy explained what happened, and Greg was taken to a room to be seen. The first nurse came in and helped stop Greg's wound from bleeding, though he was clearly going to require stitches. Then a second nurse, without any warning, and without confirming Greg was the correct patient, lifted Greg's right shirt-sleeve, and stabbed him in the arm with a needle, administering a Tetanus shot.

Greg screamed at the second nurse, yanking his arm away, causing the tip of the needle to break off, still in his arm. Now, not only did he need stitches, but Greg also needed to have a needle sliver removed from his arm.

Later, before he could be allowed to leave the hospital, Greg was required to have blood drawn. He wasn't sure why, but knew he wanted to go home. So he consented. He waited patiently for the third nurse to draw his blood, knowing his veins are awful; and, just as haphazardly as the Tetanus nurse, the blood drawing nurse randomly stabbed a needle into Greg's right arm and started shifting it around, as if she were switching gears on the track at the Daytona 500.

Greg hates needles.

"No!" Greg yells as the six Gentlemen hold him down on the bed in his cave-like room.

"Scream all you want sir," says the first Gentleman. "There's nobody here but us."

Watching the syringe move towards his neck, Greg squirms and tries to pull him- self free, but it's useless. The Gentlemen are much stronger than he is. There's nothing he can do, and as the needle punctures his jugular, a single tear rolls down Greg's cheek.

"Haha," the first Gentleman snickers on his way out of the room. "Sweet dreams."

Greg is alone, again.

Chapter 23

The packed clay is like a frozen lake beneath Greg's naked body moments before an onset of frostbite. He can see across the room as the fog descends from his vision. Wooden beams meet at the corner of the man-made ceiling. The air feels damp, and visibility is minimal without a source of light. A resounding pain suggests he's been beaten again, he assumes by his father. It wouldn't be the first time.

Through a wall of fatigue Greg manages to crawl to the nearest wall, where he's able to sit and prop himself up. There doesn't appear to be any furniture in the room. He looks for the toilet, but judging from the smell, it's too late. He wonders what he did this time.

Greg's mother made an egg salad sandwich once. He hates egg salad, but he didn't have it in him to deny her attempt at culinary art. On this particular Friday afternoon, school had been cancelled due to tornado warnings, and while his brothers remained at the baby sitter's house, Greg was home watching movies with mom.

A couple hours prior he'd been in the back yard playing, and Greg noticed what looked like chocolate candy that had fallen from a wrapper. He thought it was his lucky day. First there was no school, and now he'd found what some other kid, possibly his brother, had likely lost. Being the ignorant child that he was, Greg immediately snatched the treat from the grass, tossed it into his mouth, and began chewing. He knew it wasn't candy after the first bite. It was cat shit, and with every bite of egg salad he swallowed, that was all Greg could think about.

Hoping to make it through the meal, Greg asked his mother for something to drink. Like so many other children his age, he was given a container in the shape of a small barrel, like the ones used for ale in all of the old movies. However, this barrel was filled with an unidentifiable orange juice-like liquid. If children his age had been able to relate to alcoholics, this tasty beverage would have been their addiction.

With the drink on the table beside him, and a cat-shit sandwich staring him in the face, Greg turned to see if his mother was looking. His plan was to down the drink, throw the sandwich in the trash, and call it a day. There was always another meal later in the day after his father returned from work. Unfortunately, when Greg turned back towards his food, his elbow hit the addicting drink, knocked it over onto his plate, and the orange liquid swarmed his lunch. Not knowing what to do at that point, Greg went back to the living room and left the mess for someone else to clean. Had he known that someone else was going to be his father, he would have done it himself.

His father's car pulled into the driveway as the sun began setting later in the evening. Greg could hear him shut the car door, entering the house a moment later through the kitchen door. His father wasn't in the house for ten seconds before Greg heard him scream his name. Hoping he just wanted to give him a hug, Greg sprinted to the kitchen, only to see the orange sandwich still sitting on the table. He tried to hit the brakes and run the other way, but by the time he had come to a complete stop, his father had grabbed him by the back of the neck, and lifted him off the ground.

"Boy, what is this?" His father grunts, slamming Greg's face down into the orange mess. "Why is this sitting here? Was there something wrong with your lunch?"

Greg began choking on soggy bread and orange cat feces. He would have tried to reason with his father, but the only thing that ever earned was a beating worse than the one originally intended.

"You're going to finish your lunch, and you're going to finish it now." Greg's father pushed his face down a little harder. "Do you hear me boy?"

The choices available were rather limited. Greg considered sucking in the disgusting clumps and waiting until his father let go, at which point he would have turned and spit it all in his face, but decided against it. Instead, he just sat motionless, face down on the plate until he saw his brothers come walking in the door with their mother close behind. That was the cue. Knowing his father always releases him when his mother catches him in the act, Greg waited for the pressure to go away. As soon as his father's hand was gone, Greg spun around in the chair, pulled his right arm back, balled his hand into a small fist, and plunged it forward into his father's crotch, causing him to momentarily drop to one knee.

Greg knew he'd bought himself the world's worst beating, but he wasn't going to stand around to wait for it. With his father taking a moment to catch his breath, Greg bolted down the hall towards his bedroom. He could hear his father screaming, "You're dead, boy," but that wasn't going to stop him.

Into the room with the door locked, Greg started tossing all of his belongings behind the door. His father was going to have to work to reach him, and he did. After a minute or two, Greg could hear him trying to unlock the door.

"You better open this door right now!" He screamed, but Greg had already made his decision, and his father was not going to get any help from him.

Greg's father eventually gave up and decided to kick the door down. Once past the barricade, and with the determination of a bull chasing a red curtain, he trudged across the small mountain left in Greg's trail, and as his father's fist made its way towards him, Greg smiled as though he'd just gained entry to Wonka's factory.

The room in which the gentlemen left Greg's sedated body reminds him of the basement in which he awoke after his father beat him within an inch of his life. The difference being Greg hasn't eaten any cat-shit recently, and bowls of oatmeal are delivered by the sixth Gentleman throughout the day.

Chapter 24

Amber Jane D'Marco stares at the number scribbled on her hand through a fit of tears. She has no idea who Kent Lawson is. Amber tracked down one of Greg's high school classmates on an online site for people looking to stay connected with friends from the past; and it says Kent is Greg's best friend, and if anyone can tell Amber how to contact Greg's family, it's Kent. She dials the number, and the phone rings only once.

"Yellow," a high-pitched voice answers.

"Um," Amber mumbles, "hi. Is Mr. Lawson available?"

"You got him," he responds. "Who's this?"

"My name is, uh," Amber's nerves have a hold on her. She can barely remember her own name.

"Well, Uh," says Kent jokingly, "What can I do you for?"

"Haha," Amber chuckles, which helps a little, "I'm Amber. I got your number from a friend." She promised not to divulge her source, though she feels a little dirty being so sketchy about it.

"Really?" Says Kent in a questioning tone. "I didn't know I had any left. Nevertheless, here we are, talking, sorta." He stops, but Amber doesn't say anything just yet. "I'm assuming you're calling to do more than tell me your name. So, let's have it." Proper grammar isn't his thing.

"I apologize Mr. Lawson," says amber softly, "I'm calling because I need to locate Greg Roberts' family." She hopes this will work.

"What?" Kent asks, confused. "Why do you need to reach Greg's family? And you can call me Kent, it's okay."

"I'm sorry for the confusion Kent," says Amber, "I'm just trying to understand what happened to him. I'm guessing by the sound of shock in your voice that Greg never told you about me."

"Well, Amber," says Kent, "You're right. I don't know anything about you. But that don't matter. How'd you know him?"

"We're supposed to be getting married in three months," Amber says, proudly. "I don't know what happened, but I can't just sit and do nothing about it. Will you help me?" She can't hide the helplessness in her voice, still sniffling from crying.

"Okay, okay," says Kent, "don't go all coo-coo on me now. I don't know what you're up to lady, but if you wanna talk to Greg's family, I can give you their names and phone numbers. Can I send them via text message to the number you're calling from?" He's never been able to tell a woman *no*.

"Yeah," says Amber, happily surprised. "That'd be great. Thanks so much."

"Just do me one favor," says Kent, "if you find what you're looking for, lemme know."

Amber tries to respond, but Kent hangs up before she can say another word. A minute or so goes by and her phone vibrates, Kent followed through with his text message. There are two names with phone numbers, one for Greg's brother, and another for his mother. Now Amber can get some answers.

Wondering what she may learn with her new information, Amber clutches her favorite picture of Greg in her arms, rocking in place, remembering the day she met the man of her dreams.

The sounds of carnival rides and games mix with the scent of the world's unhealthiest fried foods. People come in droves for days on end to spend their hard earned money on the freak show that is the Los Angeles County Fair. Live music, horse racing, and all of the entertainment scams one can stomach come together for one unforgettable week.

Amber and Bonnie like the fair because it's a cheap thrill. They met during their freshman year of high school, and have been best friends ever since. The fair was Bonnie's idea, but there's little about which they don't agree. Both graduated from cosmetology school before age twenty, and they went into business together a year later. As a matter of fact, with both measuring at an average five feet and six inches tall, with long black hair, and chocolate brown eyes, if they were to omit the details, one might think they're twins.

There's one game at the fair they play every year. Only this year a creepy old man disguised as a clown who has clearly not showered in days has decided to cheat Amber out of her prize. If anyone knows how the game works, it's Amber and Bonnie. The declared rules to the game state that if someone, anyone at all, manages to successfully toss three rings around the red beer bottle amidst the sea of green beer bottles, that lucky individual will win a brand new television like the one on display behind the water proof shield at the back of the attraction. No other rules are present, nor are they made known prior to the rings leaving Amber's hands. However, when she tosses all three rings together and they cling to the red bottle like dog hair to a hand covered in superglue, the disgusting clown decides to create his own rules.

"I'm sorry young lady," says the clown in a coarse tone, almost choking on the snot running down the back of his throat, "You'll need to toss them one at a time to be eligible for the grand prize. Haha," sweat drips from his nose and runs down his diarrhea-brown teeth as he laughs, "For this toss, you may pick from the third row of stuffed animals found on the wall to my left." His eyes run up and down Amber's body, while running his greasy hands through his hair and licking his lips through a hole in smile where the teeth have rotted away as a result of his methamphetamine addiction.

"Excuse me," says Amber, disgusted. "Keep your eyes up here," she quickly points to her face, "You didn't say anything about this before you let me toss my rings. That rule isn't posted anywhere near your little tent here. That television is mine." The surrounding crowd chimes in with a growling agreement. The filthy clown goes to take a pink stuffed pony from his wall, and a young man steps forward.

"Excuse me sir," says the young man sternly, "I think you owe this beautiful young lady a TV."

"YEAH!" The crowd reinforces his statement.

"Now, you can give her the prize owed to her," the young stud asserts, "or I can see to it that your hand never accepts another dollar at this fair." The clown wipes his eyes and looks at the shining knight. "So, what do you say?" The young man's voice gives Amber chills. No man had ever stood up for her before. If feels nice.

Though he tries to fight the brave man's threat, the old clown sees looks of persecution among the crowd, and he gives in. Amber can't believe it. She was certain she was leaving with nothing, and that her county fair days were ruined.

"Thanks," Amber says to the kind man, blushing. "You didn't have to do that for me. I should know better than to give my money to con-artists."

Feeling like a hero, the young man smiles at her. Seeing a gorgeous woman blush always melts his heart.

"My name is Amber," she continues. "How can I make this up to you?" She sets the bait to see if he'll show any interest.

"Nice to meet you Amber," he responds with a smile, "I'm Greg."

It's been a long time since Amber has shown anyone romantic consideration, but Greg's smile crushes her defenses.

"You don't owe me a thing," he says. The look in Amber's eyes suggests disappointment. "But," Greg adds, "should you feel obligated, I'm always up for a cup of coffee." He figures the line to be harmless enough. The smile on Amber's face makes it official. She's his.

Tears form a puddle on the glass frame, and Amber speaks aloud as though Greg is there. "Where are you?"

Chapter 25

Amber's alarm goes off as the sun starts to shine over the surrounding hills the following morning. Her head hurts, likely because it took a bottle of whiskey to fall asleep the night before. However, she doesn't have time for a personal pity party. She takes a moment to gain her consciousness and heads to the bathroom, where she brushes her teeth, takes a shower, wraps her hair in a bun, and gets dressed in a mere twenty minutes. The coffee pot is ready with wake-up juice, and Amber grabs the phone. Who should she call first? After a couple sips of coffee, she dials the first number.

"Yo, this is George, leave your –" Amber ends the call.

"Shit." She curses aloud. "Well let's try his mom." She punches the seven digits into the dial and waits.

Ring, no answer.

Ring, still no answer.

Ring.

Ring.

"Sorry I can't take your call. Leave a message and have a blessed –" Again, Amber ends the call, tossing the phone onto her couch.

"Dammit!" She screams. "Why does this have to be so difficult?"

Determined she won't allow herself to go crazy by sitting idly by, Amber goes to her computer and does a web search for the first number she called. A few names pop up, but only one she cares about, George Roberts, Greg's brother. Amber clicks the link next to the name on the screen and it takes her to a website attempting to sell her free background information on George Roberts based on the number she entered for a low one-time payment of twenty dollars.

"Fuck it," Amber mutters to the stale air in the room. She grabs her credit card, enters her information, clicks a button to 'Order Now,' and waits for the information to hit her email. Ten minutes pass and she receives a new message. Anxious to have *something* to go on, Amber opens her email and is surprised to see what her money bought. The page is almost entirely blank, with the exception of a number, the name of a street, and a city.

Twenty dollars just doesn't buy what it used to.

Convinced it's enough to work with, she scribbles the information onto a piece of paper, grabs her keys, and sprints out the front door.

The address from the email is a good twenty minutes from Amber's house. A mile or so down the road she can't help but think about Greg, and a tear comes to her eye. She looks at herself in the rearview mirror and tells herself she needs to be tough, but she simply can't focus on anything else.

By the time Amber hit the first signal light, small drops of water begin to pitter-patter on her windshield, and she realizes it's starting to rain. Amber likes rain. It reminds her of the first weekend she ever spent with Greg. His Uncle had a log cabin in the woods up north. It was a hefty drive from home, but well worth the trip. They arrived early in the evening on a Friday, and the rain left them with little choice but to stay inside.

They unpacked what little luggage they brought with them, and then Greg prepared dinner while Amber took a shower and put on a fresh set of clothes. When Amber was finished, she walked out to the dining area, where the table was set with plastic forks and knives, paper plates, red all-purpose *SOLO* cups, and a single candle that bounced light around the room as it flickered. Each plate had a peanut butter and grape-jelly sandwich with the crusts cut off, a handful of potato chips, and another handful of animal crackers. The cups were each filled with lemonade made from a powdered mix and had a few pieces of ice.

Greg was seated at the table with the world's biggest smile as Amber looked on in amusement. She burst out with a belly full of laughter and could not contain herself. It was the poorest looking meal she'd ever seen, and yet it was also the most romantic. They said little as they ate their gourmet meals, smiling at one another with each bite.

Upon the meal's conclusion, Greg grabbed the plates, cups, and utensils, while Amber walked across the room to look at the wildlife through a window near the fireplace. Greg tossed the items in the trash and then made his way towards her, stopping for only a moment to start a small fire. The flames crackled as they found pockets of air in the ignited logs and a sense of warmth filled Amber with joy.

"What are you thinking about?" Greg whispered in Amber's ear, standing with his arms wrapped around her, both gazing out at the world.

"This place is amazing," Amber replied. She was happier than she could recall having ever been before.

Greg squeezed her like a teddy bear, while using his chin to slowly move the hair resting upon her shoulder, exposing her neckline. He bit the lobe of her ear ever so gently before whispering to her, "This is just an old cabin. It's *you* who is amazing."

The hairs on the back of Amber's neck stood up, partly from bliss, but also because his advances tickled.

Suddenly, Amber slams her hand against the rearview mirror and shouts, "No!" The car jerks to the right, just missing a young boy playing in a puddle in the middle of the street. The wheels burst into shards as they hit the curb. The vehicle bounces up and over the sidewalk, sending a set of mailboxes into the air. The car finally comes to a stop in a patch of grass; someone's font yard. A cloud of steam from the air bag slowly dissipates. Amber can hardly breathe. Then a metal box slams down upon the windshield. It looks nothing like it did mere moments before, but she can still make out the name *Roberts* painted in giant white letters on the side. She has arrived.

Chapter 26

Greg wakes up to the sound of the door to his room unlocking; the unmistakable sounds of metal components turning, followed by the squeaking of hinges as the door opening gives him a headache before he can get out of the bed. The Gentlemen enter as a pack, much like they did the day prior.

"Sir, we need you to come with us." The first Gentleman sounds as friendly as Greg remembers.

"What now?" Greg snaps. He's never been a morning person.

"Please sir, it's better if you comply willingly." The Gentleman stretches his right arm out as if to shake Greg's, and helps him to his feet.

"What time is it?" Greg asks, assuming he won't get an answer.

"It's oh five hundred hours, sir." The Gentleman's response comes as a surprise.

"Okay," Greg hesitates, "0500 of when? What day is it?" He figures the first answer was given too easily. There must be a catch.

"0500 of today, sir." The Gentleman utters in a frustrated tone, also unexpected. "Now please, sir, let us proceed without further delay."

Greg takes the trip back to the divided room, again escorted as though he's a prisoner walking to his execution. Once back inside the curious room he decides to take a seat on the floor against the wall farthest from the room's partition. Not ten seconds later, the stone-like wall disappears again, and Dr. Campos is sitting at his desk, reading what appears to be a medical file, and he's reading it rather intently.

"Good morning Mr. Roberts." The Doctor speaks but does not look up from the paperwork before him. "I would ask you how you are feeling, but you have yet to show me that you are capable of being truly reasonable."

"Huh?" Greg doesn't know what else to say. He was sleeping, though he has no idea as to how long he'd been in his prison-cell of a room. The next thing he knows he's jostled awake by large men, and now he's being what, interrogated again? "Dr. C, I'm not quite sure what's going on."

"This is precisely what I mean Mr. Roberts," the Doctor takes a deep breath mid-sentence, "you continue to disappoint me with your *beat-around-the-bush* antics, and it is becoming quite tiresome." The Doctor pushes his chair back from his desk, stands up, and walks towards the glass divider. "It's really quite simple Mr. Roberts –"

"No, Doc," Greg interrupts the tangent, "You're not understanding. I was just asleep. I don't know how long I slept. Hell, I don't even know what day it is. But if you expect me to be ready for whatever *this* is at five o'clock in the damn morning," he stops for a moment, checking to make sure the Doctor is really paying attention.

"Mr. Roberts, if I –"

"You," Greg interrupts him again, "are going to have to man-up and give me some damn coffee. There's no way in hell I'm going to be able to have a serious conversation with anyone, let alone a nut like you, without some caffeine."

"Fair enough, Mr. Roberts." Dr. Campos walks back towards his desk, presses one of his mysterious buttons, and says aloud, "Bring our guest something to help him wake up, and be quick about it." He turns back towards Greg and continues, "Now Mr. Roberts, you say you aren't awake, and therefore are unable to assist me with my endeavor. I am going to help you with that issue, and then we are going to get down to business." The Doctor glares at Greg, as if looking directly into his soul, and asks with groan, "Do I make myself clear, Mr. Roberts?"

"Whatever you say Doc. *Whatever you say.*" Greg sighs and waits for his coffee. During the silence he thinks about the recording he heard the last time he was in the room. The voice was clearly that of Jeanne. Greg still can't wrap his brain around it.

How is it possible? Is this all an elaborate hoax? Am I dreaming?

Anything would be more believable than what the Doctor suggests.

A moment later the door swings open on Greg's side of the room. The Gentlemen enter with their semi-Nazi march, only this time they aren't empty-handed. No, this time one of the Gentlemen has a large chair, the sort of chair you'd expect to find in a dentist's office, and he's carrying it as if it's a bag of feathers lightly sitting upon his shoulder. Two of the other Gentlemen grab Greg's arms while the chair is set up only a foot or two away from the room's glass divider.

"Wait!" Greg pleads. "What are you doing? What is the meaning of this? Somebody answer me!" But the Gentlemen say nothing, not even to one another. They drag Greg across the room, force his body into a sitting position in the chair, and strap him in as if he were being buckled into a shuttle waiting to launch into outer space. The Gentlemen move through their motions as though they had been practiced several times over, like a fire drill.

With all of the confusion surrounding his choice-less seating, Greg neglects to see Dr. Campos leave his office. Once the Gentlemen are convinced the restraints are correctly in place and Greg isn't able to move even an inch, they leave the room as quickly as they had arrived, and Greg hears the door close across the room behind him.

Nothing happens for at least five minutes, which feels more like hours. Greg sits motionless thinking about everything that has happened. He had been plagued by a terrible entity of some sort every time he tried to sleep; tormented to the point that he believed himself to be losing his mind.

Maybe that's it. Maybe I really have gone off the deep end.

Then again, his mother, his brother, hell, even the family dog had been looking at him like there was something wrong with him for years. The crazy is nothing new, hence his seeking out

Dr. Campos in the first place. He's supposed to be the master of such mental breakdowns, or at least he was. Now Greg's strapped onto a chair waiting for he knows not what, and all because of a name he hadn't heard in years.

Another ten or fifteen minutes pass and Greg sees there's nobody in the room in front of him, and thinking he's now alone, a single tear falls from his right eye and slides down his cheek like a bar of soap down the side of a bath tub, stopping just under his chin, where it hangs on to his face for dear life before plunging down to his shirt-covered chest. He would start bawling, but the harness on his head is stretching his face so far that he can't even blink, let alone cry.

"So, Mr. Roberts," Doctor Campos says, "are you awake yet?" He's been standing in the room observing Greg the entire time. He waits for an answer, knowing none can be given. The Doctor slowly struts across the room until he is standing just over the right shoulder of the chair upon which Greg is fastened.

"I apologize, Mr. Roberts," the Doctor continues, "I forgot. I designed your seat to prevent one from actually being able to move enough to render an audible response. Therefore," he whips his head around the side of the chair, though still standing behind it, and explains to Greg the circumstance in which he finds himself, "Mr. Roberts, I am going to tell you what will happen next. If you are now awake and alert enough to understand what I am saying, make any kinds of noise now, and I will take that as your acknowledgment."

Greg tries to speak, but the Doctor is right, it isn't possible. Even if there was coffee to drink, he'd be unable to open his mouth even to sip a straw. So, he grunts as a reply.

"Very well Mr. Roberts." The Doctor is delighted to gain some compliance. "You are sitting, at least I think it's still considered sitting, in a chair that you will not be able to get out of until I have deemed it appropriate. I assume from your response a moment ago that you now realize how very little you can actually move, and you will remain just as such, again, until I have deemed otherwise to be appropriate. In a moment my team of assistants, the Gentleman as you now know them, will arrive with a cart containing my tools, which will be needed for our next round of *Q&A* if you will." Dr. Campos nearly cracks a smile at the thought of what comes next. "I want to be up front with you, Mr. Roberts," he charges on while taking a pair of latex gloves from his pocket and puts them on his hands, "This procedure is going to be extremely painful at first. However, you can minimize the extent of the pain by simply keeping yourself from fighting it."

Greg's motor skills flare to scowl, but his face doesn't move.

"I don't want you to be confused, Mr. Roberts," the Doctor continues, "You don't have any choice in the matter. I will complete the procedure with or without your cooperation. I have morals Mr. Roberts, and those very morals tell me that giving you a chance to decrease your overall suffering is the right thing to do."

The door opens behind Greg again, and he hears the Gentlemen's march, as well as the wheels of what must be the cart of tools to which Dr. Campos previously referred.

"Thank you Gentlemen," says the Doctor. "Wait outside. I will notify you when our guest is ready."

Greg hears the Gentlemen march back out of the room. Dr. Campos grabs the edge of his tool cart and wheels it over to Greg's right side, where the Doctor will be standing for the procedure.

"Mr. Roberts," the Doctor resumes his explanation, "In a moment I am going to clamp your right eye open. I know this doesn't sound pleasant, but it's really not so bad, as long as you relax and let it happen." He pauses and takes a couple of breaths. "The hard part is what follows, Mr. Roberts. I am going to be using a special serum, my own design of course," pride is clearly among the Doctor's downfalls. "My serum will need to be injected into your tear duct," he explains without hesitation, as if pushing a needle into someone's tear duct is a common occurrence. "Now, I know your mind is probably racing, pondering the thought of the pain you're about to feel, and questioning by sanity" and the Doctor is right, "but as I mentioned before, you can tense up and be in tremendous agony or, if you allow yourself to avoid your immediate reaction, it will hurt moderately and be done."

Greg again tries to say something, this time out of sheer terror, and again is unsuccessful, letting out a hoarse, almost painful sounding hum.

The Doctor grabs his first *tool*, "This, Mr. Roberts, is a speculum," holding it so Greg can see. It looks like a hybrid between a pair of long tweezers and a vice clamp. "I imagine you've seen these in movies, or perhaps even in infomercials for various eye surgery programs," the Doctor boasts, "it's used to hold your eye propped open so that a surgeon can access it without difficulty. In many instances, it looks as though the subject's eye is going to fly out across the room, but I assure you Mr. Roberts, you are in no danger of losing any body parts at this time."

Greg wishes he could take solace in the fact that he's going to get through this intact, but all he can focus on is the thought of a needle being anywhere near his face.

"I'm going to put it in place, Mr. Roberts," the Doctor doesn't slow down for even a long breath, "and when I'm done, I'm going to release the device that is currently stretching your face. You still won't be able to talk, as the primary straps will remain fastened, but you will be able to blink your free eyelid."

Without even a moment's hesitation, Dr. Campos leans over Greg's face, the speculum in one hand, and with the other, he uses his index finger and thumb to push the top and bottom lids of Greg's right eye in opposing directions.

Greg tries to scream, but can only groan. He tries yelling, "No! No! No!" but it's all generic tone to Dr. Campos.

When the lids have stretched as far as they can, Dr. Campos puts the speculum in place. It cups Greg's eye while holding the lids out of the way. Dr. Campos then presses a valve on the back of the headrest and Greg's left eye is released from the contraption holding it open. After blinking the now free eye several times, tears stream down his face.

Wishing the nightmare would end and he'd wake up, home in his bed. Greg looks over at the Doctor with his free eye and is overrun by shock when he sees the syringe. It's filled with a neon-mint-green liquid that would almost surely glow in the dark. Greg actually thinks the liquid is beautiful, until he sees the Doctor unsheathe the needle itself, like an executioner wielding his instrument of death.

Greg remembers all of the old war movies he's seen and he can't recall ever seeing a blade in a warrior's hand that looked half as terrifying as this needle.

"Now, Mr. Roberts," says the Doctor, "we have arrived at the moment I mentioned previously. I'm hoping, for your sake of course, that you have decided to let this happen. As you can see, you have no power to prevent it."

Dr. Campos doesn't wait for Greg to respond, or even acknowledge his statement. He takes the index finger of his left hand, puts it just under the edge of Greg's right top eye lid, and pushes towards the top of the bridge of Greg's nose. This makes any remaining flesh around the eye completely taught, giving the Doctor optimal conditions for accessing the tear duct. He then squirts some artificial tears into the exposed eye.

"The drops, Mr. Roberts, will help lubricate the syringe."

Greg can't help his reaction. He grumbles, grunts, groans, blinks his free eye, cries, you name it. But all is futile.

Dr. Campos aligns the end of the syringe with Greg's right tear duct. Greg sees only a blur out of his right eye, and his nose blocks the tip of the needle from his left. A second later he feels freezing cold metal stabbing into what he thinks may be his brain. His free eye closes as tears are gushing now. Greg would yell out, but his mouth is still fastened shut. Instead he vomits up and back down his throat with such a force that it actually dribbles out through his teeth and lips, running down to his chin, and free falling down to the well collected pool of tears.

The Doctor notices the greenish oatmeal like slime on Greg's face, and with the needle still sticking out from Greg's eye, uses his left hand to hit another valve on the headrest, this time releasing Greg's chin so he won't choke, suffocate, and die.

"AAAAGGGHHHH!" Greg gurgles aloud in indescribable pain.

Dr. Campos plunges the solution out of the syringe, into Greg's tear duct. His right pupil expands and then contracts, then rests fully dilated. The pain is immeasurable. Greg's motor functions tell him to bring his hand to his face, but he can't move it. The taste of upchucked bile is the furthest thing from his mind as he feels his brain go cold, as if placed in liquid nitrogen. Then a second later, Greg falls limp.

The Doctor checks his patient's vitals, walks over to open the door, and instructs the Gentlemen to return Greg to his room.

Chapter 27

The journey begins. A dense fog sets in, making it difficult to see more than a few feet down the path on which Greg is traveling. The coarse ground feels cold beneath his feet. It's during this moment he realizes his feet are bare. Unable to remember whether he forgot his shoes or intentionally neglected them, he continues forward. Dark and mysterious trees begin to appear along the edge of a peculiar property line, sending chills down Greg's spine. If there is a forest filled with these same trees, it is a forest in which evil dwells. Nothing good can exist beyond these monstrous plants, yet still he moves on and, eventually, a driveway appears.

Do I stay or do I go? Greg ponders the thought.

If you've ever heard a story with a castle on the top of a hill at the end of a very long dark path, then you can imagine what is waiting for him. The hike takes the better part of thirty minutes. Greg is forced to climb over large granite rocks and crawl beneath massive fallen branches, each appearing to block the path, almost intentionally. Yet he can't convince himself to stop.

When he arrives at the Victorian palace of a home, Greg is puzzled to find that there are no doors or windows visible to the naked eye. He walks the entire perimeter, twice, and still, nothing. A house with no way in, and if one were to be stuck inside, no way *out*. The outer walls are covered in numerous markings of an ancient Egyptian style, or so Greg assumes. Between the fog and the thick clouds overhead, it is extremely difficult to make sense of what he sees. So, Greg closes his eyes, stretches his right arm forward and begins to run his fingertips along the wall. After a few minutes he hears what sounds like thunder. The earth beneath him begins to shake. Greg opens his eyes and there it is. The wall has a void in the shape of a doorway, from which a rush of cold air is escaping. Figuring he hasn't come this far just to run away, Greg's curiosity is now peaked.

Two steps through the new found entrance and Greg is already at a loss for words. What appeared to be a very large stone house is much more than meets the eye. The ceiling is high above the ground, much higher than Greg's eyes can see. The walls shoot straight up on all sides, painted in a mid-night blackish-blue and covered with silver dots. From where he's standing Greg feels as though he's walking through space.

After wandering along for a moment or two, he loses track of where he is, and is forced to rely on the feeling of his feet on the floor to be sure he doesn't trip. Just as the massive structure seemed from the outside, there are no doors or windows. It is an endless fortress of nowhere.

A little ways down what Greg guesses is a hallway, he comes to a giant mirror. He stops for a minute to look at himself, and the reflection catches him by surprise. The figure in front of him is a young boy of eight or nine years of age. He's short and tubby, with curly brown hair, a widow's peak, what looks like a baby's butt for a chin, tattered old clothes, and bulky round feet that look like little loaves of bread. Suddenly Greg understands what he's seeing; it's himself, only as a child.

Carrying on, Greg comes to a tall spiral staircase. On the way up, his mind considers the possibilities of where he could be going.

"Who owns this place?" He asks himself aloud. "And how has it been kept secret?"

He feels both amazement and fright at the same time, but for some reason, maybe ignorance, he continues on. Left foot, right foot, left again. Up, and up, and up, further and further. It seems as though the climb will never end. And just as Greg considers giving up, he's there, the other end of the stairs.

There's an old wooden post-sign on the wall:

WELCOME TO FLOOR 13

Greg knows he didn't climb a mere thirteen floors. There's no way. He had to have climbed at least fifty, maybe a hundred floors to get here. Regardless of the count, once at the top, he's faced with two choices, left or right. Neither one seems to be different than the other, but Greg is filled with an instinct that something isn't right. It's sad that it has taken him this long to truly become worried, but it is what it is. He can't quite place why, but Greg is filled with a fear as if he were staring death directly in the face.

To the left.

As he makes his way from the stairs, Greg stretches his arm out again and finds a wall, and quickly realizes that there is another wall on his other side as well. It's another hallway; that or it's a tunnel in the air. It's hard to tell after everything else that has happened, and honestly, neither would surprise him at this point.

Moving forward, Greg feels a door on his right, then another, and another. They're very generic and somewhat disappointing in the overall scheme of things. There appear to be rooms spread about fifteen feet apart. Curiosity being the curse that it is, Greg opens a couple of the doors and walks in, but there is nothing to be found in any of the rooms. There's simply more nothing.

Back in the corridor another burst of cold air passes by Greg, only this time he gets goose bumps and begins to shiver. The sound of an elevator door closing echoes from the other end of the hall behind him. Greg turns around and his heart stops beating.

At the far end of the hall, Greg sees a figure, a person, a thing; he's not sure which. All he sees for certain are bright yellow eyes, bloodshot and filled with hatred, staring out from a musty black cloak. He hears it breathing, and every time the figure exhales, Greg feels that cold breeze.

The figure chuckles under its breath and speaks the words, "Never again."

There they are, at opposing ends of this nothing, equidistant from the staircase. Greg doesn't wait another second, and decides to make a run for it.

"Left, right, left, right, I can do it." Greg cheers himself on with the hope that he can get to it before the cloaked figure does. After a few steps he notices the dark figure isn't running at all. Actually, the figure is moving forward in a calm manner. Greg thinks, no, he *prays* he has caught the strange being by surprise. *Maybe I'll make it.*

Greg gets to the stairs a good thirty feet before the mysterious creature and makes the right turn onto the stairway, thinking gravity should be an ally in his descent. However, he only makes it down the first few steps before Greg feels sharp pains shooting up through his feet, as if he's stepping on razor blades. He slows down long enough to reach down with his hand and sees that the stairs are suddenly covered in thorns, like those from a rose bush. Even worse, the mysterious figure is now right behind him.

"What is going on?" Greg cries out, hoping for an answer. Now fearing for his life, he deals with the pain beneath his feet and takes off on his way down again. Step after step and floor after floor disappear behind him. He looks back and finds that the dark figure is nowhere to be seen. It's not safe for Greg to stop, but the urgency for expedition briefly subsides.

After a while longer Greg notices that he has traveled much farther than thirteen floors, than fifty floors, even one hundred floors, yet there is no end in sight. With each step, he feels as though he's moving deeper and deeper into a large freezer. He can feel the cold in his bones.

Finally, Greg reaches the bottom step and notices that it isn't the floor on which he began. He doesn't know where he is, not that he had much of a clue before. He turns in circles, picks a random direction, and continues running. A couple hundred yards later and Greg can see a small ray of light coming from around a corner. It must be the way out. He picks up the pace.

Just as he's arriving to the corner, Greg sees a bright doorway. Sun light is shining through from the other side. He can see that the floor is plain concrete, nothing special at all. There are wooden beams above him, much like those of the basement room where his father often left him to think about his choices.

What is going on?

Finally, Greg turns the corner and runs into a stabbing pain, and those bloodshot yellow eyes of hatred stare into his own, stopping him dead in his tracks.

There it stands, six-foot eleven-inches with the girth of a heavyweight fighter, wearing what looks like a hooded graduation gown, black and covering it from its chin to the floor. Its face is a faint pale white, like that of repeatedly recycled paper. Veins are sticking out of its neck; filled with blood so dark they look black. The hair on its head is oily and long, down past what seem to be shoulders. It's wearing a large-brimmed hat, which casts a shadow over its eyes and nose, which stops just shy of a disgusting smile filled with razor-sharp, yet decaying teeth.

Greg sees it glance down and feels compelled to do the same. That sharp stabbing pain makes sense. The dark figure takes a step back and a knife appears from Greg's stomach, followed by a stream of blood. Greg looks in its eyes and quivers. Those eyes are bright, even through the shadow, staring right into Greg's eyes as it whispers, "You fail me." There's a brief pause while it flares its icy-breathed nostrils, and then continues, "You'll never fail me again."

As the light approaches from behind the devilish being, Greg sees another shadow in the light.

"Sir," says a voice, "please come with me."

Greg rubs his eyes to get a better look at who is in the doorway.

"Sir," Greg hears again, "the Doctor is expecting you. Let's go. Don't make this harder than it needs to be." It's one of the Gentlemen, Greg thinks, and then he sees more clearly, it's all of the Gentlemen. Greg spins around. He's back in his cell. It was the dream again, the same one that started Greg down this demented path.

"Sir," the Gentleman says, "I won't ask again, please come with me." Nap-time is over.

Chapter 28

Amber slowly opens the driver-side door of her car and climbs out onto the lawn upon which her vehicle is located. She takes a moment to collect herself, looking back at the splintered wood posts where mailboxes used to sit, then turning around to see if she has caused any more damage, at which point she is greeted.

"Hey, miss," says a portly man as he walks towards her. He's of average height, but above average weight, with fluffy brown hair, brown eyes, and is dressed in athletic shorts, a mustard-stained white sleeveless T-shirt, and black flip flops. "Are you okay?" His concern appears to be genuine.

"Oh," Amber thinks about what to say, given the landscape behind her, "I'll be alright."

"I don't know about that miss," says the man, "you look like you're pretty shook up. I reckon the mailman's in for a little surprise." He looks her over, checking for signs of blood, hoping the off road racer before him isn't going to pass out. Once he's convinced she isn't dying, he walks over to the car, grabs the mailbox that's imbedded in the windshield and says, "Well, looks like you got my last name already here on your window," referring to the name 'Roberts' painted along the side of the box, "Folks here know me as George. So, miss, who are you?"

"I'm Amber," she replies. "I sure am sorry about y –" it takes her amount to process what he said. "Did you say your name is George?"

"I did indeed," he answers.

"George Roberts?" Amber clarifies.

"Um, yeah, that's what I just," he pauses briefly, then asks, "wait, why?"

"Why what?" Amber's still foggy from the accident.

"I just got done telling you my name, and then you emphatically ask me if I just said my name is what my name is, as if you're looking for something, or some*one*?" George thinks he's being clever, but he's not that bright.

"I'm sorry, I don't mean to startle you," Amber can hardly believe of all the things she's apologizing for, her manner of speaking comes before the mess she's left in this poor man's yard. "As it turns out I *am* here looking for someone, and it appears as though I have found him, as I came here in hopes of speaking with you."

"In hopes of speaking with me?" George is puzzled. "You sure do have a funny way of putting things miss."

"Please, call me Amber," she insists.

"Okay then, Amber," says George. "What exactly brings you to my humble home? You selling something? Religion? Politics? A self-cleaning turbo vacuum with built in beer holder and ice cream scoop?"

"Haha." Amber can't help but laugh. "Well, Mr. Roberts," she says.

"Hey, hey, hey," George interrupts her, "if I'm supposed to be calling you Amber, you better plan on calling me George, and not *mister*. Mister was my daddy, well, more like my step-daddy, I think." He scratches his head, having confused himself. "But, nevertheless, I'm just George."

"Okay then, just George," says Amber. "I'm here to speak to you about your brother, Greg."

Unsure of what to make of Amber's statement, George takes a step back and waits before answering, "My brother Greg?" He asks. "What could you possibly want from me in regards to him? Especially now?"

"Well, *mist –*" she catches herself, "Well, George, if you wouldn't mind, I have some questions I'd like to ask you. Is there somewhere we can sit and talk?"

George thinks about it, looking into Amber's eyes, hard, as if to find the answer he seeks. "I, uh, suppose so," he says, "Come on in." Amber follows George across his lawn, across his front patio, and into his living room just inside his house. "Have a seat on the couch if you like." He points to a fluffy grayish sectional under the front window, behind the coffee table, which sits upon a dark burgundy carpet. *Humble* is definitely putting it nicely. The house is more homely than anything else.

"Can I get you anything to drink, Amber?" George asks, making his way towards the kitchen.

"No thank you," she answers, "I hope to take up as little of your time as possible."

"Suit yourself," says George from the other room, "I'm grabbing a brewsky myself. It's drinking time somewhere. Might as well be drinking time here too." A few seconds later he returns with a cold beer, pulls a wicker chair up to the other side of the coffee table, and takes a seat. "So, Amber, what do you want with my brother?"

"Based on your candor with me in your yard," says Amber, "I'm guessing your brother has never told you about me."

"What do you mean?" George asks.

"We're supposed to get married, George," says Amber assertively.

"And just when was this supposed to happen?" George questions.

"Not was, George," she answers, "Is. We're supposed to get married in just a few months."

"I don't see how that's possible, Amber," says George, "I just don't."

"I'm sure it comes as a surprise," Amber continues, "as I didn't even realize Greg had any living family until very recently. He always kept that part of his life secret, as part of his past."

"Okay, Amber," says George, "I can see we're on completely different pages here. Are you sure you came to the right George Roberts?"

"Well, I don't know," answers Amber, "You are the brother of Gregory Allen Roberts, are you not?"

"I am," says George, "But is there any chance there's another George Roberts with a brother of that same name? Because I just don't see how I can be who you're looking for."

"I got your name and phone number from a friend of Greg's," she explains, "Kent Lawson. Do you know him?"

"Yep," says George, "Sure do. He was Greg's best friend for the longest time. But, what's that got to do with the price of Milk of Magnesia? I still don't get why you're here now asking me about Greg."

"What do you mean?" Amber asks.

"You should go see our mamma," says George. "She lives not two blocks from here. I can give you her address. Then, I'm going to need you to go on your way."

"I don't under –" Amber tries to speak, but is cut off.

"I'm sorry," says George, "I just won't have any more of this conversation today." He scribbles his mother's name, address, and current phone number on a scrap of paper and hands it to Amber. "Take this and kindly get out of my house."

Amber accepts the small note and walks out of the house, scratching her head. The chat ended almost as soon as it started. "What just happened," she asks herself as the door closes behind her. She goes to get back into her car, but sees the front wheels were destroyed in the crash. Instead she looks at the piece of paper George gave her and in a fit of frustrated tears, makes her way towards the other side of the neighborhood by foot. She shouldn't be surprised. Why would a stranger tell her anything? Clearly Greg hasn't told his brother about Amber. Why is that?

Chapter 29

Back at his desk behind the giant glass wall, Dr. Campos hears the door close in the adjacent room.

"Well hello again, Mr. Roberts," says the Doctor without looking up from what he's reading. "Welcome back."

"Fuck off Doc," Greg replies. "Just what the hell did you do to me?"

"Now, now, Mr. Roberts. Have you learned nothing?" The Doctor asks, closing the folder on his desk. He stands up from his would-be throne and walks towards the partition. "You are powerless in all of this, Mr. Roberts. It would be –" he stops to acquire the desired word, "*wise*, yes, wise of you to cooperate from this moment on. I dare say, Mr. Roberts, your life now depends on it."

This is a first. The Doctor is making actual threats. Greg is livid, and he has always struggled with a lack of choice.

"What do you want from me?" Greg asks, almost whining. "You drugged me, brought me to God only knows where, interrogated me, played me that confusing tape, tortured me, and now you're threatening to what, kill me?" He looks at the Doctor expecting a response, but nothing happens.

"I have to admit Doc," Greg continues, "considering what it took for me to actually be in need of your help, I'm not so sure dying is the wrong choice."

"Mr. Roberts," says Dr. Campos, "I have all I need to assure your survival for as long as I need." The Doctor grimaces at Greg as he continues, "only when I have determined you to have no further use will I allow you to perish. Do you understand me Mr. Roberts?"

"Doc," Greg begins to reply with an arrogant smirk, "You still haven't told me what you did to me. You're making demands of me, but I don't know the rules to this particular game you're playing."

"Game, Mr. Roberts," says the Doctor, snarling, "I can assure you this is no game. You want to know what is going on, and I'm going to tell you. In the end Mr. Roberts, you will have told me two things; what happened to Jeanne Burns, and where she is."

The Doctor then walks back to his desk and flips open a panel exposing a button Greg hadn't noticed before. Its color is the same shade of green as the substance that was injected into Greg's tear duct. Dr. Campos presses it and nothing appears to happen. Then the Doctor covers the button back up with the panel he'd opened and walks back across the room as though nothing has changed.

Greg can only sigh. He knows there's nothing he can say to Dr. Campos that will suffice, because he doesn't know what happened to Jeanne, nor her current whereabouts. It's a mystery he gave up on years ago. But the Doctor seems determined to get what he wants, and he's determined to get it from Greg.

"Mr. Roberts," says the Doctor, "you may not realize it, but your side of the room is quite sophisticated."

Greg looks around the room thinking something must have changed, but sees nothing new; a lot of concrete, a door, and the glass wall looking through to the Doctor's office.

"There's no use in looking Mr. Roberts," says the Doctor. "The room hasn't changed a bit. However, it is built to monitor any subject within. For example," the Doctor walks to the wall at his right, pulls on a handle on the wall, and a giant screen rolls out facing towards Greg.

"Nice TV Doc," says Greg.

"This is no television, Mr. Roberts," says the Doctor, who now reaches into the pocket of his lab coat, and pulls out a remote. He presses one button on the remote and the screen turns on. "Mr. Roberts, I present to you, yourself. Oh, as the room you're in sees you, of course."

Greg walks over to the glass wall and takes a closer look. The massive monitor displays a human body in an X-ray-like view. The image mostly looks like an old negative of a photograph, all but the head. Greg points towards the top of the picture, as if to ask *what is that*? The head is glowing with that same neon greenish color.

"As you likely recall, Mr. Roberts," the Doctor starts in again, "You were injected with a painful serum."

"Yeah, how could I forget?" Greg answers sarcastically.

"That very serum, Mr. Roberts," says the Doctor, "Has a couple of functions. The first of which is what allows the receptors, which are built into the very room you're in, to communicate with the program running this large monitor. The room sends a signal over here, and depending on what that signal is, another signal is sent back." The Doctor looks at Greg for a moment. "Are you with me so far, Mr. Roberts?"

"As *with you* as I think you're likely to expect," Greg replies. "Look, I know this is going way off topic for you, but what are my friends and family supposed to think?" The Doctor looks disappointed in Greg's interruption, but responds in stride.

"What do you mean, Mr. Roberts?" He asks. "Are you wondering what your friends and family are going through with you missing?"

"You're quick Doc," says Greg, almost egging the Doctor on. "My fiancée is likely beside herself at this point. I was supposed to call her after our last session at your house, but clearly that hasn't happened."

"You know what, Mr. Roberts?" The Doctor asks, speaking cynically, "I'm glad you asked. It's my favorite part of my whole plan."

Greg is surprised to hear about an elaborate plan. He figured the Doctor was simply tormenting him randomly, grasping at straws if you will. "What plan?" He asks.

"I spoke with your mother, your brother, and your friend Kent," the Doctor explains. "We had a group, *sit-down*. I explained your need for immediate treatment, and with little objection, they agreed that I should be the one to administer such treatment. And," the Doctor smiles, "here you are. I'm sure they are quite capable of filling your fiancée in, Mr. Roberts. Now, if you're done distracting me, I believe I'll get back to –"

"You won't get away with this Doc," Greg whines through his teeth, pissed off, yet helpless.

"The other real function, Mr. Roberts," says the Doctor, picking up where Greg so rudely interrupted, "is much more detailed. My serum has, at this point, spread itself to your cerebral cortex. More importantly, it's focused on your visual cortex; the part of your brain that interprets what you see," The Doctor stops to grab a sip of water from the glass sitting atop his desk, then continues, "in a moment I'm going to start asking you a series of questions, Mr. Roberts, and when I do, you're going to visualize the answer that your mind understands to be the truth. If you choose to answer with exactly what you see, nothing will happen and we will move on to the next question."

"And if I don't tell you exactly what I see?" Greg asks, hoping it's rhetorical.

"Actually, Mr. Roberts," says the Doctor, "it's a bit more complex. If you do anything other than tell me the first thing your mind sees, for example, if you even attempt to think of another answer, let's say by accessing the creative part of your brain, in another hemisphere of your cerebral cortex, Mr. Roberts, at that point you will begin to feel a bit of pressure in your head."

"Pressure, Doctor?" Greg asks, "What kind of pressure?"

"Mr. Roberts," says the Doctor, "Have you ever seen a grapefruit in a vice that is slowly winding tighter?"

"I have not," says Greg, "but I can imagine what that looks like."

"Well, Mr. Roberts," says the Doctor, "If you should attempt to give me any answer other than the first thing your mind sees, the computer attached to this giant screen over here is going to send a signal back to the receptors in the walls of that room. That signal will cause the serum, now in your brain, to squeeze the inside of your cranium much like the grapefruit in that vice." The Doctor stomps his foot to assert his dominance. "At first it will only feel a bit uncomfortable, Mr. Roberts," he continues. "However, after a few wrong answers you will begin to get a migraine. After another wrong answer it will hurt so much that your sight will begin to blur. You can imagine where it goes from there."

"You're insane," Greg mumbles, "absolutely insane."

"Furthermore, Mr. Roberts," says the Doctor, "this little remote that I'm using to operate the screen," he shakes it in front of him tauntingly, "It has a little red button at the bottom. This button gives me a little," he pauses, "*discretion*, if you will, Mr. Roberts. So, if you give me an answer that the machine believes is genuine, but I myself find it insulting or otherwise inappropriate, I can just press the little red button and the machine acts as if you gave me a wrong answer. In short, if you don't cooperate, I have the ability to squeeze your brain until you either pass out or your brain becomes gumbo."

The Doctor shows a villainous smile as he takes his free hand, slowly moving it towards the remote, his index finger fully extended as it presses the red button inward. He watches Greg's eyelids flutter. Then Greg grabs his head with both of his hands. He tries yawning, like someone on an airplane trying to adjust to the cabin pressure.

"Do you understand me now, Mr. Roberts?" The Doctor asks.

Greg only looks up at this man who has lost sight of his sanity.

"I'm going to take your silence as acknowledgment, Mr. Roberts," says the Doctor. "First I am going to ask you a few basic questions to make sure the machine is calibrated correctly." The Doctor goes back to his desk, takes a seat, and reopens the folder in front of him. "Okay Mr. Roberts," says the Doctor, "Now remember, if you so much as think of giving me an answer other than what first comes to mind, the machine squeezes your brain, and if you take more than three seconds to start explaining the first image in your mind, I will squeeze your brain."

"You're a fucking lunatic!" Greg shouts.

"That will be the last time you use that foul language with me during this session, Mr. Roberts," the Doctor snaps back, "Unless you enjoy having the inside of your skull crushed." The Doctor takes a deep breath, inhaling new calming air, and exhaling the anger inside of him. "Now, what is your name?"

"What?" Greg answers, and is immediately brought to his knees, his eyes rolling back in his head for a quick second, "Aaah!"

"I warned you Mr. Roberts," says the Doctor. "Let's try this again. Your name, what is your name?"

"Gregory Allen Roberts," he responds immediately.

"And how long have you been in my care, Mr. Roberts?" The Doctor fires off another question.

"I don't know Doc," Greg replies. The machine does not send another signal to squeeze more, because Greg truly doesn't know how long it has been. He's been trapped in this prison of a facility with no real view of the outside world, and no concept of time.

"Fair enough, Mr. Roberts," says the Doctor. "Then how many siblings do you have?"

"One, a brother," Greg again responds immediately.

"Very good, Mr. Roberts," says the Doctor. "The machine is reading you perfectly."

"Glad I can help," Greg says with a bogus chuckle.

"Mr. Roberts, do you know Jeanne Burns?" The Doctor asks.

"I used to," Greg responds quickly; again, nothing happens.

"What do you mean by 'used to' Mr. Roberts?" Dr. Campos continues his questioning.

"I haven't seen her in a very long time Doc," Greg is prompt, and the machine does nothing.

"When did you last see Jeanne Burns, Mr. Roberts?" The Doctor asks.

"Seven years ago," says Greg. The machine still does nothing, causing the Doctor to pause.

"I asked, when did you last see Jeanne Burns?" He repeats the question.

"Seven years ago," Greg gives the same response, and nothing happens.

"You will not lie to me, Mr. Roberts," the Doctor is nearly foaming at the mouth in frustration, and he presses the button, causing the machine to clamp down on Greg's mind a little more.

Greg's hands grab the sides of his head again, hoping that the extra support may alleviate the pressure, though it's really a useless reflex.

"I'm ... not ... lying!" Greg screams, hoping the pain will stop.

"Mr. Roberts," says the Doctor with a grimace, "I advise you start cooperating with me." He takes a deep breath, collects his thoughts, and asks, "Now, Mr. Roberts, where is Jeanne Burns?"

"I –" Greg is breathing heavily, almost to the point of vomiting, "I don't –"

"TELL ME!" The Doctor shouts and presses the button again.

"Aaah!" Greg cries, louder, and louder still.

The Doctor pushes the button again, and again, with a smirk of pure evil across his face. Greg's eyes roll back in his head, and he topples over on the concrete floor, his body seizing like a fish out of water; Doctor Campos watches in amusement.

"Gentlemen," says the Doctor aloud, pressing one of the buttons on his desk, "Please come and take our guest back to his room. We are done, for now."

Chapter 30

Jeanne Burns' eyes slowly flutter open to find darkness, an eternal nothing. She blinks repeatedly, hoping her sight will return. She tries to bring her hand towards her face, but can't move her arm. She tries the other and it too won't move. Now paranoid, Jeanne attempts to stand up, but can't move her legs. She tries to yell out for help, but her mouth is taped shut. The only sound she makes comes out like gurgling.

A minute passes by, then five, then fifteen, and Jeanne Burns' sight begins adjusting to the dark. She can see the floor, and while looking down she sees what looks like short metal posts. It suddenly dawns on her; she's strapped to a small metal chair. Looking around the room she sees nothing else. No matter how much time passes, Jeanne can't see beyond the darkness. She flexes as many muscles as she can, hoping what binds her to the chair will break. Jeanne tries rocking back and forth, until she falls over backwards, smacking her head on the cold hard ground.

"Stop it," a gristly voice says from across the room, "stop it now!"

Jeanne's eyes widen with terror, and suddenly the chair is whipped back into a sitting position, with Jeanne still strapped to it. She tries to scream, but is still muffled by the gag in her mouth.

"Silence!" The voice demands, "you will do as I say."

Where is that coming from?

Several more minutes go by, and Jeanne isn't making a sound. She closes her eyes and thinks back to anything she can recall, anything that will tell her what is going on. Images of the weekend by the pool scroll through her mind. She was wearing her favorite teal two-piece bikini, catching rays of sun with her firm stomach.

"That was days ago," utters the voice from somewhere in the room.

Jeanne is startled. *How does he know what I'm thinking?* She doesn't give it much attention before she recalls her morning coffee, warm and delicious.

"Good," says the voice, "now you're getting there."

Jeanne remembers her sassy outfit; the one she'd hoped would lead to bigger things. She remembers going to work, talking to Beth before she headed out for the weekend, and–

I was supposed to have a date.

"Yes," the voice says, "Continue. You're almost there."

Jeanne tries to focus on the eerie words, but can't stop remembering. It's as if something is controlling her thoughts. She sees herself on the elevator, getting out in the parking garage, and–

Oh my God, NO!

"You fail me," the voice whispers in Jeanne Burns' ear. An intense pair of bright yellow bloodshot eyes are staring right in Jeanne Burns' face as she opens her own again. She jerks and starts to fall backwards again, but is caught in midair, and again returns back to a sitting position. The eyes are gone.

"You are going to help me with a little project," the voice says from across the room. "I'm not asking you," the voice grunts, "so, there is no point in fighting it. If you cooperate, you'll suffer much less."

A tear starts growing in the corner of Jeanne's right eye. She knows the dreams that have plagued her mind for so many nights are not dreams at all. She knows how they always end, with her lifeless body lying on the ground, drained of all innocence and beauty. She thinks about how scared the mere thought has always made her in the middle of those lonely nights, and that one building tear draws a line down her face as it falls to her lap.

Jeanne Burns winces as the tape is torn back from her mouth, taking the layer of glossed skin from her lips with it.

"I understand," Jeanne mumbles with fear.

"Let us begin," the voice asserts in a cocky tone.

Chapter 31

Doctor Campos stares at the file of Jeanne Burns through an empty whiskey bottle, his head in his hands, worn out from the lack of progress with his current patient. He was never accustomed to failure when he was in regular practice, but that was some years ago. Jeanne's case is the one that broke him; hell it's still haunting him now, though he'll never admit it to another living soul.

He goes back and forth between Greg and Jeanne's files, page by page, determined to find the missing clue to solve the riddle.

What don't I see? He thinks to himself, over and over, so certain it's going to jump off the paper and slap him across the face. It has been hours since Greg left the other room, and he's determined to stay until he finds what he's looking for. He opens another bottle of bourbon and takes a swig.

With each flip of a page the puzzle makes less and less sense, and with each drink he takes, the more convoluted the words become.

The Doctor's frustration spikes just past midnight, and he chucks his empty glass across the room, taking joy in the sound as shards of glass fall to the floor.

When the Doctor decides his mind can take no more, he snaps Jeanne's folder shut, and as the two sides come together, a small piece of notebook papers falls out of the side and floats down onto his lap.

"Where did –" the Doctor begins to ask himself aloud, but he's too drunk to finish. He adjusts his glasses and holds the paper in front of his face. There are a few words in what the Doctors recognizes as his writing:

Nightmare, Hallucination, Reality? Schizophrenia likely.

He reads the cryptic note. Then he reads it again, trying to jar the thought from his memory.

What were you talking about? Think. Think.

He thinks about the initial file for Greg, about what pushed Greg to seek him. Of all the Doctors in business, Greg chose one who is retired.

At first the words seem meaningless. Everyone has nightmares; and hallucinations perceived to be real definitely led the good Doctor to believe Jeanne was suffering from Schizophrenia. With as much liquor as he's consumed, the Doctor's logic, simply put, is absent; but he can feel something is tying Jeanne and Greg together, and the scrawny piece of notebook paper is the key.

"Just take a deep breath Manny," he hears his wife's soothing voice in his head, "You'll figure it out. You always do." She always knows exactly what to say.

Doctor Campos inhales and exhales a long breath, and flips through the pages again; first Greg's file, then Jeanne's, and back and forth, again and again. 281 pages into the back segment of Jeanne's folder, and he sees it; the answer.

"I don't fucking believe it," the Doctor says to himself with complete clarity, "It's *the* dream."

He flings Greg's folder open to same section and starts thumbing through page after page.

"It's in here, I know it." He says to himself convincingly. "Greg has been dealing with a nightmare, I remember reading it back before I agreed –" The Doctor falls silent. He was right. A debrief from Greg's first psychiatrist notes an ongoing struggle with night terrors; night terrors involving some*thing* that was haunting him.

"Gentlemen!" The Doctor presses one of his buttons and calls out with authority. "Bring him to me, *quickly.*"

Less than two minutes pass and Greg is tossed through the open door in the room he has become too familiar with these last few days. Still in a tremendous amount of pain, he's slow to get up, and he looks like he's just finished taking twelve rounds of punches from Mike Tyson.

"Gentlemen," the Doctor asks over his intercom, "why does my guest look like he's been beaten to a pulp?"

Ten seconds of silence follow before a reply comes back through the speakers.

"Compliance remains an ongoing issue, sir."

"Compliance, haha," Greg laughs and then mumbles quietly, "I couldn't comply even if I'd wanted to – can barely move, let alone *comply*."

"Mr. Roberts," says the Doctor, staggering towards the glass partition on drunken legs, "I do hope you'll accept my apologies for my little outburst earlier."

"Outburst?" Greg asks. "Is that the new word for *torture*?"

"Oh, now, now, Mr. Roberts," the Doctor replies, "The effects of my experiment are hardly permanent. You should feel much improved within another day or so."

"Yeah," Greg snaps, "I'm holding my breath in anticipation. What the hell happened Doc, why the change of tune?"

"What, um," the Doctor shows difficulty forming his thoughts, "whatever do you, uh, mean, Mr. Roberts?"

"Are you drunk?" Greg asks. "You look like shit Doc."

"My state, Mr. Roberts –" the Doctor stops for a moment and looks like he's going to puke, but it subsides, "My state is not of any concern to you. Now, tell me about this dream of yours."

"Oh," says Greg, "I get it. You've found something. Well, Doc, let's have it. What's going on?"

"I have not yet –" this time the Doctor turns and vomits in a trash receptacle. The bile and booze pour out from his insides like water from a broken fire hydrant.

"Nice Doc," says Greg. "Is this what it takes to see clearly; getting plastered?"

The Doctor continues to expel his innards for a few minutes, until the heaving stops producing anything other than entertainment for his guest.

"Mr. Roberts," the Doctor continues, wiping his mouth on the sleeve of his labcoat, "I have not made any conclusions, but I am presently interested in a note I found from one of your former Doctors." He spits onto the pile of what was formerly in his stomach several times, trying to get the taste out of his mouth. "There is a dream, Mr. Roberts, a dream from which you have suffered many sleepless nights. I want to know about this dream."

"Unbelievable Doc," says Greg. "You kidnap me, hold me against my will, torture me, and now you act like you want to do your job. Why should I tell you anything?" Greg is irate. This is the conversation he wanted to have back in Doctor Campos' office at home, not in this maximum-security facility from Hell.

"I made a mistake, Mr. Roberts," the Doctor answers. "I misjudged you, and I shouldn't have. Jeanne's case is one I've never been able to shake, and all of my old frustration returned when I thought you'd had something to do with her disappearance. I don't know how you're involved. However, Mr. Roberts, if you'll indulge me by telling me about the dream that troubles you, I may be able to make some sense out of this whole situation."

Greg's hesitant to say the least. All he wants presently is to go home. He doesn't trust the Doctor, and who can blame him? But his curiosity also has a hold on him. He too continues wondering what happened to Jeanne, and if he can help solve that mystery, then, as much as it pains him to do it, he must cooperate with the Doctor.

"It started when I was a kid," Greg begins, "eight, maybe nine years old." He continues on through the entire story; walking down a random street, the giant almost castle-like building, the maze filled fortress inside; and the Doctor doesn't say a word the entire time, not even when Greg gets to the end, when he's murdered by the mysterious dark figure. All the Doctor can do is watch and listen in astonishment, and try not to spew. The story ends, and everything is so quiet you could hear a mosquito orgasm.

"Say something Doc," Greg shouts, now directly next to the glass, as he starts snapping his fingers at Doctor Campos.

"I need to tell you a story, Mr. Roberts," says the Doctor, staring at an empty corner of Greg's room. "I'm not sure how you're going to feel about it, but it's the only logical step from here."

"Well then let's have it Doc," says Greg. Then he takes a seat on the part of floor where he stands.

Doctor Campos grabs Jeanne's file, removes the tape he played for Greg previously, puts it back in the player built into his desk, and presses play.

Chapter 32

"Ms. Burns," says Doctor Campos, "in reviewing the records sent to me from your previous Doctors, I noticed all of them have the understanding that the origin of this problem is a dream you had. Is that right?"

"The origin Doctor?" Jeanne questions. "I don't know the origin. But that's where I first saw it, in my dreams, many years ago."

"From what I can see," the Doctor says, "you described this dream to each of your previous Doctors in writing. I'm curious, Ms. Burns, did you provide copies of something you had written prior to your meetings with these Doctors?"

"No, Doctor, I didn't," Jeanne answers, "I wrote it down from memory each time, per their requests."

"Interesting," says the Doctor, "and how were able to reproduce the tale with such accuracy each time? I mean," he stops to thumb through the written recollections, "They're almost identical, verbatim, all of them." The Doctor leans forward in his chair to look into Jeanne Burns' eyes. "How often did this dream occur?"

"*Did?*" Jeanne asks. "Doctor, this nightmare hasn't stopped."

"Excuse me, Ms. Burns," says the Doctor, "but what do you mean?"

"Any time I fall asleep for more than an hour," says Jeanne, "Whether in the middle of the day or the dead of night, I have the same dream; the one you've read about in all of my files." Jeanne begins to feel overwhelmed. "Every time I go to sleep, I wander into that monstrosity of a building; more like a dungeon, to be honest. I wander around, knowing I shouldn't, knowing it's going to end the same way. Why would my subconscious think anything else would happen?" Tears slowly stream down from Jeanne's eyes, but she's too focused on the dream to pay them any attention. "I run down the stairs, floor after floor after floor, over and over, and every time it's there waiting for me around the corner, it's glowing eyes looking right into mine, telling me I'll never fail it again." Then Jeanne collapses her head down into her hands and sobs.

Doctor Campos walks out of the room and returns a moment later with a box of tissues, handing it to Jeanne. He closes her file and places it on the floor next to him, and moves his chair closer to hers.

"I'm sorry, Ms. Burns," the Doctor says in a soft tone, "I don't mean to bring about such emotions, but I want to make sure I comprehend the severity of what we're dealing with." He takes a deep breath and places a hand on her shoulder. "Whatever is happening, and regardless of the cause, you clearly need help. Real or not, I can see that this *thing*, real or not, is tearing you apart from the inside out."

Jeanne wipes the tears from her face, looks up, and it's standing there, directly behind Doctor Campos, its radiant eyes staring at her in disgust. She jumps backwards with such force that her chair flips over, sending her to the ground.

"It's here," says Jeanne, trembling.

"What?" The Doctor asks. "What do you mean Ms. Burns?"

"It's behind you," she responds, refusing to look up from the floor, too scared to see its bloodshot yellow eyes. But it's already in her head.

The Doctor stands up and looks behind him, turning in a complete circle, and finding nothing and no one, aside from Jeanne face down on the tiles near the door.

"How dare you tell this creature about me," it snarls at Jeanne, though the Doctor hears nothing. "Such a failure; you will end this now!"

"He says I shouldn't talk to you," Jeanne says, "and that I have to go now, Doctor."

"Ms. Burns, what are you talking about?" The Doctor asks, pleading, "You're in no state to leave. I think you should stay, at least until you can gain your composure."

"NOW!" It shouts at Jeanne, and as she looks up to see its discontent, the shadow lunges at her like an Olympic swimmer diving into the pool at the sound of a pistol.

"No," Jeanne whimpers, almost choking on her words, "just leave me alone."

The shadowy figure halts in front of her, no more than an inch away, exhaling its ice-cold breath onto her face. "You will pay," it exclaims; and just then, it launches Jeanne's body like a ragdoll, crashing into the wall, and then it disperses into thin air like particles of mist.

"Oh my God," the Doctor says, baffled by the sight of Jeanne flying across the room. "Are you okay Ms. Burns?"

"I'm sorry Doctor," says Jeanne, agonizing, "I – I just can't." Then she jumps to her feet, runs out of the room, and then the building in a full sprint. Doctor Campos is left speechless.

Chapter 33

"Just what are you trying to tell me Dr. C?" Greg asks, stunned.

"Mr. Roberts," the Doctor responds, "It took me a while to put it together, but, I think I've found the connection between you and Ms. Burns."

"Connection?" Greg pauses. "What connection?"

"You see, Mr. Roberts," says the Doctor, "Earlier, when I repeatedly asked you how long it had been since you last saw Ms. Burns, you consistently gave me an answer that, chronologically speaking, suggests you last saw Ms. Burns well after the recording you just heard took place. Thus, Mr. Roberts, you claim to have seen Ms. Burns more recently than I have."

Greg squints his eyes looking for the means to understand, but simply can't grasp what the Doctor is saying, and asks, "what does that have to do with anything Dr. C? Why does it matter if I've seen Jeanne more recently than you have?"

"Because!" The Doctor snaps in response, a fleck of spit shooting from his mouth and landing on the glass wall. "Mr. Roberts, Jeanne left my office that day, and the following night, she disappeared."

The story isn't adding up for Greg. The Doctor can't be right, *can he?* Perhaps the Doctor is mixing his words. "What do you mean she *disappeared*, Dr. C?" Greg asks. "You mean she never came back to see you?"

That would make a little more sense.

"No, Mr. Roberts," the Doctor replies, "I mean she went to work the next day and was never seen again, by anyone, not her parents, not her friends, not anyone." Doctor Campos stops to take a deep breath before continuing on. "It's not that people didn't go searching for her, Mr. Roberts, we did. I even helped the police and the FBI canvass known areas of interest for Ms. Burns."

"Doc," says Greg, his face now turning a darker shade of red, "how could nobody know where she went?" The conversation keeps spiraling down and out of control. "Didn't anyone have a clue as to where she was headed; and how can this even be the same girl I loved?"

"She was supposed to meet up with a gentleman, her boyfriend, after work," the Doctor explains, "He was the best, and really the *only* lead we had; but he was clean." He takes a big breath, hoping to refrain from passing out. Between the booze and his rising blood pressure, the Doctor may be in need of a Doctor if he doesn't calm down. "

"I looked for her for nearly three years," he continues, "and then I realized I just couldn't do it anymore. Still to this day, she remains missing."

"You just gave up?" Greg asks furiously.

"Mr. Roberts," says the Doctor, who is now the one pleading, "my search for Ms. Burns nearly killed me." He pulls the collar of his shirt down to reveal the large scar running down the middle of his chest. "I had to be revived by paramedics, Mr. Roberts," the Doctor's eyes seem to get almost misty with a potential for tears, "I was literally deceased; a massive heart attack, brought on by the stress of Ms. Burns' disappearance no doubt." The Doctor readjusts his shirt and wipes his face with his vomit-covered lab coat sleeve, "so don't you sit there and snap at me as though I didn't do everything I possibly could." After a long pause, the Doctor says in a shameful tone, "Ms. Burns is the client who ended my professional career."

"I, uh," Greg, feeling one small ounce of guilt, which makes no sense given all the Doctor has put him through, stumbles to find a response. "I don't know what to say Doc, this is all too bizarre for me." He tries to sound confident; but how does one stand strong on a point when he can't even fathom the point he's trying to make? "I still don't get why you're struggling with the existence of our relationship Doc," Greg says, moving along.

"You see, Mr. Roberts," says the Doctor, still trying to collect himself, "the fact you convincingly stated that you saw Ms. Burns seven years ago concerns me."

"But why Doc?" Greg asks, almost moaning. "When did Jeanne go missing?"

"That's what's so concerning Mr. Roberts," says the Doctor, "Jeanne Burns has been missing for more than ten years."

The air escapes Greg's lungs in record time. He can't believe it; it's not possible.

"No way Doc," says Greg in denial, "There's no fucking way," he stops to take a couple of breaths before apologizing, "sorry for the language."

"What makes even less sense, Mr. Roberts," says the Doctor, regaining control, "is that Ms. Burns disappeared on her twenty-eighth birthday."

"But," Greg responds, half expecting to wake from the dream, "she was only twenty-one when I last saw her Doc, and that was only seven years ago. Something just isn't right here. *Am I dreaming?*"

"I know, Mr. Roberts," says the Doctor, "you've maintained the same facts throughout these interactions. It's what led me to look at this in a different light."

"Meaning *what* Doc?" Greg asks.

"It's the dream," says the Doctor. "You both shared the same exact dream; you know, the one with the crazy ghost in a castle?"

"*Ghost?*" Greg asks, "It's no ghost Doc. I don't know exactly what it is, but a ghost it is not."

"Nevertheless, Mr. Roberts," the Doctor proceeds, ignoring Greg's claim, "both you and Ms. Burns had the same *exact* dream. You both wrote it out, word for word. I don't know what it all means," he stops to sigh, "at least not yet."

"I give up Doc," says Greg, "I have come to the conclusion that I'm never going to get where you're going. So, if you are going to get to a point, please make it."

"Think about it Mr. Roberts," says the Doctor, "Ms. Burns tells me about her dream the day before she turns twenty-eight, and then disappears; and a decade later you come to me, suffering from the same delusion, with your twenty-eighth birthday around the corner." The Doctor jabs his forefinger into the side of his head, "*think about it.*"

"Is that it Doc?" Greg asks. "Is that your big reveal?"

"Clearly, Mr. Roberts," says the Doctor, "You are connected to Ms. Burns in a way no Doctor has been able to prove, until now." He begins to show an evil grin on his face, "Mr. Roberts, you're my second chance," he rubs his hands together as if he's sat down at Thanksgiving dinner and is pondering all of the wonderful options staring at him from serving trays. "My second chance to find her."

"Great Doc," says Greg, "now you've lost your mind." He contemplates his next statement, worried about what the Doctor may do to him. "I doubt it makes any difference Doc," he decides to see where this delusion is going, "but there was one instance where Jeanne actually appeared in my dream."

"WHAT?" The Doctor asks emphatically. "I don't see that in your file, Mr. Roberts."

"Well Doc," says Greg, "that's because I've never told anyone."

When Greg first started having his awful recurring dream, he read every book he could find about dream interpretations. Later on, when Jeanne disappeared, Greg worried about what Doctors and headshrinkers would have to say about the small piece of information he's now unveiling for Dr. Campos, and he chose to consciously deny that it ever happened.

"Okay, Mr. Roberts," says the Doctor, "I think you need to tell me about how your relationship with Ms. Burns came to an end."

"But Doc," Greg tries to assert.

"But nothing, Mr. Roberts," the Doctor cuts Greg off, "you need to tell me the entire story of the end of you and Jeanne Burns; and you need to tell me now."

Greg gets up and begins to pace around the room. He struggles with the details of Jeanne's disappearance from his life. He loved her more than he ever imagined possible, and then it all ended without warning.

"Please, Mr. Roberts," says the Doctor, "I can feel it. We're right on the brink of progress."

"Fine," Greg concedes, "but I don't want to hear any judgment out of you Doc. You got it?"

"Of course, Mr. Roberts," the Doctor replies, too drunk to honestly acknowledge Greg's demand. "I want to understand this as much, if not more than you do. So, Mr. Roberts," the Doctor pushes, "tell me about the events leading up to the time when you believe your relationship with Ms. Burns came to an end."

"Well," says Greg, clearing his throat, "as I told you before, I dropped her off at the end of our last date, as I always did."

"Right, Mr. Roberts," the Doctor cuts Greg off, "and you agreed you were going to meet up again the following evening for another date. You did mention that before."

"Yeah," says Greg, "that's what I just said." He peers over at the Doctor. "Are you going to interrupt me every time I get going Doc?" He's lost nearly all the patience he can muster. "Because this is going to take forever if you do."

"My apologies, Mr. Roberts," says the Doctor, "I will do my best to wait until you're done. Although, I must inquire, how does it feel?" The Doctor can't resist. Greg had cut into the Doctor's rants more than once, and it feels good to return the volley.

"It's great, thanks," says Greg, lying of course. "As I, sorry, *we*, both recall, Jeanne and I were supposed to meet up the next evening in the same manner as usual, at Heritage Park."

Chapter 34

Greg watches Jeanne Burns as she walks away with the grace of a gazelle, until, as happens every time their dates end, she vanishes into the shadows of the night. He gets back into his car, still riding the rush of endorphins he gets every time he's with her, and heads for home. However, shortly after leaving the park he begins to feel like something is wrong; he's not sure what, but his stomach is now turning in knots, and nausea settles in.

Pulling to the side of the road, the trusty Dodge Shadow barely comes to a complete stop before Greg jumps out and runs around the vehicle to puke on the curb. Another moment of dry heaving follows before the world starts spinning as Greg becomes dizzy, and flashes of bloodshot yellow eyes and a disgusting meth-mouth run through his mind. The wind is then sucked from and pushed back into his lungs over and over, as if someone else is breathing for him, and Greg drops to his knees.

Am I going to die? This can't be it, not now. She'll never know what happened.

Finally, as if a switch was flicked "off," everything subsides, and Greg takes a seat next to his car to collect himself. He's not sure how long he sits thinking about the obscurity of such an event; it's the first time anything like that has happened outside of his home. Sure, he's constantly reminded of the creature that kills him each night, but he's never had such a *real* feeling of distress outside of his bedroom, when he first wakes up at the end of the nightmare.

After a while Greg is confident that *whatever* has passed, and he gets back in his car and finishes the trip home.

Once in the house he makes his way to the bathroom to assure himself he's okay. There are no visible signs of damage in the mirror; no blood vessels appear to have burst, no marks that he can see on any exposed parts of his body, nothing. It's as if nothing happened. So, Greg fills the small cup he uses to rinse out his mouth after brushing his teeth, and chugs some water.

Get your shit together Greg, he stares into his own eyes, looking for that, *thing*, to show its ugly face.

It has been a long day, and most of it was great, as is any day during which he gets to hold, hug, kiss, or just look at the object of his desire; his Jeanne. Greg is tired, and while he usually has to work himself up to take on an attempt to sleep, tonight he thinks nothing of his usual routine, assuming whatever happened on the roadside must be tonight's adventure. Without any hesitation, he climbs into bed, pulls his covers up, and closes his eyes while thinking only of her.

Within moments of passing into a deep sleep, the dream begins, as it always does, on a long foggy road. However, young Greg is not the one traveling through this particular dream. Oh, it's the same dream, rest assured, but Jeanne Burns appears in young Greg's place; and the dream carries on the same as always, a ridiculous castle with far too many stairs, a ghastly demon waiting for her on the top floor, hidden in the elevator. Yes, the dream is precisely the same, with the presence of an adult Jeanne Burns instead of the child Greg Roberts. She rushes to the basement, just as Greg always does, and when the vile being rams his blade into her gut like a serial killer stabbing his prey to feel joy, Greg jumps out of bed, screaming Jeanne's name.

For more than half of his life, Greg has been accustomed to nightmares. As a matter of fact, he can't recall the last good night's sleep he had without any ghoulish interruption. He's generally used to it by now. However, this wasn't any ordinary nightmare. It was *his*; he'd never witnessed anyone other than himself being murdered in the end.

Why the change?

Greg tries to shake the creepy-crawly feeling off of his skin so that he can go back to sleep, but as soon as he closes his eyes again, he's met with the image of Jeanne Burns standing there, the bloody knife protruding from her stomach like a butcher's blade left wedged into a premium roast while he takes a customer's order. The look on her face is that of pure helpless shock, as if all the good in her was syphoned like gas stolen from an abandoned car. Greg immediately sits back up. He won't be sleeping anymore on this night.

After spending the wee hours of the morning parked in front of a continuous loop of *SportsCenter*, Greg peels himself off of the couch to shower. He has to put in a full day's work before his date later that night. Nothing marvelous happened from that point on. His boss, Jack, the royal prick, was his usual asshole self, but Greg didn't think anything of it. No, all Greg could think about was getting through the day and seeing his love; his Jeanne.

The time finally came around, and Greg drove to the park as he always does. At this point in their relationship he has a favorite parking space in front of his favorite bench. It was on that bench he and Jeanne had first gotten each other off in an impromptu grope-fest. They couldn't resist one another anymore. She was wearing one of her short skirts, and throughout their night out she'd made countless innuendoes to the paradise that was waiting for him just above the cut of the fabric. Greg probably would have attempted to ravage her in his car, but no couple should have their first truly blissful moment of lust in a Dodge Shadow, regardless of the year in which it was made. So he drove to the one place he could think of where nobody else was ever around, the bench in the park, his favorite bench.

He arrived, exited the car, and took his usual seat on the bench; he's five minutes early, a personal goal of his, one he's managed to accomplish regularly. However, the five minutes pass, and this time he sees nobody coming from the shadows; he hears nothing aside from the rustling of tree leaves in a calm evening breeze.

She's never late. I wonder –

He thinks he sees someone, but it's only his eyes playing tricks on his mind. Another five minutes pass, and then thirty, and then an hour, and before he realizes it, Greg is met by the sun rising the following morning. Jeanne never showed. This never happens, and now, recalling what he saw in his dream, Greg is overrun with fear; not for himself, but for her.

What if something did *happen to Jeanne?*

The next day passes by and Greg returns to the park at the same time as the night before, and still nothing. He returns again the next day, and the next, and the next, until a week passes and he convinces himself something awful must have happened. Greg comes to the conclusion that he can no longer sit and wait. Something has to be done. Something is wrong.

Jeanne needs his help.

A call to every local police department and hospital bares no results. Nobody has filed a missing person's report for Jeanne, or for anyone fitting her description for that matter. Greg doesn't feel like he should file the report as of yet, because the thought crosses his mind that she may only be missing from him.

Is it possible she doesn't want to see me anymore?

Greg almost cries at the mere thought, but he refuses to accept that a love can so easily be discarded. Instead, he decides to take on a seemingly impossible task. Greg will go door-to-door through the entire neighborhood until he gets some answers.

The entire neighborhood of Heritage is a couple hundred feet shy of two square miles in size. Combing the village will be no easy task, but Greg feels that it must be done. He starts at his favorite bench and walks off in the direction in which he's always seen Jeanne go. The sidewalk goes around the back site of a walled-off yard and arrives at the end of a cul-de-sac.

Every house looks the same.

The outside of each home is an off-manila color with reddish clay tile-like plates for shingles on the roof. Sure, each home may have the front door located in a slightly different place in comparison to the garage, but the smallest details aside, there's no way to tell which home houses a police chief and which a serial rapist.

Greg walks across the small postage-stamp front yard of the first house, up onto the "patio," if that's what they want to call it, and gives an authoritative knock on the door. Ten or so seconds pass without a sound and Greg knocks again.

"I'm coming," an older-sounding man's voice shouts from the other side of the house. A light comes on over Greg's head and the door slowly opens. "Who are you?" The senior citizen asks.

"Hi sir," says Greg, "I'm sorry to bother you, but –"

"I don't want any," the old man snaps and slams the door in Greg's face.

Greg knocks again and shouts through the door, "sir, I'm not selling anything. I just need to find my friend."

The door opens again and the old man sort of snorts, "young man, if you're not a salesman, what are you, a Jesus freak?" He's referring, of course, to any one of the many folks of religion who come knocking on the doors of strangers.

"No sir," Greg replies, "I'm just a normal guy trying to find a friend of mine. Her name's Jeanne Burns. Do you happen to know her?"

"What?" The old man asks. "Son, I don't know what you're talking about, and I don't know any Jenny, or Genie, or Janey, hell, I just don't know." He again closes the door in Greg's face.

Convinced the old man is of no help, Greg moves on to the next house, where he gets no answer, and then the next house, where the woman who answers doesn't speak English. It goes on like this for hours. Nobody's home, or nobody knows what Greg's talking about, or nobody in the home speaks the language. He finally takes down the address of the last house he visits, so that he'll remember where to pick things back up tomorrow, and goes home for the night.

All Greg can think about every minute of that night is Jeanne and what she must be going through to have disappeared. The very thought of anything bad happening haunts him to the point it gives him the shakes. He barely sleeps a wink that night, and while he can't really recall if he had a nightmare, it matters little since he's living in one.

The following morning Greg calls in sick to work, but he isn't sick, at least not in the typical sense. He just wants to continue his search, and he heads right back to the last home from the night before. He walks to the next street over and starts again at the first house with a heavy knock. Almost no time passes and the door flings open.

"Whoa!" A twenty-something skater-type-guy is startled to find Greg standing on his doorstep. "Where'd you come from man? How long have you been here?"

"Hi," Greg says, "I just got here. I'm –"

"Oh," again Greg is cut off; "you're the guy, right?" He starts scratching his neck just under the left side of his jaw. "I been waiting for you man, where you been, you got the stuff?"

"Huh?" Greg doesn't know what to make of the guy. "No, I don't think so, why, who are you expecting?"

"You're weird man," the itchy fellow says, "I'm waiting for you, aren't I? You got it on you man?" He reaches out his hand and gives Greg a wad of cash. Greg doesn't count it.

"Wait," Greg says, giving the guy his money back, "I'm not that guy," referring to the drug dealer the addict must be waiting for. "I'm looking for a friend of mine. Her name's Jeanne, Jeanne Burns. Do you know her?"

"Oh, I get it," the addict exclaims, still scratching, "she's got the stuff, right?"

"No," Greg says, becoming frustrated, "nobody's got the *stuff*. I need to find my friend. She's about five foot nine, has light strawberry blonde hair, gorgeous, name's Jeanne. Do you know her, or perhaps where she lives?"

"Dude, if you ain't got it with you," the guy has a one-track mind, "then you gotta bounce bro. I need my stuff."

With the drug addict being of even less use than the old man from the night before, Greg decides to move on to the next house; but it's no use. He moves on, and on, and on, house after house after house, days after day, week after week, until he's reached the end of the entire village. Nobody, not one single person knows who Jeanne Burns is. Sure, people know who's selling what, who's sleeping with whom, who's on parole, and who's ultra-rich, but nobody can tell Greg anything that will help him. It's time to involve the police.

Chapter 35

"Hello, my name's Greg," he calls the office of the San Bernardino County Sherriff the following morning, "I need to report a missing woman. It's my girlfriend Jeanne Burns. Please help."

"Okay sir, hold on a moment" the receptionist responds, "Can you give me your name again, as well as your address, and telephone number? I want to send a detective over to speak with you."

"Absolutely," Greg's almost relieved to hear someone willing to help. "My name's Gregory Allen Roberts," he continues with his address, his home phone number, his cell phone number, the color of his garage door, the description of the pathetic used-to-be basketball hoop hanging from the roof, and instructions to ring the doorbell rather than knock.

"Thank you sir," says the receptionist, "I'm confident one of our units will find you. Someone should be to you within the next hour. Is there anything else I can help you with?" Greg feels as if the woman has just taken his order and is asking *would you like fries with that*; but he's probably just overreacting.

Greg goes out to his garage, grabs a lawn chair, drags it to the front yard, and takes a seat. Despite the doorbell utilization instructions given, he's going to be ready and waiting when the police arrive. He doesn't want to waste another moment. He brings a large glass of water with him, as it dawns on him that he has a rather large headache, likely because he hasn't been eating or drinking regularly since all of this happened.

Fifty-nine and one-half minutes pass without any signs of a traveler in the neighborhood when a stereotypical Ford Crown Victoria turns the corner at the end of the street. However, the car isn't marked like the average police officer's cruiser. No, this particular vehicle has no marks at all, which is just as telling as the other extreme. The car is a dark midnight blue. There are no hubcaps or flashing-light fixtures.

The unmarked car pulls up to the sidewalk in front of which Greg is sitting. The driver's door opens and out steps a man, short, no more than five feet three inches tall, but built like a professional weight lifter. He has muscles on top of muscles. His head is shaved as smooth as a chrome ball bearing, and his navy blue fatigues stick to his body as if they were painted onto his flesh.

"Are you," speaking to the only person sitting in a chair in their front yard while removing his sunglasses and looking at the name jotted on his small pad of paper, "Mr. Roberts?"

"I am." Greg responds, now getting up from his seat and walking to the end of the yard to meet the man, "and you are?"

"Detective Nathaniel Pratt, sir," the small yet large man answers, "I'm with the Sherriff's office. Did you call in a concern about a, let me see here," as he checks his notepad again, "oh, a missing woman?"

"Yes sir," Greg says, "thanks so much for coming. It's been like pulling teeth to get anyone to help me. Do you want to come inside?" Greg points back at his house.

"No sir," the detective rejects Greg's offer, "I don't see the need. How about you tell me what's going on; who's missing?"

"My girlfriend, sir," says Greg. "Her name's Jeanne Burns." The officer takes note both of the name and relationship.

"Okay," says the detective, "and can you describe her to me, her age, hair color, eye color, anything of that nature?"

"Of course," says Greg, "she's twenty-one years old, five-nine, reddish blonde, sparkling blue eyes, slender, really a gorgeous woman, sir."

"And how long has she been missing sir?" The detective asks, keeping in mind that anything less than 24 hours doesn't count as a *missing person*, and that really anything less than 48 hours may just be someone who went away for a couple of days and neglected to tell everyone.

"Well, sir," Greg replies, "It has been about six months now." The detective stops writing mid-sentence and looks up at the man giving the report.

"Excuse me sir?" The detective now thinks this is something else, perhaps a woman who stopped speaking to a man for a reason. "Did you just say she's been missing for six months sir?"

"I did, yes," Greg answers, "Six months almost to the day."

"Ever consider the fact she's not missing sir?" Detective Pratt's not impressed. "Is it possible she just doesn't want to see you Mr. Roberts?"

"Not at all Mr. Pratt," says Greg.

"Please sir, call me detective."

"Oh, okay, detective," says Greg. "I know what you're suggesting isn't possible."

"Really?" Asks the detective with little seriousness, "and why's that?"

"Well detective," says Greg, "one night we went out, as we often did, and at the end of the night, also per usual, we planned our next date, which was to be the following night. We kissed. We were happy. But she never showed."

"And what about this," the detective looks back at his pad of paper, "Jeanne? Any friends or family have any idea what happened to her?"

"No," says Greg, "but that's only because I've never met any of them."

Detective Pratt opens his mouth to speak before Greg's words hit him, causing him to quickly close his mouth and take a deep breath. Like everyone else Greg told the story to, the detective thinks he's playing games with him. However, Detective Pratt is a professional, and he isn't going to let Greg know what he thinks just yet.

"How long have you and this," the detective looks at his notes again, clearly not a man with a great memory, "Jeanne, been dating?"

"This is probably where I lose you detective," Greg says sheepishly. "We had been dating for the last four years before she went missing." Detective Pratt rolls his eyes, closes his notepad, unclicks his pen, and looks directly at Greg's face.

"Sir, are you feeling okay?" The detective asks. "Are you on any kind of medications, prescribed or otherwise?"

"What?" Greg is caught off guard by the questions. "No, I'm fine detective. I'm not making this up. I went door-to-door through Heritage looking for her and nobody knew who she was or where I could look for help."

"Heritage you say?" The detective pretends to believe him. "What part?"

"All of it," exclaims Greg. "I knocked on every door in Heritage over the last six months, which is why it has taken me so long to call the police."

Detective Nathaniel Pratt ends the initial conversation shortly thereafter. He goes through the motions, gives Greg his business card, tells him he'll look into it, and will get back to him if there are any other questions or developments; but the detective never contacts Greg. Instead, Greg calls the detective a week later.

"This is Detective Pratt," says the steroid-bound freak of an officer on the other end of the phone.

"Hi detective, it's Greg Roberts. We spoke a week ago."

"Right," says the detective, "you're worried about your missing girlfriend."

"That correct," says Greg. "I'm just calling to see what, if anything, you've learned thus far?"

"Actually," the detective's voice catches Greg's interest; "I can't find anyone fitting your description in any database as living in the area. There was one close, but not really."

"What do you mean by *close*?" Greg asks.

"Well, Mr. Roberts," says the detective, "a few years back there was a twenty-eight year old woman of the same name who went missing…"

Chapter 36

Amber D'Marco strolls along the half-mile of sidewalks from George Roberts' house, past several almost golden-vanilla houses, all with red clay tiles covering their roofs, on the way to the home of Marion Roberts, Greg's mother. She sees a father and son playing catch on one street and a couple of brothers playing *Hide & Seek* on another. The walk doesn't take long before she's there, at another house that looks like all of the others.

She knocks on the door, waits a moment, and then rings the doorbell. No answer. She tries again, and still, no answer. Marion isn't home. Amber lets out a loud sigh in a tone of defeat and begins to cry. The one thing she can't see herself living without is Greg, and she's terrified that he's been hurt. Unsure of what to do next, Amber calls a taxi to come pick her up, and bring her home. She'll have to start over again tomorrow. She's drained.

When Amber was a child, from about the ages of six until the age of sixteen, her family had a pet cat, Frosty. He was a snow-white bobcat with a small patch of black on the top of his head. He wasn't really a bobcat, but that's how Amber referred to him, because he was born without a tail. Frosty was the best pet anyone she ever could have had. He consoled her when she was down, and played with her when she was up. His favorite foods were donuts and French-fries, and no matter what was going on in Amber's life, she could always count on Frosty to be there to cuddle with.

Frosty had an amazing personality as well. One spring he sat outside on the family porch, patiently waiting for Amber, or anyone for that matter, to open the door. He had a surprise, and he was quite proud of the gesture he was waiting to display. Eventually, Amber's mother opened the door, expecting to find the morning newspaper, stunned to find Frosty, with a snake slithering and twitching, hanging from his mouth.

"What is that?" Amber's mother asked aloud, as if the cat could respond.

Knowing that this was his time, Frosty dropped the snake at her feet and looked up for approval. The great hunter had returned with sustenance, or at least a nifty toy. But, the leader of the family didn't respond with approval, or even with acceptance. No, Amber's mother screamed at the top of her lungs and started dancing in place. She hated snakes, but how was Frosty supposed to know that?

Seeing that his surprise didn't get the reaction he expected, Frosty quickly swung his right paw and cut the snake's head off at the rain-dancer's feet. Frosty had personality all right.

One day Amber returned home from school to find her cat was nowhere to be found. She'd had a pretty upsetting day, *high school girl drama*, and she wanted her kitty to help her feel better. She went back outside and started calling for him, "Frosty!" She said over and over. She even tried an inverted whistle, smacking her lips together and inhaling, but he didn't come. Amber then went in a turned on the electric can-opener, a sure-fire way to get him to come running. It was mean, considering it wasn't time to eat, but she hadn't thought that far.

Frosty never came back, and Amber spent countless days searching the neighborhood, even nearby neighborhoods, hoping to find her favorite fluffy feline. When she finally realized her best friend was gone, Amber died inside, just a little. She cried for days, worrying that something terrible had happened, when, in all likelihood, Frosty had become ill, and an old man of a cat at that point, and wandered off into the wild to rest in peace.

The loss of Frosty still torments Amber today, every time she sees a cat, or any white pet; and if she reacted that way when her cat went missing, you can begin to imagine what she's thinking not knowing what has happened to Greg.

The cab pulls up to her house, Amber pays the driver, including a generous tip, and sees a sight for sore eyes; a much older model Dodge Shadow is sitting in her driveway. Forgetting to thank the cabby she sprints to her doorway with all the miraculous hope she can contain.

"Greg!" Amber yells out as she bursts into the entry way to her home. "Greg!" The twenty-something man comes down the adjacent hall and enters the room.

"Hey, babe," says Greg, "how are –" he's met by a giant bear hug that catches him by surprise. "How are you?"

Amber burst into tears, her face planted in Greg's chest, leaving an image like that of a *Rorschach Inkblot* in his shirt. He grabs ahold of her and helps her to the floor, cradling her by the shoulders along the way as she collapses, still sobbing to the point she begins to choke.

"Amber," says Greg, concerned, "what's going on, what's the matter?"

"Where have you," Amber tries, still bawling. "Where have you been?"

"What do you mean?" Greg asks. "I'm right here." He hopes she won't push him further.

"No," Amber shouts, "Where have you been? I've been looking for you for days."

"Ah," Greg sighs, "I'm sorry babe. My cell phone died and I forgot my charger in the bag in our closet." The truth would only make things worse. He needs to think of something, and fast.

"What do you mean?" Amber asks, becoming incensed, "You couldn't pick up a phone and call me?"

"Well," Greg responds, feeling like a dog with his tail between his legs, "this is a little embarrassing, but I don't actually know our phone number. I usually go to where it's stored in my phone when I call you." It's technically true.

"Ugh!" Now Amber's fit to be tied. She just spent the better part of the last two days pining over every memory she has of she and Greg together, wondering if they were the only memories they'll ever make, and it's all because he doesn't know her phone numbers.

Bullshit.

"Amber," says Greg, "I'm sorry. I hope you didn't worry too much. I'm fine. Honest."

"*Too much?*" Amber makes a distorted face at him. "I've been everywhere I could think of to look for you. I called Kent. He gave me some information for your mom and brother. I went to see George, and he acted like there's no way in hell you and I are getting married, which is a whole other issue I have. Then I tried to go and talk to your mom, but she wasn't home; and I crashed my car, and shit, I forgot to say *thank you* to the cab driver that brought me home. So, sorry, but yeah, I worried. I worried a lot. I thought," the tears start flowing more rapidly, again, "I thought something awful happened to you. You can't just disappear on me like that. I can't take it. I just can't. I don't know what I'd do if anything ever happened to you."

"You talked to Kent?" Greg asks, his face showing signs of an emotion somewhere between sorrow and alarm. "You talked to Geor –"

"Yes," Amber cuts him off quickly, "You were nowhere to be found. Literally nobody could tell me where you were Greg. Does that not register for you? Do you not get how all of this has affected me?"

"I know, I know," says Greg, "I just, well, I wish you hadn't gone to my family."

"Why Greg?" Amber asks, in no joking mood. "Why is your family some big secret? We're getting married this summer. You can't keep stuff from me; that's not how this works."

"You're right," says Greg, "I'm sorry. I should have, I don't know, done something to let you know where I was and that I was okay; but I promise you, I'm never going to leave you. I love you."

Amber leans into her loving man, squeezes him tight, and gives him a kiss. She's just so glad he's okay.

Chapter 37

Doctor Campos stops Greg in the middle of his story, something he indicated he would try to avoid, "Mr. Roberts, you mean to tell me the detective with whom you spoke knew about Jeanne Burns going missing ten years ago?"

"Yeah Doc," says Greg. "What of it? It's not the same girl; not my Jeanne."

"But how would you know that Mr. Roberts?" The Doctor asks, now able to sit in his throne-like chair without puking.

"Detective Pratt," Greg answers, still parked on the cold cement next to the glass partition, "told me the woman who went missing ten years ago was twenty-eight. My Jeanne was only seventeen or eighteen years old at that time. This was three or four years later, which would have made that Jeanne Burns at least thirty-one. It just can't be her."

"What ever happened, Mr. Roberts," the Doctor asks, "To the detective's investigation into the woman with whom you were so madly in love?"

"It ended Doc," says Greg. "He gave up looking almost as soon as he began. Truth be told Doc, I never found another living soul who was willing to help me look for her. After a while I assumed the worst."

"Which is what, Mr. Roberts?" The Doctor asks.

"I have to go based on the belief that she was real Doc," says Greg, "though I hear how skeptical you are."

"I'm not skeptical Mr. Roberts," says the Doctor, "I just don't know where to go from here."

"I get it Doc," says Greg, "it all sounds crazy. Perhaps a little *too* crazy, but it's real. It all happened. At this point I have to figure when I let her leave my sight that last night, someone must have kidnapped her, who knows, it would have been easy enough down one of those dark sidewalks. The fact that she's never reappeared can really only mean one of two things Doc, neither of which are comforting."

"And what, Mr. Roberts, are those two things?" The Doctor asks.

"Either my Jeanne is dead, Doc," says Greg, "or she's still being held captive by some maniac. For all I know, some sexual deviant with an unmarked panel van was stalking her for weeks leading up to her disappearance, and he just waited until the perfect moment arose. She was a gorgeous woman Doc, I know I keep saying it, but some lifelong sex addict with a thing for violence likely saw exactly what I did and took it." Saying it aloud makes Greg's heart hurt all over again. He's never cared for anyone the way he cared for Jeanne Burns, not even his current fiancée, and even now all these years later, it's still eating away at him.

"You sound so certain, Mr. Roberts," says the Doctor. "Why is that?" He still wonders if Greg had something to do with his patient Jeanne Burns' vanishing.

"I'm not one to believe in coincidence Doc," says Greg. "I had that dream, she died, and then, well, I'm almost certain she really did."

"Is this why you are here, Mr. Roberts?" The Doctor asks, exhaling loudly. "Are you here because your childhood dream killed Ms. Burns?"

"I'm here because you're holding me captive Doc." Greg retorts.

"Yes, okay, Mr. Roberts," says the Doctor, rolling his eyes, "but, is this why you sought my help?"

"Not exactly Doc," says Greg, "I mean, I guess it all seems to be related, but that's not really what caused me to reach out to you."

"No, Mr. Roberts?" The Doctor stops, having been convinced he was right. "Then tell me, please, why did you come to me?"

"I don't believe I'm long for this world Doc," says Greg, "and the more you and I seem to talk, the more I see the end waiting for my arrival."

"Please explain what you mean, Mr. Roberts," says the Doctors, "What is going to happen to you?"

"At first I thought it was just me Doc," Greg says, "But from the sounds of it, this has all happened to at least one other person before." He takes a moment to collect his thoughts before continuing. "What's really difficult to accept is that I loved a woman who apparently either didn't exist or lied to me about her age, and that she went through exactly what I'm going through now. That much, sadly, seems quite clear now. She met her evident demise on her twenty-eighth birthday, according to the records and recordings that you possess, and now I am sitting here before you, telling you I am set to meet the same fate upon my birthday, which is quickly approaching. So, Doc, what I thought I came to you for is not really what matters. It seems as though I arrived on your doorstep so that I could learn more about what is waiting for me."

"What is waiting for you, Mr. Roberts?" The Doctor asks. "And how is it that you ever had a relationship with Ms. Burns if what I have told you is true?"

"*It*, Doc," Greg answers, "*It* is waiting for me. As for your second question, Doc, I think *it* is capable of making you, well *me*, see anything, whether real or not. None of this made sense before now. However, between the nightmares, the evil dwelling in the shadows, and what the fortune teller told me, I am likely going to experience whatever Jeanne went through those many years ago."

"I'm sorry, Mr. Roberts," says the Doctor, "but did you say *fortune teller?*"

Chapter 38

For Greg Roberts, a birthday is nothing more than a reminder for him to answer that annoying question of "How old are you?" with the current number, and he got out of bed on his twenty-seventh birthday as if it were any other day ending in "Y." He has no plans to party, to celebrate the anniversary of his birth with drinks amongst friends, or even to take the day off of work. With any luck the day will pass just as the every other day passed. However, as the saying goes, "If it weren't for bad luck, [Greg] would have no luck at all."

His first scheduled client is a nineteen-year-old girl named Josie. Like so many of Greg's clients, Josie is addicted to methamphetamine. Her mother was an unfortunate bystander who needlessly took three nine-millimeter rounds in the chest during a bank heist because one of the robbers forgot the safety was off on his modified fully automatic handgun, leaving Josie in the custody of her stepfather. Meth was easy enough to come by, and thinking about all of the despicable things she would be forced to do once she walked in the door at the end of each day, it provided the escape Josie needed to survive.

About a year after her mother's death, just at the start of her freshman year of high school, Josie's stepfather gained an interest in her body. As is often the case, it started with inappropriate comments and innuendo, which progressed into *random* undesired touching, and eventually full on sexual episodes. She was forced to have three abortions by her sixteenth birthday, which was about the time her stepfather decided to include her younger sister Kelly in the family affair.

Kelly first learned she was pregnant on her fifteenth birthday, two years ago today. When her stepfather insisted on an abortion the same as he always did with Josie, she walked herself off of a sidewalk in front of an oncoming bus. The note blamed Josie for not protecting her, as well as her mother for marrying the man who stole her innocence. All of this can only begin to showcase Josie's need for therapy.

Happy Birthday Greg.

The day progressed on the same as it began. Greg met with a sex addict, an ex-convict, a preacher turned Atheist, and a transgendered rape victim; *just another day ending in "Y."*

Before leaving the office for the day, Greg comes across a business card he doesn't remember receiving. The front of the card displays the name in all black capital letters "THE MASTER," with a small address and phone number scrolled across the bottom. Wondering if perhaps someone gave him a message on the card, Greg flips it over to find a single phrase, "Master your destiny." Still no recollection of where or when this card first surfaced comes to Greg's mind. However, given the birthday he's just experienced, Greg feels oddly inclined to visit this *Master*.

The drive across town is slow, as is the case every day. It takes the better part of thirty minutes to travel four miles in the rush-hour traffic, and while Greg is in no hurry, sitting bumper to bumper under the sun is not the peaceful conclusion to the day he could really use. Nevertheless, he remains patient until he reaches the end of a long winding driveway matching the address on the business card he'd found. There's nothing mysterious in the air, and there are no funky decorations of any kind. As a matter of fact, at the end of the pointlessly curvy path there is only an old 1970s single -wide mobile home with a canopy-like sign showing the words "THE MASTER," again in plain black capital letters. If Greg didn't know better, he would assume the location was vacated and waiting for a waste disposal company to remove the remaining structure from the property. Once he has parked his infamous Dodge Shadow, Greg takes a minute to contemplate what is looking more and more like a bad idea, but his decision is already made.

Stepping through the only visible doorway, Greg finds the interior of the skinny hallway-shaped building to be in stark contrast to the exterior. The floors are solid gold, polished to a clarity allowing Greg to notice his tie is crooked in the reflection. Enormous crystal chandeliers hang down from a vaulted ceiling an impossible ten to fifteen feet above his head. The walls glimmer like diamond dust in a beam of light. Sure his mind is yet again playing tricks on him, Greg steps back outside to look at the disgusting dump of a building, and upon re-entry he realizes his eyes are *not* be deceiving him, his jaw, agape in awe.

Greg steps forward to what looks like a desk and finds a small sign, also in gold, which instructs, "Please take a seat. THE MASTER will be with you shortly." Greg turns around and takes a seat on a small golden couch lined with what feels like a cloud, it's that soft. No sooner does his ass hit the seat than the panel in the wall behind the desk separates from the wall and slides to the left, revealing a massive figure. A dark-skinned man standing seven feet tall, nearly five hundred pounds, and covered in jet-black hair steps forward. The wall then reseals itself.

"Greetings Gregory," the monstrous man says with a rumbling bass-filled voice, and a smile shining through his hefty beard and mustache, "I am The Master. Welcome to my humble home."

Caught completely by surprise, not because of the size of the man, rather because he already knows his name, Greg is frozen still.

"Sir," The Master says, waving his hands at Greg, "are you okay, sir? I did not mean to frighten you."

"No, that's okay," Greg finally gets some words out, "I am just surprised to hear that you know my name. How is it that you know who I am, exactly?"

"I am The Master," he says. "A prophet of sorts; an oracle if you will. I see and hear all, therefore I see, hear, and know all. I am The Master."

"I don't mean to be rude," says Greg, "but that sounds awfully rehearsed. *I am the Master*," he teases.

"Ha ha ha," the Master laughs, shaking the chandeliers above, "I see you do not remember me, Greg. We have met before. This is why I know your name."

"We have?" Greg nearly accuses him of lying.

"Yes Greg," says the Master, "Do you not remember? You were with someone else that day; perhaps that is why."

"Someone else, huh?" Greg is stumped. "Who was I with? And what do you mean by someone *else*, who am I with now?"

"The answer to your second question is not of importance right now," says The Master, seeming mysterious. "However, regarding your first question, we met when you were here with Amber."

"What?" Greg asks with no recollection of such an event.

"That too is not of importance right now Greg," he responds. "As I said, I see and hear all, therefore I see, hear, and know all. I am The Master. What is of importance is your reason for being here this evening. So please, come with me out back and let us see if we can't put you in control of your destiny Greg."

The panel on the back wall opens again, and Greg follows The Master into the pitch-black hallway leading Greg knows not where. They proceed forward without making a sound, with only the noise created by their footsteps and breathing to keep from feeling abandoned. Though it doesn't take very long to reach the next room, Greg cannot believe they went as far as they did given the size of the building. Then again, nothing else has made any sense thus far either.

Into the back room Greg finds a seat much like the one located by the front desk on one side of a four-person card table made entirely of inch thick glass. The Master takes a seat upon a large stool on the other side of the table, offering Greg a glass of water. As he sits down, The Master looks at the woman standing behind Greg, the woman Greg has no idea is present, Jeanne Burns.

"How does this work?" Greg asks.

"It's quite simple Greg," The Master answers, "I am aware of who you are and why you are here for reasons I cannot explain to you in any manner that will make sense. Your lack of understanding is not your fault, but I am not capable of making you understand. Instead I will simply say that today is your twenty-seventh birthday. You exist in a world where seeing is believing. I, on the other hand, do not. I exist in a world where *time* is subjective, and while something may be happening in a specific moment in your world Greg, that very thing happens in my own at the same time as every other thing. Like I said, I cannot make you understand, but I must always abide by my vow to be honest, no matter the cost."

Greg looks like he wants to interrupt The Master, but has no idea what to say to such an outrageous notion.

"You sit before me today, Greg" The Master continues. "With a presence you do not recognize, nor can you acknowledge, as it is not currently visible to you. And while it will not be pleasant to hear this fact, you have precisely one year to live."

Normally Greg would burst out laughing and then walk out, but The Master's words hit him like a jack-hammer hits a sidewalk identified for replacement. There's no way what The Master says is true, and yet, Greg believes every word he hears.

"I'm not sure why I'm saying this," again Greg fumbles for the words, "but, thank you."

"You are welcome Greg," says The Master.

"I do have a question though," says Greg, "Why do you believe I am incapable of acknowledging something I cannot see?"

"That, Greg," The Master eases into his response, looking at Jeanne, still standing behind Greg, almost like a chaperone, "is the real kicker. You would not recognize it as a presence. As a matter of fact, you have failed to do so before. You have seen the terror within the shadows at night; you have even seen it as glorious as an angel in broad daylight; but you cannot begin to accept the truth, as it is beyond the understanding of man, which again, is not your fault. You did not pick your shell, but you are a slave to it just the same. Therefore," he pauses again, as Jeanne nods in his direction, "I am not in a place to discuss it. For now, let us say that some joys in life come with great sacrifice."

Greg nods in a faux state of understanding, standing up from the glass table, and follows The Master back to the front door.

"I am sorry your fortune is not more favorable," says The Master, bowing his head.

Greg walks back out to his car, unusually at peace, despite The Master's prophecy. He is not charged any money for The Master's services, and when he attempts to return a few weeks later, Greg will find the rickety mobile home is nowhere to be found.

"Mr. Roberts," says the Doctor, chiming in where Greg leaves off, concluding that the alcohol has taken a toll on his mind, and that he will soon pass out with or without his consent. "I have an idea, but I will need to make a phone call before we can continue. What do you say we pick this back up in the morning?"

Greg would object, but resisting is useless. Instead he nods in agreement and waits for the Gentlemen to escort him back to his dungeon.

Chapter 39

Back in his cavernous dungeon of a room, Greg sits on the edge of his steel bed twitching from his heightened level of anxiety. He can tell that his circumstances have slightly improved, as now, instead of being a pitch black hole in the wall, his room has two small dim lights turned on above him, and his meal of the disgusting chunky oatmeal he's becoming accustomed to has been replaced by a bologna and cheese sandwich on dry sourdough bread with a side of stale potato chips and a cup of water.

As a fan of history, Greg's grandfather often referred to old clichés such as "Never look a gift-horse in the mouth." The bread sticks to the back of Greg's throat like sand as he swallows, and it's sad that such a puny tray of food can be seen as a gift, but he enjoys it nevertheless. Growing up in a family with little money and without a parent who had a knack for cooking allows him to find joy in even the worst cuisine.

Looking around the newly lit room Greg comes to the conclusion that it was more interesting when he couldn't see anything. The walls are rugged, yet dark and plain; merely jagged rock. The Doctor clearly hasn't put any effort into decorating. The toilet looks like a hospital bedpan protruding from the back wall, and the bed, if you can call it such, looks like a Veterinarian's table with a thin pad for a mattress, and without any pillows.

This room is pathetic.

Greg would try to sleep, but his mind is racing with all of the thoughts he has encountered since being accosted by the good Doctor. He decides to try to pass the time by repeating the "Warm down" exercises from his wrestling days, hoping it will exhaust his remaining energy.

He begins jogging in place, just fast enough to be quicker than a walk; he doesn't want to pull any muscles by diving right into a vigorous pace.

Is Jeanne real?

He switches to a set of jumping jacks, counting aloud, "One, two, three, *One*. One, two, three, *Two*." He continues until he reaches: "One, two, three, *Ten*."

And what does this thing I keep seeing have to do with it all?

As soon as the jumping jacks end Greg shouts, "Sprawl," and he dives to the floor, catching himself with his hands, and then standing back up, jogging.

Greg keeps going, again yelling, "Sprawl!"

How did I end up choosing Dr. Campos?

He stays down on the floor this time, completing a set of fifteen pushups before returning to his feet, jogging again.

Where is this place?

Back to jumping jacks. And the sequence repeats itself, over, and over, as long as it needs to, until Greg can't take any more.

"Sprawl!" He shouts out again.

The giant steel door flings open and a Gentleman stands in the doorway, "What is going on in here?" The Gentleman looks to the ground to find Greg doing more pushups.

"I'm, trying," Greg struggles to speak without stopping his count, "*ten*, to regain focus, so that I can sleep.'

"Well, keep it down in here," says the Gentleman, "and stop all the yelling."

"*Fifteen*," Greg gets back to his feet, again, jogging. "Okay, sir, *Sprawl!*"

Another ten minutes of wearing himself out, and engulfed in sweat, Greg ends his workout by lying on the cool concrete floor, breathing heavy. His entire body tingles from the sensation of cold rock on the wet skin of his arms and face. It reminds him of a date he thinks he had with Jeanne. They went to a roller skating ring where they played loud techno music while strobe lights danced around the room. Greg managed to lose control on his way around the slick floor, and when he fell, Jeanne fell with him. They decided not to get back up right away, but instead chose to lay there on the cold ground, exchanging passionate kisses, and on the floor of his concrete cell, he still can't get her out of his mind.

It took a while to finally convince him to sleep, but having rid himself of any motivation to stay awake, he now finds himself passed out on the veterinarian-style table. He shakes from the chill of falling asleep soaked in a cold room. The Doctor didn't provide any blankets.

Two hours into a peaceful slumber Greg is startled by the sounds like those of firecrackers above him. He's jostled awake and hurries to stand up where he immediately feels stabbing pains in several parts of his feet. The cutting feeling sends him back to a sitting position, where he's able to reach down to touch his feet, and he notices something, several things, *shards*, are sticking out of the balls and heels. Greg grabs ahold of one and pulls it out like the ancient sword of Arthur from its mystical stone. It's a piece of glass. He now realizes the firecrackers he heard were the light bulbs exploding, as he's sitting again, in pure darkness.

"Aaaaaahhhhh!" A woman's voice screams from the far corner, echoing throughout the solid room. Greg spins his head to the right, in the direction of the goose-bump inducing sound.

"What are you doing?" The chilling voice asks, sounding vaguely familiar.

"What do you mean?" Greg responds, uncertain about what the voice is asking.

"You cannot trust Dr. Campos," says the voice.

"Who are you?" Greg asks. "Who is there?" His eyes squint as he tries to find the source.

"Do you not recognize my voice Greg?" The voice asks, almost disappointed.

"Huh? No," says Greg, pulling another sliver from his foot, "I have no clue. What do you want?"

"You mustn't tell the Doctor anything else," the voice demands in a stern tone. "Do you understand?" Greg sees now, there is a pair of luminous blue eyes looking back at him, also familiar, though he can't figure out why.

"I don't understand anything at this point," says Greg, irritated, "Not you, not where I am, not what's going, none of it."

"Dr. Campos will betray you," says the voice, snickering. "He's only interested in his own agenda. He never intends to help you."

"How can you possibly know that?" Greg asks. "And who the hell are you? Tell me, now."

"You'll know soon enough," says the cryptic voice, "but you must be patient. I'm here to help you Greg. However, if you keep telling the Doctor these," the voice stops for a moment, perhaps hesitating, "*stories*, yes, stories, the Doctor will only become more obsessed with finding his precious Jeanne, and you'll never be free. Just think about everything he's done to you already. Has he once done anything that actually *benefits* you, or has everything been what he's asked for, when he's asked for it?"

"Well, yeah, but –"

"But nothing," the voice cuts Greg off. "He is using you, and you must not let it continue. Heed my warning."

"How do you now all of this?" Greg asks, but gets no answer. He waits a moment, but gets nothing, and the eyes he saw previously are gone. Having successfully removed all the fragments from his feet, Greg walks over to the corner where he heard the voice, but finds nothings. Whatever she, or it was, it's gone.

Chapter 40

Greg Roberts lies in bed still drenched in sweat. The atypical visit from an unknown woman in his cell has him rattled, which, given the events to this point, is a normal state of being. He needs to sleep if he's going to have the patience to deal with Dr. Campos in the morning, but how can one rest when the world seems to be going crazy around him?

Who was that?

Greg's mind wanders, still hearing her screams, trying to place the familiarity of the voice and its crystal blue eyes.

More importantly, what if she's right?

It dawns on him that the Doctor may be making amends as a game plan for obtaining what he believes will lead him to Jeanne Burns.

But I really don't know where she is.

As the ideas continue swirling in his head, Greg doesn't notice that he actually falls into a solid state of Rapid-Eye-Movement, or REM sleep. Somehow his body has taken solace in the total state of chaos. Naturally, this won't last very long.

Thirty minutes pass and the massive metal door to the room flings open and crashes with a thud. A handful of Gentlemen file in one after another, grabbing Greg's limbs and head, lifting him from his perch while the sixth Gentleman uses a sharp pair of scissors to cut the clothes off of Greg's body. Not entirely certain that he's awake, Greg doesn't resist whatever is happening to him. Once his body is completely bare, the Gentlemen set him down on the cold stone floor.

The Gentleman with the scissors walks out into the hallway and returns shortly thereafter with a fire hose.

"Let her rip," he says, hose in hands. Greg hears the roar of what must be water coming his way just before he is hit with a blast to the face that feels like Bruce Lee has just landed a signature chest-caving punch to his jaw. The hose kicks a little in the Gentleman's hands as it spits its monsoon-like force, pushing Greg across the room, scraping his exposed skin across the wet cement. Greg would object, but the fear of having the bottom half of his jaw ripped off by the water crashing upon him renders him silent.

Finally, the aquatic lashing ceases, and one of the other Gentleman steps forward with a tin bucket. He grabs the bottom of the bucket with one hand, while his other hand remains firm, gripping the top, and then he swings both of his hands towards Greg as a large puff of powdered soap clings to Greg's body. Now he looks like a man-shaped sugar coated donut. As soon as the bucket-carrying Gentleman is clear, the hose fires another burst of haymakers at Greg, rinsing him clean; and when the Gentlemen determine him to be ready, they toss a bundle of new black scrubs at Greg.

"The Doctor is waiting for you," says one of the Gentleman. "So, make haste and get dressed."

Greg manages to find his way to his feet, where he quickly puts on his new shirt and pants, and then he follows the Gentleman to his other place of sanctuary, the partitioned lab. Greg doesn't know how to feel about the room where he has been twice tortured, but he knows it's not any worse than the prison cell where he's allowed to eat and sleep.

When Dr. Campos enters the room on the other side of the glass wall, he notices that Greg looks to be not only soaked, but his skin also appears to be bright red, and almost raw, as if someone had scrubbed a layer from his body.

"Mr. Roberts," says the Doctor, "what happened to you? Why are you so, *red*?"

"Haha," Greg laughs aloud. "Are you kidding me Doc? Your men just pelted me with a high-powered hose, covered me in soap, and then pelted me again."

"I do apologize, Mr. Roberts," says the Doctor, concerned, "I did not realize –"

"Save it Doc," Greg stops him, "after everything you've done to me, I'm not about to believe those hoodlums did anything other than what you requested."

"I assure you, Mr. Roberts –"

"Just *stop* it Dr. C," Greg cuts him off again, buying, at least a little, into what his mid-night visitor said. "Enough with the lies, *okay*?"

Dr. Campos walks over to his intercom and presses a button to page throughout the building as he commands, "From now on, Mr. Roberts is to be treated with the utmost respect. The order to treat him as hostile is hereby revoked." He turns back to speak to Greg. "Again, I do apologize Mr. Roberts. I forgot, likely in my drunken stupor, to lift the order before we parted company last night."

"Sure," says Greg, "whatever you say Doc. They said you want to see me. Here I am."

"Right you are, Mr. Roberts," says the Doctor, "I am going to play you another recording, and –"

"Again with the recording Doc," says Greg, his tone rising. "When will we get to the point of all this?"

"Mr. Roberts," says the Doctor, "I need you to be patient. The recording I want you to hear is important. However, you may find it *disturbing*. I cannot yet divulge the history of the recording, at least not until you've heard it. What I can tell you is the authorities believe, just as I do, that the person heard in the recording is Jeanne Burns."

"What does that even mean?" Greg asks sarcastically, "The *authorities* believe. You're all smoke and mirrors Doc."

Dr. Campos goes to his desk and again opens his file on Jeanne Burns. He removes what appears to be a compact disc, a step up from the previous cassettes, and the Doctor goes through the same motions as before; a piece of the desk raises up, exposing a CD player, into which the Doctor inserts the disc he just removed from Jeanne's file, and then the player slides back from whence it came. Then the recording begins to play.

Chapter 41

"I understand," says Jeanne as the recording begins. "What must I do?"

There is a long moment of silence followed by the sounds of metal scraping against a stone-like surface. Wherever this is happening, the room must be either massive or extremely dense, perhaps solid concrete walls, like a bunker, as even the echo plays out into Greg's ears.

"Wait," Jeanne finally speaks, "where are you?" Another silent pause follows before she continues. "Oh – okay." The sound of frantic tears ring clearly, coupled with strained sobbing. Then more scratching and metal scraping echo.

"Why can't you just get it over with?" Jeanne asks, almost choking on the words.

The moments of silence between each sentence Greg hears seem as if Jeanne is listening to someone else speaking to her, but there's nothing at all on the recording.

Who is she talking to?

Then Greg hears something being cut, though he's unsure of what. Jeanne coughs, and eventually covers her mouth, muffling the sound.

She has a free hand.

"You want me to do what?" Jeanne asks. The words are spoken with the utmost clarity, as if she had been in a trance and the magician has just snapped his finger to awaken his hypnotized subject. "I can't possibly –" More nothing, not even the faintest breathing. "Okay. Fine. I've picked it up. Are you happy now?" Her tone switches to one of anger. Jeanne is all over the place.

What is going on?

"You keep saying I'll never fail you again," Jeanne's insistent. "How is it that I've ever failed you to begin with? How is it even possible?"

BANG, BANG, BANG. A series of identical noises pierce Greg's eardrums.

What was that?

"What the hell are you?" Jeanne screams her question. "Why won't you leave me alone?" Now the sound of Jeanne Burns choking resonates before a scream that seems to fade away from the recording, followed by the squishing impact of what sounds like a body hitting an adjacent wall. Everything goes silent, for ten minutes.

"What's going on Doc?" Greg asks. "What just happened?"

"Patience Mr. Roberts," the Doctor replies, "that's not the end."

A loud strained cough shakes the speakers on Greg's side of the partition, with a subtle wheezing following suit.

"Just kill me," says Jeanne, weakly. "Do it." Jeanne's footsteps are faint, but noticeable, as is the sound of her ass hitting the seat back in the center of the room. "Happy now?" She asks. "Is this where you want me?" More nothing.

What is happening to her?

"I've known today was coming," she says. "I know I tried to ignore it for the longest time, but part of me, deep down, always knew. It's why the Doctors could never help me; because you're not a mental condition. You're not just a fucking nightmare." Jeanne's fighting away the tears and nerves. "You're evil incarnate."

"Doc," Greg interrupts, "Who is she talking to?"

"Go – to – Hell." Jeanne says.

BANG! Something metal makes a clanking sound against the floor. The recording stops.

Chapter 42

Dr. Campos stands next to the glass divider between himself and Greg, grimacing.

"That, Mr. Roberts," he says through clenched teeth, "is the last known record of Jeanne Burns. Nobody knows where it took place or what actually happened. The authorities have identified the four separate loud bursts of noise as gunshots, but they can't make out what, if anything was hit by three of the fired rounds. The last shot, however, sounds as though it was pressed against something, their guess is that it was Jeanne's head."

"It can't be," says Greg, shaking his head in disbelief. "Doc, I need you to play the recording one more time."

"And why is that Mr. Roberts?" The Doctor asks.

"Patience Doc," says Greg snidely, "remember? *Patience.*"

The Doctor plays the recording from the beginning once more, watching Greg who is listening closely.

You keep saying I'll never fail you again.

"That's *IT!*" Greg shouts, recognizing what Jeanne is saying. Those are the same words he hears at the end of his life-long nightmare as the demented yellow-eyed demon plunges his blade into Greg's stomach.

You'll never fail me again.

"I know what she's talking about Doc." If he truly *knew* what she was talking about, he wouldn't sound so excited.

"Are you saying, Mr. Roberts," says the Doctor, "that you know where Jeanne Burns is located?"

"No Doc," Greg replies, "just that I know what she's talking about. I've heard those same words thousands of times."

"Really?" The Doctor says as skeptical as ever. "Do tell, Mr. Roberts."

The words, though already in his head, hit Greg's twenty-seven-year-old ears with a chill, and his body thrust him from sleep into a kneeling position in the middle of his bed. The motion is belligerent, and it startles Greg to consciousness. As his eyes open, he finds himself staring at himself in wall-sized mirrors stretching from one end of the double closet to the other. The fog from his mind begins to clear, and his heart comes to a stop.

He's there, standing behind Greg's reflection.

How can that be?

At first it looks like his father, but he's dead. Yet, there he stands. It's not until he looks closer that Greg realizes it's not his father at all, not unless his father suddenly has bloodshot yellow eyes glowing in his head. The figure in Greg's reflection is that gruesome devil from his nightmare.

"You'll never fail me again," the dark figure whispers with authority.

Quickly, Greg jumps out of the bed, and as he goes to turn around, he feels the sharp agonizing pain in his gut, just as he always does at the bottom of those endless stairs. Blood begins spewing from Greg's abdomen like water from the Bellagio fountains in Las Vegas when his attacker withdraws the blade. Greg tries to apply pressure to the wound, but it isn't helping.

In the movies, this is the point where his eyes pop open and Greg sits up in bed, and the audience groans with thoughts of, "I knew it was a dream." But this isn't a movie. Greg isn't waking up. Unsure of what to do, he runs out of his bedroom and down the hallway. There is a bathroom at the end of the seemingly endless corridor. Once inside, Greg locks the door and turns on the light. His hands and clothes are drenched in the molasses-like fluid that was previously part of his insides. He uses his left hand to turn on the hot water in an effort to wash the blood off, but it isn't working. Soap, shampoo, rubbing alcohol; none of it works.

This can't be real.

In disbelief, Greg covers his eyes, takes a deep breath, and looks in the mirror again. There is no blood, no wound, and no man in his bedroom. Something in Greg's mind manifested his nightmares into his consciousness, and he couldn't tell the difference. For the first time in years, Greg was scared. It's all in his head.

After taking a long and hot shower, Greg climbs back in bed, where he stares at the ceiling fan until it's time to get up and face the new day. As he lies there mesmerized by the spinning, he begins to think about The Master and his prophecy.

Perhaps he is right.

"Don't you see Doc," says Greg, "those words are the key. Jeanne and I are connected. In what way? I don't know. But this much is true: both Jeanne and I are, or in the past tense in her case, plagued by some*thing* dark, some*thing* evil; and it is obsessed with my failure. Why else would we suffer from the same nightmares, the same *hauntings*, if you will?"

"I find myself saying this a lot," Says the Doctor, "but, I'm sorry, Mr. Roberts. I think the time has come for me to call in someone with a better understanding of such things."

"What do you mean Doc?" Asks Greg. "We're finally on to something. We can't just stop now. Though I didn't get it before, *this* is clearly why I came to you. Unexplainable things have been happening to me for countless years." Greg is clearly becoming overwhelmed with a sort of joy, born out of what was complete ignorance previously. "And then I end up in your, *custody*, I supposed we'll call it that, custody; and this isn't the first time you've dealt with someone in this predicament. We are meant to conquer this together Doc, I can feel it."

"We aren't stopping, Mr. Roberts," says the Doctor, "but I know an expert in the area towards which we are headed, and I must have him here if we are to be successful."

Though Dr. Campos is sure Greg is right, and as much as he wants to hear more, he's reminded of the look on Jeanne Burns' face when she saw *it* over his shoulder. He knows he should have brought in his expert then, but didn't, and Jeanne paid, evidently with her life. Refusing to allow the same fate for Greg, Dr. Campos puts an immediate end to the session and asks the Gentleman to walk Greg back to his room.

Jeanne knew about It, Greg ponders the thought back in his dark and cozy cinderblock-like suite. His legs are bouncing as he rocks back and forth in the corner closest to the door, too nervous to venture any further in.

"If you keep down this path Greg," the woman's voice returns, "you'll never see the light of day."

"Prove it," says Greg, fresh out of patience.

"Nothing good can come from talking to that hypocrite of a Doctor," says the voice, ignoring Greg's demand.

"Whatever you are," says Greg with confidence, "you're wrong. You'll see. The Doc and I are going to win this fight."

"You'd be wise to yield to my warnings boy," the woman's voice cracks a little, sounding a bit more like a man for a short moment. "You have two choices, do as I say, and maybe you'll live a bit longer; or ignore me, and find yourself in an early grave."

"And I suppose you're going to be the one to kill me then?" Greg asks. "Why should I listen to anything you say? I don't know who, or *what* you are. Hell, I don't even know *where* I am. For all I know you're just another one of the Doctor's parlor tricks, here to test me, to test my resolve. Well I'm done. You hear me? *Done.*"

The voice says nothing in return, and Greg assumes, much like last time, that she's gone. He doesn't care. He can't take much more of this solitude or the shitty food that comes with it. He's going to get through this night and then, with any luck, he and the Doctor's *specialist* will find the resolution to everything, the nightmares, the missing girl, the creepy shadows, *everything*.

Still rocking in place, Greg focuses back on one of his fondest, yet saddest memories of his grandfather, the man to whom Greg always looked up.

Chapter 43

Picture a man in his senior years. He's not astonishingly tall, but he's not short either. The hair on his head is whitish-gray and slightly combed across his scalp to cover the area where hair no longer grows. His outfit consists of a white t-shirt, which is covered by a mild-toned, checkered, short-sleeve, dress shirt. The shirt is tucked into his dull slacks, and it's all wrapped together by a plain black belt. If you can see him at this point, then you're only missing one thing; this man almost always has either a cigar or a pipe in his hand. No matter where you are, if you're with him, you can smell the tobacco. That's the man Greg's remembering.

As the car comes to a stop, Greg feels an anxiety unlike anything he's ever felt before. His stomach is turning, his heart is pounding, and he's sweating in places where glands shouldn't sweat. The cause of this panic is hard to understand. They've had many conversations in the past. Yet, his body is telling Greg this is going to be different.

Greg emerges from the vehicle and immediately surveys his surroundings. Nobody is around, so things may proceed in peace. Just like so many times before, he's already outside when he arrives. He makes his way past a bed of flowers as Greg stares at him. The ground beneath his feet feels soft, like fresh cut hair that has been conditioned to perfection. Knowing that his visit won't be short, Greg finds a clear spot and takes a seat. Once settled, Greg looks at him and speaks, "Hi Grandpa. It has been far too long, and for that, I apologize. There are some things on my mind, and I know that talking to you about them will leave me at ease."

The conversation has not started, and already more memories are flowing through Greg's mind as if they're happening right then and there. One thing that always comes to mind when he visits his grandfather is yard work.

As a young boy, Greg always followed him everywhere. On days when the lawn needed to be mowed, he would either sit in a red wagon that would attach to the back of the lawn mower, or he'd sit in his grandfather's lap. It was never a question of wanting to join him, just a matter on of *how* Greg would like to join him. He would put a smile on his face and off they'd go.

In the autumn months, Greg would show up at his grandparents' house and help rake leaves. He hated raking leaves, but if that's what his grandfather was doing, then so was Greg. The yard was huge. They spent hours out front and it felt like they'd hardly made a dent in the work that needed to be done. However, once they were ready to take a break, Greg's grandmother would make them lunch. Greg remembers dropping his rake and running into the kitchen through the back door. There really wasn't a reason to be in a rush. No matter how quickly he got there, the bread would still be frozen, and he'd have to wait for it to thaw before he could eat. As a child, Greg's thinking was that the longer it took him to eat lunch, the longer it would be until he had to return to raking. His grandfather's thinking was always that eventually they'd be eating dinner later.

Dinner was an event in and of itself. Greg's grandmother would prepare a wonderful meal that covered the dining-room table. There was a bowl full of chicken, a bowl filled with steamed vegetables, and a basket filled with bread. Greg would have a normal-sized glass of whichever beverage he wanted at the time, and his grandfather would have his six-ounce glass of milk. They would start eating, and all was well. Greg had a tendency to scrape every last shred from the bones when he ate meat. That's how his grandfather ate, so Greg followed suit. His grandfather would eat everything on his plate without taking even a small sip of any liquid. Once he was full, he'd grab his six-ounce glass and down the milk with which it was filled, signaling the end of the dinner event.

With a smile, Greg looks at him and says, "I miss the old days Grandpa. It has been far too long since we last played Pitch."

When his family lived in Georgia, Greg's grandparents came down from New Hampshire for a while. One afternoon his grandfather sat Greg down and placed a deck of cards on the rickety table in front of him. He said that the basics to the game he loved to play were high, low, and jack. It sounded like a foreign language at the time, but he spent a substantial amount of time, and tested a lot of his patience, until Greg understood the game that was known as Pitch. After that day, Greg and his grandfather sat down to play frequently, and they were almost always on the same team. Once he felt that Greg was competent, they talked about onions.

Lectures were a trademark of Greg's grandfather. It wasn't often that Greg would spend time at his grandparents' house without getting a thorough speech about whatever his grandfather decided was a good lesson for the day. They weren't short and sweet either. Greg's grandfather would spend forty-five minutes or more to make one point.

"Greg," he'd always start, "a man's word is his bond. A man is nothing without his word."

At the age of nine, he sat Greg down and told him that it wasn't good to make promises, especially ones that are hard to keep. If Greg went through life without ever breaking his word, people wouldn't question his worthiness. Greg can still hear the words in his head as if he is standing in front of him at this exact moment.

Baywatch is on the television and his grandfather looks at him and says, "Greg, no matter what you do, never disrespect a woman." There are some basic rules when it comes to women. Boys don't hit girls. When an opportunity to open a door for a lady arrives, be sure to take advantage of the situation. The biggest misunderstanding among young men is that you don't have to be in a relationship with a woman to hold a door for her. It wasn't an exact science, but it made sense.

"Greg," again his grandfather starts, "if you're going to have an idea, you might as well make it a good one." That may be the phrase that Greg quotes the most. Greg has always been a thinker. For whatever reason, he likes problem solving. Besides, any time he wanted Greg to sit down and talk, he'd send him to the freezer in the basement to get a chocolate-covered ice cream. He was going to be serious, but he wanted Greg to be happy as well. A time would come when Greg would long for those lectures.

As a result of being his grandfather's shadow, Greg gained tremendous respect for the man. However, he didn't know everything about him. Like most teenagers did, his mother made some choices that upset his grandfather, to say the least. She left his house as a teen and moved away with an older man. To hear her tell the story, her father practically disowned her the day she left. He went so far as to say that any children she had with this man would not be his grandchildren. This was no joking matter.

Greg has heard a lot of stories about his birth and the things that happened as a result. The first time his grandfather saw him, he forgot about, or at least ignored, his disownment of Greg's mother. Things weren't the way he wanted them to be, but that wasn't his priority at the time. Something about Greg opened his mind and his heart. Greg's father may have corrupted his mother and stolen her from his grandfather, but he was the surprise piece to the puzzle. His grandfather loved Greg from day one, and Greg loved him.

The truth comes from his mouth, "You know Grandpa you were always more of a father to me than my father was."

Once his parents were divorced, Greg only saw his father a couple times before he turned ten years old, and then never again. He didn't have any awesome wisdom for Greg. All he really tried to show him was how to correctly shade a sketched picture. After a few minutes his father would lose his patience with that and all expectations were out the window. Greg often wonders if he only came to town to fight his mother in court.

After a few years of living close enough to visit his grandparents on a regular basis, his mother re-married and moved his family to California. Greg tried to fight the big change. His grandfather meant too much for him to move across the country. Who was going to teach him about life? With whom was Greg going to play pitch? There was no way that his mother could give him the lectures he needed. His family had moved enough, and 3,000 miles was just too far. Greg can still see his grandfather standing in the driveway as they drove away. It hurt to even think about it. This man had been Greg's hero.

Life in California was different. Greg didn't know anything about earthquakes or racial diversity. There must have been a few lectures he missed. When things didn't make sense Greg would call his grandfather. His summer vacations often included a couple weeks back in New Hampshire with his grandparents. Greg could ramble on for days just trying to make up for lost time. No matter how long he wanted to talk, or even what he wanted to talk about, his grandfather would listen. Most times he would rationalize his stories into something basic, something that Greg could easily understand. Once Greg got the picture he'd move right into whatever he had to say.

His grandfather could have told him just about anything, and Greg would have treated it as gospel. He still remembers the first time Greg mentioned that he was disappointed in one of his classes. In reality, Greg was bored out of his mind. All of the information sounded the same as what he'd been told the year before, when he was in school in New Hampshire. It was very difficult for Greg to stay motivated, and that's what he told his grandfather.

"Grandpa," Greg would begin, "Math is so boring. I don't understand why I have to take the same tests every week." His grandfather stopped Greg from speaking any further so that he could say his piece.

"Greg," again, as he always began, "everyone has to know how to do math. Some people take longer to learn things than others. Just stick with it and you'll be fine."

That's all it took. The words left his lips and met Greg's ears through the phone. There was no unbelievable wisdom in those words, but they were spoken by his grandfather. He could have told Greg that his teacher was retarded, and that Greg should have quit the class. He would have done exactly that.

George, Greg's younger brother, was a special boy when they were young children. He and his brother had the pleasure of being in their grandparents' care one day, and George decided he was going to test his limits. He knew that his grandfather didn't like anyone messing with his things. Next to his recliner in the living room, his grandfather had a tray covered in an organized fashion with a pipe, pipe cleaners, fingernail clippers, a pocketknife, an ashtray, and a coffee cup. George decided that he wanted to play with his grandfather's things. He was warned twice, but George couldn't resist; knowing him now, Greg's not sure that George would have resisted even if he could have. After the third time George refused to listen, his grandfather headed to the basement.

When his grandfather returned to the living room, he had a machete. Without any hesitation, he looked George directly in his eyes, grabbed his arm, and stated that he was going to cut George's hand off. Greg became hysterical, and began to scream in an attempt to plead his brother's case. No limbs were lost, but Greg's grandparents didn't take the two of them into their care at the same time again. After all of that, Greg felt like his brother was the one who was out of line. His grandfather could do no wrong.

Greg eventually got over girl cooties, and at the age of seventeen he got into what would turn out to be a serious relationship. That summer he went to visit his grandparents again. It was the first time Greg had a girl to talk about. His grandfather tried to tease him once or twice, but Greg couldn't hold it against him. All Greg wanted was for his grandfather to tell him that he was proud. It didn't matter what Greg did to make him proud, just that he was proud. Greg hoped that his grandfather would approve of the choices he had been making.

A phone call came shortly after Greg's nineteenth birthday. Greg and his mother had to catch a flight to New Hampshire. They eventually arrived at the hospital and Greg wasn't sure what to think or how to feel. There his grandfather was, lying down, eating ice chips, and appearing to be clueless. The man that was Greg's image of strength was bed-ridden. His grandmother, a couple of his uncles, his aunt, and his other uncle's wife were present. Greg didn't know that any of them could have been ready for that moment.

It was like another one of those things you see in the movies or that you hear about in stories. The family had to decide what to do. Greg's grandfather was going to continue having miniature strokes and that was all there was to it. If it wasn't going to be the strokes, then it was going to be diabetes, or a problem with his heart. Knowing how his grandfather would feel if he had to make the decision himself, the family came to a conclusion. Obviously they weren't going to kill him, but they weren't going to allow him to suffer either.

"I'm sure you don't remember Grandpa, but your daughter almost went to jail."

Greg's grandfather had been moved to the Rochester Manor, a local rehabilitation facility, from the hospital. His mother spent most of that time by his side. However, his Uncle's wife was a pain-in-the-ass from day one. It was her duty to get in the way and act like she was the one in charge. She tried to get between his mother and his grandfather and it almost ended in bloodshed. Greg still doesn't know how she restrained herself, but his mom didn't even try to hit her. She just stayed by him. Any and all disagreements, whether from a point of pride, stubbornness, or refusal to let the other be right, were no longer a factor. They had reconciled their differences. The slate was clean.

After the level of anger decreased, Greg stood at the foot of his grandfather's bed. He was smoking his thumb. All of those years of packing and smoking a pipe, he didn't even realize that he wasn't holding one in his hand.

Greg tried to speak to him, but very little came out. He looked up at Greg with a smile across his face. His eyes became glazed and he said, "Greg," even demented, the speech started the same way, "There's a chocolate covered in the freezer down in the cellar if you'd like one." It was nineteen year old Greg that was standing there, but his grandfather was seeing him as he was seven or eight years prior. Greg may not have been that little boy anymore, but it was he, his partner in crime, and he knew it. It breaks Greg's heart to see it in his mind. Greg was the problem solver, and he couldn't solve this problem. How could it be that Greg could be there to make things right for anyone and everyone else, but he couldn't make things right for him? Failure was all Greg could feel.

The conversation carries on from there, "I'm sorry that I froze in front of you that day Grandpa. I didn't know what to say." Greg's mind is telling him to fight the tears, but his heart doesn't want to hear it. "What do I do now? I've had so many things happen in this life and I can't make sense of it all." Greg now rests on his knees, as if praying, or *begging*.

"I came here with the intention of explaining some things," Greg continues. "That girl you teased me about almost got the best of me. I made it out alive, but not by much." Each word exists from his mouth slowly in an attempt to refrain from breaking down. "All I have ever wanted to do is make you feel proud of me. I remember everything you told me. My word is my bond and I don't make promises. There is a lot of pleasure in holding a door open for someone. My ideas are great. Am I missing anything?"

Silence rushes over Greg like a dense fog over a pond. Everything is leading to this point and still he doesn't know how to say it. When all else fails, Greg just let its out. "A day is going to come when I want to get married Grandpa. But, how do I know that I have made the right choice? The girlfriend I have now is wonderful. We don't argue about anything. She makes me happier than I imagined I ever could be again. However, I still need your approval."

There it is, in plain black and white. The tears are falling from Greg's eyes uncontrollably, and can't see the world right in front of him. "There isn't an amount of time that is going to bring me the lecture I need. I could sit here all day and play games with you, but you won't be able to point me in the right direction. It's okay. You've given me what I need, and I won't let you down. I love you Grandpa. I'll see you again soon."

There Greg is, kneeling in the grass, his head, pounding from all of the tears. He can hear his heart beating inside his skull as if it wants to explode. The time has come for Greg to depart. He leans forward, places a rose on the ground, kisses his grandfather's head stone, rises to his feet, and, just as he turns to head to his car, a hand grabs Greg's ankle, pulling him back to the ground. Stunned by having the wind partially knocked out of him, Greg looks back to find those crisp yellow eyes with intense streaks of red staring back at him as the mammoth-sized dark figure, dressed to the nines in his cloak and hat, his face a pale white with black lines engraved like cracks into his shadowy flesh climbs out of the grave.

"You will never fail me again."

Chapter 44

While the average man can recall the general events of his wedding day, Doctor Emmanuel Campos remembers his commitment to Martha Cruz on their day of Holy Matrimony for the wrong reason.

The ceremony was held at a local golf club just off of Interstate 215 in San Bernardino on a beautifully sunny Saturday afternoon in the spring of 1986. Seeing his bride to be in her elegant white gown for the first time nearly brought Emmanuel to tears. He knew at that very moment that he'd made the best decision of his life. The vows were exchanged without any difficulty and after the customary confirmations of "I do," the newlyweds and their guests all migrated to the clubhouse, where good laughs, good food, cold beer, and delicious cake were enjoyed in a music-filled environment of love. However, this isn't what Dr. Emmanuel Campos remembers about that glorious day nearly thirty years ago.

Francis Armand Dubois is a particularly unusual fellow. At an average five feet nine inches tall, and weighing a dainty one hundred twenty-five pounds, this mysterious mid-forties man is easily underestimated. His blue eyes and chipper smile are the last among the crowd leaving an extraordinary reception, as he is tasked to gain a moment of the groom's time before the honeymoon officially begins.

"Greetings, Mr. Campos," a boney hand reaches out in politeness, "Or is it officially Doctor Campos now?"

"It is actually," says Emmanuel, "And who may I ask are you? Are you related to Martha?"

"No, Doctor," the atypical man responds with an uncanny sense of urgency. "I'm afraid I haven't officially met anyone here today. My name is Francis, and I am hoping to have a moment of your time before you bound away on a magical trip with your gorgeous bride."

"I'm sorry, *Francis*," Emmanuel says, unprepared for anything unrelated to his magical day. "*Now* hardly seems like an appropriate time to talk. As you can see, I'm quite, *busy*." He continues smiling, doing his best not to seem rude, though all he can really think about is being alone with his new wife.

"I completely understand Doctor," says Francis, still as polite as can be, "but I really think you should hear what I have to say sooner rather than later. I assure you, if it was not of the utmost importance, I would not be bothering you at such a time as now."

"Sweetie," Martha says, taking her husband by the hand, "Are we go – *Oh*," she sees the scrawny man, uncertain of where he came from. "I'm sorry. You're still entertaining a guest."

"That's okay dear," says Emmanuel, "we're just wrapping up, and then we'll be on our way."

A mid-thirties Dr. Campos draws a business card from his tuxedo pocket, *Always have them ready*, he thinks to himself, as he hands the card to the suspicious man.

"Please, sir," he says to Francis, "call me in two weeks and I will give you all the time you need to tell me your story."

Mr. Dubois tries to object, but before he can utter another word, Martha pulls the Doctor away, leading him out the front doors and into their freshly polished luxury limousine.

Dr. Campos thinks about that chance encounter as he dials the number one his telephone.

Ring, the line on the other end sounds once.

Ring, a second time.

"Hello?" A voice answers.

"It is happening again," says the Doctor. "Just like last time."

"Where are you?" The voice asks.

"I'm at the facility," the Doctor responds.

"How long?" The voice asks another question.

"A week at best," says the Doctor, "I should have called you sooner, I know."

"Yes, you should have," the voice confirms. "Be that as it may, now is better than last time. At least this one's still alive."

"What do you recommend?" The Doctor asks for advice.

"Do *nothing*," the voice answers, "I will be there at sunrise."

The voice on the other end of the line hangs up and Dr. Campos follows suit.

He is coming here. Hopefully he will succeed where I have failed.

Chapter 45

With Greg having left under the guise of an emergency at work, Amber D'Marco finds herself struggling to sleep alone, especially given the barrage of events from the past few days. She thinks about the way everyone spoke to her about Greg. George acted almost as if he doesn't have a brother outside of acknowledging him by name. Kent seems wary about Amber calling, but it's possible that could be chalked up to a best friend trying not to rat out his buddy if he's uncertain about what crisis Greg has gotten himself into.

After the sleeping pills fail to accomplish their primary function, Amber starts wondering the worst.

Is he seeing someone else? Where was he really? Would Greg turn his phone off so that nobody could find him? What is he really hiding from me?

Knowing how responsible Greg usually is, she can't help but consider every possible terrible scenario, no matter how ridiculous it may be.

Is his name even Greg? Is Kent in on it?

THUMP. Amber hears something, maybe a trashcan, bounce against the house, but thinks nothing of it. The Santa Ana winds are awful at this time of year, which could cause anything from a nearby yard to crash into the fences and walls.

THUMP. The sound gets a little louder; still, Amber doesn't give it any attention.

CRASH! The third time sounds more like a dumpster slamming into garage door, alarming Amber ever so slightly. She thinks about caring for only a moment, and then returns to her insomniatic obsessing.

THUMP, CRASH, BANG, RUMBLE! The house starts shaking, as if swaying back and forth like a boat stuck out to sea in a hurricane. Amber can't ignore it any longer. She crawls out of bed at a rather sluggish pace, maybe brought on by three doses of pills. Once she gets herself wrapped in a robe and has the lights turned on, Amber walks out of her bedroom, across the house, and out into the driveway. The noise and shaking stop. The neighborhood is filled with the sounds of dogs and cats singing tunes of anguish. Expecting her neighbors to saunter out into the street as well, Amber waits to learn the worst is over.

When Amber finally realizes that she's still all alone, and that nobody else will be joining her in the street, she thinks to herself, *typical, how selfish.*

THUMP. Amber hears the sound of the trashcan again. Tired of standing around, she walks to the side of the garage where the gate to the back yard is latched to a fencepost cemented onto the house's foundation. The trashcans are located a few feet beyond that point. There's a combination padlock that slows her down, but she eventually works some magic and gets through the gate. She notices the motion-sensor flood lights on the side of the house haven't turned on. Amber tries waving her arms and jumping up and down, but she remains in the dark, with nothing more than the little glow of a street light out front to guide her.

THUMP. Again she hears the noise, but the trashcans don't appear to be moving. Amber gets a bit of a chill and the hairs stand up on her arms and neck.

Well this is exciting.

She almost laughs, as it would at least be better than crying.

THUMP. Still she sees nothing.

What is that?

Amber creeps in closer to what she thinks is making all the noise, but now she's not so sure.

THUMP. It eventually makes sense, at least she thinks, *there must be a raccoon or something trapped inside.* That wouldn't account for the whole world bouncing beneath her moments ago, but Amber's too tired to put two and two together. She stretches her right arm out, while her left hand holds onto the dangling sleeve. Taking a deep breath in and back out, Amber quickly grabs the lid and yanks it off the trashcan; nothing. It's empty. There isn't even any trash inside.

Great, get yourself all worked up for nothing.

Then she attempts to put the lid back from where she grabbed it, and Amber sees what, in her opinion, is the scariest thing on the planet; a Black Widow spider is on the top of her hand.

"Aaaah!" Amber shouts, flinging her hand and tossing the trashcan lid into the neighbor's back yard. She turns and runs back around the front of the house and back inside, her arms flailing the whole way. The red-hour-glass-spotted arachnid flew off somewhere between the scream and the front door closing. Standing in her living room doing what looks like a modern version of a Native American rain dance, semi-jogging in place, Amber strips off her robe and underwear and checks every visible speck of her skin for more tiny black would-be assassins.

She eventually comes to the conclusion that there are no more bugs crawling on or around her, and Amber makes her way towards the kitchen, leaving the previously shed garments on the floor for someone else to pick up and destroy at a later time.

I'm not going to sleep for a week, she thinks, guzzling a glass of room-temperature tap water, her heart still racing. Amber then grabs the cordless phone on the counter and calls Greg, hoping he'll answer and be able to talk her off of her mental ledge, but it goes straight to voicemail.

What the fuck?

She'd be irate, but between the death scare and the pills, Amber is just too tired to throw another fit.

Putting the glass in the dishwasher, Amber turns out the kitchen light and heads back to her bedroom. She's surprised by the yawn that stretches across her face, but welcomes it all the same. Her short tanned legs are burning from the midnight workout with each step she takes. Another five feet through the doorway and Amber turns to close the door behind her; and, as if out of nowhere, a figure in the shadow of the corner jumps out at her, causing her to clam up and stumble backwards.

"Oh my God," Amber trembles, "Greg, you scared the shit out of me."

"I'm sorry," Greg fumbles for the words, realizing his *pleasant* surprise isn't working out as he planned. "I didn't mean to scare you. I'm back and wanted to surprise you, but you weren't in bed like I thought you'd be."

Amber grabs ahold of Greg and wraps her arms around his body, clenching her hands together in the small of his back.

"I've had the craziest night," she says, kissing his cheek. "I'm so glad you're here."

"Really?" Greg says sarcastically, an evil grin growing upon his face.

"Oggggrrrd," Amber wails out in agony, releasing her hold of him. She starts to retract from the man of her dreams and looks down. Another thrust hits her as a decaying hand surges the knife deep into her intestines.

"Ha, ha, ha," a creepy tone chuckles in Amber's ear.

Gazing back at her attacker's face Amber finds an unsuspecting pair of blood-shot eyes glowing bright yellow deep in Greg's face. When he presses down with his hand causing the long sharp blade of his knife to cut through Amber's insides on its way to puncturing a lung, Amber gasps aloud and opens her eyes to find a ray of sunshine highlighting her face while her alarm clock blares to the heavens.

The sleeping pills must have worked after all.

Chapter 46

"Good morning Gregory," an old skinny man smiles from the other side of the glass divider, "I do hope you are well rested. My name is Francis Armand Dubois."

Greg has been returned to his interrogation room, only today he has been given a plush beanbag sofa of sorts to sit on, a tall carafe of piping hot coffee to enjoy, and *ham & cheese croissants?*

"You must be the Doc's specialist," says Greg. "So, what it is you do?"

"Not so fast Gregory –"

"Will one of you please just call me Greg," he snaps at Francis, still not fully awake.

"Absolutely Greg," says Francis. "Is that better?"

"Yes, thank you." Greg replies with a fake smile. "I take it you're the charmer of the group," referring of course to his substantially upgraded accommodations.

"I wouldn't say that I'm a part of any group Greg," Francis replies. "But if you find me charming I can't say that I will complain about it." The man pulls the Doctor's throne-like chair, which must weigh nearly as much as he does, close to the glass wall, loosens his shirt cuffs, and takes a seat. "Now, Greg, are you comfortable?"

"As comfortable as one can be in captivity I suspect," says Greg, regrettably enjoying the changes from the comfort of his new seat. "Why does that matter?"

"If we are to discuss your impending doom," says Francis, "then, Greg, your environment might as well be as pleasing as possible, don't you think?"

"Glad to see you aren't going to beat around the bush," Greg jokes. "So what is this doom you're talking about?" His face fills with delight, almost like having an orgasm, as he sips coffee from a crystal mug.

"Simply put Greg," says Francis, "you're going to die in less than a week. That is, unless you work with Doctor Campos and I. Even then, I can't promise your survival." The words should concern Greg, but his will has truly been beaten out of him, and at this point, he can't stop thinking about the taste of the roasted beans in his cup.

"What is this delicious brew you've given me?" Greg asks, wishing he could chug the piping hot drink, just to be able to have another.

Francis shows an uncommon smile across his face. "I'm glad you like it Greg," he says. "That is *Kopi Luwak*. It's a high quality roast, very expensive." He can see he's earning good will with the Doctor's *guest*.

Kopi Luwak is a coffee made through a unique process. An animal known as the Asian Palm Civet selects the highest quality coffee berries, which sounds harmless. However, once the Civet has chosen which berries are best, it eats them. The berries then go through the Civet's digestive system, and once processed, the *Kopi Luwak* company takes the digested coffee berries, roasts them, grounds them, and sells it at an astoundingly high price. In short, it's its shit coffee, and it's amazing; but Francis is going to leave that tidbit out.

"Let's have it Frank," Greg says, still not taking things seriously, and without questioning the foreign coffee brand. "Tell me about my *eminent demise*."

"I'm going to tell you a bit about myself, about what I am, about what I have seen, and about what I may be able to do for you." Francis stops to see if he has Greg's attention, and though he's slurping coffee like a dehydrated Ethiopian at a well on the other side of the glass, Frank can tell he's all ears.

Francis Armand Dubois was born before the start of World War II in Paris, France. Having seen enough of the Germans in the city streets of his hometown, Francis' parents left France and moved to the United States. He was told his mother was killed shortly after the family's arrival on American soil, and his father was presumed dead ten years later when he left for work one morning and never returned home. Francis spent the next couple of years in a Catholic orphanage coming to terms with what happened to his parents before making the journey into the world on his own.

In the 1950s and again in the 60s, Francis learned about two other people, a man and a woman, who also mysteriously *died* or disappeared, much like his parents. Then Francis disappeared for two decades. He tells Greg that during that time he was physically in a state of hibernation in a cave at the northern most point of Alaska, while he mentally and spiritually chased after the *thing* he eventually learned had been killing folks, always a woman, then a man, then another woman, and so on, including killing his parents when Francis was a child.

"I learned to let go of my physical connection to the world Greg," he said. "Vowing to hunt down the *thing* that killed my family in *its* world; a world that exists just beyond our comprehension."

It was in this alternate world where Francis found his ability to see a person as no other person can. Through Francis' eyes, when looking at someone such as Greg, at whom Francis is currently looking, those who have been marked by that *thing* that killed his parents, that killed Greg's beloved Jeanne, they have an almost inverted shadow. Instead of the shade casting out behind whoever Francis is looking at, depending on the position of the sun, a dark, almost tar-like shadow seems to cling to the body of that person. While Greg can't see what Francis it talking about, his body is covered in the murky anti-glow.

Francis has long awaited the chance to end the demon-like killer, and Greg is his best chance. A man not entirely of religion, nor entirely of science, Francis Armand Dubois is considered to be an ecclesiastic expert of the paranormal.

"I have read your file Greg," says Francis, "as well as Jeanne Burns' file, and I am certain your day is coming."

"How is it that the nuts are the ones running this asylum?" Greg asks, feeling like he's the only sane person in the, *wherever* he is.

"Nobody here is crazy Greg," says Francis. He sounds like a college professor; so sure of what he's saying, "Especially not you. That figure in the shadows, those nightmares, they're all real. When you see that *thing* coming after you, it's merely your mind making a brief leap to the next world over."

"Why should I believe any of this?" Greg asks.

"I have no reason to lie to you Greg," Francis responds with one long breath. "Every seven to ten, sometimes as long out as fifteen years, *it* comes close to our world, close enough to find the next victim; and that is when the unlucky soul finds his or her way over into his *castle*, as you and Jeanne have called it." He stops to inhale. "Think about it Greg. How many times have you seen something move without anyone touching it? How many times have you known someone was following you only to find yourself alone? I know you don't believe in coincidence, it's what makes you strong. That's why *it*, wants you."

"And what about Jeanne Burns?" Greg asks, momentarily forgetting about the coffee. "How did I fall in love with her and carry on a relationship for four years if she was already dead?"

"That's the beauty of *Its* power Greg," Francis responds. "There's no sense of time in the other world, at least not how humans perceive time."

"Yes, but that still doesn't explain Jeanne loving me in this world," says Greg, intelligently.

Francis is surprised to hear Greg brush past the concept of time he just revealed, but then again, The Master is not from this world either.

"Everyone in this world has a sort of, *life-force*, if you will, similar to what major religions consider to be the human soul," Francis' story becomes more intriguing. "When one of us dies, that life-force lingers around for a short period, looking for any form of life to cling on to before dispersing entirely. It's how some have come to praise a concept of life after death, as there are those who are more in tune with their life-force than others."

"What you're telling me," Greg tries to put the pieces together, "is that I was dating Jeanne's *life-force*?" The notion sounds preposterous coming from his mouth.

"Not exactly Greg," says Francis, continuing his lecture. "From what I have been able to deduce thus far, I think this *thing*, waits until its prey turns twenty-eight, and why twenty-eight I don't know, but that's when it kills him or her. This releases the life-force, and the only life form present at that point is that *thing*. So I assume that *it*, is feeding off of that force. I also wonder if consuming a life force provides an ability to project the former physical image."

"If I understand you," says Greg, picking through Francis' lesson, "you're now saying that I was sexually involved with that – that horror in my nightmare?"

"Sadly, yes." Francis pulls no punches. "Can you think of a better way to become attached to someone?"

He's not sure if it's the tone with which Francis speaks, the look on his face, or his intricate understanding of what nobody else has understood, but Greg can tell the puny man in front of him is dead serious.

"How is it that you know so much about others this has happened to?" This is Greg's best question in days.

"Whatever *it* is," says Francis, "*It* always records the deaths. And, depending on the technology available, the recordings are more understandable as time progresses. *It* started with photographs, then audio, and suspect we'll have digital video before long. That may even be what *it* has in store for you." Francis tries light humor, but Greg isn't interested. "I simply found various recordings of suspicious deaths and disappearances over the years and combined with my new understanding of the worlds, was able to determine which were recording of *Its'* prey dying."

"But how did you know?" Greg persists.

"Anything that *thing* has ever touched bears an anti-glow similar to *Its'* prey," Francis replies, impressed with Greg's intellect. "So, if a tape or disc of a recording has that same quality, I know they were killed by *it*."

The door on Francis' side of the glass opens and in steps Dr. Campos.

"I'm sorry to interrupt," says the Doctor.

"Nonsense," says Francis. "You have arrived precisely when you needed to."

"You guys are quite the pair," says Greg, sitting back on his cozy seat, now resuming the consumption of his third cup of shit coffee. "Tell me, how did you two come to be in business?"

"Funny you should ask, Mr. Roberts," says the Doctor, happy to know his patient is cooperating. "Shortly after my honeymoon, I met with Mr. Dubois here and he explained to me a lot of what he has explained to you, with one minor exception."

"Which is what Doc?" Greg asks.

"Actually Greg," says Francis, "the good Doctor is my half-brother."

"What?" Greg reacts with surprise,

One showers me with comfort and lavish brew. The other tortures me for days. And they're related?

"Yes," says Francis, "it's true. A couple of years after my mother disappeared; my father took an interest in a local woman. However, he didn't have the heart to subject me to a second mother, so he started a second family across town. I learned about your Dr. Campos after my twenty-year slumber and approached him at his wedding. I felt bad lying about not being related to him, but I didn't want him to be consumed by curiosity, or worse, *fear*, at least not on his honeymoon."

"Only you were going to pull me aside and tell me about your crazy scheme involving a second world that day," says the Doctor. "Not just about the insane notion of an unknown sibling."

"That was different," says Francis. "That was business. *It,* was set to strike again."

"But Doc," says Greg, "your last name is Campos."

"Our father wasn't going to give a boy his name if he wasn't married to his mother Greg," says Francis, explaining his father's morals. "So Manny here has his mother's maiden name."

"Look, Mr. Roberts," says the Doctor, "I feel bad about the way I've treated you. I didn't want to involve my brother, hoping that what you are going through is mental, and not, *paranormal*." He chokes on the last word.

"Part of you has known this whole time Doc?" Greg asks, disappointed, but not shocked.

"No," says the Doctor. "Denial is one of my weaknesses Mr. Roberts. At first I refused to accept that my brother has always been right. We've never agreed on any of this, at least not until now. Jeanne paid with her life because of my ignorance, and that's what finally hit me."

"So what does all of this mean Doc?" Greg fires off another question.

"It means I'm going to let you go Mr. Roberts," says the Doctor, feeling it's only right.

"Are you crazy," says Francis frantically, putting his hand on the Doctor's chest. "We can't let him out of our sight, or it will never work."

"We will be in touch over the next week Mr. Roberts," says the Doctor. "As we will need you to return to us before you officially turn twenty-eight."

Just then the door behind Greg opens and a single Gentleman enters, who walks over to Greg, and places a black clothed bag over his head.

"Do not fight, Mr. Roberts," says the Doctor in the other room. "We are going to take you to your car."

Chapter 47

Wiping the vomit from her lips, Amber D'Marco gets up from her knees, puts the toilet seat back down, and brushes her teeth. The images of those fiery eyes and the knife protruding from her stomach made her sick.

Out in the kitchen she calls work to notify them she won't be going in today and starts brewing a pot of coffee; anything to get the taste of murderous puke out of her mouth. Her hands are still trembling.

It just felt so real.

She can't take her mind away from it. Again she tries to call Greg, who still hasn't returned home, and again she gets his voicemail.

Dammit!

She doesn't know what could have been so urgent that a mental health worker had to be gone for the entire night, but Amber does know that she isn't going to sit around waiting for Greg either. She's going to get to the bottom of all of this; and she's going to start, just as she did before, by calling Kent Lawson.

"Yellow," Kent answers before the first ring sounds in Amber's ear, the sound of a table saw buzzing in the background. He builds sheds at his house and drops them off in customers' back yards.

"Hi, Kent?" Amber says.

"Yep, who's this?" Kent asks.

"It's Amber, the weird lady who called you the other day." She re-introduces herself.

"Ah," says Kent, "and what may I do you for Ms. Amber?"

"Well, I'm at a bit of a loss. I know you weren't aware I existed the other day, but I'm assuming you know about me now.

So, I'll just come out and say it. Things with Greg are a little, *weird*."

"Yeah, how's that?" Kent asks, still cutting the trim for his latest masterpiece.

"He's just so distant," says Amber, "and I can't find anyone who can tell me anything about him. I find it odd that nobody can tell me the slightest detail. I mean, you've met him, right?" Her suspicions grow as she hears her own words.

Don't you lie to me.

"Um," Kent thinks about his approach, "sure. He and I were the best of friends. But that was a while ago."

"Oh, I see," says Amber, the sickening feeling in her stomach growing more. "Greg led me to believe you were still close. *Hmmm;* would you know anyone else who might be able to help me?"

"Didn't I give you some information the other day?" He asks, rather annoyed. "Did that not work for you Amber?"

"Yes and no," says Amber. "I spoke with George, but he was of little help. I went to speak to his mother, but she wasn't home. I guess I could always try her again."

"I tell you what," Kent prepares to offer more assistance. At this point he'll do whatever it takes to get her to leave him alone. "Greg always sought out professionals when he had the sort of issues you seem to be having. Last guy he saw was a fellow by the name of Campos. *Emmanuel* I think. I'll send you his information, well at least what I last had on the guy. Maybe he can offer you whatever it is he tried to offer Greg."

"I'm confused," says Amber. "What did he try to offer Greg?"

"I think you should ask him," says Kent, "I'll send the information now." He hangs up without saying *goodbye;* then follows through with Dr. Campos' name, address, and phone number.

This better not be a waste of my time, she thinks, *I'm running short on patience.*

Chapter 48

As the flesh and bone encrusted slug exits Jeanne Burns' skull, the demon-like figure stops the recording and lashes out to catch his victim before she hits the cold cement beneath her. The dark being tosses the steel chair out of the way and lays Jeanne's body in the center of the room, still convulsing. Though her last bit of life has not yet escaped her, the transformation has already started.

Jeanne Burns' life-force slowly separates from her flesh as her final twitch of muscle memory flares. The foggy dim-glowing aura hovers over the lifeless carcass seeking the closest being available for a reprieve. The nightmarish creature lowers down to its would-be knees, gazing over its newest prize.

The cloud of energy begins to fizzle every so subtly, when the life-force abruptly finds itself in a vacuum. The deadly shadow appears to open its mouth and inhale with enough power to propel a small jet. Every microscopic piece of dust gathers among the particles of Jeanne's aura, the ground shaking, and a pitchy noise capable of shattering bullet-proof glass reverberates from wall to wall. The gun, the bullet casings, even the audio recorder start swirling in the atmosphere above the smoky spirit of Jeanne Burns.

Once the demented beast is certain all of its victim's energy is now its own, the creature rises back to its feet, reaches its arms out in front of its body, and swings its hands together for one astounding clap. A burst of shockwaves soar out from its body, registering 5.4 on the local Richter scale. With the life-force refreshed within a new home, the daunting figure is rejuvenated.

Jeanne Burns' useless body combusts into a ball of fire; and flames collapse upon themselves inward towards the center of her lifeless mass. The spectacle is bright, and beautiful, if only one could see it. As more time passes the skin and bone begin to turn into molten rock; it's unlike anything known to man. She isn't reducing to ash. No, instead the fiery rock begins to compress closer and closer together, as if destroying itself from the inside. It isn't long before every sign of what was once Jeanne Burns disappears, leaving only a charred print on the ground. As far as this world is concerned, Jeanne Burns is no more.

"You will never fail me again." The being from another world snorts in disgust at his victim's weakness. With the task at hand now complete, the repulsive monster removes the disc from the audio recorder, which will be delivered to Jeanne's useless Doctor, so that he may pine away without ever knowing what became of such a beautiful specimen.

Until next time.

Chapter 49

Like a torture victim escorted to an undisclosed location, Gregory Allan Roberts finds himself in the custody of stereotypically large, less than intelligent, military loving freaks, with a black bag over his head. He smells the distinct aroma of jock-strap-sweat mixed with knockoff body spray. He can tell they've walked him onto an elevator, and that it is descending several floors, while the muscle-bound men's stink settles into Greg's nose hair. The trip down takes well over a minute, which suggests wherever this *facility* is located, it's at the top of a very large structure.

Greg hears the ping of a notification bell followed by the gliding doors opening before him. The steroid centerfolds nudge him forward out into what Greg can only assume is a subterranean, *garage*; more of a basement for vehicle storage. The squeal of tires on pavement sounds familiar coming towards him, and a burly automobile comes to a screeching halt directly in front of him.

"Sir," one of the Gentleman says, "keep your head down. We're going to assist you into the vehicle."

"Be careful gents." Greg hears Francis is already in the car, "We don't want any more harm coming to the young man."

Greg takes two small steps forward and his knees bump into a metal *bar* of some sort, likely where he needs to step up into his chariot. The brutes keep him from smacking his cranium off of the top of the frame, and Greg realizes upon scooting into the back seat that he's not in any small compact scrap of tin. No, he has a lot of room, and the pleasant odor of freshly treated leather comforts his nostrils, replacing the vile stench of his previous escorts. Greg is in the back of some sort of large luxury vehicle, and based on the impact of his knees, that high up, he's guessing it's a SUV.

"Is all of this necessary?" Greg asks.

"Absolutely, Mr. Roberts." Greg now knows that Dr. Campos is coming along for the ride as well. "We thought it best if we personally see that you are safely returned to your car."

"And where exactly is that Doc?" Greg asks. "Are we going back to your house?"

"No, Mr. Roberts," says the Doctor. "It's a ways down the road; a mutually beneficial location if you will. We intend to drop you off there and send you on your way, assuring everyone that nobody can pinpoint our facility's whereabouts."

"And why would your torture chamber's location matter now?" He continues with the questions as the vehicle pulls out into daylight, though it seems more like sundown through the bag.

"You have been missing for several days Greg," says Francis, "and we don't know who may be looking for you. So we aren't going to chance it."

The Doctor lied. He never told anyone where I was.

Greg doesn't respond. Arguing has achieved nothing thus far; why would it now? The ground beneath the car feels rough, like dirt, or stone gravel. Every few feet Greg bounces in his seat when they hit a bump or rut. Eventually the sound of the wheels changes to a familiar tone, the constant humming of pavement.

Now we're on a road.

The trip feels like it's passing at a snail's pace, but in reality it's only seven minutes before the SUV veers back onto a dirt road, bouncing and bumbling along. It's windy out. The Santa Ana's rock the vehicle back and forth, and Greg can hear the swirling sound of dust clouds slapping against the windows. There's a loud smack and a subtle crinkling in front of him.

"Shit," Francis says, "another windshield down." It must be his vehicle, and something must have broken the glass at the front.

"How much further?" Greg asks.

And don't give me any crap about patience.

"I didn't take you as the *Are we there yet?* type Mr. Roberts," says the Doc, chuckling. "We will be there momentarily."

The Doctor's idea of a moment is vastly different from Greg's. It's another fifteen minutes through dirt, divots, and ditches, before the tires slide to stop. He hears the doors in the front of the cab open, and then his own door opens shortly after. Francis helps him down out of the back and removes his black bag of a blindfold.

Is it dusk?

Greg can't tell if it's early morning or almost night. He doesn't know which way is north, so a guess is the best he'll be able to conjure. He's been captive for days, or so he's told. Time doesn't pass by the same when you're kept in a hole in the wall of an unknown cave.

Time doesn't pass by the same in a lot of cases to hear the Cuckoo Twins tell it.

Greg turns around to see a sight he never thought he'd enjoy. His old pile of scrap, the Dodge Shadow, just as he remembers it, without any luster.

"If you simply drive straight in the direction your car's facing Greg," says Francis, "you'll find your way to a local street where there's a gas station. The clerk working the register there can tell you how to get home."

"Remember, Mr. Roberts," says the Doctor, "we will be in touch in another day or so. It's imperative that you answer when we call."

Then Dr. Campos and Mr. Dubois get back into what Greg now sees is a late model Cadillac Escalade with off-road tires and a roll cage mounted on the interior, and his captors ride off into the distance.

What the –?

Chapter 50

Riding back to the hidden facility, Francis Armand Dubois sits in fuming silence, staring angrily at his brother, incensed by his decision to release Greg against his better judgment. The young man, who they just released into the wild, is most certainly going to die; Francis believes he can intervene and save his life; and yet Dr. Campos shows no interest in Greg's overall safety.

"Why are you glaring at me with such contempt brother?" Dr. Campos asks.

"You know why," Francis snaps back, his head bumbling about as the Escalade rolls through another sandy pothole.

"It will all work out," the Doctor tries to convince him. "Mr. Roberts will return to us, I'm sure of it."

The vehicle is bouncing up and down making its way across the rough terrain, leaving the brothers struggling to communicate effectively.

"How can you be so sure?" Francis asks, using his hands to brace himself against the truck's passenger-side window frame.

"I have spent an absurd number of hours with our ill-fated friend Mr. Roberts," says the Doctor confidently, not even bothering to look where he's driving. "The one conclusion I have reached beyond any reasonable doubt is that he needs to *know* what happened to his long lost love, Jeanne Burns. We have given him the only hope of understanding that he's ever had. He's going to come back to us when we ask."

"Yes," Francis responds, not buying into his brother's assurance. "But we have no guarantee that Greg will not be taken while he is out of our cus –" he's nearly strangled by the restricting seat belt, "custody." Francis reaches down and undoes his buckle, believing full well that he's less likely to die if he removes the taut straps that are suffocating him altogether.

"What do you mean brother?" The Doctor asks, veering the vehicle to the left, back onto gentle asphalt. "You have convinced me that Mr. Roberts is safe until his twenty-eighth birthday, which is still nearly one week away. What harm can come to him before then?"

"Have you considered any other alternatives?" Francis asks in a still pleading tone. "I just gave Greg a thorough explanation of the creature lurking in the shadows. What if he takes that knowledge, and in a bout of fear, takes his own life? Then what? I'm here for that *thing*, not your need to solve past mysteries."

"Brother," says Dr. Campos, "you underestimate me. Mr. Roberts is not capable of suicide. If he were, this conversation would not be taking place, as he'd still be shackled in his cell. We will call him soon, and he shall return to us. Just wait and see."

"But why even take that chance?" Francis can't see his brother's reasoning.

"Will you please –" the Doctor stops to focus on the sharp left he must take back into the endless desert, "trust me, just this once?"

Francis offers no reply. It's too late now. The deed is already done. Greg is already gone. He turns his head from his brother and stares out into the endless plain of dirt and rock. The remainder of the trip back to the secret facility goes without another word.

Chapter 51

Ring. Amber sits with the phone pressed to her ear.

Ring. Still no answer.

Ri – A suction-like noise splashes through the phone, followed by a fast click coupled with a sort of electronic distortion, and then a dial tone.

I know they didn't just hang up on me.

Amber, livid, dials the number again.

Ring. The line picks up on the other end this time.

"Wrong number!" Amber hears a woman shout through the phone in a coarse tone, and again the line goes dead.

Ring. Amber is not giving up.

I have all day, she thinks to herself.

Ring. Again the line is answered.

"Stop call –"

"Please don't hang up," Amber begs the woman not to ignore her call.

"Oh," Miss Paxon says on the line, "who is this?"

"My name's Amber," she says bashfully, "I'm trying to reach Dr. Campos. I'm hoping he can help me with something."

"I see," says Miss Paxon, her voice like that of an old smoker, "My apologies. I thought you were the persistent man from yesterday who keeps trying to sell me a timeshare. What did you say you want?"

Amber waits a moment, surprised by the gruff woman's tone, uncertain if she's called the right place.

"I'm looking for Dr. Campos," she says, raising her voice assuming the woman on the phone is old and losing her hearing. "Have I called the right number?"

"Well yes, you have," the surly woman responds, "but I don't think he can help you miss."

"Please ma'am," Amber says, expecting to hear the line go dead again, "it's really important. My fiancé Greg is one of his patients."

"You said Greg?" The old woman heard her right, but she isn't going to admit to knowing what Amber's talking about. "Greg who?" She hopes Amber will give in and end the call there.

"Greg Roberts ma'am," Amber says, still uncertain of whether or not she's looking in the right place. "Dr. Campos helped him, or so I'm told. Dr. Emmanuel Campos. Is this his number?"

Amber's stomach is turning. Something is off. This curt woman is hiding something.

"This is the correct number," Miss Paxon says, "but the Doctor is no longer taking on patients. I am sorry, but he can't help you. Perhaps someone else can be of greater service."

"No!" Amber yells into her phone. She's had enough. All of the polite approaches have gotten her nowhere, and she isn't putting up with it any more. "I will not look anywhere else. Someone is going to help me, and by God, if Dr. Campos has information about my soon-to-be husband, well then I need to know. Do you understand? Now, please let me speak to the Doctor." The release of energy feels good, despite the dire circumstances instigating the call.

"The Doctor is not able to speak with you miss," the grouchy woman puts her foot down. "Better yet, let me make this crystal clear; Dr. Campos no longer has the ability to speak. Therefore, he cannot help you with whatever nonsense you are referencing. Now, do *you* understand?" She slams the phone down, sending an ear-piercing twinge into Amber's head.

Son of a bitch!

Amber chucks her phone across the living room, causing a mirror to shatter just above her faux fireplace as it smashes into hundreds of tiny pieces.

The sight of glass particles exploding to the floor pushes Amber over the edge. Her face lets loose with every emotion her mind can convey in a short burst. Anger sends her couch cushions and pillows down the hall like a sack of flour from a baker's hands; bitterness tears the pad of paper she has been using to take notes along the way into small pieces; suspicion breaks the picture frame holding her favorite photo of she and Greg as it slams down upon the end table next to her; and finally a sorrow-filled frustration pours from her eyes as she hunches over at the sight of her decimated home.

Amber stumbles into the next room over, her guest bedroom, where she has a spare cordless phone. She pounds seven digits into the number pad and screams a tone of agonizing disgust when she gets Greg's voicemail yet again.

WHERE ARE YOU?

Chapter 52

Life is a petri dish of choices; does Greg try to follow the Doctor and his brother, or does he try to find his way home? Hell, what if he should decide to just head north and get away from all this madness? Not everything is as black and white as *right versus wrong*, which presents a fifty-fifty chance of stumbling on the best choice, even by accident. What about the multiple-choice questions? With Greg's future looking rather grim, he has to decide how he is going to live the last week of his life. Call him prejudice, but right and wrong pales in comparison.

With his graduation from high school, Greg's protection from the real world was gone. Fast forward ten years and his original goals of attending a big name college, obtaining a degree in psychology, and locating employment as a psychologist are almost history.

He settled for a less-than-ivy-league school and altered his career plans to accept permanency as a mental health counselor, which is a liberal title. The truth of the matter is Greg listens to drug addicts and morons whine for an hour at a time while getting paid far less than anyone should for putting up with such drivel. Add a co-dependent relationship gone awry, a revelation about imminent doom, and several days of torture at the hands of a "professional" and you have a recipe for disaster, sitting with his hands clenched with white knuckles around the steering wheel of his Dodge Shadow in the middle of the High Desert.

As Greg hits the accelerator he can't help but reflect on not only the past several days, but on his entire life leading to now. There's a chance that this long drive down through the endless field of dust clouds and sand will be the end. Miles of emptiness with only a pair of dull headlights showing the way provide the perfect opportunity for Greg's demise. Anything could happen, and nobody would know about it until the sun rose the following day, assuming he would be found at all.

Eventually, Greg's focus returns to the lack of road, and in that second, a coyote runs in front of his car. He slams on his brakes and spins the wheel to the left. The car stops just shy of the doggish animal, his face with a look of disappointment, sitting still, staring at Greg as if he should have crashed, as if that was the intention.

With his heart racing Greg takes a deep breath, looking towards the sky as if to say, "Really, God? Really?" When he returns his gaze to the wild beast he finds that the coyote is no longer there. Greg turns his head left and right looking for where it could have wandered, but sees nothing beyond the fits of sand whirling about. Another deep breath taken and he sets to continue his drive to he knows not where, when suddenly, like an image superimposed onto a desert landscape, Jeanne Burns appears before the bleak beams of light in front of Greg's car.

Jeanne's clothes are tattered, torn, and covered in soot, like she's been stranded in the sandy abyss for a lifetime. Cuts and bruises cover most of the visible parts of her body. She looks like she's hurt badly and yelling for help. Greg's head shakes in disbelief, and by the time he's done shaking, Jeanne Burns is sitting beside him in the passenger's seat of his car; her seat; his Jeanne.

"What is going on?" Greg asks, almost joyfully horrified to see her. "Where did you come from?"

"I've been here all along babe," says Jeanne through crusty dehydrated lips, "I've been waiting for you to pick me up."

"That doesn't make any sense," says Greg, "Why are you wandering around the desert?"

"Because you deserted me Greg," says Jeanne with a creepy smile, "I waited for you, and you never showed. I thought you loved me Greg."

"I do love you, but," Greg's mind is playing tricks on him, as it seems to be accustomed to doing, "you disappeared. I looked everywhere for you, but you were nowhere to be found."

"How can you say that?" Jeanne's face turns to one of sorrow. "You were everything to me Greg, and you abandoned me."

"I did no such thing," Greg exclaims, a frustrated tear escaping his eye. "I spent six months trying to find you. I thought, we all thought you were dead."

"*We*? Who is *we* Greg? You mean that snake, that terror of a Doctor?" Jeanne snarls at Greg. "I told you not to trust him, but you just couldn't do what I asked; you just had to tell him about us, didn't you? This has all been a part of his plan. He left me out here, waiting for you. This is what he wants."

"What the hell are you talking about? It's been seven years Jeanne. *Seven* Years! Does that even register to you?" Greg is playing right into her trap.

"Oh, come on now honey, you know better," the evil grin returns to her face. "It's been much longer than that. You and I," she stops to see if Greg can sense it coming, "we go back, much farther back."

"Huh?" Greg is trying to solve the riddle, but he can't see past the appearance of his lost lover.

"Baby," Jeanne says, turning away from Greg momentarily, "we go back more than a decade, closer to two, ha, ha, ha." As she turns back to look Greg in the eye, his heart stops cold for a quick second as he finds those bleeding yellow eyes glowing in her sockets like a lonely yield signal blinking on an abandoned road in the dead of night. "*You fail me.*"

Greg can still see the tears streaming down his mother's face from when he visited her in recovery. She drank to the point that she nearly died from alcohol poisoning. Alcoholism runs rampant in Greg's family, and although he never investigated how far down the family tree it went, he was made aware of his genes early in life. Greg's mother loved to drink, needed to drink, and did so frequently. At six years old, it's hard to understand why your mother looks exhausted all of the time. The flowing tears were those of remorse. His mother had been lying to Greg for years about what was wrong with her. Hell, she had been lying to herself. When she finally began to feel her life slipping away, the self-abuse came to an end.

He doesn't remember most of his twenty-first year. Life sucked and Greg didn't want anything to do with it. His heart was broken. He wanted to do anything he could to forget about her and everything she had ever meant to him. It was the worst thing Greg had ever felt in his life. She left a void in Greg's life that he would never forget. The very thought made him want to vomit.

Though he began to enjoy drinking from time to time before his relationship ended, and despite everything he had witnessed his mother go through, the emotionally crippling events of Jeanne's disappearance sent Greg's world into a downward spiral. His roommates hosted poker games every night after work, each filled with all the booze anyone could consume. When Greg watched a game on television, he drank. When stress was pushing him over the edge, he drank. It didn't matter whether or not he had a reason, he didn't need one. Greg drank.

It wasn't until the one-year anniversary of the disappearance that his eyes would open. Greg woke up with his face in the toilet of a home thirty miles from where he had been drinking, and he had no recollection of how he got there. The experience was life changing, and it made Greg think about everything he had been through from the time of his birth to that toilet. Acting like a child was no way to live. She was gone, and no amount of liquor was going to bring her back.

Greg didn't realize it at first, but sitting face-to-face with the fiery-eyed demon in the middle of the desert, he was still allowing Jeanne's departure to ruin him from the inside out; and then, "AAAAAAAAAAAHHHHHH!" Greg slams his foot down on the gas, closes his eyes, and screams as loud as he can. Either *it* will leave him alone, or Greg is going to drive blind until he hits something and ends them both. *So help him God.*

The impact never comes, and the ghastly creature doesn't say another word. A mile or two more, bouncing around the endless wasteland of dirt, and Greg opens his eyes to find he's alone, and coming to a road with a small gas station on the other side, just as the Doctor said there would be.

"Hi sir," Greg says, winded, his car waiting by the pump, "I don't have any money –"

"You Greg?" The old man behind the gas station counter interrupts with his question.

"I am," Greg responds without a hint of surprise.

"You're all set. You can fill'er up." The man says with a smile.

"Are you sure?" Greg asks.

"Yep," says the old man, "the Doctor already took care of you."

Greg doesn't hesitate. He doesn't care about the reasoning. He just wants to get back to somewhere he recognizes. The old man confirms that Greg can follow the road to the right of the station for about ten miles and he'll end up back by the main freeway, which will take Greg home.

Ten gallons and as many miles per hour as the Shadow will handle and Greg makes it home, to his bed, and passes out within seconds of his head hitting the pillow.

Chapter 53

Amber D'Marco's knocks are greeted at the front door by George Roberts, which catches her by surprise, given that she is standing on the front steps of the home of Marion Roberts, Greg and George's mother.

"C'mon in," says George who is apparently expecting the visitor, "Mama's in the back."

Amber follows Greg's brother through a narrow breezeway attached to the kitchen, then through the dining room, the living room, a television room, thinking *good Lord this is a long house*, and finally out onto a back porch, where Marion Roberts, an average sized woman with graying curly hair and pastel-blue eyes, sits rocking back and forth in her favorite wicker chair.

"Welcome, *Amber* is it?" A look of confusion washes over Amber's face. "Oh don't worry a bit. Kent called George and said you might be coming by, so naturally, my Georgie came down to wait for your arrival. He seems to think you're a particularly troubled young lady." Marion Roberts is as blunt as a person can be. Her father didn't waste any time with fluff and neither does she. "So what is this craziness about you and my oldest baby Greg?"

"Gee, I don't know where to begin," says Amber, unexpectedly flustered. "I'm trying to find out as much as I can about your son, Greg."

"Well, okay then. You've come to the right place," says Marion Roberts, a smile on her face. "There's nobody who knows more about Greg than his mama. What is it that you want to know?"

"I won't waste your time with any of the small stuff, I'm sure you're a busy woman," says Amber, trying to appeal to Greg's mother. "I don't know what has happened, but lately I've felt like I'm missing something, like something isn't –"

"You know what might be a good idea Amber?" Marion Roberts interjects. "You should go down and take a look at my boy's room. I bet you'll find all you need to know down there. I'll have George show you the way."

Marion gives her youngest son a nod and George motions Amber to the doorway back into the house, "This way." He guides her back through the previous rooms and across the breezeway, passing the door Amber came in when she arrived, and out into the garage.

The Roberts have lived in the home for nearly four decades. The tall house was built when a local contractor purchased, and then leveled, the local orange groves where the village of Victoria now sits. The only multiple-story home in the neighborhood at its inception, it sits back from the street in a dark corner of the world. It was also the only home with a quasi-basement hiding beneath it among the foundation. This is the area that was converted to become Greg's bedroom. The air was always chilled, and it was easier to watch movies at night with everyone else sleeping two floors up, which gave Greg the illusion that he lived independently from his family for several years. If you were standing in the middle of his bedroom at any given moment, you would assume it was a good place to be if you wanted to be left alone.

Amber enters Greg's room descending a set of wobbly wooden stairs beneath a rusted metal door in the center of the garage floor. The room is dark as George closes rusty entry behind her. The distance from the last step, Amber finds, is about ten feet from the closest light switch. Even once the light is on, the cold and damp space is spooky.

"Hello?" Amber calls out but nobody is there. She thinks about retreating.

This was a stupid idea.

She decides to take a look around despite her gut feeling that she should go.

After a couple of steps, Amber hears a dull click, and suddenly a light is shining around a corner to her right. Her initial thought is that George has accessed the room from another entry point and is trying to mess with her. However, as she looks around, Amber realizes there are no other windows or doors leading into the room. The only other point of access is a small vent, maybe a single foot wide and another foot tall on the far wall ahead of her.

That can't be George.

Growing more concerned, yet still not deterred, Amber quietly steps forward, turns the corner to her right, and finds a sole television sitting on the floor in the corner turned on. The light was from the snow-filled screen.

"What in the?" Amber whispers to herself, making her way across the room. As she approaches the TV to turn it off, the volume suddenly jumps from subtle noise to a blaring roar. The static feels like shish kabob skewers as it stabs her eardrums. Amber presses the power button to make the noise stop, but nothing changes; it won't turn off. Instead, she rips the power chord from the wall, and the eerie silence returns.

When the pain in her head subsides, Amber tries to make her way back up the stairs, but the door is still closed, and it won't open. She bangs her fist on the door, calling out, "Hello! Open the door. Let me out." But still the door doesn't open.

Amber goes back down the stairs and walks over the vent, shouting again, "Hello. Somebody help me. I'm trapped!" She hopes the vent goes somewhere other than an air conditioner.

At the young age of seven, Amber D'Marco's best friend was a ginger-haired, freckle-faced, boney bag of a girl named Terri Biffle. Terri's family moved into the house next door a couple years prior, and with few other children on the block, she and Amber became acquaintances by way of circumstance. Nevertheless, they ran back and forth, rolled around in the dirt, and played with toy tea sets as if they were sisters.

Amber's father had entered his name into a drawing for a new refrigerator-freezer, the kind with self-sealing doors, at the local hardware store, and he won. It was a very exciting moment for her father. The delivery men carried the new appliance into the home, and at the request of Amber's mother, carried the old lever-locking unit out to the curb for trash pick-up.

There was little to do for fun at the age of seven that didn't require playing outside, which was a vague description of an event at best. A day after the new fridge was installed; Amber and Terri were playing *Hide & Go Seek*. Amber was a ninja-grade hider, and Terri was a less than stellar seeker, especially with her undiagnosed Attention Deficit. On this particular day, Amber's hiding place was so good that even the police couldn't find her for three days. Her picture had been placed in the newspaper, the neighbors had all been questions, and little Terri Biffle felt awful about her lack of seeking skills.

It wasn't until the garbage men came by on *bulky-item* day that anyone could figure out where little Amber D'Marco had gone. Then, when the man on the back of the dump truck opened the old refrigerator on the curb, checking for dead animals or other broken belongings, he found seven-year-old Amber curled up in a ball inside, barely breathing.

Amber hated small spaces from that day on.

Staring to feel claustrophobic in Greg's subterranean bedroom, Amber paces back and forth across the chilled space, still occasionally shouting, hoping maybe George forgot about her. Her palms start to sweat and she starts thinking that this is all part of some sick plan to take her hostage.

Is this even Greg's room? Is this even Greg's family? Is Greg even Greg?

She can feel more tears coming, but then she hears a muffled sound of doors closing above, and footsteps nearing the metal doors.

"Sorry about that Amber." It's George at the top of the stairs. "The door locked when I closed it. I have to go get the key. I'll be right back."

Amber is relieved. She isn't going to be cut into a million pieces and fed to the family cats. Anxious, she turns off the light and starts back up the stairs; and again, a light clicks on behind her with the obnoxious sound of eardrum shattering white noise.

How is that even possible?

She unplugged the wretched thing, and nobody has come or gone during the time she has been down here. Nevertheless, she turns around, back down the stairs, around the corner, finding the snowy TV glistening in the dark. Then she remembers, she never plugged it back in.

It's powering itself.

Determined she isn't spending another moment at the Roberts' house, Amber runs back up the stairs, where George is now opening the door, back across the garage, into the breezeway, out the front door, down to the curb, and into her rental car, where she turns the ignition and peels out.

Amber gets two miles down the road and slows down enough to find her cell phone among the many things packed into her purse. She brandishes the smartphone like Excalibur raised in King Arthur's grip, earnestly commanding the device to call Greg.

DAMMIT!

Voicemail.

Chapter 54

Greg Roberts met Kent Lawson on his first day of high school in Latin class. Ms. Z started the day by telling all students to take out their pencils and paper, as they were "going to need them." Shortly thereafter the class learned that every year there is a Roman festival or forum, and that the freshmen serve a particular service during the festivities.

"Can you believe that we have to be slaves?" Kent asked Greg on their way to the library to pick up their books for the year. "I'm Kent," he followed up by extending his hand to shake Greg's, and they were the best of friends from that point on.

When summer vacation came around, Kent and Greg hung out at the movies, visited each other at home to play video games, and spent countless hours on the phone talking about whatever it is that young teens talk about, mostly girls.

Between their junior and senior years at Etiwanda High, Greg got his license and his first car, a used 1993 Ford Escort hatchback, jet black, with a dull grey interior, and automatic seat belts. It already had more than 100,000 miles on it, but Greg didn't care, it was his, and he drove that thing everywhere. Greg reminded Kent on a daily basis that only one of them had a car at that point, and about a month after Greg got his set of wheels, he picked Kent up on a Friday evening to head out for some fun.

Dinner was a couple of double bacon cowboy burgers and a chat about their current crushes, Jennifer Valencia and Courtney Gendron. Both Greg and Kent were sixteen, neither of them having a single clue about women, love, or even being romantic, and it showed. All they could do was giggle and laugh as they chowed down their greasy meal, joking, "Oh, the things I'd like to do to her," and "I bet she's great at giving head," letting their immaturity be heard by anyone else in the eatery.

After they stuffed their faces, Greg and Kent headed to the local fun park, Scandia, for two rounds of miniature golf. Throughout their years as friends, whenever things got rough and they needed one another, the serious conversations always began during a game of mini-golf. They'd make their way through the course with ease, until they reached the most frustrating hole, a flat piece of fake felt-like grass with a giant volcano-*ish* mound in the middle. In order to win the round, you had to successfully tap the ball up the side of the hilly structure and down into the hole which sat like an ice-cream cone in the center. The trick was to hit the ball just hard enough to get over the lip of the hill without causing it to roll over and out the other side, where the ball would wander off a good ten or so feet, causing you to have to try again.

The really scary feature of the their favorite hole was the fact that directly next to the golf course was the 15 freeway, and if the hill proved to be more than either could handle, Greg or Kent could smack their ball with all their might, using the irritating hill as a ramp, and sending the ball out into the middle of unsuspecting 65 mile per hour traffic. Thankfully, on this night both Greg and Kent were able to get their golf ball into the difficult hole after only a few attempts.

When golf had become a bore, Greg and Kent headed to the Ontario AMC movie theater; a thirty-screen multiplex attached to the Ontario Mills Mall, to see the new Godzilla film. It doesn't take much to entertain teenage boys, and a less than stellar monster thrashing through New York City easily did the trick. After the credits rolled and the pathetic mocking ended, Greg drove Kent home. Outside of Kent's parents' house they shared a few more laughs, including another jab at Kent for not having a car.

"You know what?" Kent asked Greg with as serious a face as a teenage boy could have, "I hope your car blows up on the way home." Then Kent, with his feelings apparently hurt, turned and stormed through the front door of his parents' home, slamming it behind him. On any other day this would seem like nothing, but this wasn't any other day.

Greg retraced his route back to the freeway, made his way into the first lane, and proceeded towards home. Everything was great. He and Kent had a lot of fun and Greg had won both rounds of mini-golf. However, Kent would have the last laugh.

About half of a mile before the off-ramp for Foothill Boulevard, Greg heard a loud pop followed by a column of smoke billowing out from under the hood of his car. Greg quickly swerved over to the breakdown lane and got out of the vehicle. His car was on fire.

With no idea what to do, and with Greg not getting his first cell phone until he was twenty-one, he began to walk towards the call-box just a tenth of a mile from where his car was left burning. Unfortunately, Greg never reached the call-box to get an emergency vehicle out to his car. Ten feet before he reached the yellow box on a pole, another vehicle, an old Ford model truck, swung into the breakdown lane heading straight at Greg, with a young ignorant, and seemingly drunk teenager screaming noises like that of a Banshee at Greg. Startled by both the truck and the screaming, Greg tried to take a step back, where his foot hooked the curb at the edge of the freeway, sending him down the steep hill upon which the freeway sits.

The trip down through brush, dirt, thorn bushes, and various pieces of littered trash ended as Greg's body rolled forcefully into a chain-linked fence extending the length of that stretch of freeway. Greg was able to get up and dust himself off. The scratches, though bleeding, were minor. At the end of the fence near the off-ramp Greg had intended to take, he could see Wal-Mart was still open. His goal now was to walk the half mile to the road and make his way towards the payphones outside of the store. However, and again unfortunately, there was a coyote standing between Greg and his path to safety, looking at Greg as if he was a meal sent from the heavens.

The rabid-looking dog-like creature never did attack, though he followed him all the way to the road while Greg gingerly proceeded expecting to be mauled at any second. He was able to call his mother, who collected Greg from a bench outside of the store, and they traveled back to his car, which was no longer burning. A tow-truck brought the torched Escort to Greg's home and left it at the end of the driveway. Greg would later learn that his engine had indeed exploded.

The following day, Greg called Kent to make sure he was home, and then arranged to have his mother drive him over to Kent's house under the guise of spending a day playing video games. Upon their arrival, Greg knocked on the front door, and when Kent opened it to greet his guest, Greg punched him square in the nose and left.

Eleven years later, after his best night of sleep, and following the most unusual week of his life, Greg is knocking on Kent's door again.

"You aren't going to hit me, are you?" Kent Lawson asks from the other side of the door, mostly joking.

"I suppose that depends on whether or not you have it coming," Greg responds sarcastically. "You don't have anything to do with my insane Doctor do you?"

"What Doctor?" Kent asks, opening the door to invite his best friend in, exchanging a brotherly hug.

Kent Lawson is just over five and a half feet tall, muscular build, with a crooked lump on the bridge of his nose. He lives in Southridge Village at the far end of Fontana, California. His home is another typical cookie-cutter-model on a postage stamp lot in the dry hills, which often appear in the news engulfed in flames. Kent's parents moved out of town, leaving their house to their oldest child.

"It was a joke," says Greg, "I know you don't know about my Doctors."

"We're talking plural now, Doctors?" Kent hands Greg a beer as they make their way to the barstools just beyond the kitchen. "You know I've been getting some calls wondering where the hell you've been. Your mom's worried sick. She said it's not like you to go days without talking to her."

"That's why I'm here," says Greg. "I went to see a psych-specialist about a week or so ago. I don't even remember how long ago it was now." Greg still doesn't know what day it is.

"A psych Doctor?" Kent's ears perk up. "You trying to have your fortune read again?" He refers to Greg's previous encounter with The Master, about which Kent still remains skeptical, assuming Greg just had too much to drink that night.

"A psychiatrist actually," says Greg, his eyes squinting at Kent's candor, "but thanks for the support."

"It's about time you got yourself some help," Kent says. "I told you that last year. I even told you that back when you were hung up on that *Jeanne* girl that nobody you know ever met." He has a way with words when it comes to his long-time friend.

"Look Kent," says Greg sternly, "I need you to be serious. Can you do that?"

"You know what that means don't you?" Kent asks, assuming they'll be heading to the Scandia for some rounds of putting.

"I really can't today," says Greg in return, "I know it's where we always go, but things have been crazy, and I don't know who else I can trust."

"Okay man," says Kent, disappointed. He really thought it was his turn to be victorious. "Hit me. What's going on?"

Greg starts from the beginning and tells Kent about everything; the creature in the dark that has haunted him for several years and the nightmares that started as a child; the many Doctors who have told him he's crazy; him seeking out Dr. Campos; the Doctor kidnapping and torturing him; his impending doom being around the corner; the potential fact that Jeanne Burns never existed, at least not when and where Greg thought she did; Francis Armand Dubois; being released in the middle of the desert; and now standing in Kent's house unleashing it all as if it were a connect-the-dot sequence in a Quentin Tarantino film.

Ring. Greg's phone alerts him of an incoming call.

Ring. "It's him," Greg says to Kent, "the crazy Doctor who tortured me."

"Well don't answer it stupid," says Kent, rolling his eyes.

Ring. "Hello," Greg rarely takes Kent's advice.

Chapter 55

Someone in Greg's office made the first phone call. At twenty-seven years of age, he had passed away. There had been an accident, and the understanding was that Greg had died at the scene. The first person to find out called another co-worker, and with few people having Greg's contact information, the endless game of phone-tag began.

The primary contact in his personnel file, in the event of an emergency, was Greg's mother, but her phone number was no longer in order. An office manager was contacted, but she didn't have the information needed to make the next call. Instead, a few more calls were placed to others that were higher up in Greg's circle of friends. One of them had his mother's new number, and so the woman "in the know" placed the call. Naturally, nobody answered. The message that was left said to return the call immediately upon receipt.

While the time passed, the word began to spread; news of a colleague's sudden demise left a bad taste in the office's collective mouths. More details were not available, and tears began to fall. Who knew that when everyone wished Greg a good weekend, it would be the last time anyone would see him? What would everyone have said if they knew he would not be returning? Was he going to be missed? Now that Greg was gone, did everyone know what they had in him as a friend, as a family member, as a co-worker?

A couple hours after the message had been left on her answering machine; Marion Roberts retrieved and returned the urgent call without any delay. The messenger made an inquiry regarding Greg's health. Somewhat confused by the entire ordeal, his mother stated that, to the best of her knowledge, he was doing well. The messenger began to question Marion's certainty, and asked her if Greg owned a motorcycle? Even more confused at that point, she responded with, "no."

After telling Marion Roberts that her oldest son had supposedly met his maker a couple of towns over, denial became the response. Still unsure about what made Greg's mother so certain, the caller asked her how she knew that Greg was okay? It was at that time that Marion explained a recent phone call she'd had with her son Greg between the time of the first message and the returned call.

Greg never owned a motorcycle, nor did he consider owning one. However, on that day, there was an accident in Upland. A middle-aged gentleman was killed when his motorcycle struck another vehicle and the impact shredded his body like cheese in a food processor. As the police went to inspect the rider's belongings, Greg's business card was discovered among them. How that led anyone to believe that he was the one harmed will likely remain a mystery forever.

He never told me about this. Amber D'Marco exits the article about the misreported death, returning to her search on Google.com, looking for answers to her many questions about her newly-mysterious fiancé. She had decided to get a cup of coffee at her favorite café, the one where Greg picked her up for their first official date. The coffee shop has free Wi-Fi internet, and Amber is running low on energy.

She clicks on another link, taking her to another news report; this time Greg really was involved in an accident. A passenger train struck his car, which had stalled on the tracks, and before he could exit the vehicle, the train sent him flying more than a hundred feet. Amber shakes her head in shock.

Gregory Allen Roberts was pronounced dead at the scene.

Amber continues clicking away, article after article, eventually finding one she simply can't believe.

Man's body missing after terrible accident. Local authorities remain clueless.

Gregory Allen Roberts presumed dead.

Nothing is adding up. In one article Greg was thought to be dead, but it wasn't him. Then he was in another terrible accident and determined to be dead before paramedics could help. Now the papers say his body went missing.

Disgusted with everything she sees, she decides to write down the names of all the newspapers that had anything relating to the stories she found online, and finally it hits her like a backhand across the face. The dates of all the articles are nearly ten years old. Certain there's a better explanation, Amber does what virtually nobody does anymore; she gets in her rental car and heads for the local law library.

Chapter 56

"Mr. Roberts," says Dr. Campos, echoing through Kent's kitchen, "how are you feeling?"

"What do you want Doc?" Greg asks his caller on speakerphone, wishing he had listened to his friend's logic.

"Mr. Roberts," the Doctor responds, "I told you we'd be in touch, and here I am, getting in touch with you."

"I get that," Greg snips back into the phone, "but what do you want?"

"It's important, Mr. Roberts," says the Doctor, as calm as can be, "that you meet me at Francis' house immediately. We'd like to discuss our plan with you."

"So there's a plan now?" Completely skeptical, and with good reason, Greg can't let it all go.

"Yes, Mr. Roberts," says the Doctor, "and if you'll come join me at Francis' home –"

"I'm in the middle of something Doc," Greg stops the Doctor from finishing his sentence.

"Mr. Roberts," says the Doctor industriously, "will you please take me off of speakerphone?"

"Sorry Doc," says Greg with joyous denial, "you called me. So either hurry up, or hang up."

"Have it your way, Mr. Roberts," says the Doctor, concerned that whoever's with Greg won't understand, "I can think of nothing more important than hearing what we have to say. It may very well save your life. Now, I am asking you, please, will you come –"

"I don't even know where your brother lives," Greg cuts him off again.

Dr. Campos gives a loud sigh followed by silence, making sure Greg is paying attention. "Mr. Roberts," he says, "I programmed the directions from your home to Francis' house into your phone before we released you yesterday. Simply bring up your map application and follow the green line."

Greg ends the call without saying goodbye and without confirming he'll be on his way shortly.

"Who in the name of all things holy was that?" Kent asks, not knowing what he just overheard.

"How many times have I told you I'm not crazy?" Greg asks, and sees Kent preparing to make a sarcastic reply, "at least not as crazy as you think I am."

"Are you going to tell me who that was now?" Kent doesn't let him off the subject.

"That's the insane Doctor who took me hostage," says Greg, as if the statement is completely normal.

"You're not really going to see that man, are you?" Kent's concern for his best friend grows deeper.

"I have to," says Greg, grabbing his phone and keys, "he's the only one who seems to understand what's happening to me."

Kent would try to change his mind, but that's never worked before, and he can see by the look in Greg's eyes, it's not going to work now. Instead, he walks his best friend to his car and tells him, "You better call me after all of this is sorted out. I want to know you're okay."

"Thanks Kent," Greg says from behind the wheel of his precious Dodge Shadow, "now may be a good time for some prayers." Greg drives away.

A couple of right turns followed by a sharp left, and ten minutes of unoccupied road, Greg arrives at the home of Francis Armand Dubois, whose house is nothing like that of Dr. Campos. It's a simple villa at the end of a dead end street. There are no trees in the yard, no metal gates, and no statues. There are absolutely nothing remarkable about Francis' home. If the Doctor hadn't programmed the directions into the phone himself, Greg would assume nobody lived in the abandoned-looking house.

Greg parks by the curb at the end of the flat driveway, where Dr. Campos walks out to greet him. "Thank you, Mr. Roberts. I wasn't sure you would come." Greg doesn't respond. By now he's figured out that saying anything to the Doctor may lead to ten minutes of irrelevant bickering; a revelation Greg wishes he'd experienced when they first met.

Dr. Campos leads Greg beyond the driveway, down a walkway made of pieces of cracked stone, faded by years of sunlight, and into the home of his brother. There are three steel folding chairs, dented and misshapen, looking like they'd been used during a WWE pay-per-view to bludgeon one steroid-enhanced freak or another. Greg, Francis, and Dr. Campos each take a seat around a folding table that is covered in stains and gum, reminding Greg of his old beer-pong table, which had been broken one night, ironically, by one of his roommates who had body-slammed their other roommate through the table's center, snapping it in half. He recalls something about an argument regarding who was the better baseball player, Ted Williams or Ken Griffey Jr., which was a farce any way.

"I'm glad you could make it Greg," says Francis, placing a large toolbox-looking chest on the table between them. He opens the chest-top and removes several pipe-like pieces, one of which has a padded handle, and another has what looks like the end of a metal detector.

"What in Christ's name is that?" Greg asks, starting to remember how Joe Pesci was offed in Goodfellas, in an empty house in the middle of nowhere.

I don't see any plastic tarps.

"Greg," says Francis, "I'm going to give you a brief lesson about the *thing* that is after you. Let us not argue over any of the details, and just listen to what I'm about to tell you."

Greg nods his head in agreement and waits patiently.

Francis Armand Dubois goes on to explain that there is nothing fancy about metal detectors. They utilize varying radio frequencies, and when pointed in the direction of a conductive metal, an audible tone sounds through a pair of headphones worn by the detector's operator. The tones vary depending on the conductivity levels of the metal being detected. For example, Iron and Aluminum Foil have some of the lowest conductivity levels, which cause low audible tones to ring through the detector; and

Silver has one of the highest levels of conductivity, which causes a higher audible tone to ring through the detector.

"That's great, but –"

"Greg," Francis stops him, "we have an agreement. Please, let me finish."

Francis continues his presentation by telling his audience of two that the creature that is after Greg, while able to vaporize into thin air and disappear from this world, emits an extremely low level of conductivity. *Its* conductivity is so low that the average metal detector would never be able to detect it. However, the now constructed set of pipes on the table is a modified metal detector; one that Francis was able to craft from his knowledge of the demon-like being, which he has gained over his several years spent in *Its'* world. As fate would have it, Francis Armand Dubois has created a means to detect where the *thing* that is going to kill Greg is located.

"Excellent brother!" Dr. Campos exclaims.

"Whoa, whoa, whoa." Greg interjects, "not so fast. How far out can this thing detect?" He assumes the answer will be less than impressive.

"You're quick Greg," says Francis, impressed. "As you're likely assuming, that *thing* can only be detected within a range of," he bobs his head back and forth, coming up with an estimate, "probably a maximum of five feet."

"So –" Greg's sentence is finished as soon as it starts.

"It will have to get next to you for us to help you." Francis' words cause Greg to gulp in fear.

While Greg looks on in disbelief, Francis goes on to explain that he's equipped the metal detector with an Electromagnetic Pulse device, or *EMP*. The plan is, in short, to wait for Greg's birthday to arrive, and when the dark creature comes to take him, Greg will alert Francis, who will then set off the EMP. For a reason that isn't explained, Francis believes the EMP will disorient Greg's assailant.

Francis carries on, describing an extra feature of the EMP-capable metal detector. In addition to detecting and disabling demons, it also comes with an evaporation-based stun gun not from this world. During his decades abroad, Francis studied a water-evaporating system used in the creature's alternate world, which allows one to fire water through a semi-hose of a tube, similar to the one built into the pipe-like handle of the metal detector, and upon firing out of the tube, the customized low radio frequency at which the creature from the shadows can be detected sends an immeasurable amount of energy through every atom of water, causing it to simultaneously vaporize, taking just an infinitesimal bit of the dust found in almost all air-filled environments of this world, and turning it into a microscopic powder. Then, if the vaporized powder shot hits its mark, Francis has an undisclosed weapon, about which he says nothing else, which will destroy the evil that intends to kill Greg.

"You're insane," says Greg, feeling like he's talking to a prominent writer of Science-Fiction novels, "and yet, I almost believe you. What does that say about me?"

"*Almost*, Greg?" Francis is disappointed, certain that his plan is near-perfect.

"Well yeah," says Greg, "I just fall short of belief knowing that I all but have to let this thing kill me before you can do anything about it."

"*It*, Mr. Roberts," says Dr. Campos, who Greg had forgotten was even in the room, "is going to kill you if we do nothing."

Greg takes a deep breath, his knees knocking with anxiety.

"Can I take your lack of response as agreement Greg?" Francis asks.

"I need a night guys," says Greg. "I know we're short on time. I know my birthday is in a few days. But I need to sleep on it. Can I give you my answer in the morning?"

Francis looks at his brother, worrying again that, once Greg leaves them, he may never come back. Dr. Campos looks back with the same determination she had on their less than happy trip back from the desert, and Francis takes what his brother said about trusting him to heart. "Sure, Greg," he says in a moment of blind faith.

Back in his car, thinking about the outlandish idea he is to consider, Greg heads for home. He knows the hour must be late, because there isn't another car on the road. Then again, Francis did live on an abandoned road. The Dodge Shadow chugs through the neighborhood and back across town.

At the end of Greg's street there is a set of railroad tracks in the middle of a field of dirt. They used to be blocked by a large brick wall, but amidst the many shopping district additions, the wall had been removed, and the street had been extended the extra mile down to the local stores. It's one of the few changes Greg ever approved of in his life, as if his opinion actually matters. Tonight, as his car rolls on, almost crossing into his block, Greg sees a woman sitting in the middle of the tracks; it's Jeanne Burns.

Stopping to take a closer look, Greg leans his head out the driver-side window, and his engine stalls out. Alarmed by the notion that his trusty steed has quit on him, he turns the key in the ignition, praying the engine will turn back over; but nothing happens. The Dodge Shadow has driven its last mile; and, sitting in his seat, overwhelmed by the last straw breaking, Greg curses at the heavens above.

"Son-of-a-bitch! God dammit! Mother-fucker!"

The profanities spew one after another like rounds firing from a machine gun. Greg kicks and screams, throwing his fists forward in a fit, eventually punching his rearview mirror, sending a charge of vibrations into the windshield which cracks, leaving a massive web of glass to look through. Then, when Greg has expelled all of his anger and energy, he unbuckles his seatbelt, and as he turns to open his door, the lead car of the night's last commuter train plows into the dead vehicle, sending Greg and most of the Dodge Shadow flying down the track as the Amtrak tries to stop.

When the smoke and passenger screams subside, the conductor steps down from the train, sprinting towards the limp body among the wreckage, yelling at someone on the other end of her radio to send an ambulance to their location.

Greg Roberts may not see his twenty-eighth birthday after all.

Chapter 57

Amber D'Marco remembers the research project from her senior year of high school. She and three other students created a ten minute skit summarizing the Manhattan Project, which eventually led to the atomic bombings of Hiroshima and Nagasaki, Japan. They always liked the library, because every newsworthy story, no matter how relevant, both locally and nationally, was kept on microfiche and archived in a special section of the fortress of a building Amber now enters.

She finds her way towards the far back corner, where the old technologies, such as physical newspapers, are kept. She's required to give her photo ID and pay a nominal fee of $10.00, which allows her to view any articles she desires, with the option to print up to 100 pages before having to submit an additional fee.

The microfiche is stored electronically which is nice, because it will allow Amber to look for the pages she seeks, and with the press of a button, a robotic arm will deliver the film-stored pages like a CD in a jukebox.

The process takes Amber all of ten minutes. She finds every article from every local paper for the year; only that year was ten years ago.

The downside to sifting through printed pages is that you can't perform any sort of word search or shortcut. You literally have to read through page after page until you hopefully find what you're looking for. It takes Amber nearly six hours and three lattes, but later, rather than sooner, she lands on the one she's looking for.

A man fitting Greg's description down to the slightly gapped front teeth did go missing. Much like the pages on the internet suggested, the authorities had no idea what happened. There was an accident, but not the one involving at train. This accident was days later in the middle of nowhere.

Amber notes the source, *The Associated Press*, shocker; and then moves on to the next paper for the same date. It too tells the story of a man gone missing following an accident. As does the next paper, and the next, and the next. There's mention of a previous accident, as well as Greg's almost comical near-death experience, in which he wasn't even involved.

Then Amber reads something unusual; the local authorities made reference to another missing person, Jeanne Burns, who had disappeared almost ten years prior. She too was never found.

Strangely, what stands out the most about all of the stories, which are all supported by the same source, is the other people who were found at the scene of the accident. One, a man Amber doesn't recognize and doesn't care about; and two, a retired psychiatrist by the name of Emmanuel Campos. Her hand lets go of the fourth latte, sending burning hot liquid down her chest and into her lap.

I must speak to that Doctor.

Chapter 58

Clink. Clink. Clink.

"Help!" Greg cries out. "Somebody help me."

Clink. Clink. Clink. He tries to use his arms to flag for help, but through the dizziness and fog he doesn't realize he's handcuffed to the bed.

"Please help me!" He screams again.

"Now, now, Mr. Roberts," a friendly nurse says, rubbing his forehead gently, "I need you to settle down. Can you do that for me?"

Greg tries to look at the kind woman speaking, but the world is only shades and colors. "Who are you?" He asks. "Where am I? What happened?"

"Just calm down, Mr. Roberts," the nurse continues rubbing his head, "Everything is okay. You just had a little, well," she stops herself, "I'll let the Doctor tell you about all that."

"Doctor!" Greg yells. "What Doctor? No! I don't want to see that man again. Please, not Dr. Campos. He's a lunatic!" Images of a needle stabbing him in the eye cause him to tense up.

"Sir, Mr. Roberts, please, you need to calm down." The nurse, removing her hand now, sharpens her tone. "I have to get the Doctor. He'll know what to do."

Greg tries to shake himself free. He'll do anything to cut himself loose so he can flee from that madman, neglecting the fact that he can't see a damn thing. He would rather run face first into a wood chipper than spend another minute in the care of Dr. Emmanuel Campos.

"Is there a problem here Mr. Roberts?" A man with a thick accent from India asks.

"Who's there?" Greg snaps. "What's happening to me? Why can't I see?"

The short man stretches his arms out from his lab coat, grabbing Greg's medical chart. He flips through a few pages, listening to the nurse whispering in his ear.

"I am Dr. Rajib, Mr. Roberts," the little man says, difficult to understand. "There's no need to fuss. The restraints are for your own protection."

Restraints? What restraints? Is that why I can't move? Question, after question assault Greg's mind.

"It says here, Mr. Roberts," the heavily accented Doctor continues, "that you tried to commit suicide by parking your vehicle in front of a train."

"That's a lie!" Greg tries to jerk himself free again with no luck. "My car stalled, and now I'm here." His wrists start to bleed from the constant tugging against the handcuffs.

Dr. Rajib goes on to tell Greg that his car stalling precisely in the center of the tracks is awfully coincidental, and that fact isn't the only unusual piece of information about Greg's current status in the hospital. When Greg arrived, having just returned from five minutes among the dead, he began ranting about a missing woman, Jeanne Burns, who he believed was dead, but had appeared on the tracks a moment before he stopped his car. When the police officers who followed the ambulance from the site of the accident were cuffing him to the bed, Greg started shouting obscenities, raving about an evil Doctor and his insane sibling sidekick. Nothing coming from Greg's mouth made any sense.

While everything sounded like the ramblings of a mad man, the officers were required to report the claims in case there was any validity to the statements. As it turns out, there is an old cold case. A woman, Jeanne Burns, did go missing about ten years ago, and the authorities never found any evidence to help them find her. Additionally, the only person, aside from her Doctor, who had ever said anything to the police about a missing woman of that name was Greg, four years after her disappearance.

"Sons of bitches!" Greg screams again, now rocking his bed back and forth, hoping it will break him free as it topples over and crashes to the floor.

Dr. Rajib urgently calls for a team of orderlies. Greg is struggling to breath as the weight of the hospital bed is pressing him into the floor, pushing the oxygen from his lungs. A group of well-groomed men dressed in white and blue scrubs rush into the room and act without further instruction. They're able to quickly grab the four corners of the bed and tip it up, allowing air to flow back into Greg, burning like fire rushing along a kerosene soaked path. With Greg still touching the ground and the bed propped up slightly above his body, the police officer steps in, and as Dr. Rajib administers an injection he explains what he is about to do.

"Mr. Roberts," he says, "I'm going to sedate you. Then the officer will free you from your restraints. These men will escort you to the psych ward on the other end of the building, which is where you will be when you wake up. I'm sorry to do this to you Mr. Roberts, but until you're stable, and until we're better able to assess the situation, we must admit you for your own good."

Greg's mind tells him to fight, but he can barely move, still gasping for air. The burning of the oxygen making its way back into his lungs blocks the pain of the needle in his neck. Again, Greg's world goes black.

Chapter 59

The psychiatric wing of the hospital looks more like a remodeled hotel that was never finished than any type of medical unit. The floors are pea-soup-green linoleum, old and cracked, peeling from every corner, and stained with black mold. There are plenty of windows, but each is covered in flaking lead-based paint, and like most hotel windows on upper floors, they don't open, which, given the current inhabitants, is a bonus.

Each of the patients, if that's what you want to call them, gets out of their beds at the sound of a bull-horn right around sunrise and walks out to the only common room, where first they line up for their morning medications, fed by way of tiny paper *Dixie* cups.

Once dosed, the inhabitants gather around various round tables, also topped in linoleum, standing atop rusty bowed legs. Some tables have checkers or chess waiting for anxious players, while others have dominoes and decks of cards. For those not interested in bingo-less social gatherings, three rows of folding chairs sit by a corner beneath a television, which tunes to one channel, PBS. These are the choices, day after day.

If you aren't crazy before you arrive, you will be by the time you leave.

Determined he's going to find a way out on day one, Greg Roberts stands up on what he believes to be the sturdiest of the dated tables.

"Everybody," he calls out to his fellow cuckoo birds. "Aren't you tired of this place?"

The group just looks at him, heads tilted, as though Greg is a strange alien from a planet unknown.

"Yeah!" A short old man, covered in his own drool, shouts out from the back of the room.

"Aren't you sick of being told where you can and can't go?" Greg continues what's beginning to look like a motivational speech.

"Yeah!" Another patient, a younger woman with a shaved head joins in.

"Aren't you tired of eating pills from a cup three times a day?"

"Yeah!" The support grows to five patients.

"Wouldn't you like to take control from these, *oppressors?*" Greg pushes his crowd a bit further. "Wouldn't you like to show our captors that we won't stand for their tyranny?"

"Yeah!" All but one of the nuts chimes in with agreement.

"So who's ready to bust out of here?" Greg looks down at eighteen pairs of hands. He knows most of them can't improve their circumstances, and that some even belong on the unit; but he does not belong here, and he will do whatever it takes to break free. "Then come with me!"

Greg hops down from the table, a band of crazies behind him in support. He trudges across the common room, heading straight for the first nurse he sees.

Veronica Belmont graduated two months ago. The youngest daughter of a local contractor, she completed high school early and immediately entered nursing school, where she studied hard and became the youngest student in school history to complete the courses and become a Registered Nurse.

While flying through nursing school is a feat, the first job she could land was on the psychiatric wing of her local hospital. It's her first day on the job, and when she turns around from the nursing station to find Greg Roberts fist connecting with her jaw, she realizes she isn't meant to be a nurse.

Veronica's body drops, unconscious before she hits the floor, with four teeth dribbling out of her mouth on the way down. The crowd just looks on in amazement. They were ready to follow Greg out the front doors, but they didn't consider the fact that they'd have to assault anyone along the way.

With the room quickly in disarray, the receptionist sitting behind bullet-proof glass at the med counter hits a red button hidden under the corner of her desk, causing several red lights to flash throughout the unit, which are accompanied by the screeching sounds of the security alarms.

Being that the majority of the committed patients suffer from one mental deficiency or another, when the full-scale alert begins, the doped-up crowd becomes both frightful and enraged.

Timmy Evans, the fat slob that he is, starts smacking himself in the head, screaming for the nightmare to end.

Sammy Quinto, an average sized man who has the strength of ten men when he gets rattled, lifts Ella Tremblay, a paranoid deaf mute with violent tendencies, who happens to be just shy of seventy years old, over his head, and tosses her like a sack of potatoes across the room. Along with Ella's left arm and hip, the floor breaks her fall and knocks her dentures out.

Johnny Cunningham, the evil genius of the group, standing a dominant five feet tall, grabs one of the chairs beneath the TV, folds it up to better wield it like a weapon, and as the male orderlies and security guards make their way into the room, Johnny unloads.

He swings the brown metal chair like a baseball bat, with his hands gripping the legs tightly together. His first haul connects with the bridge of a security guard's nose, sending streams of blood shooting forward, where they eventually land on the orderly in front of him.

Johnny rears back and swings again, this time hitting Donna Pintone, a mid-twenties suicide survivor with blonde hair, square in the throat, crushing her wind pipe. Donna grabs at her neck with both hands, choking, as the life escapes from her with each passing second.

Finally, a second wave of help arrives, each member carrying tasers which are aimed at the most violent offenders among the group. Greg sees the scene as it's about to unfold and starts to run at the security guard closest to him, shouting profanities the entire way. His less than quiet approach gives away his attack, and as soon as the electric current renders him unable to control his seizing, the rest of the room comes to a complete standstill.

Timmy, Sammy, and Johnny all throw their hands to the sky, with the brown chair dropping to the ground. Donna Pintone is gone, though a team of nurses is rushing to do what is ultimately a waste of time. Donna finally got her wish. Ella Tremblay continues to cry out in agony. The riot is over.

Patients are remanded to their "rooms" for the remainder of the day. Greg uses his time alone to plan his next attempt for the following morning.

Chapter 60

After three days of breaking windows, throwing chairs, and organizing his fellow nuthouse residents to riot, Greg is sedated again.

"Take him to room S-5," says Dr. Rajib, looking down into Greg's glazed-over eyes. "We have no other choice. I don't think the man formerly known as Greg Roberts is in there at all."

Room S-5 looks like an old supply closet that has been gutted. The ceiling sags from old water damage, there are holes drilled into various points in the wall where supply shelves used to be, and the floor is covered in stains even the Doctors can't identify. However, two years ago, with the help of some wealthy friends in the state legislature, Dr. Rajib was able to get a statute passed, allowing his hospital to perform Electroconvulsive Therapy (ECT) on disadvantaged patients suffering from extreme breaks in reality; breaks like the one Dr. Rajib believes Greg has suffered.

The bulky male orderlies fasten Greg to a flat table in the middle of the disgusting room. With straps around his wrists, elbows, biceps, ankles, knees, and quadriceps, as well as two straps around his waist and lower chest, Greg is going nowhere. The final piece is an archaic headpiece that fits like the type of helmet piece a man being executed in an electric chair might wear.

Once Greg is set to go, Dr. Rajib places two paddles, each at the end of a long rubber-wrapped bar, to Greg's temples. Each paddle is connected with a wire to a machine that looks like an old-era radio that has a set of knobs protruding from the front. With no hesitation at all, the Doctor gives a nod to his assisting nurse, who turns the nob to 800 milliamps. Dr. Rajib can see Greg's eyes flutter.

What the hell is George thinking?

That's the first conscious thought in Greg's mind. He'd just rolled out of bed at the crack of noon, dressed nicely in some old tattered sweat pants and a well-worn t-shirt, unlocked the door to his man cave, and proceeded to the ever so tiny area known as the living-room. There George sat, slouched down in his chair with a giant glass of orange juice in one hand and Greg's birth right in the other. Greg was the first-born son. That remote belonged to him. Naturally, Greg dashed over to him like a hobo trying to catch a train out of town at dusk, made his presence known, and stole back that which was his. The little man in George tried to fight it, but Greg was not going to lose the real-man challenge. George had lost the battle before it had even begun.

Several studies have contemplated what it means to be a man. Greg once knew a guy named Chris, who had very few friends, and Greg understood why. In Chris' mind, he was a man's man, whatever that *cliché* was supposed to imply. Most of Chris' life was spent talking about guns, arguing about politics, and watching porn. If you were a male and didn't do all of those things at least once each day, Chris would contend that you were not a real man.

When the pilgrims landed in North America and then later created colonies, things were done in a very specific manner. The man of the house worked to provide for his family day in and day out, while the woman of the house cooked, cleaned, and took care of the children. When a man woke up in the morning, it was the woman's job to make sure that his clothes were clean and ready for him to wear. It was also the woman's job to make sure that the man of the house came home to find a warm meal waiting for him. Hunting, socializing, speaking, decision making, fighting wars, and many other things were all for the men to do.

If you were to ask a truly neutral party, he or she might argue that women were the original slaves of white men, but it wouldn't last that way forever. Women gained some rights a few centuries later. Until the twentieth century, men were really the only people with any power in this country. Obviously things aren't as extreme as they once were, but they won't permanently vanish either.

Nowadays, some people think it's football and beer, while others may just think it's chewing tobacco and scratching their genitalia. For thirteen-year-old Greg Roberts, being a man was ownership of the remote control. George was nine and Greg knew he couldn't stop him from having it.

When Greg wakes from his brain therapy the next day, the last thing he remembers is standing over his brother George, sitting there, slouched down in his chair, with a giant glass of orange juice in one hand, the remote in Greg's, and nothing else.

Chapter 61

Amber D'Marco parks her rental car at the end of the driveway in front of the home of Dr. Emmanuel Campos, a man who, in Amber's opinion, is the key to explaining everything that is happening with her future husband Greg.

Dr. Campos' home is no longer the spectacle it once was. Gone are the tall marble columns. Gone are the smoke-breathing gargoyles and electrically-charged gates. There are no more vines, and daylight illuminates the path to the front door with ease. All of the things that gave this once cryptic home its allure is gone. When Dr. Campos' health faded, his insurance had to have the house renovated, inside and out, to allow for medical access, day and night. Now, aside from its still massive size, Dr. Campos' house looks like any other home in an average neighborhood, which, on this block, makes it stand out like a black eye.

Knock, knock, knock, Amber taps her knuckles to the cream-colored front door.

I better get some answers, she thinks to herself, waiting for someone to greet her; but nobody responds. There isn't a noise that she can hear from where she stands.

Knock, knock, knock, her hands wrap harder against the door this time. Again, nobody answers.

Amber steps back from the door and looks up to a window on the second floor, where she can see someone close a set of blinds.

Someone is home.

She waits another moment, assuming whomever she saw will be opening the door soon; but she's wrong. Nobody is coming.

"I know someone's in there," Amber calls out to the house, now pressing the doorbell she'd failed to notice when she first arrived. "Hello!" She continues pressing the button and shouting, her anger growing by the second. Then Amber balls her fist, preparing to punch the door, and as she pulls her arm back to throw her entire body behind her grenade-like hand, the door flies open; but it's too late. Amber punches the scrawny old woman in the doorway right in the eye, sending her backwards and to the floor.

"Oh my God!" Amber cries out. "Are you okay? I'm so sorry. I didn't even –"

"What do you want young lady?" The woman asks from the tile, apparently unfazed by the blow to her head. She slowly rises from the ground, and Amber tries to help her up. "Don't touch me!" She snaps. "You've done quite enough."

"I really didn't mean to," Amber feels terrible. She's just assaulted an elderly woman for no reason.

"Let us step outside," says Miss Paxon, holding her left eye, which is already starting to swell.

"I think we should get some ice," says Amber, trying to be helpful. "Is there any ice in the kitchen? Can I go get some for you?"

"No!" Miss Paxon snaps. "You may not enter the house. It's not safe." She pulls the door closed behind her as they walk out to the front steps.

"What do you mean it's not safe?" Amber asks. "Is something wrong inside?" Skeptical about every person she speaks to, Amber worries she's about to be sent away empty handed, again.

"The master of the house is not well," says the coarse sounding senior citizen. "Any visitors increase his risk of infection. So," she continues, "we don't allow anyone in the house. But you can speak to me. What brings you here?" Miss Paxon guides Amber over to a small bench by the front yard, where both of them take a seat.

"My name's Amber," she replies. "I called here recently, but–"

"I hung up on you," says Miss Paxon coyly. "I do apologize for that. The master of the house was ill that day, and those damn telemarketers, they act as if they have no souls at all."

Amber is stunned by the old lady's words. "You don't need to apologize to me," she says, "I'm the one who just decked you." She tries to get a look at Miss Paxon's eye, but she's keeping it covered for the moment.

"I guess we're even then," the old woman chuckles. "So, Amber, what brings you here?"

Amber starts her story from the day Greg left. She explains the attempts to reach out to friends and family, the weird feeling she keeps getting, the hallucination she had in her bedroom, and the fact that Greg is missing again now. Just talking about it brings all of the emotions up from the past, however many days, she can't even recall.

"What did you say your fiancé's name is again?" Miss Paxon asks, almost stumbling over the words.

"His name is Greg," Amber replies, "Greg Roberts. I'm told he's a patient of Dr. Campos."

Miss Paxon's right eye widens, the left remains hidden by her hand. "Oh boy," she says. "You believe Mr. Roberts is a patient of Dr. Campos, *now?*" The old woman's voice crackles at the thought of what Amber's implying.

"Well, I did," says Amber. "However, I'm not so sure what's going on at this point." She goes on to tell all of the details of her internet search for articles pertaining to Greg, which led her to the library, where she studied several pieces of microfiche, and in the end, the stories all suggested Greg disappeared a decade ago. "I'm at a loss with it all, and I'm just hoping someone can explain what's happening."

"I see," says Miss Paxon in a disturbed tone. "The master always said someone would come looking for him; Greg that is. Can you wait here dear? I'm going to get something that may be of use to you."

Amber nods with approval, as Miss Paxon gets up from the bench and makes her way back into the house, closing and locking the door once inside.

Finally, some answers.

She finds the wrinkly-skinned dwarf of a woman, with silver hair and rotted teeth, quite peculiar, but given some of the recent days' events, nothing should come as a shock. All she wants is the truth, which seems to be the one thing nobody wants to give her.

About five minutes pass and Amber hears the door unlock before it reopens. Miss Paxon returns with a sandwich bag full of ice pressed against her eye in one hand, and a small yellow envelope, approximately six inches by six inches, in her other hand.

"Dr. Campos would like you to have this," Miss Paxon says, handing the envelope to Amber.

"I –" Amber struggles to find the words, "I don't get it. What is this?"

Miss Paxon proceeds to tell Amber a story, a story that she won't possibly be able to understand, at least not until she returns home and reviews the contents of the envelope she's just been given. Nevertheless, Miss Paxon tells Amber about Dr. Campos' last two patients: a woman named Jeanne Burns, who disappeared a good twenty years ago; and Greg Roberts, a man who Dr. Campos thought he could save, but who also disappeared, about ten years after Jeanne Burns.

"That's crazy!" Amber exclaims. "We're supposed to be getting married. What you're saying can't even be possible." She's beside herself, filled with frustration, feeling like she's wasted another trip.

"I know what I say seems that way," says Miss Paxon, "But, if the man you are to marry is who you say he is, the contents of that envelope should give you some answers." The elderly woman then returns to the house, closing and locking the door again, and Amber is left sitting in the front yard, alone, more confused than ever before.

With little other option, Amber has to return to her rental car and drive home.

Chapter 62

Greg, still recouping from having his brain fried, is introduced to a man he swears he's never seen before.

"This is Dr. Campos, Greg," says the orderly escorting him to the front desk in a condescending tone. "He's going to be taking care of you from now on."

When Dr. Campos found out his only patient, following a terrible accident with a train, had been committed to the psych wing of the local hospital, he immediately went to the courts to get an order issued to have Greg placed in his custody. Now, having signed all of the proper release forms at the reception desk, the Doctor is waiting to take his patient home.

"Happy Birthday Greg," says the Doctor, an attempted friendly smile on his face. "Do you remember me?"

Greg shakes his head violently, like a child in denial.

"That's right," says a nearby nurse, "Greg's twenty-eight today. How exciting."

If she only knew.

"That's okay," says the Doctor, "I'm going to take you away from this place. Would you like that?"

"Yes," says Greg softly, his eyes widening with hope, "yes please."

A nursing aid brings Dr. Campos a wheel chair to make the transportation easier. Greg sits down and tries to roll away, but he bumps into the wall a few feet away.

"Now, now," says the Doctor, leaning over to whisper in Greg's ear, "Mr. Roberts, I need you to behave yourself until we get to the van." He smiles back at the orderlies, the receptionist, the nursing aid, and a handful of schizophrenics looking on to pass the time. Then he pushes Greg in the wheel chair down the hall to the nearest elevator. Once inside and descending, the Doctor's tone changes in an instant.

"What in the hell were you thinking, Mr. Roberts?" He shouts at his patient, glaring into his eyes.

"Why are you yelling at me?" Greg asks clueless and scared, like a child kidnapped from a toy store. "What did I do? Where are we going? Who are you again?"

"This is no time for games, Mr. Roberts." The Doctor is in no mood to play twenty questions. "You nearly got yourself killed? Do you realize how lucky you are to be alive?"

"What?" Greg hasn't the slightest idea what the stranger is talking about.

"Are you seriously trying to tell me you don't know what's happened to you, Mr. Roberts?" The Doctor grows scared, wondering what those quacks did to him.

The elevator reaches the bottom floor. Dr. Campos pushes his patient across the lobby and through the automatic doors, out to the loading area, where a large white van sits waiting for their arrival.

"How's he doing?" Francis Armand Dubois asks from the driver's seat as Dr. Campos hoists Greg up into the back seat.

"He's not," says the Doctor, who, frankly speaking, is pissed off. "I don't know what they did to him, but he's completely out of it." With Greg buckled and ready to go, the Doctor slides the side door shut. "Let's go," he yells the command at his brother.

Francis and his brother bark back and forth at one another for the next thirty miles of road. Francis blames his brother for letting Greg go in the first place, while Dr. Campos just wants Francis to step on it. They must make it to the facility, where the components of their plan wait, assembled and ready to do the job.

"At least we got to him," says Francis, "*It* had a chance to take him as soon as midnight struck, and that damn judge friend of yours couldn't get us the paperwork we needed until this morning." He jerks the van off the road and presses the accelerator to the floor, despite the bumpy terrain.

"We need to make haste brother. Otherwise this argument is useless, wouldn't you agree?" Dr. Campos grunts his rhetorical question, fuming. "Right now we just need to get there before it's too late. Is this as fast as this heap can go?" Also rhetorical, as well as redundant.

"We'll be fine brother," says Francis, "I'm just trying to beat the sun before it disappears behind the hills completely."

The van bounces off divots in the ground, and Greg's head shakes around as if he were mounted to the dashboard as a novelty.

"Where are we going guys?" Greg asks, not really expecting an answer.

"Home Greg," says Francis, "we're going home."

"We sure do live a long way away," says Greg, seeing the never ending stretch of dirt through the windshield. "How much further until we get to your house?'

Francis looks at his brother, his eyes stabbing at Dr. Campos' face with concern. "What's wrong with him? He doesn't seem to know anything."

Dr. Campos flips through the pages of Greg's medical record the hospital had been kind enough to give him. "Shit!" He shouts. "They fried him. Those idiots!"

"What do you mean they *fried* –"

The van suddenly turns off and rolls to a slow stop and the world outside turns pitch black. Francis turns the key, but it's no use. It's as if Francis' own EMP has been used against him. Then, before anyone can react, the van is sent sailing, its back end curls up and over the front, flipping through the air. The vehicle slams back to the ground, rolling over and over, glass shattering and spitting across the desert.

Dr. Campos is ejected through the void where the windshield used to be, slamming him down to the earth, where rock and glass tear his bare arms and face apart. Fifty yards beyond his body the van rocks back and forth on top of Francis Armand Dubois's body, cutting him in two, leaving a swimming pool of blood soaking into the dry earth.

Greg, still fastened in the back seat and dazed by the accident, uses his left hand to feel for the buckle, hoping to get himself out of the decimated vehicle. Then, suddenly, the door is torn from the side of the van and sent flying across the open field. A dark, cloaked figure stands there, staring at Greg with a pair of flaming yellow and red bloodshot eyes, snarling through a mouth full of rusty razors for teeth. Greg feels the world turn ice cold, as if he were suddenly standing in Alaska, outside on Christmas day, wearing nothing but a pair of briefs. Then, whether from shock of seeing its face, or from the rush of blood to his head, Greg passes out.

"Ha, ha, ha," the demented being laughs at his prey's limp body.

Greg is taken.

Chapter 63

Back in her living room, Amber D'Marco tears the edge from the small yellow envelope that Miss Paxon gave her. Reaching her index finger and thumb inside, they emerge holding a single, unmarked disc.

What in the...

She looks at the disc, flips it over, and finds nothing to suggest what information it contains. Anxious to learn what secrets it may contain, Amber puts the disc into her DVD player, and turns on her television. Within a few seconds, a video begins to play; it's Greg, and he's all alone.

Woozy from the crash, Greg Roberts sits on a steel chair in the middle of a concrete room in front of a video camera. Tiny beads of blood drip from the gash in his brow, splashing down onto a large soot-like imprint on the ground beneath him. The room is frigid and moist, and Greg's bones hurt from the chill rolling down his spine.

He slowly lifts his head to find a giant shadow standing before him, grimacing.

"We're here at last," the demonic creature speaks with a ruthless and broken tone. "I have been waiting for you Gregory. This has been a long time coming."

Greg spits a wad of bloody mucus at his captor, which passes through him and lands near the tripod holding the camera in place.

"Who," Greg starts to ask, but stops to rephrase his question, "*what* are you?"

The filthy being gets in his face, glaring into Greg's eyes. "You know exactly *what* I am. Do you take me for a fool?" Every word comes harsher than the one before. "I have been with you every step of the way. I know that pathetic brother of your precious Dr. Campos told you about me."

"What are you talking about?" Greg asks, still unable to recall anything that's happened. "What do you want with me?"

"That's just it," the dark creature hisses at Greg, "I want *you*. And now I have you."

"What?" Greg doesn't comprehend.

Just then, the shadowy figure reaches a boney claw, his hand, out from his cloak, gripping Greg's throat with his skeleton-*esque* knuckles; and with his hostage virtually cut off from his flow of oxygen, the dark assailant leans in as close to Greg's face as possible. Its eyes press against Greg's, and as the disgusting being expels the freezing cold breath from its mouth, all of Greg's lost memories are forced back into his mind.

Suddenly, Greg remembers his first day of high school, where he met Kent; his first true love, Jeanne Burns; sitting on his grandfather's grave, praying for another lecture; being stabbed in the eye by Dr. Campos, which only led to further torture; and the prospect of being saved by Francis, who is now dead. All of it is absorbed back into Greg's memory in an instant flash of icy breath.

"Now" it says, moving slowly back from Greg's face, "Let us begin."

"Haha," Greg laughs without any humility, "I knew this was going to happen. You killed her. You killed my Jeanne. I heard it on the recording the Doctor played for me. This was always to be how it ends."

"Yes, Gregory," it says, displeased with Greg's careless tone. "This is how it ends." The shadowy beast points to the floor under the left side of Greg's chair, where Greg finds the weapon that will end his torment; a nickel-plated Colt M1911, just like the one his grandfather kept under his pillow at night.

"I suppose you expect me to pick that up?" Greg asks with a smirk on his face. The fear did not return with his memory.

"That is entirely up to you," the ghastly creature snorts.

"Why'd you do it anyway?" Greg asks. "Why, Jeanne? Why'd you use her to get to me?"

"Would you have preferred this face when you were day dreaming of making love to your *soul mate*?" The dark captor points to its gruesome mug; its eyes burning in their sockets. "Everything has gone as I saw fit," it continues. "I knew taking Jeanne would make my next victim, you Gregory, that much easier to seduce."

Greg seems confused, but also doesn't seem to care. "So you seduced me? Is that how it works?"

"The first encounter is always the hardest," says the beast, "As there is often a lot of resistance. I have to be able to infiltrate you, and that's harder to do when you run away. Hence the advantages of using a nearly flawless specimen like Jeanne Burns, but that's not everything."

Looking down, Greg now sees the gun glimmering in his left hand. He tries to let it go, but he's unable to move his fingers.

"That's the real kick in the pants," the evil being speaks in a near whisper as he moves in close to Greg's right ear. "Once I'm in, I'm in control. Ha, ha, ha."

"So, The Master," says Greg, "That's you as well?"

"No, Gregory," the creature says, "but I did leave his card on your desk. I thought it was only fair that you knew the end was coming. Again, the less you resist the truth, the easier it is for me."

Then it happens. Amber watches as the man of her dreams, alone and in a dark empty room, without any notice, and without any reasonable explanation, lifts the gun up from his side, places it again his temple, and pulls the trigger, sending bloody fragments of brain, skull, and bullet out the other side of his head. The horror causes Amber to choke on her own breath, which brings tears to her eyes and snot shoots from her nose.

"Nooooo!" She cries out, falling to her knees. The envelope falls from her hands, and a piece of paper creeps out from inside, fluttering down to the ground, facing up so she can read Dr. Campos' words:

To whomever this disc is imparted, I offer my sincerest sympathy; because, if you indeed sought out this information, it would appear as though you are next.

Epilogue

Amber D'Marco looks upon the perfect specimen, six and a half feet tall, short black hair recently cut for a leaner look, and divine hazel eyes. His shade of light mocha glistens through the beads of sweat running down his muscular legs.

She doesn't know whether to stay in the shadow and continue watching as Ronald Vincent furiously packs the remaining contents of his storage unit into the nearly full *U-Haul* trailer attached to his brand new truck, or to strike now while the rest of the city sleeps.

With everything that's happened over the past few years, Ronald has decided to leave California and head east. He doesn't have a plan *per se*, but he intends to drive across the country until he either can't drive anymore, or until something amazing presents itself as a possible future. As almost anyone is likely to do, when his mind is constantly playing tricks against him, and the world around him is out to get him, Ronald figures he can run away from all of his troubles.

Amber watches him pick up a large box, carry it over to the trailer, and then back to pick up the next, over and over, like a machine with a mission.

Not yet.

After moving the last of his belongings, Ronald takes a seat on cement post designed to keep renters from driving their cars into the storage bays, slowly sipping water before beginning his journey.

"Ha-ha-ha," Amber laughs loud enough for Ronald to hear, sending a shiver across his entire body. "Where are you going?" She asks, though she isn't interested in an answer.

"I'm leaving," he replies rigidly, "and you can't stop me." Ronald's eyes begin searching for where the voice is hiding, knowing that Amber won't be able to resist for long.

"What makes you believe I intend to stop you?" Amber asks in a playfully sinister tone, like a cat using its paw to hold a mouse fastened to the floor by its tail, while the mouse's legs keep trying to run, though the end is inevitable.

"You and I both know you can't live without me," says Ronald, finishing his water and getting up to leave. "So I guess that means you'll just have to –"

"Have to what?" Amber sneers into his ear from the left, cutting off Ronald from his escape. Ronald begins to back pedal, unsure of his next move.

"I guess you're going to die Amber," he says, throwing his empty bottle at her while he turns to retreat.

"I don't think so sweetie," Amber says through a mouth full of nasty nubs that used to be teeth, her lustrous yellow eyes, highlighted in red, staring directly into Ronald's.

"*Please*," he begs.

"You fail me."

Author's Thanks

This has been a tremendous journey to this point; a journey that would not have been possible without my friends and family.

I want to thank my amazing wife Ashley, without whom I would be lost; my mother Diane, who has made sacrifice upon sacrifice throughout my life for me to be where I am today; my brothers Michael and Casey, for both their unknowing contributions to this book, and for their own courageous stories of survival alongside mine; my sister Tricia, who without a doubt, will far surpass my talents and abilities in short time; my good friend Micromachine Jess, for enduring the countless hours of my rambling on and on about life, Kevin Smith films, and the old gang from high school; my best man Richard, for all the many shared conversations and rants about religion, politics, racism, bigotry, and everything else wrong with this world, and for just being an awesome friend; my friend Adina, who, powered by an almighty pasta-ish deity in space, jumped at the opportunity to critique my work, allowing the preceding story to hit its mark; my mystery artist Alexandra, whom I've never met, but brought the image in my mind to life for the cover; and last but not least, I want to thank **YOU**, the reader, for giving [PRE]SENT a go.

I'm not making any promises from here, but I'm quite certain this is only the beginning of many stories to come.

Until next time...

Made in the USA
San Bernardino, CA
11 January 2014